The Survivalists

Book 1

Getting There

Francis Wait

D1387393

First published in the UK in April 2013 by MyVoice Publishing

Published by: MyVoice Publishing,
Unit 1,
16 Maple Road,
Eastbourne,
BN23 6NY

ISBN: 978-1-909359-14-7

Yellowstone Park

Millions of visitors head for the Rocky Mountains at Yellowstone to marvel at the steaming geysers, bubbling mud pots and thermal pools. Few of them realise the scale and depth of this natural wonder. A Super Volcano is not formed above ground but rather below it. This natural phenomenon is actually a Caldera which is formed after a volcano erupts, blowing the top of the mountain away. The resulting depression fills first with lava and then with water which forms lakes and thermal pools. The caldera at Yellowstone extends for seventy miles by thirty and is approximately six miles deep.

Scientists and archaeologists have discovered and recorded that this caldera has blown at least twice at 600,000 year intervals, the last time 640,000 years ago. It is now overdue for another eruption. If it does blow, it will spread billions of tons of rock and dust into the atmosphere blocking out the sun's rays and temperatures on Earth will plummet creating a global wide nuclear winter. No crops can be grown and millions will starve to death. The last time it happened nothing larger than a dog survived. As a measure of how much dust will be expelled, the last time it happened, two meters of dust was deposited in Iowa which is a thousand miles away.

Reports have been coming in of activity in this region with small volcanic movements happening more and more frequently. The earth in the region of the lakes has risen out of the ground by about a yard, giving rise to speculation that the magma chambers far below the surface are moving, creating unheard of pressures which could ultimately blow in one enormous explosion.

If this happens it will be catastrophic for all mankind and it is possible that out of the world's population only a few thousand people might survive.

What would you do if this happened? This is a story of what one man and his friends undertake to stay alive.

The Survivalists, Book 1, **Getting There**

Dedications

I would like to thank the following people for all the help they have given me during the process of writing this book.

Tony Flood, the author of 'The Secret Potion' and 'My Life With the Stars', (both available on Amazon), for all his ideas, suggestions and encouragement in the writing of my book.

Liz Wright, the author of 'Belle Tout - the Lighthouse that Moved' and 'From Fancy Pants to Getting There', (both available on Amazon), for her editing advice.

Christine Dudley for her alternative ideas regarding some of the more difficult parts.

Steve Lee for reading the entire book and his invaluable critique.

Publisher Rex Sumner for pointing out that the first edition needed amending and suggesting different locations.

My wife Angela for her forbearance when I disappeared for long periods during the writing process.

TWISTS IN THE TALES

Francis Wait is one of nine authors of 'Twists In The Tales', a collection of 16 intriguing short stories by the We're Not Dead Yet Writers, who also include Christine Dudley, Heather Flood, Tony Flood, Elizabeth Gibbs, Brian Jones, Ernie Richardson, Val Tinney and Barbara Fisher. Twists In The Tales is published by My Voice Publishing and is available on Amazon as both a paperback and an e-version.

Chapter One

The phone rang in the middle of the night. Bleary eyed, James groped in the general direction of the bedside table, and picked it up, fearful that something awful had happened to either of his kids. "Hello, who's this ringing at this ungodly hour?"

"Is that James?" The voice sounded vaguely familiar.

"Yes," James snapped. "Whoever you are, what on earth are you doing ringing me in the middle of the night?"

"James, mate, it's Rex. Remember me from our army days?"

How could James ever forget? In the invasion of the Falklands he'd crawled out in front of enemy fire and dragged a badly injured Rex to safety.

"What's this all about?"

"Listen. I've got something vitally important to tell you. Since you saved my life, I've owed you one, big time, now I've got the chance to save yours."

James frowned in puzzlement. "What on earth are you talking about?"

"I need your e-mail address right now. The message I send will explain everything, but you have to act on it as soon as you can. I can't stress how important this is. The US Government is keeping a lid on something that may end up being globally catastrophic. They know I have access to this information, and it wouldn't surprise me if someone was watching me right now, so I can't talk for long. I'm phoning from an outside line here in the States, and when I've got your e-mail address I'll send you some mail from this Internet café in the hope it can't be tracked down."

James grimaced, "Have you been drinking Rex? This is just ridiculous."

Patricia had stirred and sat up. "Who's that on the phone? It isn't about the kids is it? Are they all right?"

"No, its Rex, remember him? I saved his life when we were in the Falklands. I think he's having a bit of a funny turn."

"Well tell him it's two in the morning here, and put the

phone down and get back to sleep." She mumbled angrily.

Rex must have heard the conversation, "James, James, listen to me," he yelled, "this isn't a joke, I'm stone cold sober, this is for real. If you and your family want to stay alive, give me your e-mail address and I'll send you a message that will explain everything."

Still unconvinced that this wasn't a big wind up, James reluctantly told Rex how to get in touch.

"I'm going to send the message right now and I'd urge you to act on it straight away"

"All right, I will. Thanks mate." By now, James just wanted Rex to get off the line.

"Oh come on, let's get back to sleep," muttered Patricia as she snuggled down.

But James couldn't get the call out of his mind, so he went to his study and switched on the computer.

"What are you doing?"

Patricia was standing behind him.

"Rex says he's sending a vitally important e-mail, and we must act on it, as our lives depend on it."

"Oh no," Pat groaned. "He must really be having a funny turn, what utter rubbish. Leave it and come back to bed."

Just then the computer pinged and 'One new message' appeared in the corner of the screen. James clicked on the anonymous words, 'From your Pal.'

They both read the contents.

"Oh my God," exclaimed James, turning to Patricia and holding her tight. "This looks as if it's genuine and if it is we've got to change our entire lives."

Chapter Two

James looked round the room at all his family and friends. He held some sheets of paper in his hands. "Now I want you to take this seriously because it's frightening to read," he said, holding the sheets up for them all to see.

"This is a secret report from a friend of mine in America; he works in a volcanologist centre close by the Caldera in Yellowstone Park. The authorities in the US have tried to put a secret classification on it to play down the dangers. But this one got out before they reacted to the information. Now Rex, that's his name, has written at the bottom of the report that we will have to act as fast as we can. The reason is, because, as you know, there was a minor explosion in Yellowstone, last week. The Volcanologists who work there are of the opinion that if this follows the patterns of other volcanoes, there will be a series of small explosions over a period of months culminating in an enormous one." He looked round grimly. "If that happens it will threaten the whole world, and it is possible only a few thousand people may survive. We could all perish."

"Why don't you tell them what you want to do?"

It was his wife speaking, and as usual in James's view, she was trying to get her views in too quickly. James looked steadily at her, she was only a small woman but well able to make her views known. Of Irish descent, she had red hair which needed now, to be dyed, to stay that colour. But she still held all the characteristics that red hair indicated; which included the trait to lose her temper in an almighty explosion if she so chose.

"Instead of butting in, why don't you let me get to it in my own time, so I can present all the facts as necessary?"

"I agree Patricia, why don't you let him have his say, then we'll know whether to argue with him or not." The Prof spoke louder than normal, in an effort to stop the looming argument. He was a big man who wouldn't have looked out of place on a rugby field but in fact liked the quiet life on his smallholding in the country.

James had invited him and his wife Julia seated next to him, as they had been friends most of their lives. She tossed her hair which was long and lustrous, as she concurred with her husband. She was a striking looking woman who would never be beautiful, but still managed to make most men look twice at her. "Let's give James a chance first shall we? I must say I'm intrigued to learn more about this…..explosion. It sounds interesting."

James nodded his thanks at her choice of words and glared at his wife, daring her to interrupt again, and then started again. "As I said just now, this e-mail I got from Rex includes a report from a group of scientists who've been studying volcanoes; in particular the one in Yellowstone." He looked around the room. "Now if you'll let me, I want to give you some facts about this particular volcano, although to give it a better name, it is a caldera which is left after a volcano explodes with terrifying force and blows the top of the volcano away."

"Is this going to take long?" His daughter Colette spoke. She was seated next to her husband Richard, a civil engineer. She was a doctor with all the attendant worries of her profession and never seemed to have time for any social life. "Because I was hoping to go out for a drink and a meal this evening."

James felt sympathy and annoyance at the same time, because with caring for her first child and a job, she was easily stressed so her time was precious. He snapped. "If you'll let me get on with this, maybe you'll be able to get out this evening."

He ploughed on. "This disaster has been proved to have happened twice in the last 1.2 million years." He held his hands up to stop the possible disbelief that was going to surface. "It last happened 640,000 years ago and is currently overdue for another explosion by about 40,000 years. Now let me give you some facts and then you can all shout me down.

"The caldera is 70 miles long by 30 miles wide and is thought to extend six miles down. If that blows, the amount of dust and debris that will spread is mind boggling. A nuclear winter will spread over the whole globe and it is thought that it will last for at least ten years. Crops will fail, and most of the inhabitants of this planet will die of starvation. I can tell you two more facts and that the last time it happened nothing larger than a dog survived. There has been a great deal of movement in this area with all these explosions, and you heard yourselves about the last one because it was on the TV. Also the ground at one end of the lakes has risen by about a metre. Now let me ask you, how much pressure would have to be applied to raise six miles depth of ground by a metre? It would be impossible to calculate and if those pressures continue, the resulting explosion would be enormous.

"Now I want you to think about this and it's a rhetorical question. In the case of a disaster happening, what's the first thing that all the people in power who run our lives start to do? And I'm talking about council officials, politicians, forces personnel, civil servants, royalty." He paused for effect then answered his own question. "They all start to find a place to hide in for as long as necessary and then emerge to take up the reins of power again. Mostly, these people have no real skills that could be useful to anybody trying to run a community that must, in the end, be self sufficient. So I think that the people who could make this work and have the skills to do it are people like doctors, nurses, engineers, scientists, builders, electricians, carpenters, farmers, and teachers, and any person able to bring the ability to work to a community."

His son-in-law Richard raised his hand. "I can see now why you invited us. I'm an engineer, Colette is a doctor, Andrew a builder, the Prof and Julia are teachers, you've even got Victoria, who's a biologist."

James grinned; he had at last made some sort of breakthrough and got a discussion started. "Well let's look at the problem from the beginning shall we?"

He ticked off the points on his fingers as he spoke. "First, we have to find a place to live. My suggestion is that we erect a very large building and start an indoor farm; I've taken the trouble to examine possible places to select and this comes up. I think you'll agree that it has got to be well away from any other civilisation, so that would rule out most of the northern hemisphere and anyway, the fall out will probably be most severe there. And, as I said, if we get too close to any other human beings they will almost certainly try and take what we have. That is one reason why I think we will have to arm ourselves as well, but more of that later. Most of the southern continents such as South America, Africa and India, I would disqualify for one reason or another. So I think the only viable option I can see would be Australia, somewhere in the Northern Territories."

One or two of his audience grinned and some frowned, his daughter Colette was the first on her feet. "Do you mean to say you want us all to pack up everything and go with you to some godforsaken wilderness in the outback of Australia? Have you considered at all what this would do to all our lives?"

"That's the whole point, darling," James retorted, "it might just save your life."

She didn't answer but turned to her husband and snapped. "Get your coat on we're leaving, I've never heard so much rubbish coming from dad's mouth in my life." She turned to her father and said scornfully, "Why don't you grow up and stop dreaming, it's never going to happen."

She swept out of the room with Richard in tow. He cast an apologetic glance at James before departing. James sighed, he had been counting on her support. Then he stared at the remainder of his audience and asked: "Do any of you feel like that?"

His son, Andrew, who worked with James as a builder, shook his head. "Look dad," he exclaimed, "I told you at work that Victoria and I are in with you on this. Neither of us is convinced about the disaster happening, but we quite fancy living in Australia so we're willing to go and give it a try."

James nodded and said to The Prof, "What's your take on this?"

The Prof laughed, and nudged his wife. "What do you reckon then, love?"

She chuckled in her turn. "It couldn't come at a better time could it?" She answered.

Then, turning to James she explained, "We have been discussing moving to a house in Spain but we both like the idea of living in Australia, miles from anywhere. We've heard a lot about

British citizens who've been ripped off by the Spanish and we would prefer Australia."

James frowned, "You never mentioned anything about this to me, when were you thinking of going?"

The Prof shrugged and cast a sideways glance at his wife who smiled and nodded. "In a couple of weeks, we've got a buyer for the house and when that goes through we'll be gone."

James persisted. "But why, right now?"

The Prof grinned, "I'll let you know when we meet next time.........wherever that is"

He handed James a piece of paper from his pocket, "that's my new mobile number; I'm getting rid of the old one, now if you'll excuse us we've got a lot of packing to do. Oh, and don't give that number to anyone else, it's important."

They then said their goodbyes and left, leaving James nonplussed, holding a slip of paper in his hand. Patricia sat down in a chair facing him and asked. "Have you any idea of how you'll persuade Colette to come with us because we aren't going to leave her behind."

Shrugging, James answered, "I'll think of something."

A few days later the event happened which was to prove the pivotal moment that would change their lives. James got a phone call in the evening just as they finished their meal. It was their son-in-law Richard and the first words he said were, "have you seen the news?"

James shook his head before realising that Richard couldn't see him, and then answered in the negative. "There's been a huge explosion in the Yellowstone Park, and it's killed a lot of people," Richard blurted out. "But the scientists have predicted that it's not over yet, they think it can blow again but they don't know how long before it does. There's worse to come, I've got a text from my brother to tell me he was going to visit there this week during his tour of America. He's probably dead."

By this time James had Patricia holding on to his arm as she attempted to listen in to the conversation. He shrugged her off and said tersely, "switch on the TV, there's been an explosion in the Yellowstone Park and Richard thinks his brother is there."

Patricia held her knuckles over her mouth and did as she was asked. That done, she held out her hand and asked him to hand her the phone. James did so then switched on the news channel. He smiled to himself as it was obvious that although the government agencies in America had tried to keep a cap on it, the news was out. The Yellowstone Caldera was erupting and several thousand people had died. It looked as though the fallout would be large enough to lower the mean temperature of the world a little, but it was nowhere near the eruption that James had anticipated.

Then, as James watched in consternation, the announcer said that although the opinions of the scientists were divided, they all agreed this was just the forerunner of a much larger eruption and it was possible sometime in the next twelve months, the long awaited enormous eruption could occur. He shook his head in despair; they were too late and they had run out of time; he couldn't carry out his plan to save them all.

His wife put down the telephone and sighed, "Richard is convinced his brother is dead, he said he would have rung by now and he isn't answering his mobile."

She slapped him on the arm. "Listen to me; I know you and I know what's going through your head. You think it's too late, don't you? Well it's not, we can still do it and this time Richard has just said that he and Colette are going to come. This has proved the turning point for them, and the icing on the cake is that she is going to have another baby, so she wants to secure the future for the two children."

That evening they held another meeting and a very disconsolate Richard attended with his wife. Colette came over to James and, putting her arms around him she said, "I'm sorry for doubting you dad, you were right and I was wrong, we've had a phone call from America and Richard's brother is among the casualties. He's going to America to his funeral and in the meantime I'm putting our house on the market, so we can come with you."

After they had all given Richard their condolences they sat down in the lounge. The only persons missing were the Prof and Julia, James had had a hurried phone call from him to say that they were definitely going with them and would be in touch later. James had outlined his plan to the Prof and he had said to count on him financially and he would be in contact in Australia.

Colette started by asking. "Why don't you bring us up to date on what you were thinking of doing if you go to Australia?"

James nodded. "OK, here's what I think we should do. I believe we'll need about 30 people to make it viable." He held his finger up, "and I do mean people who will be useful, such as farmers and tradesmen, experts in the fields which we'll need, then we will all have to sell all our property and houses and the money we raise goes into a central pot. We can take containers with our personal possessions in them, and then we must buy some land miles from any other habitation. We'll need to build a big two-story building with the bottom floor lit by fluorescent lights and the top floor in glass. Now when I say big, I mean very big, probably 100 yards long by the same wide. When we've done that we move in and start growing all our food inside. We'll have to get all our electricity needs from one of those really large windmill generators, and all our water will have to come from deep underground, although I'm hoping that we can buy something like a farm that already has a water supply."

Colette had been listening intently to this and nodding as James spoke. "I can see the windmill and I can see the water supply, but what about the roof? I take it that if the roof is going to be glass, you'll want to use it as a greenhouse, but surely if there's that amount of dust about, within a very short space of time it's going to be knee-deep in dust and it'll be useless for growing things."

James smiled; she always had had a gift for putting her finger right on the weakness in an argument. "I take your point," he answered, "We've been using a power washer at work just lately and if we have enough water and electricity, we can clean the roof periodically with one of those."

Victoria raised her hand. "I'd like to make a comment, if I may." James smiled at her. "Go ahead, dear," he said. "This is a democracy after all."

"I have given this a little bit of thought," she said. "But surely there's a lot of things it won't be possible to grow aren't there? I mean what about coffee and tea and what will we use for medicine when the supplies run out, and they will if we're in there for possibly ten years?"

James sighed. "I agree there are a lot of things we can't grow but we will be able to take some seeds with us that will last for some time so we can grow them in the future. And as for medicine, mankind lasted for a long time using just herbal remedies didn't they? And don't forget, Collette is a doctor so I'm sure she can stock enough of the right sorts of medicine to last us. But I admit that in the end, we will have to ignore things like cancer and sicknesses that can't be treated, because for us to survive only the fit will be able to live."

Andrew and Colette looked at each other and Andrew asked, "does that mean that if you've got something like aids or cancer you'll stop them going?"

James shrugged. "More or less I suppose, there doesn't seem any point in taking somebody who will die anyway."

Andrew raised his eyebrows at this and said, "I can't believe you said that dad, you've always been someone who'd take care of people less fortunate than yourself."

James smiled clasping his hands in front of him, he answered. "Look, it's simple enough, if we do go and this catastrophe does happen, we'll be in no position to care for the sick and ill, they'll drain our resources and if somebody has to look after them they won't be able to work for the good of the community. And that will be the single most important object in our lives. How would you like it if food or medicine was taken to care for a terminally ill patient and your child needed that medicine? So if we go, I want it clearly understood that no sick or ill person is going. And whilst I'm on the subject, you can forget all the relations and friends you want to invite as well, because our capacity is limited. And for now that's my last word on the subject."

James then asked Victoria, "You're a biologist, do you think it's possible to grow the amount of food we need?"

The question seemed to amuse her and she answered. "I don't think you know how many different kinds of biologist there are James, but I will say that I have given some thought to this, and I feel that if we had a large enough area and sufficient growing medium we could grow the crops in troughs about five high and if we kept the seasons right by using lights, we could grow the same crops several times a year to ensure succession. Also hydroponics could play a part as well. And coming to that, have you given any thought to animals, I mean what about cattle, pigs, sheep, chickens, dogs, and so on, and not forgetting horses. I know they wouldn't be much use while we were inside but think of the value if we kept some alive, we might end up with the only horses in the world."

James nodded; she had started to think along the right lines now, so he carried on and added, "Of course we'll have to compost everything so we can use the resulting manure for the crops, and a side issue that could come from that is we might be able to produce our own gas from the fermentation process as well. I also thought that we should take as many computers as we can manage, with their programmes, so that we can educate the children for the future, and that goes for books; we'll probably need a big library because if this catastrophe does occur, all the TV stations in the world are going to close down."

Chapter Three

Things started to move quickly after this, and Richard left his job before going to America to attend a memorial service for his brother. No bodies had been found so the Americans had decided to erect a memorial stone to the dead. He had then offered to go to Australia directly, as an advance party, and he had instructions to try and find a property with plenty of water and also room for the building they intended to construct.

James said to him, "We'll have to find somewhere remote because we don't need nosy neighbours spreading the word about what we're doing, don't put your name to anything until we all get a look at it."

Collette was looking for a practice in the Northern Territories that was willing to take her on and as it was so far from the main areas of so-called civilisation it was almost certain she would secure the job. Victoria had been looking for work and was hopeful that she could get one in her profession. She also volunteered as chief crop grower and started to design the troughs she wanted to have in the growing area.

Patricia offered to give her services as housekeeper with Julia when she arrived, because as Patricia said. "You men couldn't clean anything satisfactorily and there is no way I'm going to let my standards drop because we're out in the bush."

They had several meetings as time went on and agreed that they would buy some computers and stockpile as many games and information discs as possible because, as The Prof had pointed out before he left, if anything did happen it would be a long time before paper came back into use and at least the children would have access to a medium where they could write things down for their school work. It was understood by them all that if the computers broke down that would be the end of it as nobody would have sufficient knowledge to repair them or produce new parts.

About a week after they had taken the decision to proceed with their plans, they met once more. James opened the meeting as usual and looked over to Victoria to start, she stood and produced a large folder from which she took several sheets of paper. "It's really very simple," she said. "Given an area of 100x100 yards and the fact that we will be on two floors with a series of troughs about five feet high, I think that it will be possible to grow enough food for probably forty people." She pointed to some of the sheets. "Some of the troughs will have to be only two in height as some of the crops are quite tall." She looked at James pointedly. "It's going to cost a pretty penny to have them all made and installed, not to mention the compost to fill them, but I'm going to have to leave the finance to you as I can only design what I want." Having said her piece, she sat down.

James only answered, "I'm sure we'll have enough money to cover all the costs." His son interrupted him and said. "Will you tell Victoria about your plans for getting in the back door dad, I'm sure she'll like to hear them?"

Victoria's head came up and she frowned. "What's going on?" She asked, "What's this about a back door?"

James stared at Andrew. "You haven't told her then?" He asked. Andrew shook his head. "Didn't see any point," he mumbled.

Victoria looked from one to the other. "Told me what?"

James grimaced, and glanced over to where his wife was sitting with a noncommittal smile on her face; she shrugged and said. "You'll have to say something to put the girl out of her misery."

By now Victoria was on the edge of her seat with impatience. "Look, if somebody doesn't tell me pretty damn quick, what's going on, I'm going to murder someone."

James grinned. "OK, you've asked for it, now I'll tell you."

Before he could say anything else his wife blurted out. "We've got a conviction in Australia and we can't enter the country legally, without being slung in jail."

James looked at his wife whom he loved most of the time and thought that sometimes he could cheerfully strangle her. He held his hand up in front of her face and said, "right now you've said enough, why don't you go in the kitchen and make us all a cup of tea while I bring this girl up to date."

She left the room mumbling to herself in such a way as to leave no doubt in his mind that he would be in for it when all the guests had left. James ignored her and turned to Victoria just as Colette and Richard stood and started to go out of the door. Colette merely said succinctly. "Heard it all before." When they had departed, James was left with Andrew and Victoria. So he sat himself comfortably and began to speak, when Andrew said. "Don't go into the entire extravagant details dad, just keep it plain and simple."

"I had intended to do just that, son." James replied. "Now will you let me get on with it without any more interruptions?"

He turned to Victoria. "Now if you listen to this sorry tale it won't take long. My wife was quite right, we have got a conviction in Australia and we will have to sneak our way in, but let me put it in perspective. We went on a holiday to Australia a few years ago; we'd saved a long time and decided to visit some friends out there and have a long break. As it turned out, the friends weren't very friendly. I think they thought we overstayed our welcome, but that's another matter. Anyway when we said we were going, a family friend got in touch and said she was planning to go as well and maybe we could all go together. We said yes and so Diane came with us. We left at six in the morning here and went to Heathrow to board the plane for Singapore. Our plane left at ten that morning so we got out of bed at around 5am. The flight took about twelve hours to Changi airport so we had been travelling now for about seventeen hours. It wasn't the easiest thing because Diane is diabetic, and she found it hard to control her injections and keep herself within the limits of her blood sugar. She had brought along some fruit, as the Diabetic Association booklet she had with her had said that some airlines, especially foreign ones, didn't serve the best food for her condition and it would help her to control her blood. As it turned out they were exactly right, and she needed the fruit."

Patricia came in with tea for all of them and then left with the comment, "don't take too long over this." James shrugged and went on. "So where was I? Oh yes, we reached Singapore without incident and went into the rest area. There was only a coffee bar open that we could see and the layover was three hours." He grinned, "we found out later that there were several cafes on the upper floor but to be honest we none of us had the energy to look for them. All of us by this time were shattered and we still had another eight hour flight in front of us. We stopped there for another couple of hours, and then wandered along to the boarding gate, and sat down in the waiting area. So by now we had been on the go for nearly twenty hours, and this is important; someone came round and gave us cards with a series of questions on them such as are we importing any wooden articles or various other substances. To be honest, I was so tired I just ticked off all the way down without reading it properly, then we handed the cards in when we boarded the plane."

He collected his thoughts and then carried on. "This is where it got tricky; we had been on the plane for about four hours when Diane suddenly took a turn and said, "I don't feel well, I've got to go to the loo." We started to help her go along the aisle but she collapsed, the flight attendants saw this and rushed along to help. We got her feet higher than her head and I was panicking wondering what to do when a hand came down and started to take her pulse, then this guy said. "I'm a Doctor." You could have knocked me down with a feather at that, as she had picked the one spot on the plane where there was a doctor, he didn't even have to get out of his seat at first; anyway he tested her blood sugar, which was OK and decided she was dehydrated, and got the flight attendant to break open the medical kit and put her on a drip. When she came round, they put her on to three seats in a row and let her rest."

He glanced at Victoria and shrugged. "It all went pear shaped after that, we got into Brisbane and when we started to get off the plane they came along and told us we should wait for a wheelchair. This arrived and they loaded all our possessions on to the trolley that came with it. Now I can honestly state that from this point on I saw nothing to say we could not bring any fruit into Australia. We picked up our suitcases and got to the Customs Desk and then the girl who had been pushing the wheelchair decided that she had had enough and she put all our travelling bags on the conveyor and just walked off. I was busy watching Diane and Patricia when I heard a voice saying. "Is this yours?" I looked over my shoulder and said yes, as it was the fruit. Then he said, "don't you know it's illegal to import fruit into the country?" I said I'm hardly importing it, as it was for our own consumption on the plane, some of it got left over. After that, they dragged me into an office and photographed all the fruit, searched all the bags and I really got the impression that I'd arrived just in time to stave off the boredom of their graveyard shift. And they looked a bit triumphant at catching another bloody Pom and let's get a bit of our own back. So a few weeks later I ended up in court in Brisbane with a young girl for a lawyer and it was a Friday and she seemed more interested in making for the Gold Coast for the weekend than defending me. The lawyers for the prosecution were by this time laying it on with a shovel and making out that I was the biggest criminal they had ever seen and I was about to cause untold damage to their economy if I was let loose ever again. They said there were big signs all over the airport about fruit importing and I should have read them."

He rubbed his eyes with his hands as he recollected what had happened, then went on. "The magistrate listened to this lot laying it on for about two hours and then this slip of a girl stood up and gave my version of the tale which was that the fruit had been intended for Diane and nothing to do with me although I had said that it was mine at the time, to spare Diane any more stress. Looking back I should have said that none of it belonged to me and I didn't know where it came from, they'd have had a job proving it was mine, as I didn't load the trolley. Her defence took about ten minutes and that was that. To be honest, by now I knew my goose was cooked and this guy could have been directly descended from those magistrates who deported the original settlers to Australia."

He spread his hands and grinned. "So there it was; guilty as charged and a three thousand pound fine or three months inside jail in default. Case closed. I went outside with the lawyer and she couldn't get away quickly enough. All she said was, "if you're going back to England ask for time to pay and do a runner. Just don't come back here again or you'll end up in jail for your trouble." "So that's what I did, I got out of Australia as quick as I could and I've never been back. Although it's the one place in the world I really would like to go back to." He grinned. "Of course now I can't go back legally at all."

"So now you've got to sneak into Australia by the back door so to speak," Victoria remarked, "have you thought about going to the Australian Embassy in London to see if you can get the charges dropped?"

James shook his head. "Won't work I'm afraid, I tried that, but the only answer I got was to go back and appeal, but that meant serving the sentence if anything went wrong, and those bloody Australians are not going to put me in prison for having fruit on me when I went into their country. After all, they imported all the fruit trees themselves anyway. And they've imported a lot worse than that, stuff that should never have been taken in, like rabbits and frogs." He shrugged his shoulders. "Don't worry about this any more, I will get in I'm sure."

The rest of the family re-entered the room so the conversation dropped and they started to discuss the finer details of their plans. It had been agreed that they would order a windmill before they knew the address for it to be forwarded to. In addition they arranged for an engineer to accompany it and oversee its erection. Their household belongings which they wanted to take with them would be loaded on to a container and shipped out by sea. All the materials for the building and eventual planting would be purchased in Australia. Finally, James said, "Right, let's call it a day if none of you have anything more?" He glanced around for confirmation and nodded when nobody had anything to add. Then he said. "You all know what you're doing now and we've all got each others phone numbers to get in touch when we get there. So I'm going to say goodbye now as I don't like farewells; so good bye and good luck and I'll see you all in Australia."

It was time for the more emotional persons amongst them to start getting tearful and hugging each other till they had all said all that it was possible to say. James looked at his son Andrew and said. "I'll see you in a few days as you're coming with me, I'll let you know where we're going and all the details when it's organised."

With that they all took themselves off and started the process of travelling to a country on the other side of the world where not one of them knew what would happen.

Chapter Four

Two weeks had elapsed since the group had had their meeting to choose what they intended to do. It had been a momentous decision for them all and none more so than for James. He looked around now and pondered over the actions they had all taken over the last few weeks.

All their possessions that they intended to keep had been loaded into containers. This had been sent to the shipping agents in Colette's name to be forwarded to an address yet to be decided. They were now living in temporary accommodation rented from one of his contacts in the property market. His business had been sold to his foreman, and the man had said. "Who better to run it than someone who had been with it from its conception?" James was very pleased about that, as the man had worked hard for him for a long time and deserved to be rewarded. He had paid a fair price for it and Andrew and himself had shared the proceeds amongst themselves as they had agreed.

He stood in their house with Patricia before they had moved out and she had sighed, "We're never coming back are we?"

Looking at her he answered with what he knew was a lie. "Don't be so stupid, if all this blows over we can come back and start again."

James was still worried about the Prof; he had left with what James could only call undue haste. He thought it strange that they had not been in touch before they went, but just disappeared.

Richard had been in the Northern territories now for some days and had sent back a few brochures he had obtained about available property's thereabouts. It seemed a likely place to make a new life, being fairly tropical and with enough water to sustain them. James privately wanted to see them for himself before committing to any purchase, but at least it looked hopeful.

Victoria and Andrew were going to marry as soon as possible. James knew they had already started to live together but they were being very closemouthed about everything; certainly neither one was saying anything about it to anyone. James and Patricia had discussed it several times and had decided to let them have their own space and do things in their own time. Victoria had had some difficulty in finding a job in that area. She had had an offer of one in Cairns which she thought it would probably be better to take and keep a lookout for one closer to home when she was actually in the country. If they were married in Australia Andrew and her could probably apply for citizenship and legalise matters. He could then work on the farm all week and meet up with her at weekends if she came up. It brought up problems about how she would be able to work on the design of the indoor farm but it was generally agreed that she could probably input enough of her work through the Internet, as she would not have been expected to physically work on the project. It was a solution but she wasn't happy about it, as she liked the hands on approach where her work was concerned.

Colette had made tentative enquiries and there was a chance she would be able to be taken on at a private practice as there was a shortage of doctors who were willing to work so far from the main areas of "civilisation" as it was put to her. Although as she said. "That was no bad thing as civilisation often brought more problems than benefits."

They had not as yet taken any steps to recruit the other members of the team, as they all agreed that it was better to see the candidates in person than take anyone unseen. None of them subscribed to the American way of interviewing people where they took psychological profiles and had them evaluated. James in particular had always interviewed employees personally and had seldom been wrong.

Andrew had also been busy with his pet projects, which included MRE, or as he put it. Meals, ready to eat. James, who had seen some service, knew it better as compo, from the term he had learned in the services as composite rations. Whatever it was called he also knew it tasted foul, but at the same time if they needed food and couldn't grow it, it would prove useful. There was always a need to have something in reserve. Andrew had managed to contact someone in Australia and had ordered quite a large quantity of MRE to be delivered when they had somewhere to store it. The windmill generator had been ordered and only needed an address to be sent to where it would be delivered and erected. The chap who sold it him had assured him that it would work quite well even at low wind speeds. This was something that he was looking forward to seeing as he had heard that sort of story many times in the past and had developed a very sceptical turn of mind when it came to promises from salesmen.

One thing they did which had not been planned was form an English Company to handle all the financial details. James's accountant, who had seen him through some good and bad times, had suggested it to James when he had dissolved the building firm. With the price of houses soaring, as they had the last few years, when they sold they had built up a sum of over £2,500.000 between them and James knew then that the pipe dream stood a chance of becoming reality.

So now they all had shares distributed according to how much each of them had invested. If anyone wanted to back out of the deal they could walk out with whatever they had previously invested. It was a solution that James had not really wanted as his opinion was that they were taking a decision for life and not for a short period of time. But as life would have it, it was a majority decision and James had unwillingly gone along with it.

Patricia came into the room and seeing the look on his face asked. "Is everything OK darling?"

He looked at her with affection and replied. "Yes its fine, I'm just going over the past few weeks and trying to sort out where we're going from here on."

"Maybe it would be nice to go out and have a drink with Andrew and Victoria before we left." Pat said.

James felt a moment of regret and then shrugged his shoulders. "Ask them if you want." And turned to other things with which to occupy his mind. He had already booked flights for himself, Patricia and Andrew to Singapore. From there he hoped to contact someone to spirit them into Australia. He made a mental note to call Richard in Australia the following day in the early morning and find out more about the situation. It would be evening there and he had more chance of contacting him direct.

There was a knock on the door and James opened it to find Andrew standing there with a large haversack.

"Hi dad," were his first words and before James could reply he went on, "I've just brought my things round for you to take. I'm going to see Victoria off and then I'll be back. I've got to stay with you now, I've given up the apartment and I've got nowhere to live until we go."

James, although speechless, had to laugh at the cheek of his son. "Don't you think a little bit of notice might have been in order?"

"I should have let you know dad but I wasn't aware that Victoria was going to leave so quickly and anyway you've got plenty of space here for a couple of days, haven't you?"

Patricia came bustling through and immediately took charge of the situation.

"What are you thinking of, keeping that boy on the doorstep." As all mothers before her had done, she had never got over the fact that her son had grown up, and to her he was still her child. James looked at Richard, six feet tall and broad in the chest, thirty years old, and still he was her boy. "Give me the bloody haversack and get off to Victoria and see her onto the train, the only thing I ask is that you come back before midnight, your mother and me want to go to bed today and not in the early hours of tomorrow."

Andrew leaned over and kissed his mother on the cheek and was gone.

Patricia smiled at James and said. "He still thinks a lot of me doesn't he?"

James laughed at this and replied. "One peck on the cheek and he can twist you round his little finger."

The next day dawned with the sun shining and in better spirits James rang Richard in Australia. He answered happily, "I've got some good news for you dad, I think I've found the ideal property, I've seen it and it looks good with loads of space, and plenty of water. I also think I've found a possible chance to for you to get into Australia with the minimum of fuss. If you go to Singapore to that Hotel Miramar, I'll leave a number for you to ring at the desk."

James hung up the phone in a much better frame of mind. He hadn't realised how much the worry had been playing on him. So it was in this happy mood that they started to pack their cases ready for departure.

Chapter Five

Singapore. They had finally arrived there on the first leg of their journey, after travelling for seventeen hours, and then they had had the trouble of finding their coach which turned out to be the most uncomfortable little vehicle James had ever sat in. Their journey to the hotel took over an hour dropping passengers off on the way. James could have sworn they crossed over the same junction several times, but, as he reflected, a lot of the roads looked amazingly similar. The hotel was much as James remembered and they were swiftly booked in.

They had slept and rested for most of the time there and now in the morning James had found himself with an appetite and was looking forward to breakfast. Patricia appeared from the bedroom ready to go just as the phone rang. James answered and to his surprise it was Richard.

"I didn't think you would be able to find us on the phone." He said, "I was going to call you later to see how you were getting on and give you this number."

Richard laughed, "The directory enquiries in Australia are very good."

"How have you been getting on?" James asked.

"I've seen a farm about 700 hundred miles out of Darwin with just about everything on it that we could possibly want. It has water, wind, good grazing for the animals, it's secluded, but with a reasonable road for transport, and the guy who is selling it needs the money badly to settle a few debts that he has on the property. There is a small township about two hundred and fifty miles away but apart from that there's no-one for miles around."

James's heart leapt, this was the news he had been hoping for. He realised how much he had been worrying about finding a place to settle. His face must have been showing his pleasure as both Andrew, who had just surfaced, and Patricia, started asking what was happening. He held his hand up to quiet them for a moment and asked Richard for the telephone number that he was using at this time and wrote it down, and then he told him he would ring back in a while.

After he put the phone down and told the others the good news they took the time to have a little celebration. James said, "It's far too early to have a drink so the best thing is we'll have some fresh orange juice." So they toasted themselves with the breakfast orange and then started to assess the situation.

James called the number Richard had given him. A strange voice answered and it was definitely a woman and Australian. James asked to speak to Richard and she answered. "Can he call you back, he's in the shower."

James asked. "What are you doing in his room while he's in the shower?"

Patricia looked up at this exchange and asked. "What's going on there?"

James snapped. "That's exactly what I am trying to find out."

The woman on the phone carried on with what she was saying, as she hadn't heard Patricia's question. "I'm not in his room at all, I'm on our bridge, and from the tone of your voice I think you owe me an apology. Nothing is going on here, and if you want to speak to my husband to confirm that you can. He's standing right next to me now."

James felt himself going red at this as he realised he had just made an assumption without any facts to go on at all. He tried to cover it up by asking what Richard was doing on a boat.

She answered. "You were just too damn quick when you spoke to him earlier," her voice still sounded snappy and irritated. "If you had taken the time to listen you might have understood when you rang."

James realised this conversation was not going too well so tried too mollify her as best he could.

"Shall we just start again with this conversation, as it's true I don't know exactly what's going on?"

The woman didn't appear to want to be mollified but just snapped. "Why don't you ring back in a few minutes? Then you may understand just what is happening." With that said she put the phone down.

Patricia by this time was practically hopping from foot to foot with anxiety. "Will you tell me what is happening or am I going to have to drag it out of you."

James brought her up to date as far as it was possible to with what the woman had told him. This took a little while, as Patricia wanted to know everything that had been said. She took the time to think over what he had told her and then came to the conclusion that at the moment all was well with her family. Although, as she put it. "You seem to have upset that woman didn't you?"

James sighed at this, as he was well aware, when it came to upsetting women it was only too easy for a man to do. But, as he thought to himself privately, the females of the species are only too ready to do battle to prove a point, if men fought over the things women did there would be far more casualties in this life. Anyway, women seemed to fight with words and men with their fists, so it was probably more civilised in its way. He grinned to himself as he thought that most men were unaware that there had even been a battle until it was all over, and their wife said something like. "Did you hear what that woman said to me?" He came out of his reverie to find her looking at him in the way that said. "Are you going to answer me or what?"

He shook his head and said to her, "I'm very sorry I didn't hear a word you were saying as I was miles away deep in thought."

She snapped at him. "You should keep your mind on what you are doing and stop that dreaming, I said are you going to ring Richard now or later?"

He was just about to say that he would do that when the phone rang; when he answered, it was Richard.

"Hi dad," he said, "I thought I had better give you a call to put you into the picture with what's going on here."

James shook his head and asked the question that was paramount in his mind." Have you found a way for us to get into Australia?"

Richard answered with what could have been the best news he had ever heard. "Simple," he said. "I'm on a large yacht sailing past the Malaysian coast with the perfect plan to get you into Australia with no bother from the customs or immigration, all you have to do is board the yacht in Singapore. Is that easy or what?"

"Richard," James answered. "If you only knew how much I wanted to hear something like that, I'm so pleased that you have come up with a plan, you won't believe how grateful I am, and also you'd better bring me up to date on what is happening there, as I think I upset some woman when she answered the call I made earlier."

"That was Leah, she can be a bit abrasive when she thinks someone has taken her the wrong way. She half owns the boat we are on now, and we're in the Java Sea on our way to Singapore. I think you've just had a little misunderstanding and when you meet her you'll get on like a house on fire, she really is quite a nice person."

Richard paused for a few seconds and then went on, "Leah just said she'd like to apologise for running off at the mouth like that, and maybe you can all have a new start when you meet."

"Sounds like a good idea." James answered. "I didn't want to offend anyone anyway,

I hope we can begin afresh when we're sitting opposite each other."

"I'll tell her that in a moment, so we'll see you in a few days. Just relax and lie in the sun until we get there." With that they said their goodbyes and hung up the phones.

James turned to Patricia and asked. "Did you get the gist of that conversation?"

She asked. "What was that about a yacht?"

James told her what Richard had said, and they both agreed there was nothing more that either of them could do until Richard arrived. They went down to the breakfast room and ate a hearty meal to set them up for the day, then up to reception to book a sightseeing trip They had talked it over many times in the past and could not understand people who were willing to invest large sums of money in a holiday and then sat around a pool all day (probably moaning about the Germans who stole all the best seats by going down at six in the morning and placing towels on the loungers). Their idea of a holiday was to soak up some of the atmosphere of the country and see as much of it as possible. In their opinion a pool was just that, a pool. It could be anywhere in the world but it was still just a pool.

On the fourth day they had been in Singapore, at about nine in the morning the phone rang. It was Richard. "Well I hope you two are ready for the off, because we arrived last night and we're in the marina waiting for you." 'At last' James thought, 'we can, at least start doing something'. He realised the enforced waiting time had been playing on his mind without him knowing, although not a true man of action he certainly didn't like hanging around waiting for events to give him something to do.

He turned to Patricia and said to her. "Are you ready to go and see Richard, he's here in Singapore?"

Her eyes widened and she answered. "How can you ask a question like that when we've been on tenterhooks all week waiting for something to happen?" She went on. "Is that Richard or not?"

"Well off course its Richard, who else do you think is going to ring us here at this hotel?"

"Are you going to let me speak to him or are you going to stand there like some stupid oaf all morning."

She snatched the phone out of his hand and promptly started to question Richard about what was happening.

Apparently Richard was not about to go into long conversations over the phone, so she had to put it down after a few minutes conversation. She turned to James and said, "we have to meet him at the marina as soon as possible."

"I suppose you got their position in the harbour as well didn't you."

"He told me to go to reception in RSYC Singapore alright." They grinned at each other and prepared to go out and had a taxi sent to the hotel and soon found themselves at the yacht club. The boat turned out to be a large yacht and when they arrived the awning had been erected on the afterdeck and there were five people sitting under it with drinks spread out over the table. On seeing them approach Richard stood and waved to them. They waved back and went along to the gangplank. Both James and Patricia suffered from a feeling of nervousness as they went on board as neither had been in this sort of situation before. They didn't like meeting four total strangers in a place where they appeared to have no control over the circumstances. Their minds were soon put at rest. Leah and her husband, turned out to be typical friendly Australians with tanned healthy skins. The husband at six foot, as tall as James, made every effort to put them at their ease. Leah was smaller at about five foot six with long blonde hair and the bluest of eyes, she was dressed in a bikini which didn't leave too much to the imagination, and at first James was hard put not to stare. However, a glance from his wife soon told him where to keep his eyes.

They were introduced by Richard, who said, "This is Leah and her husband Ray, they own this boat. These are their children, George, and his sister Jeannie, they're twelve and fourteen respectively, and a pair of monsters they are."

Jeannie pushed him "You'll regret that remark when we go swimming later," she was obviously very fond of him and from the look in her eyes, infatuated as well as she made every effort to sit as close to Richard at all times.

It was Ray who started things off by saying, "where are your manners you lot, we have guests come aboard and not one offer of a drink for any of them, they must be well and truly parched."

Everyone bustled about for a while until finally they were all seated round the table with a drink to hand. In the meantime Leah had found the chance to lean over to James and joke. "I won't bite your head off today, if you don't draw any conclusions before you know the facts."

James flushed, it wasn't too often he got embarrassed but she seemed to have a way of getting to him. She appeared to be a very direct woman, and, as James was to find out later, she had run her own business for several years before meeting Ray. Probably her way of dealing with men was to be direct and up front, but for James who had been used to the more gentle women in England it came as something of a culture shock. He held up his hands in surrender and answered. "Can we just have peace until we have time to sort out our problems?"

Leah by now had the bit between her teeth and wasn't about to let go. "So you do admit that we have problems?"

"No I don't admit that we have problems, I think that you're trying to pick fault just for the hell of it."

By this time James was getting to the point in the conversation where he was willing to let everything go and give her a piece of his mind, he didn't like mind games and that was what Leah seemed determined to play. She must have seen something in James's manner because she suddenly backed out of the exchange by saying. "Ooh, the drinks are on the table."

James thought to himself that he had better watch out for her as she seemed to be a very dangerous woman and could, if left to go her own way cause a lot of problems, pretty as she was it was better to stay as far away from her as possible. Patricia glared at James, who had opted for a beer, but knew better than to bring the subject up in front of strangers. James had seen her look and smiled to himself, as he knew the Australian custom of offering a man a drink when visited.

"Right." said Ray. "I think I had better take the floor, and give these folks here the rundown on what we are going to do from now on." He glanced around at all of them. "Anybody got any objections to that?"

Leah leaned forward and interjected. "Ooh, I love it when you are being all masterful,"

Ray glared at her. "If that's your idea of sarcasm you can stuff it, I don't have time for any funny business from you,"

"There you go again." was her rejoinder. "You can never take a joke."

"It's no joke having you sniping at everything I say?" Ray's face was beginning to go red and not from the sun. "Don't you think it would be better if we get on with what we're doing and stop all this petty hassling about?"

Leah suddenly subsided as if she had made her point and saw no gain in carrying on with her little game. "Oh get on with it then," She turned to Patricia who was sat next to her and who had been listening to this exchange with some interest. "These men are all so bloody macho, except when it comes to bedtime, then all they want to do is have another drink."

Ray, who had been listening to this remark with all the signs of exasperation on his face, chose this moment to say once again. "Can we bloody well get on with what we're here for?"

Richard slammed his can on the table in exasperation, and said. "Look you two, we've all listened to you snipe at each other all the way from Oz and now you seem to want to start in front of my family, why don't you give it a rest for a bit and allow us to get on with the business?"

Strangely this seemed to have a calming effect on Leah; she simply sat back in her chair and waved her hands. "Oh do go on and then we can get some peace."

Ray heaved a sigh of relief and started his presentation. "Well as we all know the problem is an easy one at first glance, it is to get you people into Oz without the authorities knowing anything about it. The real crux of the matter, which I might add has never been explained to me, is, why? You are all obviously English and it's only a matter of going in on any form of transport and you can stay as long as you like."

"That's not strictly true," James answered. "We know that we can get into Australia at any time, but that's only for a limited period of maybe six months. We want to stay there for a much longer time. Maybe later when we can be sure of the grounds we can ask for a longer stay officially, but for now all we want to do is enter and the less people know about it the better."

"Fair enough," Ray replied. "I won't pry any further into your affairs. So now all we need to do is get you into our fair country. This isn't too difficult as one of the advantages of living in Oz is that, generally speaking, the Aussies aren't too impressed with officialdom. I take it you're not going to be doing anything really illegal while you're there?"

James looked at Patricia and they both laughed, Patricia answered for them both. "All we'll be doing is living on a farm in the outback somewhere. If we can keep our presence quiet no one will ever know we're in the country at all."

Ray nodded. "That's exactly the same story Richard here

came up with." His face took on a look of puzzlement and he shook his head. "Although you are going to have to tell me later why anyone in their right mind would want to go and live in such a god awful place as that. You do know that at the last survey there were as many crocs as people up North?"

He turned to the others and went on. "Well as I was saying, getting someone into Oz isn't too difficult if you know what you are doing. I'll simply take you in and if any of the authorities take too close an interest we're going to have to play with the cards that we have. I'll just say that I gave you a lift from Singapore, as you wanted to go to Oz for a couple of weeks. You'll then have to sort out some visas, I know that you wanted it totally unofficial but if we drop you on a sandy beach somewhere and you are found, your feet won't touch on the way out. What we propose I'd like you to come here and bunk in on board while we sort out what we do next."

This proposal met with James and Patricia's approval so they promptly agreed. "But," as James added. "Don't forget that there is one more in our party." and he explained about Andrew.

Patricia stood up and said to Leah. "Can you show me around the boat, I think I need to go to the loo?"

Leah gave in with what for her was good grace. "OK, I'll take you round, it's not so big you'll get lost but it's best to know where you are,"

After they had gone the children wanted to go along the marina to a play area close by, so Ray gave them some money and off they went. Jeannie looked at Richard longingly and asked if he wanted to go with them. He let her down as gently as possible by saying maybe he would come along later.

"Don't wander out of the area." was Rays parting word to them. This was greeted with loud groans from the two of them, as they wanted to explore.

"I mean it," Ray said, "I want you back her in two hours from now because we're going to eat and I want to see you sitting at the table."

With that the pair ran off as fast as they could, pushing and shoving each other as they went.

"If they appear in two hours I'll be dumbstruck." Ray said.

"They're good kids but they don't take any notice of me."

He leaned forward in the manner of someone with a secret to impart. "Now we are on our own I want to know what you lot are up to, and don't give me any bullshit because I'm a bullshitter from way back and as they say, it takes one to know one. I've got some theories about the true purpose of this project but I want to check them out."

He went over to the table of drinks and got out three beers from the icebox on the side. Placing them on the table he seated himself and leaned back in the manner of one who knows he has a slight edge on his opponents. "OK, let's have the story."

By now James was in a quandary, as he didn't know how much Richard had let slip about their project. He looked at Ray and tried fishing for clues. "What do you think we are doing?"

Ray stared at him. "Let's get something straight, I'm not about to let you know just how much I've figured out. The first theory I put forward you'll agree with it straight off and I'll never know what you are thinking. You just tell me your story and let me decide if you're lying to me."

Helpless now, James glanced at Richard who looked back and said to James. "I haven't said a word about any of the project up till now, only that you want to get into Australia. If Ray has figured anything out he must have put two and two together but I'll bet he's come up with five."

Ray was listening to this exchange with some amusement. "I bet I'm not far off if you want to put some money where your mouth is."

James leaned forward and said to him in his most earnest way. "I'm willing to bet that you are miles out but it isn't about the bet or the money, I'm not interested in either of those. What would you say if I told you we aren't going to grow drugs, deal drugs, and that we don't expect to make any money out of this?"

Ray looked at him with a face that had dumbstruck all over it. To someone who had been in business all his life and fairly successful as well, the concept of anyone doing something for nothing just didn't occur to him. He said to them, "well now you have taken the ground from under me, I'd have sworn it was drugs.

I had visions of fields of cannabis waving in the wind."

James by now had the knowledge that Ray's information about their project was very limited. He decided to try out the theory he had propounded in England and said to Ray. "We're going to start a Kibbutz in the outback and live simple lives cultivating a few crops and making a bit of a living."

This information had no effect on Ray at all. "Go on, pull the other one, if you expect me to buy that story you've got another think coming, I don't believe you and that's flat. You're lying and I want the truth."

James answered with another question. "Before we get into all this any further I'd like you to tell me some of your story, how did you lot meet for example?"

"Simple," Richard, had stayed quiet up till now, as he didn't know what James had been prepared to tell Ray. "We met in a bar near the waterfront when I was looking for someone to help out with the entry into Australia. We got talking, and Ray was looking for something interesting to do as he seems to get bored with this life of ease."

Ray nodded. "Not much use having a boat if you've got nowhere to go and nothing to do. This just added a bit of spice to life, and anyway, if people like you want to come in, why not? It's better than a load of tossers from some of the countries around here, coming in and going straight on relief."

James asked him, "how did you make all the money then?"

"That was easy mate, I had a shop selling computers when I discovered I had a talent for them. I found that I could design them better than some of the rubbish that comes on the market, so I opened a little factory and made some prototypes which sold well and it went from there. In a few years I was making too big an inroad into the profits of the competition so I was given a choice, either sell out to them or face a price war. It doesn't take much to figure out what I did. I bought a nice big house in Sydney and this boat, now I just sail around and amuse myself where I can. When I met Richard up on the top end it was just another way of amusing myself. This doesn't let you off the hook you know, I still want to know what you lot are up to."

It was now up to James and he wasn't sure quite what to do about it. He said to Ray. "Look, you've put me in a difficult situation; we've all agreed that the only people who should know about this are the ones that are going to join. I don't think that you will join us, not with the lifestyle you have at the moment. That can put you in a very dangerous situation with regard to our project. You wouldn't be with us but you would know all about us, and that could be very difficult for us later. You will certainly remember later when the project is going forward. At that point it'll be too late and you wouldn't be able to come in with it. Now I am not saying you can't join, I am saying that if we tell you about it we would feel that you should join."

Ray, by now was scratching his head in puzzlement. "I have never heard so many bloody ifs ands or buts in my life, let me get this straight, if you tell me what you're doing, you think I ought to join you."

"Exactly"

"You don't give a feller much choice do you?

James considered for a moment and then answered, "If you had a lot less money I might have offered you a place by now, but I've got the feeling that it wouldn't be helpful, as your life at the moment is too good and we're looking forward to some hardship."

Ray leaned back in his chair and took a sip of his beer. He sat like this for some time and then leaned forward. "You've really set me a problem here, and I'm not sure how I'm going to solve it. You're obviously sincere in what you believe in, but you're beginning to sound like one of those religious nuts that want to go off into the wild blue yonder and live off nuts and berries. If you tell me I can live off muesli and lentils for the rest of my life you can stuff it."

This last amused both of the others and they burst out laughing. Ray was forced to sit there looking at them in bemusement until they stopped. When they'd calmed down James said. "I think we're going to have to let you into the secret and give you a chance to make up your own mind, I warn you though, if you don't want to join us I want your word that everything you're told will be in the strictest confidence. This is no idle warning either, you'll be in a position to cause us a great deal of harm, and we will take steps to protect ourselves."

Ray looked shocked at this and answered. "Strewth, you don't mess about do you, but I like that in a man. It shows that he's sincere in his beliefs."

Richard stood and said to James. "I'm glad I had the foresight to bring a copy of a programme with me in case I wanted to show it to any future prospects, do you want me to show it to Ray? I know he's got all the equipment here on board."

James nodded and said to Ray. "Do you want to view this DVD? It explains things much better visually and afterwards you will at least understand our reasons for doing this."

They called out to the women and told them what they were about to do. Patricia went a little pale when she realised that Ray knew nothing of what they were doing and she confessed.

"I thought they knew and I've been talking to Leah about it."

James grunted in exasperation. "I thought we agreed that we told no one unless we're convinced they want to join us." Patricia knew she had done some wrong and attempted to defend her actions by saying. "But I thought they knew all about it and that was why they helped Richard to come and get us, and anyway you're telling them now so where's the harm?"

"You appear to have missed the point completely don't you?" James by this time was getting very angry with her when Leah stepped in.

"Look mate, she didn't know that you've made some big secret out of your stupid little scheme did she? She only thought we knew and talked about it because of that, so back off and calm down, or you're going to have to deal with me and you won't like that I can assure you."

James could not help notice her chest was heaving with emotion and in that swimsuit it left little to the imagination. He also realised that he didn't want to antagonise this woman as she seemed to have a great deal of influence with what went on, on this boat. He paused for a moment before answering her so as to give himself a moment to calm down.

Then said. "We seem to get off on the wrong foot a lot of

the time don't we? Shall we call a peace treaty until we can all calm down and discuss it? As you said, it won't matter now that we are about to show everybody what our reasons are for coming here." He added. "There is one thing though, I still think security is going to be a big problem and I want to keep everything about the true purpose of this scheme under wraps as much as possible."

He glanced around at them seeking their approval. He went on. "Right, shall we go and see what this is all about?"

Ray brightened considerably at this. "Too true mate, it's about time we get to see what's going on."

As they started to file down into the salon James caught Richard's eye and held him back a moment, when the others were out of earshot he said to him, "don't let on about where the location of the farm is going to be, at least we can get a little security out of that." Richard nodded and they both followed the others into the salon.

It was a very subdued man that emerged an hour later, Ray obviously had a lot on his mind when they appeared. He committed what was an unpardonable sin in Australia; he helped himself to a beer without offering one to the others. James and Richard looked at each other in amusement and then went and took one each out of the icebox. As they seated themselves at the table under the awning they heard the dry voice of Leah.

"Well thanks guys, we'll have a drink as well."

She had been watching the tape with Patricia and had followed them out to the sundeck. James looked at them and asked what they would like to drink, as Ray had subsided into one of the loungers and seemed in no hurry to pay attention to any of the assembled company. They settled for a gin and tonic and an orange juice respectively, then took their seats along the side of the boat. While they had been watching the film, the sun had sunk towards the horizon, and the air had started to cool down, although as James reflected to himself, in these latitudes cool was a relative term. In England they would have been complaining about the heat in no uncertain terms. He could feel the sweat starting to prickle on his skin after the cool of the air-conditioned salon.

Ray looked over at James. "So that's the reason you didn't want to say anything to me, I can see it all now. Do you really believe that this prediction is going to come true?"'

Once again James felt the necessity to explain himself. "Look Ray, this can come true or not, no one has the ability to predict what will happen in the future, but to my mind isn't it better to be prepared if it does? And what happens if you aren't? You will certainly die whether you're rich or poor. All the money in the world won't save you if it does happen. My way you will at least have a fighting chance. The strongest instinct in this life is that of survival of the species, and I want my family to have the best chance I can give them. You can be part of that if you wish, that's all I want to say, apart from one thing. The scientists are predicting that it can happen at any time; that can mean, it will happen this year or maybe in a thousand years. Maybe even in ten thousand years, we have no way of knowing so we can only gamble. The one certain thing for us, as a community, is that we will live a lot better lives than if we were living in some of the communities that exist now."

Leah commented enthusiastically. "Hey Ray, you've said yourself many times you get bored with the life we lead; maybe you ought to try this. It may even be a way of getting our life back on an even keel."

James glanced towards Patricia who had a cat got the cream smirk on her face and was sitting next to Leah. She leaned over and said quietly. "I've had a little talk with her and it's a bit of a long story, but I'll tell you later."

Ray brightened up for the first time since they had emerged from the salon. "I can see the point of trying to safeguard your future, but it's all so airy fairy. You say you're going to open a farm and live there happily ever after. You haven't said so yet, but I assume you'll take precautions about the nuclear winter they are predicting, so you're going to have to stay there to be sure it will all go OK when this happens. So far so good, but as you say yourself, it could happen so many years in the future you would never see any benefit from it at all."

Leah asked. "Will you have any drugs or drink or anything like that there?"

"Don't be stupid Leah," James answered. "That's a way of making sure we won't succeed, you must know that drugs and even alcohol drag society down."

Ray looked up at this. "Are you against alcohol as well then?"

"No," said James vehemently. "But you must remember we can only take limited supplies with us, and if you want to look at storage space, isn't it better to pack in food than spirits? Or would you rather die drunk?"

Ray looked aghast at this revelation. "Are you saying that there'll be no beer in the entire place? You'll never get any true blooded Aussies to go with you, I can tell you."

James had now put himself into a bit of a quandary, as he liked to have a drink as much as the next man. The thought of the next few years without any form of relaxation was beginning to play on his mind. "Maybe there is a way out of this," he answered. "All the time we're building this up until we have to go, - 'Underground.' For want of a better word, maybe we can have some drink available for recreational purposes. I can even visualise taking a certain amount in with us to allow some sort of celebrations to take place. But if you, or anybody else, imagine that we are going to have regular Saturday night booze-ups you've got another think coming."

Ray appeared somewhat mollified at this but Patricia certainly wasn't happy about it and started to make her views known. "You told me that there wouldn't be any drinking allowed in this community, now you've started to go back on your word."

Leah broke in at this and said. "Hey Patricia, you've got to realise that most people drink in this life and if you try to ban it completely you're going to pile up more trouble for yourself than you can handle. You can't press your point of view on other people. That's anarchy and no one will want to live with that sort of rule, especially as," and she looked around at the others. "I think you are probably in the minority."

Patricia had a way of staring that was very discomfiting for other persons to bear. She had said nothing while this was happening, and now it was Leah's turn to get the treatment.

"You'll have to say something to me either way you know,

I don't understand what you have against drink in moderation anyway, it's never done any of us any harm."

Patricia broke her silence and answered. "I'm not against drink in moderation and never have been, what I am against is the mindless idiots drinking themselves into oblivion at every single opportunity. You have got to understand that most of the drinkers I have seen never know when to call it quits. It destroys families and its better if no one's allowed to drink." She went on. "I make no secret of the fact that I'm against drinking but I know that it is an essential part of some people's lives. If we can't ban it then at least let's make sure no one can get too much at any one time." She sat back and looked around at them.

There was silence until Ray shook his head and said. "When you Englishwomen have your say you don't mess about, but on the other hand I think you're wrong to impose your views on everyone else without putting it to the vote."

James intervened and said to Ray, "as far as votes go you haven't got one yet, so don't think you can influence decisions that are not yours to make. Until you join you can only ask for information."

"Point taken, and I'll feel a lot better having a good think before I make my mind up about what I'm going to do. I have got one question though, and I'd appreciate an answer before we go any further. I can see that you have had to have a lot of finance but where does it come from?"

James looked at him and simply said. "It comes from us, we've sold all our assets to put everything into this venture."

Ray slumped back in his chair. "Do you mean you've put all your assets, everything, into some crazy scheme that may never pay off?"

"I suppose that's about the size of it. Don't forget we aren't disappearing off the face of the earth, we're going to lead normal lives until it all happens. If someone has to have a job in Australia they're going to put their money into a central pot. That can be used to buy essentials that we can't grow ourselves. The only difference is that we'll be sharing everything with everybody else."

Ray looked happy at this revelation. "He leered at James.

"Does that mean everything?"

This was enough for Leah. "You can put that thought out of your dirty little mind," she had moved over to be a little nearer to Ray, he hadn't noticed and barely heard what she had said. It was to be is undoing as she landed a punch right over his ear. He toppled out of his chair and sprawled on the floor, he obviously didn't understand why he had been punched. Leah stood over him. "You learn from that you bastard, and think before you open your fat mouth in the future."

She then stormed off the sun deck into the salon. Patricia looked over at James in the universal meaning of here we go again, then followed Leah into the dark of the salon. Open-mouthed, Ray looked around in puzzlement. "What did I do?" He asked. James and Richard couldn't help laughing at this, and Richard answered for both of them saying. "If you don't know, you must be far more stupid than we give you credit for."

Ray looked a little shamefaced as he replied. "That woman never did have any sense of humour."

"She doesn't need a sense of humour, she needs a medal." James felt compelled to comment. Ray was obviously one of those people who blunder through life with little or no real understanding of the thoughts or feelings of his fellow human beings. "You seem to have discovered some way to annoy your wife with no effort on your part at all."

Ray crossed over to the drink table and helped himself to another bottle and raised it to them in silent question. When they nodded he flipped the tops on two more and handed them over and sat down. They sat in contemplation for a few minutes and then Ray started to speak. "I think it would be better if I told you the story and then you can understand. Basically I had an affair at work before I sold the business. When I sold it, the girl, I was involved with thought we were off into the wild blue yonder together, but she hadn't reckoned on the fact that I really love my missus and kids and I didn't want to leave them. Then the silly cow decided that if she couldn't have me she was going to spoil it with my family. She rang Leah and spilled the beans. She told her everything, so that put the kibosh on my marriage." He nodded in the general direction of the salon and added. "She's known about it for a long time now and she's never forgiven me. I thought she was going to forget it when I bought the boat and we started sailing around, but it rears its head now and again." He grimaced and added. "Especially when I start fooling around in front of other people."

James who had never felt comfortable with revelations of this kind, felt quite relieved when he spotted the two children returning along the marina wall towards them. He said to Ray. "I think we'll have to continue with this conversation another time, your kids are coming back now,"

Ray jumped to his feet and called out to the children who were fooling around as they walked along. "I thought I told you two to come back sooner than this."

They began to run and when they got nearer Jeannie shouted. "Aw come on dad we're not that late, And anyway you haven't got any food on the table yet."

Just then Leah and Patricia appeared in the doorway with a large tray, it was piled high with sandwiches and dishes of meat and salad. Leah eyed the table, which was scattered with bottles and rubbish and said. "You men had better clear all that stuff off the table if you want to get any of this food down you."

She then looked up at the two children who by now were rapidly approaching and yelled at the top of her voice. "You two kids had better hurry if you're going to get any of this grub and get your bloody hands washed first."

James flinched at her language and noise, and then glanced over at Patricia, who was wincing herself, she looked at him and shrugged her shoulders as if it was none of her concern. The men started to clear the table and everyone pitched in and helped and in a short time the food was served. Leah seemed to have got over her tantrum and even managed to smile at Ray, who glowered in remembrance of the punch he had received. When the meal had been placed on the table, they all sat where there was any available space. Jeannie managed, with no apparent effort to sit next to Richard. He appeared not to notice, but Patricia did. The meal passed without incident and afterwards James and Patricia agreed it would be best to go to their hotel and exchange their accommodation.

Ray got on to the shoreline and called a taxi, which took them to the hotel. When they arrived they saw the management and rearranged the booking with them. James paid their bill with his card, then went with Patricia up to their room to pack. Andrew came to the door and they quickly brought him up to date with the developments in their schedule. He seemed quite happy about the plans, and so, within a very short time they were in a taxi once more heading for the Marina.

On arrival James had the foresight to call a man to help with the luggage, and they went down to the boat. Leah was waiting for them on the sundeck with the inevitable drink in her hand. When she saw Andrew she sprang to her feet, and fluffing up her hair came to the gangplank to greet them and James introduced Andrew to her. She seemed quite impressed with Andrew, and she drew him to one side under the pretext of showing him around the boat. James watched them and resolved to have a word with Andrew later. It wasn't beyond the bounds of possibility for Leah to try to use Andrew to get some of her own back on her husband. That was one scenario James was determined to prevent. He thought prevention is better than cure and decided to talk to Andrew later. Ray appeared and shouted out. "Right now, get yourselves aboard, I'll give you a hand to get your luggage stowed away, we've got an early start in the morning."

James looked at him in puzzlement and asked. "What are you talking about? I thought we weren't leaving port yet."

"Your right," Ray answered. "We aren't leaving yet but I want us to go out on a shakedown cruise to teach you something about running a boat, if anything happens out there when we're going over I want you two to be able to help out. There's nothing worse than to run into trouble and you don't know what you're doing."

At this Patricia looked really worried. "I don't know the first thing about boats and I'm not sure I want to learn."

"Don't worry your pretty little head about anything dear, I'm sure everything will be just hunky dory," said Ray

Patricia caught the tone of Ray's voice and flared immediately. "Let's get one thing straight before we go any further, I am not a 'little woman', or a 'dear', so don't start your condescending tones with me. There's a lot of things in this world that you can't do, and a lot more that I can do, so start off by thinking that some of us aren't natural born sailors and we need some encouragement before we step on a boat and start sailing."

Ray held his hands up in mock surrender saying. "Hey, I only meant it as a joke, there ain't any malice in what I say."

She replied. "You might think it is a joke but let me tell you something, I was brought up by very strict parents, who didn't understand things like going to the beach or swimming pool, so I was never taught to swim. I don't mind going on big boats but the thought of going to sea in this tin pot little excuse for a ship petrifies me. I'm only doing this for the good of everybody else, so you can start off by being a little bit more considerate towards your passengers."

Ray had never come across anybody who couldn't swim before, and it showed on his face as he answered her. "The first thing I'm going to get out for you is a lifejacket and you are going to wear it at all times when you're on this boat at sea. I'm sorry you're petrified but there's nothing I can do about that. You'll just have to do the best you can. And just what is it you can do that I can't?"

She triumphantly answered him. "The list is endless matey, you men think you have it made when you make money and get a bit successful in life, but don't forget where you get the babies from. And having said that, who wipes their dirty bottoms, I'll bet you haven't done that more that twice in your life."

Ray coloured and was about to come back with a nasty remark when Leah spoke "Go on then darling tell her just how many times you have changed their nappies."

He snorted and replied. "I happen to think that making a bit of money for a better life is more important than changing dirty nappies."

Leah wasn't to be outdone, "If you men ever stopped to think about all the work that's done behind your backs when you are at 'work'," she emphasised with her fingers. "You might have some understanding of what actually goes on in this world." She pointed at Patricia and went on. "That woman has probably done more actual work than you in this life and a lot of its work that you wouldn't stoop to doing, but it's necessary and needs doing. So you cut a little slack here and try and have a little bit more understanding about what other people can do in this existence."

Patricia clapped her hands. It was obvious that the age-old battle of the sexes had two more protagonists on the side of the women. Ray, by this time was only too ready to admit defeat. He turned to James and tried a weak grin, looking for an ally. "Here they go again, these women are always going on about how important their housekeeping is, but they never stop to think they wouldn't have a job if we didn't earn any cash for them would they?" There was no way that James was going to get involved in this sort of argument, he felt it wasn't only pointless but also destructive to the harmony of life in any community. So he attempted to change the subject. "What time are we leaving in the morning?"

By the expression on Ray's face it was obvious what he thought of James's attempt at defusing the situation but nonetheless he decided to go along with it and looked at his watch. "Okay, so it's now 10 and we need about 8 hrs. So give us an hour to get to bed and we get up at 7am tomorrow and after breakfast we'll set sail. We can go out all day and get a fair bit of training in. Now, I want you all to pay attention. This is not a game we're playing, it's dead serious and I don't want anybody sloping off. What we do tomorrow is training for what could be life or death, I know it sounds melodramatic," he grinned at them. "Especially from a bloke like me, but it only takes one mistake out there and it could kill us all or at the very least cause serious damage. So I want you to pay attention when you're told something," he pointed to Patricia. "You've got to get over your fear of sailing so I want you to make the effort and try and enjoy it. It's a great way to spend some time, if you think your going to be sick, take some tablets in the morning, but don't take too many as they make you drowsy. You'll probably be better off if you don't take any and face up to it as you might not get sick."

Patricia by this time had had quite enough of being dictated to so she threw him a salute and shouted. "Yes sir, affirmative sir."

Leah snorted when she saw the expression on Ray's face, she

said. "Come on Ray you were coming on a bit heavy handed there."

Ray glowered at her. "Maybe I was, but everything I said is the truth, and I want these people to know how serious it is out there. If we get caught in a situation I want everyone to be able to turn their hand to helping with it."

"All right, all right," By this time Leah was showing her annoyance. "We all understand you think it's dangerous out there but the long range weather forecast this morning said it would be fine for the next week, just a bit of a blow, and that's how you said you like it."

Ray's face by this time said it all, he was getting exasperated himself, and it looked like they were in for another blazing row. James stepped in front of both of them. He raised his hands and said, "I'm sure we understand the seriousness of sailing with amateurs and we're willing to learn as much as possible in the short time available. I'm also sure that we won't be too much of a problem to you, but that will only come if everyone is taught in a calm and collected manner." He turned to Ray. "If you go round with all this anger beneath the surface, you'll only end up making people nervous, and it's going to cause a lot of stress." Then he turned to Leah. "You aren't helping either, you keep on stirring him up with no reason that I can see, and the end result is, he doesn't know where he is with you and he takes it out in anger. Only at the moment that anger is directed in the wrong direction, so let's try and do the job in hand and get on together."

The pair of them looked a James with amazement on their faces. It was probable that neither of them had been spoken to like that for a very long time. Ray grinned when it had sunk in that someone had told him what he could or couldn't do, but he seemed to take it in the spirit in which it was intended. Leah on the other hand turned on James like a cat with all her claws out.

"Just who do you think you are? Speaking to me like that. You are nothing but a guest on this boat and if you think you can dictate to me what we do around here you've got another think coming. You're only here because I said we could help you out but if you want to cause trouble your feet won't touch until they're on that bloody dock over there."

She had flung out her arm in what was meant to be a dramatic gesture, but unfortunately it knocked over the drinks table so various bottles, glasses and assorted implements went flying all over the deck. She stared at the mess for several seconds before it seemed to register what she had done. Ray however, was only too happy to tell her.

"Aw fer Christ's sake Leah just look at the bloody mess, you and your sodding temper, well the cleaning up is down to you, so you'd better break out the mop and bucket and get to it."

She turned and stared at him, "you clean it up yourself you lazy bastard, I've had enough of you for today so find another bed to sleep in tonight." With this final word she flounced off. The sound of the door slamming made them all wince. It was Ray who broke the silence. "Don't worry about her, she'll be all right in the morning, she must just be a bit stressed with all this going on."

Patricia, ever the peacemaker, asked Ray where he kept the cleaning materials. He led her over to an unobtrusive little cupboard and silently watched her get out mop, bucket and broom. She got quickly to it and with their help a few minutes later everything was spick and span.

She looked at Ray and asked. "What do you do with all the glass and broken bits?"

He seemed to be in a bit of a trance, but jumped and said. "Dump it overboard."

Patricia didn't appear to understand, as a lifetime of being tidy wouldn't let her just dump things like that.

Richard came to the rescue saying. "Think about it, nobody is going to stand on it are they. It won't be seen ever again will it?"

She answered. "Do you know, I'd never given it moments thought until just now, but I suppose you're right? It just never crossed my mind. I suppose all ships and boats dump a lot of stuff over the side?"

"It is a big problem with all the shipping on the oceans now, heavy stuff like glass is no problem but it's the oil and plastic containers that are causing a lot of trouble."

So Patricia emptied the dustpan over the side. She looked at the spot on the water in contemplation for a moment, then turned and said to them with. "I could get quite used to this life you know, one dustbin never seems enough does it?"

Ray looked a bit puzzled so she enlightened him and said. "We're only allowed one dustbin in England you know, and it really fills up quickly."

He shook his head. "You women think of the strangest things. What do you imagine you'll be doing when you're living miles from anywhere, do you think they'll be coming a hundred miles along a dirt road to empty your dustbin?"

She looked appalled at her husband. "Is that right? Aren't we going to have any services on the house at all?" James replied. "Haven't you been listening to any of the discussions we've been having just lately? We'll be living too far from anywhere to have that sort of thing, and anyway the last thing we want is visitors all the time. Some people are just too nosy for their own good. The only services we're going to have are the ones we provide ourselves. That means water, electricity, rubbish disposal, sewage disposal, in fact anything to do with us living there. It'll all be down to us to provide for ourselves." Patricia who seemed to realise just what she was about to give up and she pulled her face in a parody of disappointment and chagrin. "I thought I was going to get at least some luxuries in this life, but now you seem to be taking them all away."

Richard broke in now and said teasingly. "You won't be watching too much television either if this disaster does happen, because all the television stations will be closed."

Patricia's eyes widened in shock and she said. "But how will I know what happens to 'Neighbours'?"

This cracked them all up and they all started laughing, with the exception of Patricia, who didn't really find it amusing to discover out that her favourite programmes were going to disappear. The laughter however was brought to an abrupt halt by the Leah's screaming voice.

"Will you lot shut that bloody row up and get to bed or I'll put a stop to this caper of yours so fast you won't know what hit you." This had a far greater effect on them than even she could have expected. They abruptly stopped all the noise and looked at each other like little children who had been caught stealing cakes. They wanted to laugh, but, at the same time they had guilty looks all over their faces. Patricia tried not to giggle but her shoulders were by now heaving with suppressed laughter; soon all of them were trying not to laugh. By now they were making almost as much noise as they had previously. Leah appeared in the doorway with a face like thunder. She shouted at them, "I'm gonna give you one last chance to get to bed and then you've had it. Now shut up and move," They all filed past her trying not to look at her face, or it would have set them off again. She waited till everyone had gone past her except Ray. Then as he attempted to walk past her she said. "Where do think you're going?" He turned in surprise and answered. "To bed of course." Leah grinned evilly. "Not in that bed you're not, your place is up forward in the cabin, there," Ray blurted out. "Aw come on Leah, that's just about the most uncomfortable bed in the whole boat and the cabin's so small I can't even put my arms out straight." She thrust her face forward until it was almost touching his, and she hissed. "Maybe you should have thought about that before you opened your big mouth. Now get up there and don't think you're getting in my bed tonight." She turned before he could make any more protest and slammed the salon door, he heard the key turn in the lock and sudden awareness came to his face. He called. "Leah, I won't try to come in but don't lock that door, if anything happens you won't be able to get out quickly." When he heard the lock click he shrugged his shoulders in resignation and walked off to his lonely bed.

Chapter Six

The next day dawned bright and clear with some tendrils of cloud high in the sky. At first light it was a little chilly but with the promise of a warm day later. Ray was a good as his word and he roused them promptly at 7 am, he seemed none the worse for his ordeal in the forward cabin but Richard couldn't resist a little dig at him.

"Did you sleep well Ray?"

Ray merely grunted in reply and glanced over at Leah, who was just emerging from the salon accompanied by the children. She seemed to be in a good humour and greeted them all with a cheery. "Good morning."

She turned to Patricia and said. "We might as well start off right, we have this system aboard and it boils down to this. We women seem to be relegated to the kitchen around here while these men, being the macho things they are, sail the boat. So, can you give me a hand in the kitchen? We've got to get breakfast for this lot before we set sail."

There seemed no sign of the foul temper that had appeared the previous day so Patricia mentally shrugged her shoulders and followed her down to the galley. On arrival there it soon became obvious that Leah wasn't one of life's tidy people in the kitchen. Patricia was appalled at the mess it was in, and as she was one of those people who found it difficult to keep quiet about the things that bothered her, she turned to Leah and said, "There's no way I'm going to work in this kitchen until it's cleaned up, I can't abide a mess and everything will have to wait until I get it sorted out."

This seemed not to faze Leah at all. She didn't seem too bothered about the mess but merely said. "His highness up there might have something to say about that, but if you want we'll clean up first, but let's be quick about it."

The pair of them set to and it didn't take long to start getting the place clean and tidy. While they were working Leah explained her reasons for the untidiness. "I hate having to work down here when we're in port and all that lot are sitting around expecting the drudge to just bring food to order for them. Not one of that lot would even dream of entering here and giving a hand."

Patricia felt compelled to reply. "You're the cause of that and you don't strike me as the type of person to let it go that easily. I can't understand why you don't stand up for yourself and give them some orders of your own."

"I suppose I'd better tell you what really happened then you'll understand why I don't say anything. When we started on the cruise we had a cook and a cabin boy. They both showed an interest in me but the cook was a student on a holiday job, great looking guy. It all started with a little flirting. We got a little too interested in each other and to cut a long story short, Ray found us in a compromising position." She paused and a dreamy expression came on her face. "We hadn't gone the whole way but it wouldn't have been long. Anyway the upshot was they both got the sack and I was left to carry on in the galley. So now I can't say anything about getting some more help around here, at least until he gets over it."

"So." Patricia answered. "It seems you're both as bad as one another."

She tried telling Leah where to put various items on the shelves and how to clean the surfaces. But Leah was having none of this and replied. "If you don't like the way I do things around here why don't you do them yourself and I can go on deck and sit with the men. I'm sure you can cope very well without any help."

She started to walk out of the door but Patricia realised instantly she had said something wrong and immediately tried to put it right by saying in her best conciliatory manner. "Oh no Leah I'm sure you know best around here and two heads are better than one when it comes to doing things in the kitchen."

Somewhat mollified Leah came back into the galley and together they began to prepare the breakfast. It was probably because it was such an easy meal to prepare that it was finished in a very short time, and they appeared on deck with full plates. When breakfast was over they cleared away, Leah and Patricia washed up, and then had to stack all the dishes and plates in cupboards as everything in the kitchen had to be fixed tightly down.

Leah remarked as they were doing this. "You wouldn't believe how much can fall on the deck when we're at sea, the first time we went out it must have cost Ray a 100 bucks for replacements."

This of course did nothing to allay Patricia's fears about her setting sail. As it turned out Ray had hit on a scheme to distract her mind while they set sail. He had already been along to the Marina office and settled the bill for harbour dues. He pointed out to James who had accompanied him for the walk. "The thing is, we can say we're just going round the bay but there's nothing to stop anyone from keeping on going, and then they get stuck with the bill and nowhere to send it. So we pay up every time we leave harbour."

Turning to the orders of the day, he went on to the upper deck and addressed them all. He started by saying. "Richard I want you to take her out of the harbour under power on the diesel engine, because I don't want to raise sail in the harbour. Andrew, you go with Richard and learn what you can about steering this craft. I'll give you some lessons later about the way we do things. You kids are in charge of drinks hot or cold, and your mother." He looked at Leah who was leaning on the door with a cynical smile on her face as she watched him trying to be captain. "Can you help prepare them?" He asked her.

Jeannie started to say she wanted to help Richard on the steering, but shut up quickly when she saw the look Ray was giving her. "I also want you two kids to make sure you don't get under anyone's feet, and if you see any loose objects lying around, for pity's sake pick them up and put them away. Patricia I want you to come with me, I've got something to show you."

He turned to the rest of them and said. "Leah, you cast off the bowline on my word, and I'll cast off the aft line. Start the engine Richard, and give her a little throttle and steer right when she gets under way. Just follow the marker buoys out to sea."

With that he went to the line aft and called out to Leah to let go and not to forget to coil the rope the way he had shown her. When she had cast off he waited a moment for the boat to swing out and then released the rope as Richard raised the engine revs. Slowly the boat left the jetty and nosed out into the channel. Patricia looked down at the water, which was now on both sides of the boat and felt the vibrations of the engine beneath her feet. The nervousness she had previously felt was becoming more obvious and started to show on her face.

Ray had deliberately left out James when he had been giving orders, but now turned to him and asked, "Do you know anything about these boats with sails?"

James felt obliged to laugh at the expression Ray had used. "Very little." He answered shaking his head.

Ray nodded as if he had been expecting that answer. "No bother, I'd rather have it like that anyway, you can pick it up the right way from me as we go along,"

He turned to Patricia and raised his voice a little, "stop staring at that sea and pay attention to me. I want you to listen to what I am saying now, as this is very important and this is where you start learning."

Patricia, who had indeed been staring at the sea; jumped and looked at him, Ray went on. "I want you both to stand here with me and look forward on the ship." He pointed and said, "That's fore."

They both crossed over to him and did as they were told.

"Now," he said. "Point to the right side of the boat." This they did. He then said. "Do you agree that that is the right side of the boat?" They both nodded their agreement. Ray shook his head and said. "Loud and clear if you will, I want this to go right down into your subconscious, so sound off."

He had their full attention now. They both chorused to him. "Yes we agree."

He grinned at them wickedly and said. "Now turn round," Once again they turned round and faced backwards this time. He pointed again and said, "That's aft."

"Right," he said. "Now point to the right side of the boat."

This time it was evident that there was going to be even more confusion, as James had pointed to the side they had previously agreed was right, but Patricia pointed to the side that was now on her right.

Ray held his hand up to stop them and said, "Now do you get

the point I'm trying to make? This is the reason sailors have devised another scheme to make it easy to identify which side is which. What I want you to do is learn a very simple way of identifying which side of the boat you are on."

He faced them forward again and pointed to the right side of the boat and said. "This will never change, this is the right side of the boat and I want you to always think of it as starboard, it also has a green light." He pointed to the other side of the boat. "This side is the left side of the boat and it's referred to as port. It also has a red light."

He went on. "This is the most important thing you must learn, to give you an easy way to remember, this is what I learned when I first started. All three of the words red, port, and left, are shorter than the other three words, starboard, green and right. Now I can't stress how important it is to have this in your head, as sometimes we won't have time to correct you and you'll have to get it right first time."

He proceeded to test them both by shouting the different words at them while they were facing in different directions until he was satisfied they had absorbed the basic knowledge he was trying to instil in them. By this time they were just about to clear the harbour and the first of the swells started to catch the boat. He grinned at Patricia who up till now had been completely absorbed in the lesson. "You've forgotten to be sick haven't you?"

She in her turn gasped and grabbed for a handrail close by. But it was a purely reflex action and soon she let go and proudly stood without holding on. By now they had left the harbour and were experiencing the first swells of the sea. James had been out in boats several times in his life, so all he had to do was appreciate how great it felt to have the wind in his hair. On such a fine day as this he could only feel a sense of happiness and he was beginning to appreciate what old sailors called the 'lure of the sea'. They looked at each other and smiled as they realised that it wasn't such a bad adventure so far, and they were enjoying the day after all. Ray looked at this exchange and a twinge of envy crossed his features.

"Right," he said, "now I'm going to get some sail on this boat; and while I'm doing it I want you to watch what happens so you can practice later."

They observed him go aft to where the others were clustered around Richard, who was holding the wheel. He appeared not to notice that Leah was standing closer than was necessary to Andrew. From where Patricia stood she could see that their hips seemed to be touching and her hand was resting on his arm. Small signs maybe, but to another woman it gave off signals that she couldn't ignore. Their eyes met across the boat and both knew what the other was thinking, and although it wasn't war yet, the battle lines were drawn.

The boat had been designed so that all the setting of sails and necessary work could be carried out from the cockpit at the aft end. So now Ray said to Leah, "I want you to show these landlubbers how to set sail on her so they can see it can be done with very little strength." He turned to Richard. "I want you to keep hold of that wheel, as you've done it before, and we can see how you have to adjust the steering to compensate for the drag of the wind."

He cut the engine so the boat wallowed a little in the water. For the next few minutes it got a little hectic, as Leah wound on the windlass and the sails went up, making the boat swing round to take the wind fully from the rear. It leaped forward over the water and buried its nose into the waves, A few splashes of spray came over the side and soaked James and Patricia who were still amidships where Ray had left them; Patricia gave a little scream and wiped her face. James looked at her but was surprised to see her smiling and enjoying herself.

Ray shouted out to them. "Come on down here and get some training in, this ain't no pleasure cruise you know."

His face was beaming which took the sting out of his words, so they promptly followed his suggestion and joined the others in the cockpit. Ray shouted out for the children to come up out of the salon and when they appeared he said. "You two can go and make us a nice hot drink, and bring us something to eat, like chocolate biscuits. This life at sea gives us a good appetite."

The two of them scampered off to do his bidding and he said to them all, "We'll keep on this heading for a bit while we have some refreshments and then we can get down to some serious training." He spoke to James and said. "I want you to show Andrew what I showed you earlier about which side of the boat is which, and I want you, Patricia, to learn something about steering this boat in a while."

Her eyes widened and she appeared about to protest, but he stopped her by pointing his finger and saying. "It'll do you no good to try and get out of it, we might have to make you do it in an emergency and I want to be sure that you're at least capable."

She realised there was nothing to be done but to agree to his request, so she accepted with the best grace she could. By this time Richard had been on the wheel for over an hour and wanted no more to do than sit and relax, as it was a tiring experience for him. He gladly handed over the wheel to Ray who took a grip firmly and beckoned Patricia over to join him. She approached him with some trepidation as she had never in her life done something like this before. Ray first of all showed her what the compass looked like and what she had to study. He then said. "Now come here and hold on to the wheel with both hands and get the feel of it, I'm going to steady it from behind you. Don't worry I'll help you hold it for a while till you get the hang of it. Just keep the heading on the compass as I showed you."

Patricia looked wildly about and said. "How do we know where we are?

"Don't worry about that for a minute." Ray answered. "If you look about you, there are no other ships for miles around, so there's no chance of colliding with anyone else. Just watch the compass needle and try to keep it in the general area I showed you." The children reappeared with some drinks for them so they could enjoy a good hot cup whilst the boat was keeping a straight line.

Patricia drank while Ray held the wheel for her so she could drink, he then stood behind her for a few minutes and helped her steer the boat, and slowly as he felt she gained more confidence he slackened his grip on the wheel. By this time she was so absorbed in what she was doing she barely noticed. The boat kept its course with hardly any effort on her part. With the wind just off to her side the boat sped through the water and before long Ray let go completely and stepped back a pace. Patricia didn't notice this and for several minutes she steered the boat on her own. Finally she looked down at the wheel and realised what he had done, she gripped the wheel firmly and pulled on it in panic. Ray leapt forward and put a steadying hand on the wheel saying. "Don't pull, but do it gently and she'll respond, your doing great."

Patricia looked round at him in triumphant excitement. "This is the greatest experience I've ever had. Can I carry on for a bit?"

Ray answered. "Sure you can but don't forget there's more to steering than just going before the wind. You've got a long way to go yet."

He let her have her head for a while longer, so she could get the whole experience of it and then said. "Okay Patricia, I'll take over now. I want James and Andrew to have a go while we're on this heading."

She handed over reluctantly and sank into one of the bench seats around the cockpit. "That was the greatest." She enthused, plainly she wanted to go back and do it again.

Although he had said nothing up till now James had been quite frankly astounded. He had no idea that his wife would take to sailing so quickly and she seemed to have a natural bent for it. He had little time to dwell on this though as Ray beckoned him forward and gestured towards the wheel. James mentally girded his loins and stepped into the breech. He grasped the wheel and held it tightly hoping that all would be well. Before he had time to take a breath the boat had bucked under his hands. Ray leaped back and steadied it for him. "Just go gently with her and she'll treat you right," he said to him. "It's not like a car that you've got to keep on the straight and narrow, she'll sway about a bit but just let he have her head and watch the compass. Keep a couple of points either side of the direction you're sailing to and she'll be alright."

James tried to follow his advice and slowly he got to feel how the boat would try to pull in the other direction to the one he wanted to go. He tried to keep the line set for him by Ray, but was nowhere near as successful as Patricia. Patricia was staring in his direction with a look on her face that said plainly that she thought he couldn't even steer a boat. Ray kept James at it for some time, as he wanted him to absorb as much as possible of the handling characteristics of the boat. It was more than an hour before he was satisfied that James was ready.

Then he beckoned Andrew to take his place on the wheel, Andrew proved an adept pupil and very quickly got the boat on the right course. All too soon the time came round for something to eat. Leah had wisely decided that it would be better if she did the preparation of the food without the help of Patricia, as she was off in a world of her own with the boat.

She appeared at noon with a selection of sandwiches and cold cuts of meat and they allowed the boat to drift along under the mainsail only, they then spent a lazy hour discussing the different ways of handling a boat. Ray gave them some more lessons in navigation and also how to recognise the direction other boats would be taking if they passed them at night. This would be easy for someone who knew the side the lights were on, and as Ray pointed out they should have committed that to memory.

By this time the sky above them had started to darken slightly and the waves were getting higher. Ray looked worriedly about him and said, "Just keep her on course for a bit I'm going below to check on something."

James nodded but something in his manner raised a seed of doubt in his mind. He took a moment to steal a glance at Patricia and it was evident she had caught the same idea. Leah stood up and followed Ray down the steps to the chart table. All the instruments needed to run a boat in modern times were there. There was no doubt that when Ray had outfitted the boat he had spared no expense. He had radar, radio, global positioning, barometer, and an up to date weather satellite map, in fact everything to run the boat in the safest possible way.

The two children appeared carrying hot drinks for everyone and as they accepted them Jeannie smiled and said. "Don't worry, Dad always has to check out the weather as soon as he sees a cloud on the horizon."

This had just the opposite effect, Andrew and Richard went into a huddle, talking in low tones before they too went. James smiled at Patricia and said. "I don't think there's much to worry about, it doesn't look too bad out there does it?"

She looked at him as if he had suddenly gone crazy. "Can't you see why they're all worried or is there something wrong with your eyes?"

James had to agree with her, the sea was turning an angry shade of grey and the sun had been covered by cloud. There was a chill in the air, and James shivered even though he had a jumper on. In moments the waves seemed to get higher and angrier. He blinked and shook the idea out of his mind as some sort of fantasy, but there was no doubt that the waves suddenly looked dangerous.

Ray came back up the steps trailed by Leah, and spoke immediately. "We'll have to get back to harbour as soon as possible, it may be nothing much but in these waters who knows. We seem to have run into a bit of a squall, but you never know what's round the corner so to be on the safe side I think we'd better turn back."

He turned and spoke to all the others who had followed him up into the cockpit. "I want you all to do what I want you to do, immediately, and without question." He carried on without waiting for an answer. "Patricia, I want you to take the wheel for a bit until I get things sorted out. Kids you get below and batten down everything that's loose. Leah," he was about to go on when she drawled, "I know, get something brewed hot and put it into flasks, and prepare some sarnies to go with the drinks."

He grinned in. "That's it love, do what you're best at."

She flushed and was about to give him an angry retort when events took an ugly turn as a large wave smashed into the bow and washed straight over the decks, drenching them all. Ray had the presence of mind to grab the wheel, as Patricia had been about to take it from James.

He shouted to her. "Keep it more to the wind for a bit, it's only because she drifted that that happened."

She took the wheel back from him unenthusiastically but he had no time to offer her any more advice. He said to the other three men. "I want you to give me a hand to bring in this sail, we've got too much up there and it'll snap the mast if we don't get it down"

He looked over at Leah who up till now had seemed frozen to the spot, and shouted to her. "Snap out of it and get below and do what you were told."

This time she had no answer for him so went to do as he said. He turned to the men and said. "Well come on then, let's get going or we'll be in serious trouble."

They immediately went with him and with a combination of hard work and luck managed to get the sails down and put in their place one he referred to as a storm sail. They then had to fold down and cover the sails and get all the ropes stowed away. It wasn't easy work but they managed to get it done although they were all soaked and frozen before they had finished. When they were done he said. "Okay that wasn't too bad was it, now go down and dry off as best you can and grab a drink, tell Leah to bring one up for me and Patricia as well. We'll have to get on the best we can for a bit. You've got ten minutes at the most, so make the best of it."

They went down the steps to do as they were told and Patricia and he were left on the deck, he sat down on the bench that ran around the cockpit and said to her. "You're doing quite well, you know, you seem to have a knack for it."

She answered. "You must be the most sexist man I've ever come across, why do you have to persist in idea that women can't do things that men can do?"

He was about to answer when another large wave came curling towards them. He saw the look on her face as she spied it approaching, and jumped to help her turn the wheel towards it to lessen the impact. The boat rose in the air from the bow end and suddenly Patricia found herself looking at the sky. The bow rose and rose until it seemed as if it must turn upside down, just when it was about to do so, it capped the wave and plunged into the trough just behind. As it crashed down a chorus of yells and screams came from the salon accompanied by the sound of crockery smashing to the floor.

"I think we've just lost our hot drinks," he muttered dryly. The door was flung open with a crash and Leah's voice screamed out. "Next time you want to go over a wave like that give us some warning, and you've just lost your drinks." then the door was slammed shut.

Both of them looked at each other and burst out laughing, they had nearly died and Leah's greatest concern was over some spilled drink. When they had stopped Ray looked at her and said. "Can you hold her like this while I go below a while? We've got some hard decisions to make." She nodded and he went on, "Will you accept that we've got to make our minds up about what we're going to do from now on, and it will probably have to be a majority?"

Patricia knew she had to make her mind up, but asked him what he recommended. He wouldn't answer her directly but instead said. "Each person has to vote what they feel, not what I tell them to." Having said that he left her and went below.

When he arrived in the salon a scene of chaos greeted him. All the drinks and sandwiches had been thrown to the deck and everyone had been trying to pick everything up but had merely succeeded in spreading it further as they stumbled about. As soon as something had been placed on the table it had been thrown off again. They were trying to get into wet weather gear at the same time, and this had added to the confusion.

He raised his hands in a calming gesture and shouted above the din, "Alright, alright, let's have some calm round here, I want you all to stop what you're doing for a moment and sit down while we have a talk about what we're going to do."

They gradually calmed down and sat on whatever available seats they could find. He waited until they had settled down and then went on, "the first thing I want to tell you is that this weather has just blown up from nowhere, I didn't get a chance to speak about it before as things can happen very quickly at sea, as you saw. I don't think it's going to be too bad but, I'm certainly not a prophet. For the moment, however, it's certainly here. What we have to decide now, is what we're going to do."

He looked around at the group and grinned when he saw their solemn faces. "Don't worry folks." He joshed. "It's not going to be the end of the world."

He was rewarded with some hesitant smiles and Leah snorted. "All right lover boy, get on with it. We've got a lot to do down here."

He shrugged and went on. "We can turn the boat and try to go back, that's one option. The other is to run before it, but there's no telling how long it will blow. If we try to turn round we'll have a hard time making it back to port, as we'll have to tack all the way against the wind. If we run before it we'll run out of supplies, as we didn't stock up before we left port."

James raised his hand to speak. "How much supplies have you got aboard?"

"Probably enough for three or four days." Ray looked at Leah for confirmation. She nodded and answered. "That's supposing you don't mind eating out of tins and having cold drinks as we can't cook in this weather."

James glanced at Richard and he gave him the permission he needed to make the decision on his behalf. He turned back to Ray and said; "I think the best solution is, we turn back to port, if it takes us two days to get back, so be it. But if we go on we're certainly going to run out of supplies, and," he grinned. "I don't fancy trying my hand at fishing for food just yet."

"OK." Ray was happy to take the decision. "I think you've just chosen the best way for us. Now I want everyone to help out and give Leah a hand clearing up here. I'm going to relieve Patricia on the wheel and let her dry out."

He went out of the salon leaving them to cope with food and drink all over the floor. Andrew looked round and remarked. "I think in some cases it's better to be the captain than the crew. At least he avoids all the mess."

They all smiled and Leah commented. "He's always avoided the mess dearie, right from day one."

By this time the boat was pitching around all over the place and as Patricia came down the steps to the salon, her first words were. "Ray said he wants the men on deck in a few minutes to set sail and help him when he swings the boat round. He's going to have to go sideways on to the waves, when he does and it can get dangerous."

Leah looked up and said. "You men get out of here now. You're bloody useless when it comes to cleaning up anyway, I'll do it with the kids." She pointed a finger at them. "You tell that husband of mine to give me a few minutes, and let me know when he's going to turn. I don't want another episode like the last one."

With some relief the men trooped out of the door, only Andrew looked back at her and joked. "Sooner you than me."

She answered. "Don't worry, I bet you'll have your share of doing this before we hit port again." But she was talking to herself; they'd all gone above.

She looked at Patricia who by this time had collapsed into a seat, her face showing the strain she had been under. "You look dead beat dearie, there's a few drops of water still hot. Why don't you get a quick rinse and then change it'll make you feel a bit better."

Patricia sighed with relief and went to do as Leah had suggested. Her bones ached with weariness from holding the wheel and it was as much as she could do to rinse her face and hands. Finally she was done and she stumbled along to the cabin to get a change of clothes. When she came out she found Leah waiting with some oilskins for her.

"Here you are." Leah said. "Get these on when you go out and tie the neck up real tight and put the cap on over it. It helps to stop the water getting in. That stuff you've got is no good for bad weather on a boat."

Patricia nodded her thanks and began to don the oilskins. Leah stopped her with a wave of her hand. "Don't go out there right now, you get some rest. You're going to need as much as you can get in the next couple of days. I've seen this happen before and it can get worse before it gets better. Right now there are four men on deck, they can handle everything for a while."

Throwing the waterproofs on a seat Patricia slumped down alongside them and within moments had closed her eyes. Leah stared at her speculatively for a minute and then started to work cleaning up.

Up on deck the rest of the party were struggling to get all the rigging under control. Ray had produced lifelines for everybody, he had given them out with the shouted instructions to clip them on at all times. The wind was howling now, tearing the words away almost before they had time to understand what he had said. James looked at the sea around them and felt a shiver go up his back, they looked mountainous to him and constantly in imminent danger of curling over and swamping them. Each time the boat seemed to surmount them with just a few inches to spare.

Ray screamed in his ear. "I said, get hold of that line and heave when I tell you."

The shock brought James to his senses and he grabbed for the line and paid attention to what Ray had been saying. Andrew was holding on to the wheel like grim death and Richard had another line similar to James in his hands. Ray poked his head down into the salon and shouted to the women. "We're going to turn any minute now, hang on."

He started to give his orders, "Get those two small sails up now and Andrew, you be prepared for the extra strain. When we turn she'll heel over, but don't worry she always comes back up. You two get the lines tied down as soon as they come tight and wait for the wind to swing from the starboard, when it does, slacken them off a bit and let the wind take the sail on the port side. It'll snap the boom over but let it go, don't try and hold it too tight. Try and hold it on a centre line with the boat. Are you all ready?" He looked at all their unsmiling faces showing the concern about this move and started laughing. "This is the way to live, right lads?" He seemed to be positively enjoying himself, and if they had asked him he would have agreed. There was something in him of the sense of adventure and a liking for risk. James felt himself warm to the man as he bounded over to Andrew on the wheel and put his hands alongside Andrew's. "I'm going to help you here." He shouted.

He glanced round at the rest of them and took in at a glance how they were faring and nodded in satisfaction. Then he took a deep breath and yelled, "We're going now." He turned the wheel with Andrew, and the boat slowly started to heel over and go across the waves, as it did they grabbed hold of the boat and pushed with terrible force on one side. A large wave appeared from nowhere, and they looked up at it from the trough. It seemed to tower over them as if it was the sea taking revenge on them for being so presumptuous as to travel on its surface in such a puny little craft. Time stood still for a moment and they saw the wind tearing spindrift off the top as the wave curled over them. By now the boat was leaning so far over it seemed impossible that it would ever right itself. Ray was shouting something incomprehensible at the wave, and exhorting the boat at the same time. Slowly they climbed up the side of the wave. James could hear crockery breaking and smashing below and the sound of Leah's voice cursing and swearing.

It seemed an eternity to James before the wave slid slowly beneath them and the wind was back, tearing at the lines they held. Ray started to yell again to let them out a little but not to leave slack but they had already done the right thing. The sails filled and helped to pull the boat round a little further. James heard Ray shout, "Let's get this beauty round into the wind before the next monster comes along."

They wallowed for a moment in the trough behind the wave, and then started to slowly come back to the opposite direction they had been travelling in. The waves were still as large, but now the boat could climb them better. Ray held the boat steady on a tack so that it had the wind as a controlling force and could be steered with the rudder, and then he relaxed a little. He glanced over his shoulder at them and yelled over the noise of wind and sea. "See, I told you she could do it didn't I?" He held his expression for a moment. "It was bloody close though wasn't it?"

He handed over control of the wheel to Andrew then went down to open the door to the salon. But before he could get to it, it flew open and Leah came flying out. She threw her arms round him and gave him a passionate kiss on the lips. It came as a surprise to Ray and almost knocked him over. When she stopped kissing him she shouted. "You crazy bastard, I thought we were goners there."

Ray held her at arms length and looked into her eyes for several seconds while she grinned in delight at him. "I take it I don't have to sleep in the cabin again tonight then?"

She laughed and answered. "Is that all you men think about?" But it was plain to see that the argument was over and they were back together again.

Patricia and the children came up on the deck to see how everything was going. They had come through relatively unscathed with little damage so Ray decided to call for drinks all round although it was still difficult to hold them without spilling any. With the amount of sea spray coming over them from the bows it was probably the saltiest beer James had ever drunk. It took two days of slogging back and forth to make it back to harbour because the weather stayed rough for that time, and as Ray said. "When we set sail, it was forecast as a bit of a blow, but if that's the case I'd like to see what a real blow was like. Talk about understatement."

James had the last word, "We'll all have to have a look at the weather report before we go out again."

Chapter 5

They had been back in harbour for two days before the subject of sailing for Australia had come up, the boat was now in good shape, and they had all turned to and helped. Even the children had had to work with them and, on the morning of the third day Ray decided to take Leah and the children out for a sightseeing tour. James, Patricia, Richard and Andrew gathered on deck after breakfast for a conference. The budget was uppermost in James and Patricia's minds, as they had to think about stocking up for such a long time.

They were attempting to work out a list of how much food one person needed for a year, which was proving an impossible task, as they couldn't reach agreement on the amount each would need for one day. Andrew listened to the argument raging back and forth for some time, until finally he could hold himself in no longer.

"I know you don't like to listen to me as, I'm the youngest and you think I don't know anything. But you're going about this the wrong way." He interrupted. "When I was in the army I had to work in the quartermasters stores for a while."

There was a collective groan from the others as he got on to a subject with which he would bore the pants off from anyone who would listen. "All right, All right, I know you think I go on, but let me finish and then tell me I'm wrong. As I was saying, the quartermaster had to order the food for 600 men in my regiment and the Army laid down guidelines for him to follow. Now the Army had it down to a fine art how much food a man had to have each day to sustain him, and they put out a list to guide him. Well I got to see that list and it was pretty impressive."

He looked at them all in turn and said. "How much margarine or butter does each of you eat in a day, including the cooking, such as pastry?"

He waited for a moment not really expecting an answer.

"2oz." Patricia guessed.

"Not even close," Andrew was scathing. "That was a guess right out of the back of your head. You're not even in the same area."

"All right, then you tell me how much it is then." Patricia was by this time getting a little hot under the collar. She didn't like guessing games and Andrew was her son. She felt he shouldn't make her look a fool.

"Okay," Andrew was enjoying his small moment of victory. "It's actually 1/16 oz." They all looked incredulous and started to speak at once. The loudest voice of them all was Patricia's. "How do you arrive at a figure like that? I've bought for a family and we use far more than that."

Andrew waited until the furore died down. "It's really very simple when you think about it. If you order food for a lot of people the portions that each of them need are quite small but if you add it all up you'll find that they end up as large amounts. "And, "I've seen the orders that went in and they were down to really small amounts like salt and pepper." He grinned at a sudden memory. "They never gave us enough HP sauce though, when it came it disappeared in one day. I saw one guy who put at least half a bottle on one dinner, and then there wasn't any for tea. What I'm trying to say is that if you wait until we're there, we can contact somebody who will give us something like that list. It's going to save you a lot of guesswork, and don't forget the Army has been feeding men for a long time. What I suggest you do is write down what you want in toiletries and things like that. Then when we get established we can order the food to come. You're going to need to build storehouses first anyway."

Richard hadn't said much until now but pointed out, "You can't really order up these things at the moment, as you aren't sure just how many people you are going to have or even how many of each sex will be there."

"I would assume that we're going to have mostly couples, so that shouldn't make any problems with the counting." James had planned this all along and he meant to keep to it. "The last thing we want is for single people to be running around causing trouble by making up to the married ones."

Patricia had listened to this and now interrupted. "One thing has been puzzling me in all this preparation, what happens if one partner dies or decides they don't want to be with the other one any more? After all in our modern society we have divorce courts but we won't be big enough to have all that paraphernalia."

James pointed out that initially they would have contact with society, but had nothing more to offer in the way of solution, other than to say. "We've got to cross certain bridges when we come to them, as we're going to be a society on our own. At some time every one who's affected will have to be able to put in their two pence worth at the time." He pulled on his chin for a moment while thinking and then went on. "I think we'll all have to think of our morals and our way of life when we do this, it won't necessarily be the same as in a normal society. If you think about it, with only a limited amount of people in the community, interbreeding will happen within a very short space of time."

Patricia looked up at this. "What are you saying? That we allow cousins and brothers and sisters to breed? Or are you saying we all ought to breed with each other?" Her face had gone quite red at this and she looked at her husband as if he were the devil incarnate for suggesting such a thing.

"Look, don't fly off the handle with me for bringing up ideas that have to be considered. Ordinary common sense should tell you that we don't have enough people to separate family ties. If you take an example with twenty people, that makes ten couples, if they have one child each, that's a potential of five of each sex. If they marry and have children, the kids will be forced to have babies with a blood relative. I'm not too good with numbers but it is inescapable with such a small community that interbreeding will happen. The only alternative would be if you could find other communities and arrange marriage between them." He raised his hands. "What are the chances of that happening?"

Patricia was aghast. "But you've seen the results of interbreeding, look at the royal families in Europe. For years they had their share of sub normal children because of interbreeding. They had to marry so called commoners to improve the stock.

And," she pointed her finger at him. "You lived in Belgium with me for some time when you worked over there, how many idiots did you see caused by this very same problem."

She was well into her stride by this time and no one dared to intervene. "You used to joke with me that because the average Belgian wanted to marry and live in the same village without moving, most of them were related to each other. Look at all the sub normal people we saw. Do you remember you used to say that even the laws had to be passed by idiots?"

"Yes but you should remember that they never missed a trick when it came to the money though, every time I had a dispute with them about money they always won. Even the government seemed to load the system against foreign people working there."

James had said many times he had only met two or three people who didn't try to cheat him and he could only think of two people that he could call friends in the whole country. In his mind it had been one of the worst times of his life and he had been quite relieved when he stopped working there. Any mention of it was guaranteed to raise his blood pressure.

By now James was getting to dislike the way the conversation had turned and attempted to change the direction. "There is another thing that has been worrying me about this and that's the question of clothes while we're in there. Is it possible to order enough material for ten years and have someone make them as we go along? Otherwise we're going to have some sort of fashion parade with everybody trying to get one over the others."

"That's one thing that I agree we ought to be doing." Patricia replied. "Maybe we can do some sort of deal in tracksuits for evening and hard wearing overalls for the day, oh." She had a sudden thought. "And maybe different colours for the sexes."

"There is one other thing that I've been thinking about, and I think it will have to be discussed and that's the question of women and the time of month. When it comes to periods with ten women that's going to be a lot of sanitary towels to provide."

Patricia raised her eyes to the sky in despair at the stupidity of men. The men in question all hung their heads and glanced at each other in confusion. This subject always seemed to create uncertainty in their minds.

"Haven't you heard of reusable towels? We'll just have to provide enough for them and keep washing them." James raised his head to look at her, it was obvious from his expression that something else had occurred to him. "I've heard that when women are living together that their cycles synchronize after a while."

Patricia nodded in agreement. James groaned aloud. "Can you imagine ten women all with PMT at the same time? Nobody's going to have a chance."

Although she had been offended by James's remark, Patricia had to admit he had a point and resolved to make enquiries as soon as possible into this problem. She supposed Colette might have an answer. Meanwhile she retorted to James that maybe if he had ever had to go through some of the things that women had to bear there might be a little more understanding from men. This seemed to put a stop to any further discussion, and they agreed to each make a list of purchases that they thought would be needed for the future. "After all," as Richard said. "If we all make a list separately there is a chance we won't forget anything."

"Are you kidding?" James mocked him. "How many times have you gone on holiday and forgotten something? I bet every one of you has done that at least once. When I was working abroad I lost count of the times I left something important behind."

"Well then." Richard was scathing. "Just remember if you leave it behind this time you're going to have to wait ten years before you can go back and get it."

This remark sobered them up for a while and they all retired to separate parts of the boat to compile their lists. With one final instruction from James. "Put everything down that you can think of, even if you think that someone else might write it in. It'll be better to have something down twice than forget it. We can do a compilation when we get together later."

It was after some time when Ray, Leah and the children came across the gangplank after their day out and found all their passengers scattered about the boat with paper and pens in hand. Except for Richard, who had started to do what had become for him, an obsession. He had got out a computer game and was busy punching keys, completely oblivious to everything going on around him. Andrew wandered over and started to watch as he played the game, occasionally making a comment about his progress.

Ray looked at Patricia and James who had put down their writing materials when his family had come aboard, Patricia had started to make a fuss of the children and was asking them about their day. They were excitedly telling her where they had been and what they had done and their chatter carried on as they went outside.

"These two guys are just the sort of customers who'd make me a fortune when I was running my own company." Ray told James grinning at the two of them.

It wasn't certain if they had heard what he had said as the response was no more than a grunt of acknowledgement. They were both transfixed by the little figures on the screen. James, who had seen this sort of thing before felt ashamed that they thought no more than the next move of the game. They certainly didn't take any more notice of Ray or him, it was as if they had been mesmerised. He looked at Ray and Leah and shrugged his shoulders. "I don't know what to say, and I've never come across this sort of thing before, except when they brought out television in the old days. That created the instant moron situation as well. It seems to affect some people more than others though. In those days I thought it was the fascination of something new."

He paused for a moment and thought, and then went on. "I think you could draw a correlation between the amount spent doing something like this and intelligence but I don't think that's the whole answer. Some very intelligent people are addicted to these games as well. How about you Ray? Are you addicted as well?

It was Leah who answered first. "He was as addicted as these two were ducky, he spent hours on that bloody computer."

Ray looked at her with disbelief at this remark, shook his head and said. "I can't believe you said that, did you think when I was on that computer all the time I was playing these stupid games? I was doing that so I could earn enough money to keep you in the style you seem to have grown accustomed to. I was putting the bloody things together, not playing on them, and another thing, when I played on them it was so I could show the punters how the games worked."

Something in his voice had got through to Richard, he raised his head to listen, only to find that he had lost a life! He swore then started to push buttons until he could start another game. Andrew leaned over and pointed at the screen and said something about he should go to level 3. Richard nodded and started to comply, his face rapt with concentration on the game once more. Ray watched for a moment then said to James. "All the time they spend on these was money in my bank when I had the Company. I'd rather try and invent another game than do that all day."

James nodded in agreement, although he occasionally enjoyed playing a game on the computer he had always found other things to do with it. Consequently he knew a lot about the programmes and how to run them but not how to play the games. "I think we ought to treat ourselves to a beer, before we go and eat, don't you think Ray?"

Ray beamed. "That's one suggestion I can agree with mate," he turned to Leah and commented "I hope you remembered to stock the fridge up with some tinny's. Nothing worse than a warm one, eh!"

Ray had the typical Australians' attitude to drink; it seemed to James they never stopped drinking all day. The supply appeared to be inexhaustible.

Leah sneered. "Don't worry darling the tinny's are all getting cold for you, we wouldn't want you suffering with a warm beer would we?"

Ray looked at her and answered in the same sort of tone, "Why don't you go and get some food on Luvvie, or you'll miss out on your gin and tonic won't you?"

James started to move out of the door ushering Ray before him, he wanted no part in another row between them. They met Patricia in the doorway with the children. "I'm just coming to see if we should put some food on the table, these kids are starving."

"Those kids are always bloody starving." Leah's voice had a long-suffering tone about it. "I suppose you're right though, we'll have to get something ready."

She looked over at Richard and Andrew. "I don't suppose it'd be any good asking those two to help would it?" The response she got back from those two was complete indifference. She shrugged and turned to go to the galley. Patricia looked at them playing the game completely oblivious to anything around them, and then looked at Ray and James. "While you're swigging those beers you can set the table, there's no excuse for you two to be idle even if they are."

Ray nudged James and muttered. "I think it might be an idea to do as the little woman says don't you?"

James winced, the last thing anyone could refer to Patricia as, was. "The little woman," Sure enough, she spun round and would have let fly with one of her nasty remarks. But she would have been talking to empty air; Ray had seen the expression on her face and beaten a hasty retreat.

When they arrived on deck Ray got two cans of beer from the fridge and tossed one to James. They quickly set the table and then sat down to finish the beers off. Ray said. "I've got something to ask you mate. Now hear me out before you say anything. First of all, I think your idea of this community is fairly good. You seem to be a bit half-assed about it but in principle the thing can work. I can see some areas that are going to need a bit of spit and polish, but generally speaking you seem to be on the right lines. Now, the idea has occurred to me that you've got the impression that you have enough money for the whole project. Bullshit, you haven't got anywhere near enough."

James protested at this and tried to say something, but Ray beat him to it. "Just hear me out please, and then you can have your say. I want to join your group and I'm willing to put in a lot of money for the privilege, the only thing is, I don't want to tie myself down for the next few years on some farm right out in the middle of the outback. If we can work out something so as I can be a part of the group but come in a bit later I wouldn't mind doing it"

James asked "How much money were you thinking of putting in?"

Ray grinned, "Do you think now that you have got enough cash?"

"I didn't know in the first place how much we would need

but we are expecting to earn more money as we go along. Then we are hoping to sell some of the crops we'll be growing to get some cash in. it might be a bit tight but if everybody pulls their weight we should manage."

"You'll have to earn a lot of money to put all your ideas into practice, and I don't think you'll be able to set it up without going broke." Ray was emphatic when he spoke. "Now I'm willing to put in, let's say, a million bucks. On the understanding that I can come in later."

This sum of money was a complete surprise to James, he had known Ray was wealthy but by investing £500,000 he had to be serious. He sat back for a moment to absorb this information, his mind going over all the possible computations.

"I don't deny the idea of you investing in the community to the sum of half a million quid is very tempting. But first I'm going to have to explain something to you. One of my pet hates is people who want something but don't put the time in. Now, we need bodies on the ground who are willing to work. I've got no doubt that you are, in your own way thinking you're doing us a good turn. But how do you think the others are going to take this when I say, we've got this rich guy who wants to buy a place in the future. We can take his money and he's going to join us later, put a place out for him. If I wanted to do that I could probably find a dozen investors who'd put the money in."

Taken aback Ray answered. "But you are going to need the money so why not do it?"

"Look." James felt the need to explain to Ray just what they needed. "I can see you don't want to change your lifestyle for a bit, but you have to understand that the people who are coming sincerely believe that the world as we know it is coming to an end. They're willing to go along with us and work to survive. I can't go around selling tickets to the future, because it's not about investing your money it's about investing your life and your work."

Ray considered this for a while then said. "It's like religion with you lot isn't it? You know as well as I do that it might not happen in our lifetime and you still want me to come and work on the place till it's ready. Then what?"

"I'll consider letting you have a holiday, so long of course, as you don't go too far."

"And you still want me to put in the million bucks?"

"Naturally; don't forget all the others are putting in all their life savings." James smiled at Ray, "What are you going to do with the rest of your money when you're stuck in there for ten years, and you won't have anything to spend it on when you do come out; there won't be anybody to give it to anyway."

This last statement gave Ray something to think about, he reached for two cans and handed one to James. They both had a drink whilst he thought everything over.

Then he commented, "I can see your point about everybody has to pull their weight, I don't think I'd like it if I put a lot of work into something and some rich guy came along and settled himself in. I'll tell you what I'll do. I'll put in a year of work and throw in the best computer system money can buy with lots of spares, and for the icing on the cake you can still have the million bucks. But after one year I take off for a month's holiday and no trying to stop me."

Reaching out James grabbed his hand and said. "Welcome into the community, but no moaning about how much work we've got to do. And don't forget the wife and kids come as well."

They smiled at each other while still clasping hands. Leah's dry voice said. "And what are you two hatching up that we need to know? As if I can't guess."

Still grinning, both men turned to find Leah and Patricia standing behind them with trays of food. Jumping up, Ray took the tray from Leah whilst attempting to kiss her on the cheek. Naturally he didn't quite make it and some of the drinks started to slop over. She began to complain but Ray was having none of it.

"Don't fuss Leah," he shouted. "We've just signed into this crazy bastard's community, and we're going to be working in the outback for a long time. It only cost a million bucks, cheap at the price don't you think?"

Leah stared at him as if he had gone straight out of his head. "You've promised to give this guy a million bucks so you can go and work in the Northern Territories in all that heat and humidity.

And for what? The promise that if the world maybe blows up or whatever they think it's going to do, you get a place. What if it doesn't explode? You'll have blown a million bucks."

Ray answered her angrily. "Just what you always do isn't it? Never stop to listen to anyone, just lose your rag. Don't think of anything else but yourself. Are you afraid you can't get to the shops in Sydney and buy the latest fashions? Think about the future of the planet. Think about our future, what happens to the kids if this thing does occur?"

From being a man who was trying to hedge his bets Ray had now turned into a man who was concerned for the future of the planet. James stifled a smile, as it wouldn't have been the most diplomatic thing to do for the moment. He attempted to restore peace to the proceedings. "Calm down Leah, he isn't going to lose his money; we sign an agreement to pay everybody back their investment if they leave."

She rounded on him angrily. "Tell me how you can pay back a million bucks if you've spent it on some crazy scheme to set up a community in the back of beyond?"

James replied. "We've gone through all the figures, and it does work out. We give shares in the Company to all the participants and anyone holding those shares can sell them back to us if they wish. I know the money isn't in cash in the bank, but that's natural as it's in the buildings and the equipment. It's also in the hands of the community so if anyone says, I'm out, they can go. I agree they can't get all their money back in one go, because if we paid everybody out like that we'd go broke."

Ray nodded. "Sounds like a good way to do business; I've done it myself a couple of times when I needed finance."

Leah rounded on him. "You would say something like that, wouldn't you? But you remember that money belongs to both of us and I get to say if we go or not. Now, I'm not going to waste good food again so get this lot eaten. I'm going to talk to Pat about this later and I've got one more thing to say, this is Oz we're talking about, and you may think your going to bring your stuffy Pommy ways here but you're not." She paused and looked around at them all. Then she pointed at James. "I'm up to here with all this formality when we speak to you, from now on you're Jim, you're Pat, and those other two are Andy and Dick, that's if they ever bother to come out of that stupor they're in whenever there's a computer about." With that she grabbed the tray from Ray's hands and slammed it on the table, spilling even more of the drinks. She then rounded on Pat and said. "Get that food on the table as quick as you can, I want a word with you after we've eaten." She called Andy and Dick to the table and pointed at the food; they sat down and started to eat. The food was all eaten in record time as none of them seemed in the mood for talking. When the meal was over Leah said to Ray. "I want you and Jim to go and put those things in the dishwasher and get cleaned up here, Pat and me have things to talk about regarding this. And I don't want any interruptions; this goes for you two kids as well. I want you two in bed in about an hour, and wash yourselves before you go." She looked at Ray and said to him. "Make sure they do as there're told and no nonsense from them."

They turned and left to a chorus of moans from the two children and rueful looks from Ray as she went. Pat smiled at Jim and crossed her fingers before leaving to follow Leah. Andy and Dick who had been watching all this without comment now wanted to know what was going on, and they looked expectantly at Jim. He merely said to them. "You'll find out soon enough."

They glanced at each other then went out with the children. A minute later they could hear the sounds of a computer game starting up and one of the children saying. "I want to play first, you two have been on it all day,"

Jim looked at Ray and said. "We'd better get this place cleaned up or we'll be in trouble ourselves."

They set to as quickly as possible as neither relished the idea of housework, and a few minutes later Ray slammed the door of the dishwasher shut and said to Jim, "Want to go for a walk? It's got a little cooler now that evenings coming on." Jim nodded so they went on to the pontoon and walked off down the marina.

In the cabin Leah and Pat faced each other over the chart table. Pat started the conversation. "Now you've had your say and I want to get my word in before you begin, first of all I don't think this is such a crazy idea as you appear to think. Take into consideration all the advantages of living in the back of beyond as you put it. The children are going to have a happy upbringing with lots of people around to help them with any problems, my best friend is coming and she's a good teacher. Her husband is a professor and he's got a lot of brains. I'm going to be there for everybody and to organise everything. It'll be like living on a farm with animals and farming crops to occupy them in their spare time. At first they can attend the local school if one is close enough for them so they can mix with other kids, if there isn't they can be taught by friends. We've got other children coming along so they'll have company if they want. Your husband's going to be there so you can settle down to a real family life. I can't pretend everything is going to be a bed of roses but who can promise that."

She stopped and looked at Leah, who hadn't moved a muscle and was looking at her with a serene expression on her face. Pat had been expecting a fierce argument from her and now it hadn't happened. She looked at her and asked her, "Are you all right? You haven't given me any trouble yet."

Leah's face broke into a huge smile. "Don't worry, I'd already made up my mind it was the best thing to do, all that trouble out there was just for Ray's benefit. I wanted the big lug to think he had to persuade me to go. If he assumes he's got it easy he'll ride roughshod over everything we say or do. He'll try and take over from your old man if you let him, so keep your guard up. I know that the sort of life you're going to lead will be for the best; it's just that he was right, I will miss all the shops and fashions. Still, I suppose when it's as hot as that we won't need many clothes and jewellery. Any way, who is there to dress up for? What I really want to know is what my job is going to be in all this? All I've ever done is secretarial work and I don't suppose there's going to be much call for that is there."

"There'll be lots to do, don't worry about that," Pat reassured her. "If you don't know how much mess men can make by now, there must be something wrong with the life you've been living." Her eyes took on a slightly dreamy quality as she thought of the life they would be having in the not too distant future. She looked at

Leah and asked her. "What do you think you could do if you were given free rein then?"

"Well," Leah had been given an opportunity to realise her private dreams and for a moment she was at a loss for words. Then she seemed to gather her thoughts about her. "What I always wanted to do for a living was organise everything. When I was a secretary working for someone else I was always sticking my oar in when the boss made mistakes. But the trouble was that when things turned out OK I never got the credit, if they went wrong it always seemed to be my fault. I think you're going to need someone with overall responsibility for ordering all your supplies and seeing they get delivered. Someone who isn't afraid to stand up to suppliers and shout at them until the right things get sent. I look at the people you have here and they all seem to have a specific job and you think Jim is going to do the ordering, but he'll be far too busy building everything to have time to organise supplies. Another thing, I know Aussies better than you and they need some careful handling. If you say the wrong thing to some of them its very likely to go wrong. And don't imagine it's the money they're thinking about, if their pride gets hurt that's just as important. And anyway, when it comes to men I have a way of getting the best out of them."

Pat thought to herself. "I wonder what her way could possibly be?" but then dismissed the thought as disloyal to her newfound friend. Some people had an unfortunate way of putting things and maybe this was the reason. She just said. "What happens if the suppliers you're dealing with are women?"

"Don't worry about that," came the reply. "Most women are too busy trying to be good business people to worry about what the other female looks like."

Patricia's experience with other women had never led her to this conclusion. In her visits to the hairdressers it always seemed as if other ladies were jealous of anyone who may be a little better looking than them and attempted to make them have hairstyles that were completely inappropriate. Still, she thought to herself. "Maybe its different out in the mainstream of business,"

Aloud she said. "Do you think you can handle the job then?"

The reply came with a very confident voice. "Piece of cake,

I can handle this job as easy as I run my marriage and the two kids that go with it."

Although she didn't show it, this wasn't quite the answer Pat was hoping to get. She didn't think Leah's way of running her marriage was quite the way she would have wanted to run a community in the outback. Still, trying to be philosophical about it, she thought at least we get another willing volunteer. She contented herself with one more admonition. "You'll have a very responsible job to do when we arrive; I just hope you're up to it."

Leah smiled back at her. "Don't worry about me, I can handle anything that comes my way. I'm strong and no one messes me about. The job I'm lined up for I can do, but you've got a problem and you don't even know it. Those two guys down there," she pointed into the area where Andy and Dick using the computer. There're going to cause you some serious grief if you let them go on playing those games, there're the worst thing that can happen to blokes like that. They end up thinking that it's real and losing it for the real world."

This was a problem that had been bothering Pat for some time now, as she had seen the effects that it had had on her son, now it appeared to be worse for Dick as he didn't seem to be able to function in the same way as he had previously. He certainly paid no attention to any of the goings on in the family; all he seemed to do was head for the computer at the first available opportunity. Pat also recalled that when he had been at home he constantly complained of feeling tired, simply so he could get out of helping in the house. As she and Jim had often commented, there's no job on earth that could make you that tired.

She looked at Leah and replied. "I can't agree that I don't know about the problem. My real trouble is what am I going to do about it, the only solution I've got for this is to walk in and pull the plug on them. But that only shifts the trouble to my shoulders for switching it off."

Leah mulled this over for a little while and then said. "Maybe we'll have to do something about it when we reach the property, like get Ray to install the computers later rather than sooner."

"They'll still be there though won't they," Pat responded. "I'd like to take their stupid little play station and wrap it round their ears for them."

"Oh well, maybe we'll think of something to do before we get there."

And with that in mind they walked out to relax in the cooler air of the evening.

The next day was bright and sunny with just a hint of clouds above; James looked over the side. He had just had a shower and felt refreshed and ready for anything the day threw at him. It was already warm and he only had on a pair of shorts and sandals. He ran his fingers through his hair and looked around at the scene around him. During the day the marina was a hive of activity, at this time there were only a few people about. Most of whom seemed to be like himself, up a little too early for the rest of the crew and able to potter about on their own. He found the coffee pot and put it on the burner in the galley to heat then spooned the grains into the large flask reserved for coffee. While he waited he got some cups out and put sugar and milk on the table. When the water boiled he filled the pot and carried it outside to put on the table.

From behind him he heard Leah say. "That coffee smells delicious I hope you've made enough for two." He looked at her, she was dressed much as he was, with just a T-shirt and shorts and her hair was damp from the shower. "There's one thing I've learnt in my time and that's never make coffee for one person because someone always turns up just as you've made it."

He poured out two cups and they sat in silence for a few moments, contemplating the scene before them. She turned to him and asked. "Has Pat told you about my new job in your community yet?"

At first she thought he hadn't heard the question then he nodded slowly as if deep in reflection. "Yes she has told me. What do you think you can bring to this job that I can't?"

She laughed, "Oh, Oh, here we go again, watch out for the old male ego rearing up it's ugly head and trying to prove you're better than us poor little women."

In fact she couldn't have been further from the truth, as James had no interest in the male female struggle. In his opinion women were far better at some things than men, just as men were better than women at other things. He liked women to reach their full potential, he just abhorred the women who tried to lord it over men and prove all the time they were better. He hadn't forgotten the phone call in their hotel room when she had started to roust him out when he misunderstood what had been going on with her and Dick.

"So you think you're up to the job?"

She answered his question with one of her own. "When you're working on a project how much time do you have to sit in the office or go and sort materials out? Wouldn't it be better if you were able to stay on the ground and watch everybody yourself?"

"I understand what you're saying but now I've got a question for you," James was aware of the potential disasters that awaited the unwary learner on a building site. He had sent one man to get some bandage scrim for sealing cracks in the plasterboard ceilings and the guy had returned with bandages from the site office. "Do you think you can learn all the different terms we use in the building industry to describe a range of material? Could you differentiate between plumber's requirements and bricklayers for example? Would you understand that if a carpenter came to you and asked for a beam 9"x4" it was in wood but if a bricklayer asked for the same thing, it's in concrete?"

She looked incredulously at him. "What do you take me for? When Ray first made it big we built our own house in the country, and Ray being Ray he couldn't wait to hand it over to someone else to run for him. All he wanted to do was get down the marina and watch his big boat being built; it was left to muggins here to sort out the house. I ran that job from first to last, and I did it right. And if we get the time when we're in Oz I'll show it to you to prove I can do it."

Her voice had risen higher and higher, she was in danger of losing her temper and that was the last thing James wanted to happen. He held up his hands up, saying. "Calm down, calm down, I believe you. I just wanted to be sure that you could handle the work. I know what suppliers can be like, that's all. I sometimes think they're put on this earth to make life as difficult as possible for the builders."

She sat back in her chair. "Well you've got no need to worry about me, as I can do this work and I can do it as good as anyone else, you just explain exactly what you want and that's what you'll get."

James breathed a sigh of relief for having averted another crisis, but thought that she would take careful handling to keep her happy out in the country. The boat started to come alive with voices and sounds of the others getting ready for the day. Soon everybody came to get their breakfast. Leah sighed and grinned at Jim. "Looks like I've got to go and do my primary job right now, how do you like your eggs?"

She didn't wait for an answer but went directly to the galley. Soon the smells of a good English breakfast were wafting upwards as she and Pat worked together to create the ideal meal to start the day. In a very short time the breakfast was on the table and everybody was tucking in.

Ray mopped the last of the egg from his plate and took a swig of coffee, then he glanced around to the assembly and said. "Well we've got to go sometime and the weather forecast is quite good for the next week so I think we ought to think about setting sail tomorrow or the next day. That means we've got to get sufficient supplies for the following few weeks, I don't think it's going to take that long but it's better to be safe than sorry. I'm going to need the help of everybody, so none of you had better start sloping off and that goes for you two over there." He pointed at Andy and Dick who both glanced at each other a little sheepishly

"We had no intention of sloping off as you put it." Dick retorted.

Ray looked back at him. "I didn't exactly mean you were going to disappear, I meant I didn't want you to begin playing on that computer. You loose all track of time when you start. I need you two to help me lug all the supplies back from the stores when we go."

It was obvious that Dick didn't like the way that Ray was talking to him but in his position he evidently decided that it would be better to hold his tongue. Ray by this time had moved on to other things and had started talking to Jim. "I'd like you and Pat to start sorting out the store cupboards and tidying them up to see how much we've got in them."

He said to Leah. "You can give me a list of supplies while they're doing that and make sure we've got enough for about a month. I don't think it'll take that long to get there but I want some margin for error." He looked around at Andy and Dick and said. "Can you two cast off, I'm going to go round and get some diesel for the engines."

He went start the engines and the rest cast off. At the fuel depot Ray instructed the man to fill the tanks to the brim and while he was doing that he filled the water tanks as well. He looked at Jim while this was going on and remarked. "Can't be too careful from now on so I'm going to go with a full load."

Finally they were full and Ray presented his credit card to pay. The operator took it without comment but Jim saw it was the ultimate in cards, the American Express platinum card. While it was put through the machine Ray noticed him looking and said. "Don't be surprised, when you have boats like this you have to forget how much it's costing you, if you didn't you'd never have one."

His comments were heard by the operator who grinned and said. "Get a lot of those cards through here."

"Not from me you wouldn't," Jim said. It wasn't that he didn't have cards he just didn't like to use them. Especially cards like Rays, which were almost limitless in their use. "What happens to you if you lose it then? He asked.

"Not really a problem," was the answer. "All you have to do is get on the phone and tell them; anyway if the wrong type of person tries to use that card he'll be spotted in no time."

Payment made, Ray went on board to start the engines, and the men on the dockside cast off for them and they motored back round to their mooring. On arrival at their own jetty they tied up. Leah handed Ray a list of provisions she had written out. Ray glanced over it and asked a couple of questions about which brand she wanted with certain items. That finished, he called to the children and set off for the store.

Jim was on deck when Ray came back from the store accompanied by an assistant with an electric trolley. He couldn't believe his eyes as it was piled high with provisions. Leah called out to Ray. "Are you sure you've got enough for a little journey?"

"Yeah, but you wouldn't believe how much we needed when we worked it out," Ray answered. "Don't forget there's eight of us to feed and then all the washing of clothes and us as well, and anyway you ordered a lot of this."

The next hour was spent in the loading of the stores on to the boat and trying to put them in to cupboards and hidey-holes everywhere. Leah glanced at the clock on the bulkhead and said, "it's time to eat," She looked at the children pointedly and said. "It's about time you two kids started to pull your weight around here so come and help me get a meal going,"

This of course was greeted with a chorus of moans and groans, and especially from Jeannie who had managed as usual to ensconce herself by the side of Dick. Leah went on over their groans. "Since Dick is staying here and helping today, he can get the dinner as well then you and he can prepare it in the galley while I get this mess sorted out with Pat."

Jeannie smiled in Dick's direction and grabbed his hand pulling him towards the galley. He glared at Leah and followed reluctantly. The last they heard was Jeannie saying "Isn't it great we can work together preparing food for everyone."

They all had a meal in the cabin together, it was very simple, as Jeannie had only begun to learn to cook this year and wasn't sure what to do for a meal for eight, while Dick had proved to be a reluctant worker as far as kitchens went.

While they were eating Ray brought up a subject that had been troubling him. "If this all does happen how are you going to defend yourselves?"

Jim frowned. "Defend?" he said questioningly.

"Yeah, like if someone turns up and says I'm dying let me in,"

Jim scratched his head. "I don't understand, can't we just let them in?"

Ray stared at him in amusement. "What if the geezers got twenty of his mates with him? You let them in as well?"

Jim's eyes widened. "Do you think that's going to happen?"

"Sure as eggs is eggs it'll happen, when word gets round that you're living in that place they'll be turning up and you'd better believe they'll have some firepower with them. So I'll ask you again, what're you going to do about it?"

Jim shrugged his shoulders, he was at a loss to as to what to say, he had never been in this situation before and now he had no answers.

"Leah said scathingly. "Just like a Pom, start off something without thinking it through,"

Pat rounded on her in defence of Jim. "He might be a Pom but he always looks for the best in a man, and expects them to behave in a proper manner."

Ray said angrily. "Do you think they'll come up all polite and knock gently on the door asking to be let in, forget it? It'll probably be a rocket launcher at a hundred yards or a claymore against the door, so I'm telling you now you've got to get organised and get some serious weaponry in there to help you out."

Jim absorbed this for a few seconds and then said. "I just don't know what to say, I wouldn't even know where to look for something like that."

Ray and Leah exchanged glances, then Ray said. "Look, we can get rifles and shotguns in Oz, they're allowed for hunting kangaroo and small game, but anything else we'll have to look elsewhere. I'll be making some calls and looking on the internet to see what I can come up with."

"Watch what you enter in the search boxes, because they have a watch for key words." Leah called after him. She got a wave over his shoulder as he entered the saloon.

It was an hour later when he re-appeared; he had a wry grin on his face. "Good news and bad news. The good news is that I can get some useful rifles and shotguns fairly easily, but the rest." He paused and looked around. "We'd have to take a chance. I found a guy who can supply what we want but we'd have to sail north to Thailand and hope to meet him there. I'm worried because these guys aren't like us westerners. It could be dangerous. At the moment he's on a ship bound for Bangkok but he's willing to stop off at some island in the middle of nowhere if we make it worth his while. So my solution is to put it to the vote," He held his hands up. "Kids excluded," he snapped as the children started to sit up in excitement, and he got a chorus of groans for his trouble.

"All those in favour of meeting this guy, raise your hand."

Several hands rose until just Pat had her hands in her lap.

"Why not?" Jim asked.

"I thought you'd know that," She snapped. "You just heard Ray say how it could be dangerous and now you want to sail off into the middle of nowhere at the drop of a hat trying to buy guns. We're ordinary people not some cowboys or terrorists. It's all too airy fairy for my liking."

Jim felt a pang of pity but decided to put pressure on her. "What will you do if some other ordinary people take it into their heads to try and seize over our project and turning up with some guns to do it? Are you just going to roll over like a little puppy or are you going to stand up and be counted?"

"Will it really happen like that?" She asked.

When Jim nodded "It could do." she sighed and raised her hand as well.

"That's that then." Ray said happily. "We'll be off as soon as I can get my hands on some cash."

He looked over at Jim. "How about you sport, you got any spare cash lying around?"

Jim stared at the deck. "I'm afraid not," he sighed. "We set it up so I could draw cash in OZ. "Not out here, although I could get into the bank and give it a try, how much are we going to be looking for?"

He whistled when Ray gave him a figure. "I can get some but I reckon they won't give me that much without some severe negotiation."

Ray grinned. "Thought you'd say that, so it's lucky I can lay my hands on some serious cash if I need to, let's call it my contribution to the Company Fund. Now I've got some negotiating to do to arrange what we need and a meeting place."

Chapter Six

They had been sailing now for nearly two weeks, steadily going north along the coast between Indonesia and Malaysia in the Andaman Sea and making for the Bay of Bengal. They were heading for a tiny group of islands north of Indonesia where they would rendezvous with a freighter carrying their weapons. It had been arranged over many phone calls, the salesman who went under the name of Sulim had explained that he had had a shipment of arms to go to one of the many revolutionary groups in the world. But they had to cancel at the last minute, 'probably the ruling regime had caught up with them' Ray joked. Now he had to unload them to recoup his losses, although Ray thought he was likely to have much more than they needed. They had no idea where the freighter was at present, as the captain wouldn't reveal his position, so all they had to go on was a date and a bearing. When Jim had looked worried about navigation Ray grunted sarcastically. "The system I've got for positioning is accurate right down to about three metres. So if you think we'll miss him at that range you'd better get yourself another guy."

Ray had been as good as his word with the cash and had drawn far more than Jim thought was needed. Ray had just smiled and joked, "I've been there before and you can never have too much of the old wonga." The weather to their surprise had been mostly hot without storms. The Andaman Islands, a long chain of islands were on their port side, were mostly densely wooded and sparsely populated. Ray had said their meeting place was just north of a tiny Isle called the Coco Island. He had no intention of trying to moor there, as the designated meeting spot would be ten miles further north on the open sea between the Andaman Sea and the Bay of Bengal.

Finally with much fussing with the satellite navigation system Ray pronounced they were right on target. Jim glanced around and could see nothing in any direction "Nobody's here." he announced.

Ray's lip curled. "Shouldn't think there would be yet, he's not due until tomorrow,"

"Thanks for the update Captain." Jim snorted. "If you'd chosen to share that little bit of information we might not make silly remarks, and if you think about it you should share info because if anything happens to you, we'll be left high and dry,"

"Yeah." Leah chipped in. "It ain't going to make you cleverer than us if you keep information to yourself like that, so stop trying to prove you're the big I am."

Ray glowered at both of them and would have started another argument, but Pat got in as well. "I agree with these two, you start letting everybody else know what's going on so we'll all know what's going to happen."

Ray resented being told what to do and went straight into attack mode shouting. "All right I agree with you, but let's get this boat shipshape and how about some grub? And you, Jim, you can get the sea anchor out so we don't drift too far, cos the wind and waves can push us several miles without something to hold us still."

The next hour saw a change in the boat as they stowed everything away, and finally Ray pronounced himself satisfied and they settled down to wait for the freighter to appear. While they were at a loose end they went over the arrangements for making a payment to the man selling the guns. "I want to go on board to look the guns over and I need someone to come with me, someone who knows about guns and can judge what they're like and how useful they'll be to us."

He stared at Andy while he said this; but Jim butted in. "I thought I should go instead, after all I am the leader of this group and I want to be represented when big purchases like this are made."

Almost to a man they rounded on him, with Andy the most vociferous. "You don't know enough about guns to be a good judge."

Jim said sullenly. "All right," and pointing his finger at Andy he snapped. "You make sure you make a good choice because if you don't it could cost us all our lives. And don't get only machine guns, they use ammo too quickly and you have to carry a lot of it."

Ray said to him. "I'm not going to take any money with me when I go aboard, when we've made our selection, I'll come topside and call down how much we need, you can count it in the cabin so that lot don't know how much we have aboard. It'll be risky enough anyway because we can't defend ourselves if they try to take us over. I'm going to convey the impression that we are armed and can get some guns out if needed. I'm also going to order a lot extra to be delivered in Oz so they think we'll pay out a lot more money when they get there."

Somewhat mollified, Jim agreed. At least this way he got some small authority out of the arrangements.

The following day everybody was up bright and early, the good weather had continued and apart from a slight swell the sea was calm. After they had breakfast they settled in to wait for the freighter to arrive. Dick and Andy headed straight for the video game machine and the children went on to their computer having been banned from the games that the older ones played.

About eleven am Jim glanced up from his book and saw a tiny curl of smoke on the horizon and drew their attention to it. They all crowded to the side to watch and over the next hour a ship grew steadily larger. Finally it hove to about fifty metres away and they could see it clearly. Rust streaked the sides and it was obvious that no one had tried to improve the appearance for several years. Jim grunted. "I expect they think it's a good disguise to appear like that, looks like it's a down at heel grafter doesn't it?"

"I don't expect they want too many questions when they're in port and if you look wealthy people might wonder where you got your money from."

A man appeared on deck with a loud hailer and the metallic voice boomed over the water. "I will only allow two persons to come aboard to inspect my cargo, please come over in that little dinghy you have there."

They all looked at each other then Ray snapped. "It's only what we expected so let's get on with it."

Everybody pitched in and threw the dinghy overboard. Andy, Ray and Dick slid down into it. It only took a few moments to arrive and by then a rope ladder had been lowered, they watched as Ray and Andy climbed up, shook hands with the man and disappeared into the bowels of the boat. Dick rowed the boat back and clambered on board. Jim smiled and said. "Now the waiting starts, I want everybody on alert for now, because I don't know how long this is going to take. The sea's pretty calm, I think it'll be a good ides to get closer to them."

They started the engines and motored over to the freighter. On board the boat Ray and Andy had been led to the cargo hold. On the way down they suddenly heard a shout, and then several shouts of alarm and a man burst out of a door along the passage. He ran to them and began shouting and pleading in a foreign dialect. Neither of them could understand a word that he said but it was obvious he was asking for help. Sulim barked an order and one of the men standing with them grabbed the unfortunate man and dragged him off down the passageway. His voice faded as he went further from them but it was cut off in mid cry by a shot. They heard no more and the man returned and stood by them as if nothing had happened. Ray and Andy looked at each other, it seemed as if they had witnessed a murder and nobody cared. "What the hells going on?" Ray asked.

"Nothing to worry about." Their host replied. "Just a matter of some discipline. You must understand that in my line of work it is often difficult to get the right kind of employee."

He looked at them and smiled; the smile didn't reach his eyes however and both of them felt uneasy in his presence. He was of indeterminate ancestry although to Andy's eyes he had at least some Arab in his blood. He spoke then and his voice was almost accentless. "So, now we begin, first, my name is Suleiman Ben Akbar and for tonight you may call me Sulim. And you are Ray and Andy if my information is correct." He waited for them to acknowledge this then reached out and shook their hands.

Ray frowned. "It seems that you just killed a man who was asking for our help and also you shot him down in cold blood."

Sulim raised a finger and pointed it at Ray. "Do not test my patience, Mr Australian. I am the captain of my ship and my word is law."

With that he spoke again as if nothing had happened. "I will first tell you the rules we will follow, I am completely honest and fair, and I will not cheat you in any way. My reputation depends on that. Of course it goes without saying that if you try to cheat me, I will have you killed; and your dependants as well." He added.

"This transaction is to be carried out in cash and the cash will be paid before any cargo is downloaded to your boat. You have the cash aboard your boat?"

When Ray nodded, Sulim smiled his evil smile and pointed behind them. To their surprise the second man stood silently with his hands on hips. He had on a shoulder holster with the butt of a gun poking out.

Sulim went on. "The man behind you is an associate of mine called Diman, I warn you now he is a very dangerous man so do not antagonise him, he is like the coiled spring, always ready to go off. He is here to ensure that we have fair play and that means you will not load any gun here until I say so, I do not want to have to shoot you, but that rule is absolute, do not break it. I have a small range here that you can try out the guns. Some are packed for the journey, but all are guaranteed, if you have any problems with any of them you will receive a full refund." He laughed mirthlessly. "That's of course if you survive to complain."

Ray snapped. "Shall we get on with it?"

Sulim stared for a moment. "Always the same with Westerners, never any patience, you miss all life's pleasantries when you are in such a hurry; now, what weapons do you want from me?"

"Alright." Ray answered. "Now we know what we're doing here, I need two things from you. First I want some weapons to protect a boat, a small boat not a gunboat. I want them now, today. Second I want some armaments to defend a compound. You will be paid in full for today's arms and the second delivery somewhere in Oz will be paid cash on delivery,"

Sulim bristled at this. "I will not deliver anywhere until I am paid in full, I never deal in HP."

Ray knew he was beaten on the second option so after some bargaining they agreed, half now and the rest on delivery. With a surcharge for the delivery.

Sulim smiled his mirthless smile once more. "Do not cheat

me Australian, they will be delivered and you will pay; one way or the other." He raised his fingers imitated the trigger of a gun and fired it at Ray's head.

Andy leaned forward. "There are two things you can put on that list as well and that is, I want a snipers rifle accurate to a range of two miles with telescopic sights and if possible, I also want some night sights for it as well. Probably a Parker-Hale Model 85 would do the trick and about a hundred rounds of ammo. Then I want an automatic shotgun, a Franchi SPAS-12 with an eight shot magazine would be the best if you've got one."

Ray turned to look at Andy in surprise, he didn't say much normally and now he came up with specialist equipment. Andy looked back at them all and then shrugged and smiled bleakly. "Got to be prepared for all emergencies."

He then said to Ray. "I don't mind paying for that myself if it cost's too much."

Sulim had been listening to this exchange with some amusement and now he said to Andy. "I've got just the thing for you in my store, but tell me, can you use such equipment?"

Andy replied. "If you mean have I killed anybody with it? The answer is no, but I can use sniper rifles because I was a crack shot in the Army and I was trained in their use. Also my best friend was a sniper in the American Army and we trained together in America."

The next statement from Sulim surprised them all. "I've been looking for someone with your training so if you want a job and no questions asked come back and see me."

Andy shook his head. "I could never kill another person unless it was in self defence. It's not in my nature to do that, so I don't think I'd be any use to you."

Sulim shrugged his shoulders. "It's only the first one that's the hardest." He glanced at them and went on. "Or so they say,"

Ray felt a shiver go down his back at the implications of this remark and couldn't resist a glance over his shoulder to find Diman grinning wolfishly at him. Sulim caught the movement and flicked a look in his direction.

"You don't like my little protector standing behind you, do you?" He asked.

Ray shook his head in answer. Sulim took no further action, but it served as a reminder that the man was there and armed as well.

Sulim turned to Ray and started to lay out his options. "I can deal with both your requests at this time, I think you're going to need at least one heavy machine gun with belt feed. You are also going to have to have a tripod for this gun, as there is a problem with fixing these guns on deck. They can be very vulnerable to attack because they can be easily seen and any enemy will try and knock them out first. A well placed sniper." He nodded at Andy. "Could knock out any operator with one shot, and keep everybody away from the gun. Also if you have a gun on deck where everybody can see it I recommend you have a steel shield on the front of it. I think also you should have some kind of small machine guns for close in work as rifles aren't too good for that. I personally think that a good pistol if you are at close range is an ideal weapon and I have some that can fire fifteen shots"

He grinned. "Stops them counting how many shots you've fired so they don't know when you're reloading. That can be very useful in a fire fight."

He went on. "Your second request is far more unusual, I can understand you wanting to defend your boat in these waters, but what are you going to defend in Australia? It is not a country such as mine where it is necessary to defend your house sometimes. What will you be doing in Australia that you find you need guns?"

Ray had come prepared for this question and answered. "First of all mate we don't have to tell you what or why, but to satisfy your curiosity a little bit, lets just say we think we know of a way to make a lot of extra money very quickly."

Sulim chuckled and nodded his head in understanding. He had evidently thought of several ways that they could make a lot of money, and all of them illegally, and in the way of people who make their living that way he assumed they would not want to disclose their plans.

Sulim stood and held both his hands out to Ray who was obliged to grasp them. They looked each other in the eye and shook both hands together. Both knew that if either reneged on this deal it would mean a great deal of trouble for both of them. For Ray it would probably mean his death, as Sulim would make sure he hunted him down so he didn't lose face. Sulim would lose all credibility in the international community in which he dealt. That would mean a long slow death for him as business ceased to exist.

Sulim said to them with a hint of triumph in his voice. "So, you want to see the guns now? He led them forward to a door set in the middle of a bulkhead. It had huge steel levers to lock it and swung open silently when pushed. "Shall we go gentlemen?"

There was a small staircase down to the main floor. The three of them followed him down and when they had got about halfway Sulim touched a switch on the wall. Fluorescent lights sprang to life the whole length of the hold and from his position on the stairs Ray could see the entire room was covered in racks marching in orderly fashion across the entire floor. Each rack was about head height and they were completely covered with a wide variety of weapons. Every shelf on the rack seemed to be given over to a particular sort of gun, there was one gun of each unpacked and assembled, and then beside that there were boxes stacked. Jim assumed they were of that type and was proved right as they moved along. As they went further into the room he could see there were also small missiles and grenades stacked at the other end.

There were enough arms in this place to supply an army and Ray realised that to this man they were very small fry indeed. Andy's eyes were popping out of his head at the sight of all the weapons and he started to go along the aisles examining them as he went. He bent to pick one up but was stopped by the sound of a gun being cocked. They looked back to see the bodyguard Diman standing on the staircase with a gun in his hand pointed towards them, Sulim called out to Andy. "For the moment young man, you can look but do not touch, I cannot see both of you at once but rest assured that Diman can and he is very fast on the trigger. I will explain. There is ammunition in this place and you would not be the first if you tried to load one of these fine weapons and use it to steal some of them from us. If you try to do that Diman will shoot you and he will enjoy it, we live in dangerous times and we must have security." Andy looked sheepish and placed the gun back on the rack. All of them breathed a little easier at this but Diman retained his hold on the gun and continued to point it at them. It was left to Sulim to wave a hand at him and say. "Put it away Diman, we are all friends here."

He slowly uncocked the gun but kept it in his hand where they could see it. He looked almost disappointed at losing a chance to use it.

Sulim looked at them quizzically and asked. "Now who wants to choose the guns that you need?"

The two of them had to look at each other for the moment but it was Andy who answered. "I'll check the guns out Ray, and you can keep count of how much money we're spending,"

Ray nodded as he and Sulim started to walk along the aisles together. As Andy picked out guns Sulim recounted to them various facts about them such as range, calibre, weight, strength, durability, whether they were liable to seize in operation. He knew his subject backwards and didn't try to influence them in any way. As he said. "If I try to tell customers what to buy and it goes wrong, who are they going to look for afterwards. Anyway the perfect gun hasn't been made yet. There is always another one that can do the particular job better in some way. So there must be some compromise in the manufacture so they can be used in different situations."

Andy finally made a choice of four Heckler and Koch MP5 short-barrelled rapid-fire guns with a magazine that took thirty rounds; these came with a thousand rounds of ammunition each. He then chose some Kalashnikov rifles with ammunition because as he said. "Almost everybody has these guns if they're in this business so you can swap them around a bit if needed." He also chose a Parker-Hale model 85 Mauser system sniper rifle plus ammunition with a telescopic sight, this came with a bipod as extra for stability. He then chose an FN L7 General Purpose Machine Gun on a tripod; this had a range of 2 miles, and as Andy said. "This gun will cut through an oak door six inches thick if you concentrate the fire."

Sulim smiled in appreciation of his knowledge and remarked. "Don't forget I have work for you if you want it."

Andy wisely said nothing and just acknowledged the remark with a grin. He went on to what he liked to think of as the piece de resistance, this was his prized shotgun. From the way he picked it up and held it to his shoulder it was evident that this was what he had come for. A Luigi Franchi SPAS-12 Special Purpose Automatic Shotgun that could be used either as full automatic or by pump action. It was quite short at about two feet long and the magazine, which held eight shells, could be easily changed to give different loadings. It had no sights. Andy held it lovingly in his hands and said. "I'm taking this."

Ray smiled to himself at the different things that people liked in their life. He thought to himself that he would probably feel the same way about a nice piece of mahogany furniture French polished to a deep glow. He hoped that Andy would have no chance to use his toy, but at the same time he thought it would be better to safe than sorry. After that they progressed to the order for delivery in Australia and worked out a budget to cover all the costs.

Andy then went over to the other racks and picked out some plastic explosive with various detonators. He also took some radio controlled claymore mines and grenades, several automatic pistols with ammunition, some small disposable rocket launchers, and smoke canisters completed the order. These they agreed to have delivered later as lack of space precluded them from taking them on board now.

Ray had a shock when he realised how much of their budget would be going on defence but recognised that it would probably be necessary. At last they were finished but Sulim had one more surprise for them. He led them through another door where they found themselves in a target range with one end filled with sand bags; he went to a locked cupboard on the wall and opened it. He took something out and when he turned round he was holding a rifle in his hands. If any gun could be described as beautiful this was the one. The barrel was blued steel and the stock had been waxed and polished lovingly till it shone. He held it out towards Andy and said. "This is my favourite rifle from the whole collection, and it is the only one of its kind in the southern hemisphere. A master craftsman altered it to my specification; it takes six months from the time you order till delivery. It is accurate to 13cm diameter dispersion at 800 metres in the right hands. If you shot an elephant it would stop it dead in its tracks. It's based on the Parker-Hale model 82 using a Mauser action, the sights are 4 x multiplication; the same as many armed forces use now." Andy looked at him sharply but the man's face remained impassive. He took it in his hands and stared in wonder at it. Sulim gave him five rounds and said. "Try it on the range there and tell me what you think,"

Andy slowly loaded the gun and faced the range, he turned to say something to Sulim and found himself looking into the mocking eyes of Diman. He was still holding his gun in his hand and watched Andy expectantly as if waiting for him to try and use it on Sulim. Andy smiled at him and then faced the range. Sulim placed a target on the pulley and as he pulled it down to the end he said. "This target represents a man facing you one mile away"

Ray looked at it when it reached the end of the range and all he could discern was the paper. The target was too small to see. Andy raised the rifle to his shoulder and was about to fire a round when Sulim stopped him. "You will have to rest that rifle on something because at that range a whisper of a breath will make you miss by six feet."

Andy nodded and placed his elbows on the firing bench, he settled himself, and then taking his time he fired, he didn't get up but fired the remaining rounds as well. Sulim pulled the target back to them and when it arrived they bent over it. Andy had hit the man on the target three times, and missed by a fraction the other two.

Sulim whistled. "That's the best shooting I've seen for a long time. Now, do you want to buy this fine weapon?"

Andy looked at it longingly. "How much,"

"To you because you are such a fine shot I will sell it for a discount. 30,000 Dollars US."

Ray had been watching this with interest but at the mention of so much money for a rifle Andy blanched, and looked at Ray. Then he handed the gun back to Sulim. "I would like to own your fine weapon Sulim, but there is no way I can afford a gun of such quality." He turned to Ray and said. "I think we should be going."

Sulim tried one last gambit to make Andy change his mind; "If you work for me I shall let you buy it, on the HP as you say."

Andy shook his head. "You've already got your answer to

that."

Sulim shrugged sorrowfully but led them out and up to the deck; several of the crew under Dimans direction brought up the arms they would take with them and then waited expectantly for the business to conclude. When they arrived on deck Sulim consulted his pad and said. "Now for the best part, you will pay for the arms you have now plus half of the delivery. When they arrive in Australia I will expect the other half and the delivery charge. I will tell you one last time, do not cheat me, or else."

He left the rest of the sentence unfinished. He told Ray how much he wanted and he and went to the side of the boat and called the figure down to Jim, who went below out of sight and counted out the money. He put it into a bag and tied it to a rope that had been lowered to him. Ray took charge of the money and counted it once more into Sulims hand. His eyes were gleaming when he got the money and Ray felt it necessary to say. "That just about cleans us out Sulim; we've got barely enough to get us to Oz now."

Sulim leant forward and hissed. "You had no need to say that, I am an honourable man and if I wanted, I could have killed you all and stolen the money with no comeback from any police force in the world. In my business it is always better for the client to live because they can always come back and buy more. Now you should leave." And with that he shook their hands and went up on to the bridge

Ray and Andy climbed down the ladder and the arms were lowered after them. When they had them on board the freighter tooted them and it slowly pulled away. It sailed in an easterly direction and Jim speculated he was going somewhere like Thailand or Vietnam. He would have been surprised at its final destination but chose to speculate no further. Andy and Ray brought James up to date regarding the crewman who had been shot, but he merely said. "Just don't tell the women; as that Sulim said. He is the law on that boat and we have no power to interfere."

On board the freighter Sulim said to Diman. "Get me the contact details for our friend Chang, I think they've got more on that yacht than they're letting on and that boat will be worth a lot in the right place. I want you to go with Chang on his Junk and bring the boat back, empty of course. But, with some of the women maybe as well."

Chapter Seven

On board the yacht Ray turned to the crew. "Right then, let's set sail for Oz, we're going home and you can start your new life."

They set to with a burst of energy and soon had the sails up; the boat heeled over dug into the sea and sailed south with just a spray of sea water over the bow to remind them they were under way. Ray said to Andy. "You might as well get those guns out of the packing and look them over." Then he called to Leah. "How about a tinny then after all that hard work I've been doing and some grub'd be a good thing, I'm starving."

The two women looked at each other with that expression in their eyes that said volumes. It was Pat who spoke up this time and she promptly put Ray in his place. "If you think you're going to go through the next few weeks ordering us about like a couple of skivvies you can think again. We'll do it this time because you've been doing a lot this morning, but when we're at sea and we're all working you can pitch in and help in the kitchen like everybody else."

She then faced them all and said. "That goes for everybody here, we do our share of running this boat so it won't hurt any of you to help in the kitchen, and also cleaning up after yourselves. I've got no intention of running around after a load of lazy men."

Ray spread his hands and smiled at her. "All right keep your hair on Pat, no one said you and Leah had to do it all, I only asked if we could have some grub. We'll do our share when we're at sea, won't we lads?"

All the men nodded their assent, although it was plain to see that none of them were particularly keen on the idea. Pat tossed her head and snapped. "Make sure you do pull your weight or you'll have me to deal with."

Leah pitched in. "And she'll have me to back her up, so don't think you'll get away with anything,"

The two of them then marched off down to the galley. Up on deck the men glanced at each other sheepishly and it was left to Jim to make the only comment. "Best do as she says or she'll make life difficult for you in the long run."

Ray scowled. "I hate cooking and cleaning at the best of times, I can usually convince Leah its best if she does it." Then he turned to Jim and said. "I've got to bring you up to date on what happened when we were on that boat." And he recounted the whole story to him. The tale worried Jim but he answered. "We probably won't ever see that Sulim again, is it worth our while to try and get him punished for it, because as he said to you, he is the captain and he can convince enough of that crew to back him up in any story he likes. Best not to tell the women though."

They had a following breeze and it was just enough to give them a good speed through the water and the sea was a beautiful shade of blue. The two women brought drinks and a snack back on deck, they all sipped for a while and then Ray broke the silence with a question. "Has Andy finished cleaning those guns yet?"

Andy himself answered from behind him. "You must be a mind reader Ray; I was just bringing them up for a test firing,"

He came on deck followed by Dick carrying the rest of the guns and some ammunition. The pair of them placed everything on the deck and Andy started to load the guns, and while he was doing it he said. "I want everybody to watch what I'm doing and then have a test firing themselves, after we've done that we'll clean the guns and then practice how to load and use them. All of you need to learn as much as possible about them as we'll never know when you need to use that knowledge."

He looked around at all of them and noted he had their full attention. "I want you all to learn how to fire these Machine guns as they're for the defence of this boat, there're better used on single shot automatic reload. If you pull and hold the trigger they continue to fire but as they pull to the side when they're fired you stand the chance of hitting one of your own side. So I want you to put the gun to your shoulder when you shoot it, I know if it's an emergency you won't have time but if you have, try and aim from the shoulder and aim for the chest, it makes the biggest target. Don't think you can fire guns from the hip like they do in westerns because it's almost impossible to hit anything from there."

He demonstrated how he wanted them to do it but as he did this Ray's son George stepped forward and picked up one of the guns lying on the deck. Fast as a striking snake Leah reached out and snatched the gun from his grasp. "I don't want you touching any of these." she shouted. "You get below; I'll deal with you later."

She cuffed him on the head. "And take your sister with you."

His sister shouted back at her. "We've got to learn Mum or else we'll be useless in an emergency. You might need us to help and we have to know what to do."

Leah faced her with eyes blazing. "No kids of mine are learning how to use guns and that's final, and now get below before I tan your arse in front of everybody here."

An ashen-faced Jeannie wailed. "Mum."

Jim had been watching this with some interest and stepped into the argument, it was probably the wrong thing to do with Leah in the mood she was in but he felt he had no option. "Look Leah, I know you've got strong views about the kids learning about guns but I'd like to put my point of view if I can." He held up his hand to forestall the expected outburst from her.

"These kids are going to get their hands on guns sooner or later whether you like it or not, I think you'll concede that if they get their hands on them it'd be better they know what there're doing than just fumbling around until they hurt someone else."

He pointed at Andy. "I taught him about guns when he was ten years old and he's been safe around them ever since. I know you didn't notice what went on just now when George picked up that gun did you?"

He didn't wait for an answer but carried straight on. "He made two basic mistakes when he did that." He held his finger up. "First, he pointed it straight at you, and second he had his finger near the trigger. Now it doesn't take much imagination to figure out what would happen if his finger had slipped. That isn't a mistake he would ever make," And he nodded at Andy.

"What I'm trying to tell you is that it'll be better for them to know about guns now and they'll learn how to be safe around them later."

He stopped talking and waited for Leah to blast off in her normal way, but she stared at him for long moments while the permutations were going through her mind. Finally she answered him. "They learn how to clean them, load them and handle them, but they don't fire them, understood?"

He grinned back at her. "Understood."

The children whooped and ran to the guns, only to be stopped in their tracks by Andy shouting. "Leave them alone until I tell you what to do or you'll get a clip round the ear from me, and if I give you a clout you'll never forget it."

He looked at Ray. "Have you got something we can use as a target? And I don't want bottles because they sink. Something like a polystyrene chest or even a lifejacket if you've got one spare."

Ray hurried off and came back moments later with a small surfboard which he tied to a length of cord and slung it over the back of the boat. The only comment came from George. "That's my board Dad,"

Ray looked at him, and then he looked at the board, which by now was bouncing along about fifty yards behind them. He looked back to George and asked. "Do you want to go and sit on it then?"

"I didn't mean that Dad." George moaned. "I meant it's my board and you didn't ask me if you could use it."

Ray sighed in exasperation. "Don't be stupid all your life George, it's doing no good in that locker back there, you can't use it here, and I can get you another one when we get home. For now, we need something to have a shot at and that's it."

He turned to face the others and said "Lets take down some sail before we try out these guns so were not bouncing around all over the place while we're practising." They quickly struck some of the sail, just allowing enough to give them some way through the water then he turned to face Andy without listening to George who was still moaning about his board and said. "Let's get this show on the road before it gets dark shall we."

Andy nodded and proceeded to give them a demonstration of firing the machine guns. Then he stepped back and let them fire the guns one at a time at the target floating behind, very few of the bullets actually hit it but he consoled them by saying. "We are floating around on an unstable base and it's bobbing about a bit so chances are you'll miss anyway."

Ray and Jim got several hits between them but the biggest surprise was Leah, She scored hits with almost all her rounds. And when Andy looked at her in surprise she shrugged and said. "Used to go hunting with my dad when I was a kid, I thought I'd forgotten how to do it."

"Humph," Andy snorted. "Pity you didn't say that before causing all that trouble over George touching the guns."

He then turned to the serious business of teaching them how to fire them. When they had finished firing the rapid-fire guns. He picked up the automatic pistols and instructed them in their use, saying. "These will only be useful if we've actually got boarders or the range is only about twenty yards at most."

They then tried the Kalashnikov's to get the general idea of how to use them. When they had finished he laid them all down in a pile and said. "Right, now the single most important thing in the life of a gun is to make sure it's clean, so now we're going to strip down every one of them and make sure there're nice and clean and with a light film of grease on them."

After he had shown them how to do the work he set them all to cleaning the weapons while he himself set the FN GMP up on it's tripod with a view of the surf board. When that was done he loaded it and called the men over. "I want you men to have a go at this gun but not for long as it's a machine gun and the ammunition will go too quickly if we practice too much."

They all watched as he settled himself behind it and aimed at the surfboard. He took a breath and held it then gently squeezed the trigger. The result was astounding; in less than ten seconds the board was reduced to shreds. The noise attracted all the others and they all stared soberly at the board now still floating as the natural buoyancy kept it on top of the water. Leah whistled silently. "That's some lethal weapon you've got there,"

Andy smiled bleakly. "It does a job of work that's all."

He turned to the other men. "Lets get you having a go, and then you can strip this one down and clean it."

They all tried the gun but none of them could match Andy's skill and found it difficult to control. Only Jim who had fired a Bren gun in the army came anywhere near to hitting the board. Ray shrugged it of by saying. "Looks like you'll have to take responsibility for that gun Andy."

"And what if something happens to me and I can't fire it?" Andy rejoined.

No one could answer that. He looked at the gun. "I'll clean that myself in a minute, I want to get the sniper rifle out and test it first,"

He went over to the case and got the sniper rifle out. It was a Parker-Hale M85, a model that had been used extensively by Australian forces. This was probably the reason that they had been able to purchase one. It had been fitted with a telescopic lens and Andy spent several minutes adjusting this to his personal satisfaction. When he was finally finished he took a position on the deck and fired two test shots at the board and although they hit he appeared to be dissatisfied and carried on adjusting the sights. At last he seemed satisfied and emptied the rest of the magazine into the target. Although it had been bobbing about while he was shooting he still hit it within a very small area with nearly all the shots. He nodded to himself in satisfaction and then started to strip it and clean it.

While this had been going on the others had cleaned and assembled all the other guns. They carried them all down and stowed them away while Andy cleaned the machine gun. He said to Ray when he had finished. "I think we'll have to leave this gun up here on deck as it'll take too long to bring it out if anything happens."

They discussed the different options and decided that the most likely angle for any one to attack them would be by chasing them so they fitted it on the afterdeck and lashed a cover over it. Leah and Pat had decided in the meantime to prepare some food so they ate with the gun taking pride of place on the deck. Leah glanced at the gun while she was eating and said to Ray. "I don't know how you're going to sail into a harbour in Oz with that thing sitting on deck, I reckon any customs bloke seeing that would have kittens and your feet wouldn't touch the ground on the way to nick."

"You're not far wrong there missus, I reckon I'll have to think of something else to get past the customs in Oz." Ray admitted to her. "Maybe I'll try to land further along the coast and stash them on shore somewhere till I can go back for them."

"So long as you keep them out of sight of those Abbos, you'll be OK. But if they see them you'll be a goner cos they'll shop you for sure." Leah had the Australians friendly contempt for the Aborigine people and was well aware of their capacity to do anything to get a few more quid to spend in the pub. That included either stealing the guns or turning the culprit into the police, whichever they thought would turn the most profit. It wasn't dislike of them; she just had knowledge of the foibles of a race that had been brought into the modern world far too quickly. When that happened they always seemed to take to the worst habits of the dominant race and in this case it meant drinking gambling and indolence.

The average Australian didn't seem to her to be any better; they encouraged the Aborigine nation in the bad habits as a way of keeping them down. No Australian wanted to have the Aborigines to be any better than them as to their mind it seemed as if the Aborigine Nation as a whole got far more than they worked for.

Ray furrowed his brow as he thought about this for a while, then he brightened and said. "Maybe I can sort out something for when we land I'll give a friend of mine a ring when we get a little closer to Oz."

With that they had to be content as he refused to be drawn out any more on his plans. He stood a moment later and said to Jim. "I want you to help me later to plan a rota of the crew to work in teams so we can keep going 24 hours a day, so let's go below and sort something out."

He turned to the others and said in his captains' voice. "You lot sort out the washing up and stowage of the guns and get the boat under way, we're heading south for some time now so we might have to tack a bit but I'll sort it out in a bit. With that he went down into the Salon with Jim. Once below they tried to sort out a rota that would be acceptable to everybody. The weak point in all their deliberations was that there were only two members of the crew who knew the boat thoroughly and they were Ray and Leah. The others were in various stages of readiness. They finally decided to put Andy with Leah, Dick with Ray, and Jim and Pat together. It wasn't an ideal situation as Jim and Pat had no real experience between them. But as Ray said. "If anything crops up on your shift you'll have to give me a call."

They decided to work four hours on and eight hours off, with the team that had been off for four hours doing some preparation of food for the others, with the children pulling as much of a share as they could. They would be expected to help give the team working, drinks, and refreshments as they were needed.

Ray looked at his watch and then said, "I'm suggesting you and Pat take the watch from 4 till 8 this evening. I'll put Andy and Leah on from 8 till 12 midnight and I'll come on with Dick from 12 till four in the morning. Then we can carry on from there. It's not going to be easy for any of us but it'll put you and Pat on the shifts we think will be the easiest and someone can be around to keep an eye open for you."

Jim nodded his understanding; he had had to pull shift work at some times in his life and knew how hard it was, not only to do it but to plan it as well. As it was by now gone four-o-clock Jim and Pat were officially on duty and Ray said to them. "You might as well get used to doing it from now on so you're in charge of the boat from now on, the course is south."

All the rest of the crew had gone below by this time and were going about different pursuits so they were alone with their thoughts for the first time for a long time. She looked up at him and he was struck by how much he thought of her. Never one to show his affection he contented himself with putting his arm round her shoulder, she snuggled herself into his shoulder and looked up at him. Her nose was a little red and shiny from the wind and her eyes twinkled as she gazed at him. "I hope you don't think your lucks changing just because you've got your arms round me." It was an old joke between them and he smiled at the recollection.

"I've got no time for that nonsense, even if we could find somewhere to do it in private." He answered, and they both smiled at each other in the manner of people who were comfortable with each other.

The time passed slowly as it always does on watch and it was a relief when at about six-o-clock in the evening Leah came up on deck with two large cups of sweet tea for them. She stopped to pass the time of day with them for a few minutes while they sipped at the scalding liquid.

"How do you like watch keeping?" She asked Pat. Completely ignoring the fact that Jim was there doing his share.

Pat glanced at Jim before she answered, it was just long enough to catch the look on his face and she laughed a little when she answered her. "We both like being at sea." she emphasised the "we both" when she spoke so that Jim could at least feel included. She went on. "Ever since Ray gave us that instruction course the other day I've thought that this could be the life for me."

"Even when we got caught in that storm?" Leah asked.

"Well I must admit that did make me wonder whether I was suited to the life of a seaman." Pat replied. "But I think that I could get used to a life on the ocean if it was possible." She looked at their surroundings. "It can be a bit boring though."

"You can say that again," Leah agreed, with feeling. I don't mind being at sea but I prefer to be in port sitting on the deck with a nice gin and tonic in my hand watching the world go by. Do you know? I'd love to be able to go to the Mediterranean and cruise round there visiting all those lovely harbours and sitting out in the sun so all the peasants can see you and envy you."

They all smiled at the note of nostalgia in Leah's voice although she had only been at sea for a few hours.

Pat felt she ought to say something to put her out of her misery. "The Med's probably the most polluted water in the world Leah, and the so-called peasants are just about the greediest people you'll ever meet. Tourists don't stand a chance with the average continental when it comes to financial matters. They always seem to have their hands out for money the whole time."

Leah sighed. "I guess you're right Pat. It was just one of those impossible dreams we all have from time to time. Anyway if your disaster happens as you say it will, we won't be going anywhere for a long time will we?"

She bent down to pick their empty cups up, her voice sounding very sad she said. "Just think, the whole world with no people in it, even if we travel there'll be no-one to see when we arrive will there?"

Jim broke in on her musings. "There's bound to be some survivors, there are people out there who must be thinking of doing the same things we are, and anyway the chances are some would survive just by using the materials to hand. Think about all these military installations that are deep underground with air conditioning and food for years, maybe they could survive."

She snapped back at him. "Don't be stupid; those installations have fuel to carry on for a time but not enough to carry on for years."

"I understand that, and I'm not stupid. But what you're forgetting is that mankind is very ingenious when it comes to survival and I'm willing to bet that if this does happen a lot of them out there are going to make damn sure they survive. Our problem comes when it's all over because a great deal of these survivors are going to be men, and that's going to cause a lot of trouble when the crisis is over."

Leah looked at him for a long moment. "Are you saying us women are going to be in short supply?"

"Almost certainly,"

"Well, that's going to be a turn up isn't it, you men are going to have to watch the way you treat us from now on,"

It was Jim's turn to stare at her. "That's an attitude of mind you can do without Leah, when it comes down to the nitty gritty's, a lot of men will kill rather than lose their woman, especially when there's no law out there to stop them."

Pat sensed from Jim's tone of voice that this conversation in all likelihood would itself end in bad feeling so she stepped in promptly to end it as best she could.

"I don't think any of us are going to run of with someone else so lets get this project off the ground before we think about what happens some time in the future,"

By this time the two protagonists were almost face-to-face with their fists clenched at their sides; she had to bodily step between them and push them apart. They stared at each other for what seemed like minutes but were only seconds. Jim finally stepped back and grinned in embarrassment. "This is stupid; we all need each other too much to argue about what could be happening in some year's time."

Leah also stepped back and nodded in agreement, but being a woman she had to have the last word. "Don't forget that women don't have to have men around to carry on the race, we can do without you."

This was probably the one statement she shouldn't have made to Jim. Who, although he wasn't a chauvinist certainly believed that there was a place for both sexes in any civilisation. He turned a glared at her. "If you believe that you are more stupid than I ever thought you could be." He gestured all around them. "Who supplied all this, if it wasn't a man? Who do you think made all this possible, if it wasn't a man? You need men in your life far more than you realise. Especially when half the time you can't think any further than the next hair do." This last was a crack about her taking a lot of time in the shower room because her hair had been unmanageable while they were in Singapore. She flushed and rose to the bait immediately. "You men seem to think that women are only good for one thing but you'd better remember how much we do for you."

He replied. "That's exactly what I'm trying to say to you, but it has to be a partnership. You can't expect one or the other to be dominant."

Pat broke in. "Will you two stop acting like a couple of kids and get on with being real, here we are facing a disaster and you two a bickering about which sex is the best. Why don't you realise that they both have qualities that are needed. If we lost either of you two we'd find it hard to replace you, so why don't you go about your business and forget this nonsense."

Both of them carried on staring at each other for a while as they were thinking of what to do in this situation. Finally Jim held his hand out and said. "Pax."

Leah smiled and put her arms round him and gave him a hug. "Stuff your Latin," She said and pecked him on the cheek. "We must both be born under a dominant star sign the way we go on sometimes. You'll have to forgive me; I always want to be the one giving orders."

Jim put his arms round her and hugged her back and said. "If we all do the job we agreed on I think we'll make do."

They stepped back and Leah went on. "I think I'd better be going and doing some of those women's jobs that keep on cropping up." She grinned wryly. "Like the washing up maybe,"

With that last crack she went down the steps to the salon. Jim turned to Pat and said. "She gets fiery doesn't she?"

Pat stared at him in some disbelief. "You don't do so bad yourself do you?"

They had been sailing for a week on this southerly course when Ray, who had been studying the radar sank into the other seats opposite Jim and asked. "Have you seen anything unusual out there in the way of other boats?"

Jim raised his eyebrows, had Ray suddenly developed second vision? Or had he been thinking on the same lines as Jim?

"I'm not certain as there's too much traffic out there at the moment," the answer although true conveyed something to Ray as he looked at Jim quizzically.

"Why aren't you certain? Is there something out there we should know about or not?"

Jim took his time to answer this time as he didn't want to alarm everybody on the boat but at the same time they should be forewarned. "It's hard to say but there are about three or four boats out there that are keeping course with us. In waters like this though that's what we could consider normal, other boats do travel in the same direction as us and it would be alarmist at this stage to worry too much."

Ray sat up. "Alarmist or not we'll have to keep a close watch on them and see if any of them change course when we do. Have you told Andy about this?"

"Yes of course," Jim answered. "I told him to watch the ones on course with us."

Ray nodded in satisfaction. "Can't be too careful, maybe I'll take another look too see what's going on. He stood and went to climb the steps to go on deck but stopped at the first one and turned to Jim. "Are you coming to show me then?"

His voice was heard on deck and in the nick of time Andy removed his hand from the inside of Leah's blouse and they sat hurriedly apart. Ray noticed nothing unusual in their demeanour; he was too worried about the mysterious dots on the radar screen to pay any attention to other people at that moment. But Jim following up the steps did. The pair of them were flushed and trying to pay no attention to each other, to Jim it came in a flash that something was going on between them. He decided to say nothing at the moment and talk to Pat about it later.

He followed Ray over to the radar console and the two of them spent a little time considering it, Ray finally decided to record all the movements over the next few hours before he came on duty and then make a course change to the west. At that point they should be able to spot any boat that changed course to go through with them. Jim agreed,"

By this time it appeared that Leah and Andy had regained their composure and Andy came over to see what was going on. Leah still had the wheel in her hand and when Jim glanced over at her she gave him a mocking smile back. He looked fleetingly at Andy but he seemed oblivious to what was going on between Jim and Leah. When Jim looked back in Leah's direction her smile broadened and it occurred to Jim that she either didn't care what he had guessed or she thought he wouldn't go and tell Ray. His face reddened as these thoughts went through his mind and he decided to keep his suspicions to himself for the time being.

Ray bent down and adjusted some of the controls on the radar and then turned to Jim and said. "That's the recorder working so now we'll have to wait and see if anything happens for us to see." He looked at Andy and went on. "Don't fiddle with those controls, then we can have a clear record of what happens in the next few hours, if you really are curious about it, all that happens is that it records what's on the screen every minute or so. Then when we play it, it looks like a speeded up version of the keystone cops on water."

"Been there, seen it, done it, tell me something new." Andy

didn't like being talked down to and let people know when he thought they were doing just that.

Ray glanced sharply at him to ascertain whether Andy was being serious, but he had the Australian sense of humour, which is a bit more basic than the English so he appreciated that Andy was being facetious and not taking the mickey out of him.

Andy for his part had long ago decided that he wouldn't make any jokes about penal colonies or bloody colonials, as long as he got no jokes thrown at him about whingeing Poms. He had a friend in America and when he had visited he had used the joke about colonials there but that had been met with blank stares. As he had said on his return to England, their history only goes back as far as the War of Independence. And that's based on the true story as told by Hollywood and John Wayne who according to their account had won it single-handed.

Straightening up Ray turned to Jim and said. "Not much more we can do here for now, let's go and get a cup of something and get some rest before we have to start again."

It had been noticeable to Jim that Ray's drinking since they left harbour had dropped considerably; in fact, he hadn't seen Ray touch a drop since then. As they went down to the Salon he broached the subject and asked him.

"Drinking and the sea just don't go together mate," Ray answered. "I got drunk once when I was docking in the Marina and caused a bit of damage, it cost a lot of money to smooth that one over and I swore off it there and then. I've never touched much at sea since and anyway if we get any trouble now I want to feel able to handle it."

Jim nodded in reply and thought privately that the policy was a good one. When they arrived in the Salon it was to find the other two had gone to bed so they had a cup of coffee each and retired themselves. The next thing that Jim knew was that a hand shook his shoulder and a voice said. "Christ mate you take some waking up I must say."

He opened his eyes blearily and looked up at Ray standing above him, then glanced over at the clock beside him. He blinked and the figures swam into view, three forty five am. He struggled to sit up and yawned, trying to shake off the tiredness that had him in its grip. He scratched himself and said to Ray. "That's probably the best I've slept for weeks now, do you want to go back on watch for a couple of hours while I get myself ready?"

"Up and at em mate, no skivers on this boat I've done my four hours and you can do yours, lets have you both on deck in ten minutes bright eyed and bushy tailed ready to go. There's a mug of tea on the table in the Salon and if you're quick you can drink it and still have time for a wash before you get up there,"

Having said that he turned and went out of the cabin and could be heard stomping along the passage to go out on deck. Jim looked at Pat lying next to him with her hair spread all over the pillow, her eyes were fast shut but she said. "I know, we've got to get out and right now."

Jim grinned, got hold of the duvet, and yanked it of the bed in one movement, she made an ineffectual grab for it, but it was far too late. He leapt out of bed before the expected punch could land on his arm and dashed for the door, straight out and into the toilet and locked the door. She arrived a split second later and banged on the door saying. "I'll get you, you see if I don't,"

Leah's voice could be heard from the cabin next door. "If you two don't bloody well shut up I'll get the pair of you when I get up. Now let us get some bloody sleep or you'll have me to answer to."

Jim washed quickly and as best he could, quietly. Then he went out to find Pat dressed and ready holding her tea in her hand. She silently handed him the cup with a look in her eyes that said. "You just wait, this isn't over yet." Then she went into the toilet while he helped himself to the tea.

When she came out she sat for a moment with him and whispered. "We'll have to be a bit quieter next time, on these boats you can hear everything that goes on."

Jim grunted in affirmative, then as the full import of her words sunk in he replied. "Do you think that goes for everything?"

"What do you think?" she replied. "Have you gone deaf just lately or have you got cotton wool stuffed in your ears when you go to bed. These walls might be insulated but sounds still carry through them."

Jim shook his head. "I hadn't thought about that at all,"

She looked at him in amazement. "I sometimes wonder just what does go through your head." She would have carried on giving him the full lecture on his shortcomings but was interrupted by Ray shoving his head through the door. "Righto, lets be having you, I want to get some shuteye."

When they had had time to get their bearings Ray started to explain what had happened while they had been off watch.

"First of all, I want to tell you that I haven't detected any sign of another boat following us." He peered over his shoulder at Jim and said. "That doesn't preclude the fact that it is possible there is one out there. I've left that recorder on so it's going to come clearer when we have a look later."

Ray then went over to the wheel, which at this time was in the hands of Dick and let Jim look at the compass. "If you look here you can see that we're still going in a roughly southerly direction, I want you to try and keep that heading as best as you can, you'll have to tack a bit as the wind seems to be coming at us from the West but this isn't such a bad boat to come fairly close to the wind. Pat had been listening to all this with some impatience and now she reached out and took the wheel out of Dick's hands, she said to them both. "Go on and get some rest we can cope with this now."

Both Ray and Dick grinned at her as she took command of everyone on deck but she was so pleased to get hold of the wheel she was completely oblivious to the looks they gave her and amongst themselves. She turned to Jim and said. "That sail's flapping a bit can you pull on it or something to straighten it out, then when you've done that there's some bits of equipment here that ought to be put away."

Looking at Jim, Ray laughed and taunted him. "Go on then old son, jump to it, her masters voice is calling." Then he and Dick left for the salon laughing to each other as they went.

The watch was quiet with little happening and no incidents occurred to destroy the calm so Jim took the opportunity to bring Pat up to date with what he had deduced about Andy and Leah's behaviour. He wasn't surprised to learn that she had already seen as much as for herself. As they talked it over he became aware that she didn't condemn it as much as he himself did; she explained her feelings to him. "We're hoping to set up a community in the outback of Australia aren't we? What do you think would happen if all the men but one were killed by an accident?" She went on without pause to answer her own question.

"Just conceivably the whole human race could die out couldn't it? I'm sorry to tell you darling but when it comes to reproduction the females of this generation would just buckle down and go on trying to get pregnant. They'll be round the single remaining man like the proverbial flies on the honey pot. This in itself leads me to the conclusion that the younger generation aren't going to be so choosy from now on about marriage and all the trappings that go with it. Just remember that Marriage as an institution was invented to keep the man round the home as it takes a long time for children to grow up. Well in a community such as ours that need isn't there any more is it? The men will have to stay around for all the time the children are growing up, as there's nowhere to go. You said it yourself a while back that the genes are going to have to get mixed anyway so they're just starting a bit early. The biggest problem is if Ray takes offence but it's my bet that he won't once he sets eyes on the other women. Especially if he thinks he stands a chance of getting into someone else's knickers. One thing us women know about men is that that thing in their pants can lead them round, can't it? At the end of the day it'll probably be better if everyone can have whoever they like rather than have a lot of jealousy in a small community."

Jim had listened to all this with a sense of amazement, he couldn't believe what he was hearing from his wife's mouth. She had always displayed a strong morality all her life and now she was preaching the breakdown of family life. The first thing that occurred to him as she was talking was that some men had more success with women than others. "What do you think is going to happen when two men want the same woman or one man can't get off with the woman of his choice? It's a recipe for disaster. And what's going to happen to all the kids when they don't know who their parents are?"

Don't you think that it may be better for all the kids to have several parents; you don't know much about women do you? Any woman would be a mother to another child with no problem; I know they'd all muck in together and help each other regardless of who the father or mother is. As for the problem of men getting what they want, most women are practical enough to come up with a solution to that little problem without causing a lot of bother over it. Just as long as the man has some redeeming features, and at the moment that is the case isn't it?"

He couldn't believe his ears; his wife with all the morals had done a complete turnaround and found nothing wrong with everyone sleeping with whoever they like! She had been watching the emotions crossing his features while he wrestled with the ideas she had been expounding. When he finally arrived at the conclusion she had been waiting for she pounced.

"I suppose you think that I'm saying that the same can go for you don't you? Well you'll have to think again, for a start you're far too old to be attractive to the young things we've got coming with us. There's nothing worse than an old man chasing young girls about and anyway I think you're breeding days are over don't you?"

He put his head back and would have roared with laughter but it would make too much noise and wake everybody, so he stifled his laughter and confessed. "You had me going there for a bit, I was thinking I'm getting past all that chasing around and now you were saying I had to start all over again. I'm glad it's them that have to get on with it and not me."

She was laughing with him but looked up and had to haul the wheel over to put the boat on a new tack so they busied themselves for a few minutes till they were on an even keel and set on a new direction. Then she looked up into his face and kissed him, afterwards she said. "I hoped you would see the sense of what I've been saying, it's not going to be an easy ride for the young ones if it does happen but if it does they'll have to learn how to cope with inbreeding anyway. In such a small community it's bound to be a problem but there are ways of coping with it."

Jim nodded. "You know, one way might be to think about some artificial insemination in the community so that they can get a mixture of genes. The problem would be to get a deep freeze that

119

could cope for a few years; still it's something we can think about when our resident doctor sets up shop."

They both smiled at the memory their daughter evoked in them. Pat spoke. "It will be nice to meet her when we get there won't it?"

Jim felt himself getting emotional as he always did when they talked about their children, neither of them would admit it to them but in their eyes the children were still just that and they worried about them as if they had never got past childhood. They heaved a collective sigh and got on with the business of running the boat. Around seven in the morning he could hear the sounds of stirring below and shortly after, the delicious smell of coffee wafted up from the direction of the galley and Leah poked her head up and gave them two of the cups of the drink she had prepared.

"Where are we now?" She asked them.

Jim looked at the chart he had spread on the table. "As far as I can make out we seem to be about three hundred miles of the coast of Sumatra but my dead reckoning isn't the best and I find it difficult to use that thing he's got over there." He pointed at the Global positioning device that Ray had left out the previous night." "They seem to make these things smaller and smaller so people can carry them, but the manuals get bigger and bigger so we can try and understand them. Seems bloody self defeating in the end but Ray said something about turning west to see if anything is following us."

Leah smiled at him in sympathy. "I know what you mean but if he can buy the latest device that's on the market he will. If it's electric and needs a battery the worst salesman in the world has a job on to try and stop him reaching in his pocket for his credit card. He's a salesman's dream, all he has to do is go into a store that sells these things, and his eyes glaze over. I sometimes think he should just buy the store, at least he can have them for a bit without the trouble of buying them." She shrugged her shoulders at the thought and went on. "I wouldn't mind betting he doesn't know how to work it either."

"But I do," A voice from behind her said, and Andy poked his head round the door. "And so does Ray." He went on. "He showed me how to the other day when we had a bit of spare time,"

The three of them looked at each other sceptically, even in the short time that Andy had known Leah he had proved that one thing he knew nothing about was mathematics. Jim and Pat had known for years, as they had had to read his school reports. Nonetheless he strode over to the device and pressed a couple of buttons then turned around triumphantly and said. "We're off the coast of Sumatra."

The three of them looked at each other and collapsed in their seats, Pat started it by the shaking of her body with suppressed mirth and soon the other two were laughing as well. Andy looked from one to the other of them in indignation. "So what's funny about that?" He asked.

Jim had to wave at him to wait for a moment until he could get his breath back, when he finally could speak he said to him. "We've been off the coast of Sumatra for about three days now and you come and tell us that. We wanted to know where we were within 5 yards. Like that instrument is supposed to tell us."

Andy immediately tried to bluster his way out of the predicament he had found himself in. "It's only because it's not fine tuned."

Leah gasped and said; "Maybe if we put him on Ayers Rock he could tell us he was in Australia,"

That started them off again and it was some time before they had control over themselves. At last Leah said. "Well, I reckon I'd better get some breakfast on the go before that husband of mine gets out of bed with a sore head because there's nothing to eat."

She went off to start preparing some food and Pat decided to hand over the wheel to Jim so he could steer for the next 30 minutes, till it was time to hand over to Andy and Leah. He passed the next thirty minutes steering cautiously and practising how to keep the craft on an even keel. A couple of times he overreacted to a wave with the result of complaining from below. At last eight-o-clock arrived and Leah and Andy came on deck to take over. She said in passing. "I've left some food out for you and that lazy husband of mine, if he ever decides to get out of bed. I've fed the kids and told them they can do the washing up for everybody so don't help them with it. Just eat up and get some shuteye for a bit."

That said she let them go below and eat. At first Jim had felt fine but now he had some food he felt really fatigued and immediately went to bed. His head had hardly touched the pillow before he was sound asleep, Pat looked down at his recumbent form and smiled to herself, he had had a lot to think about this night and doubtless he would be still thinking about it when he woke.

Chapter Eight

Jim came to abruptly; his head was ringing from the violent shaking he was being given. He opened one eye and blearily stared at the clock, it read 14-00 so he had been in bed for six hours. He then looked up to see who was giving him such a rough shaking and saw Dick looking down on him with concern on his face.

"Christ, you take some waking when you're out don't you?

Jim felt a little aggrieved at this, as it wasn't normally the case; he woke up quite quickly under normal circumstances and figured he must have had too many worries of late. He raised himself off the bed and yawned stretching his arms to get the kinks out, he felt a tug on the sheets as Patricia pulled them back over her and a tiny voice came out of the covers. "Sod off and talk somewhere else will you, I want to get some more sleep."

Jim grinned down at the top of her head; all that could be seen was a little curl of hair poking over the top on the pillow. It had long been a joke between them that she was a dormouse in bed and only wanted to be kept warm and tucked well in. he looked up at Dick and asked. "What's up? I was enjoying that little sleep."

Dick answered cautiously with a glance at Patricia. "I think you'd better come on deck for a closer look."

"Can I just have five minutes to do the necessary?" Jim was one of those people who couldn't get out of bed without going straight to the bathroom, but this time he was out on deck in two minutes flat. He found the others clustered round the radar console watching it avidly and discussing something they could see there.

They looked up when he approached and made way for him. Ray spoke first. "Sorry to get you out mate but this doesn't look good." He pointed at the screen and said. "Do you see that blip there?" He pointed to the screen and went on. "We're about a hundred miles east of the Sunda Straits heading south at the moment. That one is about ten miles behind us and he's keeping station about there. Every time I try a course change to the east he immediately starts on a south-easterly course to cut across and shorten the distance. What he's doing is herding us more and more southerly. I think its trouble heading our way and we can't go in the direction we need to go."

Jim stared at the screen for a moment while he pondered the problem; finally he had marshalled all his thoughts. "Three things come to mind now." He raised his fingers. "First, are you absolutely certain he's chasing us? Second, is he possibly faster than us? And third, if we keep this course, where are we likely to end up?" He looked at them and added. "I put that last one in because considering the size of Australia I don't think we'll miss it by much of we keep on this course."

Ray answered him for the others. "In answer to your first question I can say without doubt he's on our tail as I've got him on the tape for about 5 hours and he's never deviated much in all that time. On the second question, I'm not sure as he's keeping up with us but he doesn't close the distance. I think he can't go faster but it's not certain. The only thing is; if he wanted to close with us, now is as good a time as any. Whatever happens here there aren't going to be any witnesses are there?" For the last question the only thing that can be said for that is, we're headed for what must be one of the most desolate stretches of coast in the world."

"Can we go any faster?" Jim asked.

Ray nodded his head in answer to this question. "We can go faster but there is a cost, we could get that spinnaker out and use that, but it needs all hands on deck to control it so we end up with no sleep and only a few miles further forward. We'd need to be going half as fast again to leave him behind, and." He added looking at Jim. "He might have a spinnaker as well."

Jim shook his head; "Do you think he knows that we suspect he's behind us?"

"Almost certainly." Ray replied. "When I first suspected he was there I started trying to manoeuvre around to try and lose him. I know he's got radar because we can't see him visually and he's following us, but he'll have those manoeuvres down and he can see what we've been doing." He pointed to the chart where he had inscribed their course. "You can see for yourself that no one in his right mind would sail like that. And anyway, the best course for us is east and he knows it."

Jim sat down for a moment to consider this information. "One thing comes to mind in all this discussion. Are we sure this guy who's following us means us any harm? What if he turns out to be just an innocent fisherman or trader and we start shooting at him for no other reason than he's going in the same direction as us? And can we be certain this boat following us is a pirate?"

Ray answered for the others. "I know you like to play the devil's advocate and put doubts in our minds but there is evidence to support this you know." He ticked them off on his hands. "We've done a deal with a guy who knows we've got access to a lot of money, and the boat's worth a lot as well, and I wouldn't trust that Sulim any further than I could throw him, and if you're honest you know I'm right. So the conclusion I've drawn is that it's better to shoot first and ask questions later." He brought his face closer to Jim and added grimly. "Think about this, it's no use to him just to get the guns back, he has to get the boat and everything on it to make it pay. In those circumstances there's no way he can allow anyone to live, as they'll be witnesses against him. Now you'd better say to me you understand and agree with me before anything happens, because we can't afford to have anyone here who's going to hesitate at a critical moment."

He looked around at all of them in turn. "That goes for all of you, if you have to shoot, do it or you might die. Do you understand?"

He waited for each of them to acknowledge him in their own way before he relaxed his body and let Jim speak; Jim coughed and grinned ruefully. "Well I must admit you don't mess about when it comes to telling us the true situation. First of all I want you to know that I agree with what you just said." He raised his voice to include them all and carried on from the point where he had been interrupted; he got up and looked at the chart again. "Tell me I'm right if I say there are ports on the west coast of Oz?"

Ray looked at the charts over his shoulder with a frown on his face. "I've got to admit that I know very little about the ports on that side of Oz." He said. "But you've only got to look at that chart to see there ain't much in the way of civilisation along the whole coast, not till you get right down to Geraldton or Perth. And that's just about as far out of our way as you can get." He mused almost to himself. "We have to get somewhere near to a customs boat or something, but if we do that they could start asking some pretty sticky questions."

"Why don't we ambush them?"

They both turned to look at Andy. Jim was getting angry with his son who always seemed to think of violence as a way out of a problem, and Ray was merely curious as to how an ambush could be carried out in mid ocean.

He smiled at them. "I don't mean we've got to find some rocky gorge and climb to the top of a hill to wait for them, but what about making it look like an accident and we've had to stop sailing and wait for him to get close enough to attack him. Then we'd have a chance to finish the whole business in one go."

"I suppose you've thought about the women and children we've got on board here, while you're giving us these crazy schemes?" Jim answered. "You of all people should know what a machine gun can do to a boat." He stamped his foot on the deck. "That's about the hardest thing on this boat, and even that wouldn't stop a bullet. If we do something like you suggest, someone is going to end up very dead."

Another voice came from behind them. "If you don't do something there're going to kill us all anyway," They all swung round to see Pat had come up while they were talking. She went on. "Or maybe you men would be dead and we could be shipped off anywhere it suits them, and don't pretend it doesn't happen."

This thought sobered them for a while and it was Ray who broke the silence. "I'm going below for a bit, let's just all have a think and see what we can come up with." He went below and must have said something to the children as shortly after they appeared carrying a tray of drinks. They sipped them for a while as they were thinking until Pat who didn't like silence and thought on her feet started to throw ideas into the middle.

"First of all, why can't we get the Australian authorities to do something? Maybe send a plane out, I can't understand we're here in the new Millennium and these people are acting like pirates, and we're letting them get away with it."

"Sounds easy when you say it quick like that ducky," Leah answered. But don't forget you're trying to get into Oz without anybody knowing about you. Even if they would fly about two thousand miles just on our suspicions. And if they did, what could they do? We've got no proof this boat behind is doing anything wrong."

Pats head had come up when it was mentioned that they were trying to get into Australia illegally. Although it was true, she was one of life's people who always tried to stay on the right side of the law and it broke her heart to be doing something illegal.

"They don't have to know our final destination but if they speak to us, we could say we're going on to somewhere like New Zealand,"

Leah nodded in agreement. "It might work, but our problem's a bit more pressing to worry about it for the moment, it looks like we either fight or run and I'm more inclined to run than fight right at this time. I don't want anything to happen to those two there." She pointed her nose in the direction of the two children who were gathering up the crockery. Pat agreed with her wholeheartedly as she could understand a mothers concern. Andy and Dick had been talking in the background while they had been having their discussion and Andy broke in. "What about if I tried picking them off at long range with the sniper rifle? I could set it up on a tripod and get a steady firing point."

Jim sighed once more; this son of his could be a trial with his fanciful schemes. "This isn't one of your computer games where they say, alright you missed this time, lose a life, and try again. If you miss and they get a shot in, it may mean one of us dying, even you, did you think about that? They know we've got a lot of weapons on this boat and there're going to take some care when they approach us."

Ray came back up from the salon; he had a look of some satisfaction on his face. He glanced around at them and announced. "I think I've cracked it" He went to the chart and said. "Get round here and have a look at this," He put his finger on the chart at a point roughly south of their position, then announced triumphantly. "Christmas Island, I'd forgotten all about it."

Jim bent to pore over the chart for a moment. "It's Australian territory if that's what you're wondering," Ray said. "Mostly mining but it has a port and Australian Police there. They don't have a lot to do beside look after a lot of drunken Aussie miners."

Jim shook his head. "It won't do Ray, Those guys aren't going to follow us into a harbour like that, they'll just lay off a few miles and wait for us to come out again. The only thing that would happen is that they'll catch us up while were in the harbour." He breathed deeply as he thought about it. "The other thing is that your Aussie police'll have chance to check us all out, and being such a quiet place they'll do it with pleasure."

Ray didn't seem to be very despondent at this news; he just answered. "Yeah, I thought you might say that, that's why I thought up plan B."

They all raised their heads at this, wondering what was to come. Ray laughed in delight. "That got the attention I wanted." He said. "Now listen to this, I think we should get that spinnaker out and head east as we've got a following wind in that direction, now when we put that up this boat's going to go like the wind and it'll have to. I've worked it out roughly." He pointed at the chart. "This guy's about 10 miles behind us at the moment and we're heading south, so if we turn east he can sail south by east to cut us of. Now that puts him at our relative rates; which is about even, maybe four miles behind us after we've sailed east. So we'll have lost six miles. The spinnaker up will make us faster and I think we'll be able to lose him if we can keep it up."

He paused here to make sure they all understood and then went on. "The problem is that the spinnaker is good for following wind but that's all, and it takes more people to handle it when it's up. We'll have to divide into two teams and take turn about, two on and two off."

There was a babble of sound as they all tried to speak at once until finally Jim thundered. "SHUT UP." when they had all quieted down he said to Ray. "You take the biscuit don't you? First you tell us it's too risky and then you say we're going to do it. What if this all goes pear shaped and they do catch up with us?"

Ray spread his hands. "There's nothing I can do about that, and you know it. It can just as easily go wrong doing it the way we are now. We'll just have to play the cards the way they're dealt. I happen to think that it'll be better for us if we head along the north coast of Oz. If anything goes wrong we'll stand more chance of getting some help in that direction. I'm going to steer a course just south of east so that we'll be heading more in the direction of Darwin, which, if you recall." He looked Jim in the eye and said. "Is right where you wanted to go when all this started."

In his heart of hearts Jim had to acknowledge that Ray was telling them the best way of handling the crisis they found themselves in. At least in the direction Ray wanted to sail they had a much better chance of getting help and more importantly for them they could blend in better with a larger population. Although Jim had had ideas about entry into Australia legally he still had his doubts about whether the authorities would allow it; and also if they applied and were refused they would then have tipped their hand and the Australian authorities would then know about them. Up till now he had been relying on the average Australians well known contempt for anything that looked like authority. Ray had been a prime example of this as he had taken it in his stride that they were doing something highly illegal, and even helping them in this way could get him into a great deal of trouble with the legal system, ultimately he could land himself in prison.

He studied Ray while he pondered on this and came to the conclusion that he was an average sort of guy who was looking for a bit of excitement then he grinned inwardly to himself. 'He's getting more than his fair share of that on this trip'. He thought. 'I only hope he doesn't die of it'. He then looked around at all the others and found them all watching him and realised that although Ray was nominally in charge on board the boat they were still looking to him for leadership, all their eyes were waiting for his reaction to Ray's proposal. He nodded to him and said. "OK."

Ray's shoulders positively sagged with relief as he accepted the opinion from Jim. Without realising it he had been relying on his leadership to sway the others to his way of thinking. Now that the two of them were in agreement they could proceed much more easily. He squared his shoulders. "Right." He snapped. "Let's get this show on the road."

He looked over at Dick who had the helm. "I want you to keep the boat on this course for the time being until we get the spinnaker rigged, then we'll haul it up and see what this boat can do."

He turned and said to the rest of them. "Let's get the sail out of the side locker and rig it up to the mast, the only instruction at the moment is we've got to keep it tied up until the very last moment and then let it go in one easy movement. But first it has to be tied down to both port and starboard sides of the boat and a line run to the top of the mast onto that pulley there."

He pointed to the top of the mast where a small pulley swung in the breeze. They all stared upwards at the mast, which was swaying with the motion of the boat. Jim had never liked heights and it must have showed in his face because Ray grinned evilly and said to him. "I think I'll volunteer you for that little climb Jim."

Jim felt his stomach turn at the thought and went green around the gills. The mast carried on swaying and as he glanced up a shadow passed over his face as it went over the face of the sun. He was saved from further embarrassment as Andy stepped into the breech. He knew his father well and was certain that he would have gone if necessary but felt that every man has a weakness, and he was prepared to tolerate that in his father. So he said to Ray. "I think I'm going to be the best man for this job as I've done some climbing back home."

Jim silently heaved a sigh of relief and listened as Ray described what was to be done. In the end it was deceptively simple. A rope was always kept tied to the mast and this ran through a pulley at the top and down again. Ray unhitched it and fashioned a seat from it at one end with a series of knots with enough room for Andy to sit in it with both legs dangling, next they hauled on the other end to pull it tight. Ray then handed the line from the top of the spinnaker to Andy who was then hauled up the mast to the top, as he went up he had to hand himself off the mast so as not to get tangled in any of the lines which were attached to it. When he arrived at the very tip of the mast he ran the line through the pulley and then they lowered him back down. When he arrived back down on the deck the line was used to pull a block and tackle up to the top of the mast ready to haul the spinnaker up. The spinnaker then was hauled out and spread on the deck and connected to the line. Ray had Dick change course till they were facing east with the wind behind them. Then the forward sail was lowered, Jim and Andy were detailed to help him haul the sail up when he was ready and Pat and Leah held the bottom lines on either side with strict instructions not to let them out. Ray glanced round at them all to assure himself that they were all ready and then grunted. "Right, heave now."

The three of them hauled back on the rope and the sail rose in the air with a series of spasmodic jerks as they all pulled upwards at the same time. Ray watched the rope as the sail neared the top of the mast and when it neared it he called out. "OK, hold it there a minute and we'll tie it off there."

They fought to tie it off before the wind filled it and were just in time as it billowed out with a snap, Pat and Leah would have been pulled forward with the lines if they hadn't had the good sense to wind them round a cleat. The sail bulged out and the speed of the boat increased considerably as they felt the pull of the following wind. The boat heeled over as Dick struggled to get it onto the course he had been given, a little south of east. Then as it righted itself another problem showed itself. As the boat went faster it fairly flew over the tops of the waves but on the downside it buried its nose further into the troughs as well. This had the effect of bringing water cascading on to the deck making it dangerous to be there without a lifeline.

Ray shouted to them to get below for a minute and get their breath back and as the increased speed and noise made talking difficult he held his finger up to Dick to indicate he would only be a minute. Then he followed them down to the salon. On arrival he said to them. "We've got to split into two teams to handle this now so I think its better if Andy comes with me and Dick and Leah goes with Pat and Jim. Is that OK with everyone?"

Everybody nodded agreement but Jim and Pat watched Andy and Leah exchange glances before agreeing to this new development.

Jim himself was only happy that Ray seemed unaware of what was going on with the two of them.

Leah turned to the children who were hanging around waiting and asked them to make up some drinks for them and then turned to Ray and said. "I suppose you know that it's not been long since I came off duty and now you've got me going out again, when do you think I'll get some rest or isn't that important in your scheme of things?"

He shrugged his shoulders in reply, and replied. "We've all got to pull our weight as much as we can and you're no exception to that rule, it's just the luck of the draw. It could have happened to any of us, anyway I can't stop here and leave it all to Dick, I'm going out there now and I expect you to get out and help as soon as it's your turn." He nodded in Andy's direction and went out of the door followed by Andy.

Leah turned to Pat and Jim in frustration at what he had just said to her and snapped. "Bloody men, they think they can order you around as if you're a piece of rubbish that's got no other thought in its head but to obey them."

Although Pat sympathised with Leah about the way Ray had informed her she felt obliged to point out to her something she seemed to be missing. "If you took a moment to think about it Leah, he's done it for the best. All of us here have to work in a team and he's put them so that some of us have an experienced person with them, and as we've got you and they have Ray that makes the teams about equal."

Leah frowned at her in reply and said. "I think you're the one that's missing the point, dearie. I wasn't complaining about working with you but about him ordering me about. He just did it without consulting anybody else; who does he think he is?" She shook herself in frustration and muttered something about getting even with him later.

Pat could see one of her rages coming on and knew they could ill afford to have her causing any more trouble at this development in their plans, so she attempted to pour some oil on the troubled waters. "Will you please calm down Leah, we can't afford to rock the boat just now," At this, even Leah had to smile at the unintentional pun. Pat went on. "We've got to work together in the common interest for the next few days, and causing trouble isn't going to help anyone is it?"

Leah smiled, ruefully as she conceded that Pat was, as usual, right. "Don't worry," She answered. "I won't rock the boat, as you so beautifully put it. I'll just store it up for the future, when he's not quite so busy."

Jim, who was happy that potential trouble had been averted, said. "I think we ought to get out on deck now, it's almost time for our watch to take over."

The other two nodded in answer and followed him up the steps to the deck. Once there they found Ray huddled over the radar set watching the trace of the other boat intently. He said without looking up. "It's still too early to see if he's spotted our change of course yet but at the speed we're making now any delay on his part is that much better for us."

Jim answered him. "We've come up to take over this watch Ray, it's four in the afternoon, and it's our turn to stand watch."

It took a moment for the import of his words to sink in and then Ray looked up bemusedly, as if Jim had taken leave of his senses. "There's no way I'm coming off watch for some time mate." He answered. He nodded in the direction of Andy and Dick. "You two go off watch and get some rest. These can take over while I keep an eye on the radar here."

They all shuffled around attempting to take positions without getting in each other's way and finally they got it sorted out. Ray had been watching this out of the corner of his eye and when they had finished he commented dryly. "If you play about like that with no emergency I'd like to see you when there's a panic on."

Leah, who was still smarting from the comments Ray had made below, instantly swung round and snapped at him. "Don't worry darling, we know what to do when the time comes."

Jim cringed in expectation of another row between the pair of them but Ray was obviously not concentrating on her, he had already turned to the screen. "Damn." He muttered. "It looks like they've changed course to south east, now we've got trouble." He looked up at them and said. "All shore leave is cancelled for the next day or so, everybody's on watch full time for now, so if you've got any caffeine pills you might as well start taking them."

The weak joke did little to dispel any misgivings they felt at the course of event they had embarked upon but his next words served to bring home the trouble they were in. He said to Andy. "You'd better start checking out that machine gun on the afterdeck, screw the tripod down tight and get Dick to help with the ammunition. We can put a canvas screen round it for the moment to camouflage it. We might get a few minutes surprise out of it if we're lucky."

To the rest of them he said. "Get some guns out and hide them within easy reach, we don't want them to know what we intend to do before he gets too close, we should get some idea of what his intentions are by then."

They all went to do his bidding except Andy who said to Jim before he left. "Can you get my sniper rifle out and put it up by the hatch on top of the cabin, I want to be able to get to it quickly if I need to."

Jim nodded his agreement and they all went about the business of preparing to defend the boat. Everything went according to the plans they had laid with the exception of Leah who approached Dick and said. "I don't think I'll be any good trying to shoot a gun on a swaying boat so why don't I take over as loader for Andy and that'll leave you free to have your own gun."

That seemed a good idea so with some relief that he would at least get a chance to use a weapon instead of holding an ammunition belt Dick agreed; then went off to find himself a gun. One of the Heckler and Koch machine guns was still in the chest so he took that and several clips of ammunition, these he placed in his pants pockets although they made him heavy on the legs they were at least reassuring. While he was doing this he mused to himself about who had taken the other guns. Jim and Ray had taken one each but surprisingly Pat had one as well. Jim looked at her quizzically but she only shrugged and said.

"There's no way these guys are going to take me of to some brothel in the backwaters of Thailand. I'll be better off dead."

Jim couldn't help the next crack that came out of his mouth. "With your age and beauty I don't think they'll bother to transport you all the way back to Thailand, by the time you get there you'll be long past it," This earned him a well placed kick up the rear as they went about their jobs.

Meanwhile Andy had spoken to Leah about her remarks to Dick. "I thought you were going to take one of the machine guns as you were much better than anybody else in practice,"

"That's true." She replied. "But I have a feeling the action is going to be round here with this bloody great gun. Or don't you want me to assist you firing it? Anyway, what do you think this is? Scotch mist?" And she reached into a pack she was carrying and pulled one of the Hecklers out. Andy glanced into the pack and saw several clips of ammunition nestling in the bottom.

"It looks like you were in the girls guides by the amount of preparation you've been doing."

"Hmm." She answered. "It's just a pity they didn't go into the finer points of warfare."

While all this had been going on, Ray had been taking the helm to keep the boat on course but now he called out so everyone could hear. "I want you all to spread out around the boat so that if they fire they can't aim at more than one person and if you can, lay flat facing them so you'll make a smaller target. You kids, I want you down below now, and if it gets hairy I want you to run ammo to anybody who calls for it, but stay below and run in the passageways, don't go on deck unless it's absolutely necessary. If they're firing, stay down, it won't help anyone if you get hurt."

The children ran off to do his bidding and he glanced round at the others who were getting everything ready in preparation. He nodded to himself in satisfaction and concentrated on holding the boat on its present course.

Jim was inspecting all the preparations as they went on and decided that there was one further thing to be done in the way of preparing them for whatever was going to happen. He cleared his throat and called out, loud enough so that everybody heard. "Can I have your attention everybody just for a minute?"

They all gradually stopped what they were doing and looked at him expectantly. "He rubbed his fingers through his hair as he chose his words, a nervous habit he didn't know he did but that was as familiar to Pat as watching him when he spoke to her. When he was sure he had their attention he said. "I've just got a few words to say about what happens if these people catch up with us. If they are in any way connected to the arms salesman that means they can't be up to any good. If they had wanted to contact us in they could have easily done that on the radio; as they haven't I think we will have to treat any advance from them as hostile."

He stopped talking and looked at them each in turn. "That means," he went on. "We will not stop to ask questions if they get close enough to us, as soon as we can identify these people we start shooting, do I make myself perfectly clear on this?" They all stared back grimfaced and one or two swallowed nervously as they thought of what he had said.

"If any of you have any doubts, I want you to speak up now, as hesitation if anything starts, like giving the other guy a chance to shoot first will get you killed, because these guys won't give you a chance. And you're only going to get one try at killing them as they are far more experienced in this sort of thing than you, and if they are the sort of men I think they are, they will kill you. Do you all understand what I've just said?"

"He waited until they had all nodded their assent and then grinned and said. "Right, give it to them right where it hurts and follow my lead." He paused for a moment to let it all sink in and then went on. "It might never happen anyway as we stand a good chance of outrunning them, don't we?" This last was to Ray who was still wrestling with the wheel.

He hardly paid any attention to Jim who now looked round and realised that even as he had been speaking the wind had risen and was now pushing the boat ever faster. He rushed over to Ray's side and helped with the wheel, which was bucking and twisting in his hands, they brought it under control and Ray shouted in his ear. "If it gets much worse we'll have to take the spinnaker down, but I think it's only a squall and it'll blow itself out soon."

He pointed to the mast, which was showing signs of the strain it was under and had a slight bow in it. The sail was as tight as a drum and throbbing as it took the force of the wind behind it. They had been sailing under the spinnaker for only about twenty minutes up to now and Andy came over and asked. "How long before we know if we're ahead of them?"

Ray gave the control of the wheel to him and went over to check the radar screen, He had barely time to get there when there was an almighty crack and the mast broke in two about two thirds of the way up. The spinnaker collapsed with a sigh into the water and was immediately swept under the keel where it snagged and acted as a giant sea anchor. They lost all way and stopped dead in the water. Ray looked at the remains in despair but suddenly snapped himself out of it and started shouting orders to get knives out and cut it free. As they were doing that he called Andy over and said. "Get up that mast and cut the top down, leave all the stays below the cut but get everything off the top and let it drop. When that's done I'm going to get a pulley up to you, you fix it tight and maybe we can bring a sail up as far as that."

Andy ran to do his bidding but was hampered by the amount of lines around the bottom of the mast. Seeing this Jim ran over and started hacking them free and soon they had cleared enough for Andy to start climbing. He went up as fast as possible and it was only when he had reached the break that he realised he had come this far with no safety line. It was too late to worry about now so he bent to the task in hand and got his knife out and started cutting. The boat was still swaying heavily in the swell but as he cut into the various lines that were in the way he realised that the wind had eased up a little and it was getting more comfortable to be there. He cut into one line and took a moment to lash himself to the mast, this to Pat's relief as she had been watching so far with her heart in her mouth as any mother would have done. With a determined effort the sail was cut free and Ray reluctantly gave the order to set it loose. He was probably the only one on board who realised how much the spinnaker had cost but there was no time to be lost, as he had to get on with the repairs to the boat first and worry about cost later.

Andy had by now freed all the lines and the top of the mast was hanging down by one line remaining, Ray looked up and judging when the swing of the mast was best shouted to Andy to cut it down. It crashed to the deck and they stowed it as quickly as possible on the side of the boat out of the way, possibly to be used later. Ray ran back to the after deck to look at the radar readout while the others tried to rig a pulley to the top of the mast. They passed one of the cut lines which Andy had kept up and hauled a new pulley up to him, he quickly lashed it to the mast and ran the line back down to them. When they had secured it Pat and Jim threaded the sail through and it was hauled up to the top, it wasn't as big as previously but they wound the bottom round the boom and the boat started to get under way again.

Ray came back while this was going on and was just in time to congratulate Andy as he slid back down to the deck. He pointed in a roughly north west direction and said. "They're about 1 hour away on that heading but they'll be closing on us now." He looked over the side and made a quick mental calculation. Then said. "At the rate we're going now I think they'll catch us by morning, I'll work that out better when I get a bit of time later."

He looked around at all of them then nodded in congratulation. "I can only say I'm proud of the way you all came through this, you did really well and showed a team spirit I didn't expect you to have. Now lets get this show on the road again and do our best to get as many knots out of this tub as we can." They all looked at each other at this with a new expression on their faces that showed their pride in themselves and each other then they all set too and tightened everything they could and got the sails trimmed until once more they were making some headway through the water. Ray kept an anxious eye on the radar now and again but finally had to admit the other boat was catching them slowly but surely. Andy had taken over the wheel now and they were making the best course they could under the circumstances.

Pat and Leah had gone to make some drinks when Dick approached Jim and Ray. "I've been thinking about what's going to happen when these guys get in range, if I read the situation right, all hells going to break out if we all start shooting and with probably five or six guys on the other boat and all of us here armed and ready to shoot it's going to be murder. Some of us are going to die, and that's the last thing any of us wants."

The two of them looked at each other and then at Dick with

questions in their eyes. The both of them had been thinking the same but had no solution to the problem. Jim said. "Go on."

"We've got all the items necessary for us to try another way, we've got plastic explosive, detonators, and small radio signallers to set them off, and we've got Andy's scuba gear. When they get close enough I could go over one side and swim to their boat underneath and plant the explosive. It needn't be a very big explosion just enough to make a hole in their boat and create a diversion."

"How the hell do you expect to stick plastic explosive to the keel of a boat," Jim was getting angry and it showed. "Boats are made especially to be smooth and you certainly can't nail it, can you?"

Ray intervened. "He's got a point you know, but I've got some tape around here somewhere that's made especially for underwater use, it'll stick to anything. He could even go for the rudder, as he said it doesn't have to be big, especially underwater, as that makes the impact go inward."

Jim stared at both of these people, one his son-in-law the other who was proving to be a good friend. "Do you realise how dangerous this could be, if they even sniff one little thing wrong with the way we handle this," He held his finger up. "Just one, do you know what they would do, because I would do it to them if they tried this, they can drop a hand grenade over the side and you're dead with no risk to them at all."

He looked over the side and although it was now evening and the sky was darkening in preparation for night he was able to point down and say. "How far down can you see? Five, ten, fifteen metres. You'd be a sitting duck."

Dick shook his head at this little protest from Jim. "You're forgetting something in all this Jim, Ray said earlier that they can catch up with us by morning, why don't we slow down a bit and let them catch us when it's still a bit dark. Say about four in the morning."

Jim scratched his head as he always did when he was thinking, then he turned and went to lean on the side rail. He stood there for several minutes lost in contemplation. Finally he turned round and said. "I don't think they're going to be fooled if we just turn over and let them catch us, we'd have to make it more convincing. Although with a broken mast we could possibly get away with it."

Dick grinned, at least his plan had been accepted and they stood more of a chance. Ray had one or two objections to the plan though. "Maybe they won't wait till they get close to open fire or they'll have their own diver to do the same, any way Dick isn't the best at scuba diving, that'd be me or Andy. We've done far more than him."

Dick rounded on him before Jim could open his mouth; "You and Andy are far more useful to the boat than me, and anyway you said it yourself, there're obviously after the boat so they won't open fire at all if they can help it and if they do have their own diver wouldn't it be best to have a diver of your own down there to see him?"

Jim was forced to step back in the face of this passionate display from Dick. "Hey, I said I thought it was a god idea but Ray has raised point's; valid points. We've got to consider all the angles before we go off half-cocked and ruin a perfectly good plan. Now I suggest we all sit down for a while and have a discussion about this idea."

The two women by this time had returned with the drinks for everyone so they all gathered together on the afterdeck and discussed this new idea till they had ironed all the kinks out of the plan. The most worrying part they agreed was that they had to persuade the other boat to come close enough to enable Dick to swim across, as no one was certain he could go more than fifty feet underwater in a straight direction in the dark. When they had settled that, Ray Andy and Jim offered to stay on watch while the rest of them got some relaxation. But as Pat said before she went below. "I don't think I could close my eyes for a minute until this is over."

They slowed the boat down even more and then settled down to wait for the other one to catch up with them. It was a long night just sitting there waiting for something to happen. As the clock ticked on Jim sat and thought about the strange turn of events that had brought them to this boat in the middle of the Indian Ocean off the North West coast of the Australian continent. He considered that he hoped all their efforts had not been in vain, although he smiled a little to himself that the irony was that if he was proved right billions of people over the whole world were going to die. Then he cursed the greed of men like Sulim the arms salesman who were never satisfied but had to steal more than they were entitled to from any deal.

He was awakened from his reverie by a slight sound from the bow and unconsciously glanced at his watch. It read three-thirty. Jim raised his head slightly to try and see what had caught his attention; he was rewarded with a tap from something hard on the back of the head behind the ear and a voice whispered. "If you move one tiny little muscle I will pull the trigger."

He involuntarily moved his head to see whoever was holding the gun but all he had for his effort was the barrel pressing into his temple and a click that sounded loud enough to wake every body on the boat. But that in reality was probably not heard more than three feet away. His mind was racing trying to figure out what had happened to them, he could have sworn the junk couldn't have caught them yet. So what other explanation was there? He cursed himself after a moment as he realised they must have put a dinghy with an outboard to outflank them and wait for them to arrive on course. And they had just sailed into the trap like the amateurs they were.

The voice from behind said. "I want you to stand slowly and go back to the man on the helm."

Jim did as he said, as he saw no use in arguing. When he arrived he found a crestfallen Ray standing there with a man who was dressed entirely in black. This turned out to be a wetsuit that covered all his body, he assumed the man behind him would be dressed the same. This explained why they had not been spotted coming aboard. The two men conferred quietly for a moment and Jim thought he heard the man behind him say. "Only two on guard."

This meant they had missed Andy as he had been watching on the bow. Jim had been amidships and they would have had to pass Andy to get to him. Although they had trapped him, Jim couldn't help admiring the way they had done it so quietly. In the dull gleam of the compass light he could see Ray looking at him with a question in his eyes and tried to answer that he understood the question but something about the way he moved his head attracted the guard and he received another painful tap and the hissed command. "Quiet."

It dawned on Jim that they were trying to isolate the entire crew one at a time, as to have them all up and milling about would be very difficult for them to control. For the moment they wanted both of them immobilised and the next step they took proved it. They produced some plastic cuffs such as the police used, it consisted of a single strand of serrated plastic which when it was tightened was impossible to undo without cutting. Jim had his hands tied behind him and his feet lashed around the ankles. They tied Ray to the wheel so he could keep the boat on the same course, then took some tape out of their pockets and bound it round their mouths. One of them then stood in front of them and put his fingers to his lips. Jim thought it seemed unnecessary in the light of them closing their mouths with the tape. He grabbed Jim and made him sit alongside Ray so he could watch them both, the other set off down the steps into the salon.

He reappeared only a few minutes later with the children who came up the steps with wide eyes and stared at the spectacle of Jim and Ray tied up. He took some tape from his pocket and bound it round their mouths and tied the children in the same way as they had been. In the time he had been bound, Jim had tried to wriggle his hands free but it was a fruitless task, as he knew it would be. He had seen the same material used to tie electrical wires together on building sites and had tried to break it before, without success. It had been tied too tightly to allow him to wriggle his hands free.

When they were all thoroughly bound, the man set off once more, and as he went down the steps again Jim prayed that Andy hadn't gone down to be with Leah while Ray was on deck. He was at least partly right, Andy had done just that, and he was now in Leah's cabin with her. He had gone down to see her thinking that the other boat couldn't possibly catch them for another hour or two. But there is one peculiarity of boats and that is they can never be made to be quiet, he had heard the footsteps of the intruder both when he heard his father being taken captive and when they had returned for the children. The intruder was a very quiet man but when a person is familiar with all the noises on a boat it is easy to pick out strange ones. So Andy was very aware they had unwanted visitors aboard.

He waited with Leah until he heard the man go back on deck with the children and then moved silently over to Dick's cabin and shook him awake holding his hand over his mouth to stop Dick from calling out when he woke. As was normal for Dick he woke almost instantly and Andy leant down and whispered in his ear and told him the situation in as few words as possible. He felt Dick nod his head in the darkness, and said to him. "I think this guy will come to Leah's cabin now as it's next in line along the passage, I'm going to go there and see if I can drop him when he comes in. If I can, we'll only have one to deal with."

He had to leave it at that as time was going on and he had to get back to Leah before the man came back. He only hoped that Dick had enough sense to do something from the knowledge he had but they had to play it by ear. He had only time to say to Leah. "Try and distract him in some way when he comes through the door and I'll drop him from behind." He looked around the cabin, which was only just big enough for the bed and some wardrobes built into the wall, trying to see if there was anything to use as a weapon. Leah understood what he was doing and reached into her bedside drawer and pulled out one of the pistols they had bought. Andy quickly checked it to see if it was loaded and nodded in satisfaction when it was. He felt rather than heard stealthy footsteps come along the passage and signalled with his eyes to Leah who stood in front of the door on the other side of the room. She was dressed only in a skimpy top and panties, which served her as nightwear, she quickly reached up and whipped off her top, and turning round took down her panties.

Andy was treated to the sight of her lovely lithe figure with her pert bottom on display for a moment then the door slowly opened, a man came through the door and Leah turned round as if in amazement with her hands still holding the panties, it looked just as if she had been interrupted in the act of dressing. The man took in the totally unexpected sigh of Leah completely naked before him and for a few seconds forgot the purpose of his mission. It was to prove his undoing. Almost as if in slow motion he realised someone else was in the room as well and started to turn towards Andy, but it was far too late for him. Andy hit him across the temple with the butt of the gun and he went down as if pole axed.

Leah bent forward to catch him and together they lowered his inert body to the ground. When this was accomplished Andy looked at her and whispered. "You'd better get some clothes on before I forget what we're doing here."

To his surprise she folded herself into his arms and he had to hold her for a moment as she was shaking so much. Finally he pushed her back and said. "You'd better get dressed and we'll have to see about the rest of them. That guy above won't wait too long for this one to come back."

She went back to her clothes and dressed quickly while Andy tied him up as best he could with some tights from her drawer. They left the cabin and Andy checked Dick's room but he was nowhere to be seen so they started to creep along the passage until they reached the salon. When they arrived Andy glanced round to see if they were alone and then whispered to Leah. "I'll go in front as if I'm a prisoner and see if I can get the drop on him; I can hold this pistol behind me."

She shook her head violently and mouthed back. "I'll go first, it might work twice."

Andy disagreed with this, as he didn't want her to be exposed to more danger. This had absolutely no effect on her and she made her way to the steps without waiting for any reply from him. He was forced to follow her as she turned and looked at him in the dim light of the cabin; she reached out and took his head in her hands and kissed him then got hold of her top and ripped it to expose the swell of her breasts. She leant forward and whispered. "It's worked once tonight."

Andy closed his eyes and prayed the guy wasn't dancing to another tune like being gay. Leah started to go up the steps out of the salon with her head bent forward, this had the effect of making her breasts hang slightly and bulge out of the top. The second intruder had placed himself behind Ray and was holding his gun to Ray's head when she reached the top of the stairs. His eyes started to pop when he saw her coming but he was far to alert to let Andy surprise him. Andy came out fast and low as he had been taught but as he started to fire he saw it was hopeless. The man was hidden almost completely behind Ray with his gun to his ear; all Andy could see was the side of his head and he knew he had no chance of a shot without hitting Ray. For a moment he wished he could be like one of the hero's in the films who could shoot from the hip and never miss, but as life isn't like that he let his gun hand drop to his side. The man motioned with the gun to drop it and Andy had to lock the safety on and let it fall to the deck.

The man surveyed them for a while, plainly thinking which was the best way to deal with the situation, he didn't take his eyes off them for a second and holding Ray by the throat he brought the gun slowly to the side and said. "Both of you lie down on the deck with your arms out on the floor and lie perfectly still, if you move at all I'm going to kill you."

When they had both done this he came from behind Ray and roughly pulling their hands down he bound them behind them. Then he dragged them alongside the others, when this was accomplished he stood in front of them and sneered. "Amateurs, did you think you could surprise a professional with that stupid trick of exposing your breasts."

He bent down in front of Leah and reached inside her top, which was still sagging open and fondled her breasts. Ray's eyes bulged as he tried to wrench himself free to try and stop him but he was tied too tightly. The man stopped what he was doing and knocked Ray back onto the wheel. "Stay still sonny." he hissed to Ray. "Or I'll have to kill you first so she can see you die."

Just then the sea heaved as a shape came quickly out of the water trying to get onto the diving platform at the rear end of the boat. It was Dick carrying a gun in his hand. He never had a chance of levelling the weapon as the man had plainly been waiting for this to happen. He brought his own gun up to shoot Dick and Jim could see his finger tightening on the trigger when there was an enormous bang from the salon door. Jim watched in amazement as the man's eyes opened wide in pain and surprise and then the front of his chest exploded out over them all and blood seemed to be everywhere.

Jim looked at the door wondering what had happened and Pat

stepped through carrying Andy's shotgun, she came on deck and looked at the man lying there then went over to the side of the boat put down the gun and heaved until her stomach was empty. When she had finished she sank back and sat down on the floor looking very ill and shaking. Jim tried shouting at her but hardly any sound came out of his mouth, just a subdued mumble because of the tape binding it. Fortunately this was enough to rouse her and she sat up and came over to them, she went to Jim first and tore the tape off his mouth. As soon as he could speak he said. "Get a knife and cut us free as quick as you can, this isn't over yet, we've still got that other boat out there and he can't be far behind by now."

She didn't seem to comprehend what he had said at first and went about her task as if in a dream. Dick by now had pulled himself up onto the deck and had a diver's knife in his hand and set to cutting them all free. In a matter of minutes they were all untied and able to congratulate themselves on a lucky escape. Jim spoke up for all of them and said with relief in his voice.

"I don't know how they missed you Pat but I'm glad they did or we might have all been sitting there trussed up like a load of chickens."

She smiled wanly the thought of killing a man still fresh in her mind. "It must have been the way I sleep right down under the covers; he probably thought the bed was empty. Then I found the shotgun in Andy's cabin, but I didn't expect it to happen like that." The thought made her sick again and she threw up over the side again.

Jim knew that if he showed sympathy now they would lose too much time and he gazed at the others urgently. "We've got to get ready as quickly as we can because these guys are going to be catching up with us pretty soon. We got lucky this time but don't think it's going to happen every time we go into action, we all know their intentions now so let's not take any more chances. We shoot first and ask questions later, lets all get into the positions we were going to take before this happened. But first we'll have to get rid of this one, so let's dump him over the side."

Dick gave him a hand and they dragged the man over to the side and heaved him over. It wasn't much of a burial but Jim consoled himself with the thought that they would have fared no better in his position. They all left to take up their allotted positions except Pat who was still sitting in the same spot shaking her head, Jim went over to her and she looked up with tears in her eyes and said. "I've killed a man."

Jim knelt down beside her and put his arms around her, she clung to him tightly her whole body shaking. Jim could feel the tears wetting his neck, he patted her on the back thinking to himself that everybody did that in times of stress and it wasn't enough to comfort anybody. Then he pulled back and made her look him in the eye. "I know this is a shock but you've got to remember that if you hadn't done what you did, we'd probably be dead ourselves by now, those guys were professional killers and meant to kill us."

His head snapped up; the accomplice! Once again he cursed himself for his amateurism. He jumped up and ran down the steps into the salon. When he arrived he met Andy coming through from the passageway with the second man who had boarded them, he was still tied up and blood had been flowing down his temple where Andy had hit him. He regarded Jim balefully; Jim breathed a sigh of relief and went to help Andy. Andy flung the man to the floor and asked him roughly. "What's your name?"

He just looked at the floor and his lips tightened in refusal. Andy leaned forward and put the muzzle of his machine pistol under the man's chin and asked again. "I said, what's your name?"

The man sneered in reply. "Go ahead and use it, if you don't kill me now, they will when they catch up."

Jim stiffened when he heard this as it reinforced his view that there would be no escape from this situation without someone dying. He reached out and pulled Andy round so the man couldn't see his face and said to Andy. "Slit the throat of this one and dump him overboard, we haven't time for playing these macho games, if we get no information from him he's no use to us."

He winked at him as he said it, and at first Andy appeared to be puzzled but then caught on to his intention. He reached into his belt and tugged out a long knife from his belt and roughly taking the man by the shoulder he flung him down in a kneeling position. Then he took hold of the man's hair and pulled his head back so he could put the knife across his throat. Pressing the knife down so it cut into the man's neck he said. "You've just got time to say a quick prayer to whatever God you worship."

It was too much for the prisoner, he voided himself and with all pretence of bravado gone he gasped. "My name is Ali, spare me please."

Jim groaned. "He's peed himself, bloody disgusting, if we had more time I'd make him clean the deck before we killed him."

Ali twisted his head as far as he could, his eyes bulging with terror. "Please don't kill me, I'll tell you everything you want to know."

Jim thrust his face forward until it was inches from the Ali's and asked him. "How many are left on that boat over there?"

Ali hesitated and Jim stood he deliberately walked away saying to Andy, "slit his throat and throw him to the fishes, and when you've done that come and meet me in the salon we'll go over the plans for later."

He had only taken two more steps before he heard Ali cry out. "No, no, please sir I'll tell you all I know."

He deliberately made himself take another step before he heard a strangled cry come from the man and turning he saw Andy taking a firmer hold on the man's head and pulling it higher so he could cut deeply. He ran back and pulled Andy off, then reaching down he grasped the mans ear and dragged his face round he said, "If you hesitate or tell me one lie, I'll cut your bollocks off and feed them to the fishes and you can spend all eternity with no balls."

He could almost see the man's groin closing in to protect his most precious asset and thought 'You're an Arab'. And as brave as they are in battle, when they die they hope to spend the rest of eternity in the company of virgins. Although it seemed to Jim that it must have been a man who laid down that particular dream of heaven and not a woman, Ali said to Jim. "Five sir, there are five more on board."

Jim nearly laughed out loud but prevented himself from doing that and instead asked, "How many are warriors like yourself?"

"Only two sir; and three crew."

"Who are they?" Jin asked.

"Diman and one other warrior, the crew have been pirates before and have guns as well."

Ray had been listening to this exchange from his position on the helm and said to Jim. "I reckon it'd be a good idea to get the machine gun set up and take them on at long range first, don't you?"

"I reckon you're right." Jim nodded. He made up his mind quickly and said to Andy. "Let's get this one below, and truss him up so he can't do any more harm."

They half carried and half dragged him down to the salon where they looked in his pockets and came up with some more of the plastic ties he had used on them. They quickly bound him in a similar manner and wrapped some tape round his mouth. When they had finished Jim bent over him and said. "That promise I made you earlier still goes, one peep out of you and I'll still cut you're balls off and feed them to the fishes."

The man blanched and involuntarily squeezed his legs together. Jim turned his attention to the rest of the crew, he directed Andy to go and set the machine gun on the deck and Leah to help him. The children were congratulated on their bravery, and told to fetch some more ammunition. Then he turned his attention to Pat, who was still sitting shaking on the seat. "I want you to stand guard over this man here until this is finished." He handed her a small pistol. "Take this and use it if you need to, don't forget he'd kill you without a second thought so don't think about it, just do it."

She nodded in reply but Jim had his doubts about whether she would actually have the nerve to carry it out. By now, he thought, the other boat should be catching up with them. He hoped that it wouldn't come to her again, to have to kill another person. He had to leave her to it and get on with defending the boat again, so he walked out without a backward glance. When he arrived on deck he saw the preparations were coming on apace. Andy had the machine gun set up behind a canvas screen and he and Leah had a box of ammunition beside it. Ray had the boat on course and his gun was lying on the deck close by. Dick still had his wetsuit on, but he had taken up position in the bow. Jim went over to his gun and checked the mechanism and then the ammunition; he knew how fast automatic guns ran out of bullets so he set the gun to a slower rate of fire to give himself time to aim. Because, as the experts said, 'one good shot is better then a hundred bad ones'.

With the coming of the dawn, he could now see the front of the boat and make out the figure of Dick crouching down.

Ray had turned the radar set back on, as it hadn't served the purpose they had intended of convincing the other boat they were helpless in the water. He was now studying it intently and when Jim approached he said tersely. "There're only about two miles behind and coming at us fast."

Looking back over the wake he couldn't discern the other boat as it was still too dark, then he finally saw it appear. It was a junk and he could see that it was making very good progress through the water and would soon catch them. He went over to Andy and asked. "What range do you think you'd need to guarantee a hit?"

Andy glanced over at the junk and answered. "If you mean hit a man when I aim at him, I'd say about fifty yards. On dry land I could give that guarantee at a mile, but this tub bounces about so much the bullets will just keep bouncing with it."

Jim swore softly under his breath, this was the answer he didn't want to hear. It meant that they had to let the other boat get close and then they had as much chance of getting hit themselves.

Ray had looked up when he heard his boat described as a tub but only smiled at Andy's expression. "How about putting the prisoner on deck looking as if he was in charge?"

Jim shook his head. "Won't work, first they've got binoculars and second they'll smell a rat as we didn't heave to earlier."

By this time the other boat had crept perceptibly nearer and Jim could begin to make out the figures of the men aboard her. There was some movement up near its bow and snatching up his binoculars he trained them on the boat. What he saw took his breath away. They were taking the canvas cover of a gun in the bow, but no ordinary gun. It was in his experience an anti-aircraft gun adapted for firing on the level. The muzzle was very large, and Jim knew from bitter experience that the larger the bore the more damage it could inflict.

To Andy he muttered, "They've got a large gun over there, you'll have to go for that first, because if one of those shells strikes home we're dead." He went on, "They can only threaten with that gun, if they use it there goes all the profit," Jim wished he felt as confident as he sounded because if they did use it they were all going to be blown to pieces.

He could see Diman quite clearly now through the glasses doing the same to them. Out of devilry he waved to him in a friendly fashion, only to have it ignored. Diman then bent down and spoke to the gunner who loaded a shell and trained it on them. Jim saw a puff of smoke spurt from the gun and heard the whine of a shell as it passed overhead, it splashed in the sea behind them and exploded in a shower of foam. He looked through the glasses again and saw Diman studying them as well and he gave them a wave back. Jim swore softly under his breath, if they capitulated now he was sure that they were going to get killed, as there was no way any of this could be kept quiet if they got to dry land.

He made up his mind that the only way out of this mess was to fight for their lives, he put the glasses down, turned to the others and called quietly to them, "this guy thinks because he's got a big gun we're going to fold over and give up, but he's got to take this boat without too much damage to show a profit, so if we fight he's going to destroy one of his assets. I want you all to look as if you're going to give up and when he gets closer, dive for your weapons and give him hell. Andy, he can't see you on that machine gun while you're lying there so stay down and keep your finger on the trigger; I'll pull the screen away when you have to fire. All of you take your cue from me."

They all began to lower their weapons and stand in plain view and Ray allowed the boat to drift out of the wind and the sails began to flap. The boat slowed down and stopped in the water and very soon the junk approached them. When it was about a mile away they hove to and Ray saw them taking down their sails, then heard them start the engine so they could approach under power, it crept slowly through the water towards them until Jim could pick out the individual people on board. They were all heavily armed and looked as villainous a crew as one could hope to find, and when they had approached to within a hundred yards it stopped and they could see some indecision in their attitude. Jim knew Diman was worried that he couldn't see his two men but had to hope that he thought they had missed them in the dark. When it had approached to about fifty yards they saw Diman signal to the crewman on the wheel and it stopped its approach. Diman shouted, "Where is the young puppy that shoots so well? Tell him to stand so I can see him."

'This is it,' Jim thought, this is where we've got to stand and fight. He said to Andy without looking down. "There're about fifty yards almost dead in line from your gun, I'm going to pull the cover in a minute, so be ready."

He glanced quickly at the others and although they looked tense nobody had started to move for their guns, there was an unearthly scream from the salon and Ali burst out with Pat in full pursuit, he ran over to where Andy lay and shouted across to Diman. "He's here, he's here."

Jim looked in amazement at him, and had just time to think, 'how in heavens name did he get loose?' Then all hell broke loose, he bent down to pull the screen from Andy, and a hail of bullets flew over his head catching Ali full in the chest. Ali stood for a moment with surprise on his face looking down at the damage inflicted on himself and clutched his chest, trying to stem the flow of blood. But he was fatally hit and sank down without a murmur on to the deck. Jim yanked the screen from in front of Andy and he opened up with the machine gun. The rest of them dived for their weapons and started to fire at the junk, but by this time most of the targets had disappeared. Only one remained for the moment, but he was potentially the most dangerous as he was manning the gun in the bow.

Andy swung his gun in that direction and it stuttered its deadly song across the water. The bows and woodwork of the junk started to splinter under the impact of the bullets and the gun operator was torn apart as if a maniac had attacked him with a chain saw. Jim had just a glimpse of Diman cowering behind the forward cabin trying to bring his gun to bear so he fired at him to keep his head down.

Jim was mentally counting up how many crew were still on the other boat when he heard a cry of pain and Ray slumped at the wheel. Jim started to go to him but Ray waved his hand at him and cried. "It's only a flesh wound," then lay down himself but kept a grip on the wheel to try and keep the boat on station.

Leah had also started to get up to go to Ray, until she heard him claim it wasn't serious. Although worried she tried to ignore him and continued to feed the belts of ammunition into the machine gun. Andy was now raking across the junk to try and hit any one silly enough to poke their head up. For the moment no targets showed themselves, so he stopped firing to conserve ammunition and give the barrel time to cool down.

Then there was silence and Jim realised that from his position by the machine gun the noise had been horrendous, and he was now seriously deaf. He knew that there were still four men on the junk, and, if they were all armed it was still a serious threat. Then as if from a long way away he heard Diman calling.

"Why don't you throw down your arms Englishman, you know we're going to win. If you don't surrender, we're going to kill you all."

Jim smiled at the irony of someone promising to give you life while shooting at you, and knew it was better to die fighting than to let someone execute you. He called back as much to annoy Diman. "Why don't *you* surrender? We've got the best chance here, you can't use that cannon on the bow and we've got the machine gun covering you."

The answer was a hail of bullets from a gun that sounded suspiciously like an Uzi. It is capable of firing an enormous amount of bullets very rapidly. And to his ears it was like someone running a zip through their fingers. When that happens it is best to take cover and keep your head down, which they all did. Fortunately their magazine emptied in a few seconds so it didn't go on very long. When it stopped Andy opened up on the corner the fire had been coming from but instead of trying to catch the other man when he came back out he fired directly at the corner about two feet from the deck. The bullets tore through the cabin woodwork as if they were paper and they were rewarded with a scream from the other boat.

'That's two out of five' thought Jim. He felt a hand on his shoulder and looked back to see Pat lying beside him. She handed him some ammunition and he realised he was nearly out. She then said "I can't find Dick."

It was then he realised how precarious their position really was, only Andy, himself, Pat and Leah were still in the fight. Not good odds against determined enemies. Especially as two of the crew were essentially non-combatants.

"Kids OK?" he questioned her. She nodded. "How's Ray?"

She looked in Ray's direction and shrugged her shoulders. "He'll have to wait for a bit we can't get to him yet without exposing ourselves."

Jim asked her. "Has Andy got enough ammo?"

She answered. "He's got about half a box,"

"OK." Jim was satisfied for the moment. He wondered where Dick was but was interrupted by another hail of fire from the other boat, which didn't appear to hit anyone, luckily for them it must have been one of the crewmen as most of the shots were fired from another corner, the guy didn't aim but held the gun round the corner and shot blind.

Andy immediately fired back. Jim fired as well and the junk's woodwork once again splintered to pieces and this time the man staggered out into the stream of bullets they were firing. He jerked with the impact and screamed before falling.

'Three,' Jim thought. 'Now there's only two left'. Another of the enemy appeared trying to run to the cannon on the bow. He got halfway before Andy opened up but to his horror the gun jammed. He started swearing and cursing as he was trying to unblock the gun. "Calm down Andy." Jim shouted. "You'll make it worse if you try to hurry too much."

Jim opened fire himself but the man was partially protected by the cannon, and the bullets ricocheted off the armour plating in front of the firing position. The man started to run away and it seemed as if he would leave his post but a hail of shots hit the deck at his feet. Jim realised that Diman must be there and firing at him to make him stay by the gun. Jim took aim at the wall where Diman was sheltering but his bullets didn't have the firepower of the machine gun so they only embedded themselves in the wood of the junk's cabin. After what seemed a lifetime Andy got the machine gun free and opened fire again on the cannon. Several of his shots got through to the gunner who fell back on the deck and lay still.

Four, now there's only one and that's Diman. Jim stood and shouted to the junk. "Do you want to surrender now, Diman?"

To his great surprise another man with a submachine gun opened fire, Jim had no chance of moving before he was struck by a bullet in the shoulder, Diman appeared as well and started firing, trying to kill Andy on the machine gun. He almost succeeded, as Andy had swung the barrel round to shoot at Jim's opponent, but Andy had fired two bursts of bullets and the man had gone down with a cry of pain and now he was in a position to return the fire from Diman. The engagement lasted only a short time, Diman dropped his gun and held his hands in the air. Andy stopped firing and immediately asked Jim. "How are you?"

"Don't worry about me, worry about that bastard over there." Jim waved his hand in the direction of the other boat. "Keep an eye on him for a minute while I get all this sorted out."

He felt his shoulder and found a hole under his arm; the bullet must have passed right through his flesh. It was bleeding copiously and his shirt was never going to be of any further use but at least he was alive. He got gently to his feet and had started to make his way down to the salon when there was an explosion of bubbles alongside the boat and Dick thrust his head out of the water, dressed in his wetsuit and when he took his mouthpiece out of his mouth he had a triumphant smile on his face. He swam alongside so he couldn't be seen from the other boat and said to Jim.

"I've planted the explosive on the junk; it's all set to blow anytime you need it now."

"Is that where you've been all this time?" Jim exploded, "Do you realise the chance you were taking. What if we decided to run for it? How do you expect us to know where you were unless you tell someone? Of all the crackbrained schemes you come up with that beats it all. Don't you think we could have done with you here when we had a firelight going on?"

Jim threw his good arm up in despair at Dick's stupidity. Then remembered where he had been going when Dick had reappeared, so he set off for the salon. Dick clambered aboard holding the transmitter in his hand and flung it down the steps into the salon.

"What's his problem?" he said petulantly. "I did my best and all I get is abuse and moaning."

Without taking his eyes off Diman on the junk who by now had signalled to Andy that he was going to smoke and was leaning nonchalantly against the wall of the cabin with a cigarette. Andy replied. "Don't you realise how close we came to being killed or captured while you were swanning around under there? If we hadn't had this machine gun we'd all be dead by now. Just when we needed all the firepower on the boat, you have to disappear."

He turned and looked at Dick. "It was bloody idiotic to go over there while we were fighting, we needed you here."

When he looked back Diman had disappeared. He swore and shouted to Jim. "I've lost sight of that guy on the other boat."

Jim had just reassured himself that the children were OK when he heard Andy shout. He ran up the steps to the upper deck, passing Dick without a second glance, but when he arrived he could only look at the other boat in despair. There was no sign of Diman and it looked as if he had started the engine. Leah looked up from where she had been helping Pat to tend to Ray.

"I can't be sure where that bastard went, but I think he's now below decks, I thought I caught a glimpse of him when he disappeared."

Jim knew that he should order Andy to rake the junk with the machine gun to be sure they got Diman, but held back. It almost proved his undoing. Diman reappeared on the deck but this time he was carrying a long tube with sights on the side. Inside Jim quailed, it was a disposable missile launcher. He had seen them in Sulims weapons store. He shouted to Andy, "Don't let him fire that bloody missile, or we're all dead."

He cast around for his gun but he had laid it down when he went to the saloon, and it now rested on the seat there, he knew he couldn't get to it in time. The junk pulled away from them and Diman was fumbling with the launcher, trying to get it to fire. Jim heard a click from the machine gun and Andy started swearing and cursing again. "Bloody sodding guns, never do what you want,"

Jim knelt down beside him and put his hand on his shoulder. "Calm down son and tell me quickly what's wrong."

Andy was wrestling with the gun and trying to pull the ammunition belt straight, while he did this he muttered to Jim. "I need to have the belt fed through, or it catches and won't fire."

Jim closed his eyes in despair. "Doesn't anything go right for us, we've only got seconds to stop this bastard now, and all we've got is a bloody useless jammed gun."

He looked over at Diman who was still wrestling with the missile launcher and then cast around for any sort of weapon to fire at him. The deck was bare though, and he tried to concentrate on helping Andy but all he did was get in the way. Andy knocked his hand aside and grasped the ammunition belt to wrench it out so he could start loading again, Jim watched him doing this saying. "Come on, come on." Under his breath. He glanced up quickly to see what was happening on the other boat but couldn't see Diman. Jim was torn between making a run for the salon and trying to get to his gun or waiting for Andy to free the machine gun. The problem was solved for him a moment later as Diman reappeared carrying the launcher again. Jim looked down at Andy and saw the gun still lay in pieces on the deck. There was no more time left and Jim offered up a prayer that the missile would go wide. Andy was still fumbling with the gun and Jim could see that he had no chance of getting it free before they got hit. Diman had obviously decided that if he couldn't win, he would take everyone with him. Jim could see the round black hole of the missile launcher staring at them over the water and closed his eyes and tensed his body in expectation of the impact.

When it came, it sounded as if from a long way, and he realised that he had heard the explosion and everyone said you never hear the one that gets you. He looked up in amazement and saw that Diman had disappeared in a cloud of smoke and the stern of the junk seemed to be badly damaged.

"What happened?" He heard Andy as if from a distance.

Jim shook his head, slumped down on the deck and said to Andy. "I don't know, one minute I'm looking death in the face and the next I'm still alive."

He became aware of loud whooping and cheering, and looked over his shoulder and saw Dick and the children dancing around on the deck. Dick was holding the detonator in his hand shouting. "It worked, it bloody well worked, and you two did nothing but moan about it."

Leah was smiling and Pat came up from the salon carrying a medicine chest, she still looked shaky but happy. Ray raised his head and said. "Can I have a tinny now? I feel like I need one after all that."

They all stood and grinned at each other sheepishly with the realisation that they had come through the ordeal relatively unscathed. Jim became aware of Pat staring at him in horror and realised the blood was still dripping down his side; he smiled at her in reassurance and said. "Don't worry, the bullet went straight through. It looks worse than it is." She rushed over and pulled him to a seat where she could take a closer look at his wound.

Andy still had a puzzled look on his face. "That gun should never have jammed like that, I'm going to strip it down and get the manual to check it over."

Dick punched him on the arm. "Next time you feel like having a moan about something I do mate, just think won't you."

Andy groaned. "Are we going to have to put up with this from now on, he does one thing and it saves the day." He poked Dick in the chest. "Don't you realise it was me and that gun there that saved everybody's lives, I can't be sure but I think I got every one of them except that Diman."

Dick wouldn't stop chortling at him. "But don't forget he had that missile launcher trained right down your throat, if I hadn't swum over there and planted that explosive you'd have been feeding the fishes by now."

They moved off down to the salon, still arguing over the various merits of the battle leaving the others looking at each other in relief. Ray looked over the boat as best he could and said to Jim. "Looks like we'll have to get some cosmetic work before we reach any port in Oz because there ain't a copper in the whole country who wouldn't ask questions if he saw it in this state."

Jim had to agree with him when he looked around; the was everywhere to see. There was blood all over the deck and holes where the bullets had punched through. The mainsail especially, had so many it looked like cheesecloth. He stared over at the junk, which was still chugging along away from them. Pat wrenched his shirt off and brought him back to the present. She produced some rag and wiped as much of the blood off as she could. Then examined the shoulder for any broken bones, Jim winced under her probing fingers but she wouldn't let up until she was satisfied. She then said to Leah. "Both of these guys have got to count themselves lucky to be alive."

"You can say that again," Leah answered with feeling. She bent down and lifted Ray to an easier position. Andy's head appeared over the steps to the salon and he threw a can to Leah. "Better give that to the hero before he dies of thirst."

She grinned her thanks before popping it and handing it to Ray. Jim stared at him until he laughed and tossed one to him. "Didn't think I'd leave you out did you Dad."

"I'd never have thought that son." Jim replied sarcastically. He opened the can and pushed his mouth over the end to stop the beer foaming out. He took a long draft and said to no-one in particular. "Cheers"

Ray raised his can in salute and took a long swallow himself. When he surfaced at last he gestured over to where the junk was still chugging away from them. "What do you think we ought to do about that?"

Jim looked in the same direction. The junk had by now got a list to one side and appeared to be taking more water in through the hole in her stern. "It doesn't look as if it's going to last much longer does it?"

He was thoroughly fed up with the whole sorry mess and wanted to be shot of the whole lot. "If we chase after it how long to overtake it?" He asked.

Ray looked at it speculatively, and then replied. "At the speed he's going, maybe five hours. We can't make much speed ourselves unless we start the engines and take the sails down, and anyway we can only sink her when we catch her. And from here it looks like that's going to happen anyway. It's going due west and there's nothing in that direction for at least three or four thousand miles until you hit India."

Satisfied, Jim relaxed and commented. "I'll have to get Andy to make that gun more reliable as soon as possible."

Diman woke slowly to pain, he ached in many places. His leg seemed to be hurting more than anywhere else, and when he inspected it he saw that a piece of the deck had blasted its way into the thigh. Praying that it hadn't hit one of his arteries he tore his shirt into pieces and pulled gently on the wood to loosen it, it came out with a sucking sound but no great flow of blood followed it. Quickly binding it with his shirt he pulled himself upright and risked a look behind the junk. About two miles away he could see the yacht but it was too far away to make out any figures on it.

He limped over to the stern and gazed down at the hole and the water bubbling up, the boat had a definite list to one side and he knew that time was running out for it. When he went below he had reason to thank the shipbuilders who had constructed such a sturdy craft. The hole wasn't as large below decks as it appeared from above, so limping heavily now, he retraced his steps to one of the cabins and dragged a mattress back with him. He pushed the mattress into the hole and when it was wedged as tight as he could manage, he found some timbers on deck and jammed them over it. When he had finished the water had slowed to a trickle. Next he went back up on deck and dragging the crewmen to the side of the boat, he dumped them all overboard.

Turning his attention to the rest of the boat he realised there was nothing to be done about the damage to the structure so resolved to get as close as possible to the coast and scuttle it before swimming ashore. At least, he thought, it'll save embarrassing questions. He turned the wheel east in the direction of Indonesia and chugged home with murder in his heart.

Chapter Nine

They spent the next few days repairing the damage to the boat as much as possible. Jim was amazed at how many bullet holes they found in the structure and reflected that they must have had charmed lives to survive without serious injury. Both Jim and Ray got their wounds bandaged and Pat was of the opinion that they had got lucky and would heal without too much infection. Andy was more realistic and said they survived because they had the right equipment and attitude to the job in hand. They took the sails down and made more permanent repairs to the mast and were able to rig a reasonable set in place of the old ones. This gave Ray a chance to crow a little as not many yachts seem to carry another set of sails in reserve. He also worked out for them that to sail to Darwin would at their pace of 5 miles an hour take them about a month or more. Jim spoke to Ray.

"I know I want to get there as quickly as possible, but if we pull into any Australian port looking like this all the security in the world won't stop curious looking us over. I also know we're trying to patch up all these holes but you and I both know that it needs a professional guy in a boatyard to cover up this little lot. If any police or customs see us that's the end and you know it." Ray smiled his secret little smile, "I told you I was making some arrangements before all this started and now they can come into play. Before we get to Darwin we're going to meet another boat. This'll be an old friend of mine, and he's going to take the guns for us and I think it'll be a good idea if you go ashore with him, I'm going to try and get this into a boatyard I know and get it repaired without anybody seeing it. If they do I'll have to try and brazen it out. Either way it's probably best if you aren't with me if I get caught. This guy you're meeting needs to keep quiet about what he does so I reckon he'll be safe as you can get."

"What's he normally smuggle then?" Jim asked.

Ray looked offended. "Who said anything about smuggling?"

"Give me credit Ray, please. Do I look as if I came in on the last banana boat?"

"Yeah all right, but he's a regular guy. He lives well up top on a farm and I think everyone knows about him but if they shop him it's like shopping your own family up there." He thought about it for a moment. "They probably are related if they've lived up there for as long as they say cos people are pretty sparse in that district."

Jim decided that, as the man wouldn't be smuggling anything when he met them that it would be prudent not to enquire too closely into what the guy normally smuggled. Anyway they were trying to get a load of guns into the country and they themselves were illegal so who was calling the kettle black.

They sailed steadily eastwards on the endless blue Timor Sea. It was a really pleasant time for all of them for some weeks as they had dropped back into their old routine of keeping watches. The only thing that marred it for Jim was the continuing friendship between Andy and Leah. To an outsider like himself it seemed obvious what was going on but if Ray had seen anything to disturb him he gave no sign. He voiced his concern to Pat but she seemed strangely indifferent, merely saying that they had to sort it out and it was no concern of theirs. The boat began to take on a much better aspect under their repairs and soon Ray was able to pronounce. "Well it won't pass a full inspection but if you don't look too close it'll pass muster."

That evening he called Jim over to where he was making a call on his mobile phone, and when he put it down he said. "OK, my guy's going to meet us in three days at this spot here." he pointed to the northern coast. "He'll take all the guns and you three off and drop you at his place. I'm going to set Dick off somewhere on the northern coast and help him get some transport to drive about in. When you're ready the guy can drive you over to meet Dick wherever you say that'll be. I'll put him on to a nice big Ute, as he'll need something large to carry everything you'll need. Anyway, whoever heard of a farm without transport?"

Jim looked puzzled for a moment. "I've heard a lot about Aussie slang, but what's a Ute?"

"Come on mate your pulling my leg." Ray was scathing. "Everybody knows a Ute's short for Utility Truck, Jesus where'd you get your education?"

"In England, as far away from your kind of slang as I could get." Jim replied. "Don't start on the way I speak now, as you lot ought to hear what you sound like to our ears. So tell me a bit more about the arrangements you're making without asking me first."

"Yeah, all right mate, we'll let the language barrier go for a bit. What I suggest is that we make some sort of meeting place out of sight of everybody where we can transfer you and the "cargo", and I think it'll be a good idea to refer to the guns as that from now on, to your Ute and then you can drive yourselves to the farm without anyone knowing where it is."

Jim shook his head; "This isn't going to work old mate, It'd be better if you deliver them, and how are you going to get this yacht into a repair yard without a lot of questions being asked?"

Tapping the side of his nose Ray answered. "Don't worry about that, I haven't had this yacht for a few years without finding out something about the best way to get certain alterations done and no questions asked."

With that Jim had to be satisfied and he went below to arrange with Dick how he would be able to draw enough money to buy some of the supplies they were going to need. Dick handed over all the details of the property they were going to purchase and a description of how to get there in case anything happened to upset their plans. Jim looked at the rest of his team and said, "Right let's get down to some real planning. We've got to start thinking about the rest of our little crew and how we're going to go on from there. He looked a Ray and asked. "Will your mate store the 'cargo' for a couple of weeks until we get ourselves sorted out because we can't have it delivered until we have an address can we?"

Ray looked a bit worried. "You can't expect him to keep that sort of stuff too long, it's too risky. We'll have to ask him when we meet up."

Jim felt that for the moment he would have to accept this but in no way did he think it was an ideal solution. For the rest of the day they were busy planning how they were going to meet up with the other members of their group. The next few days were spent arranging their affairs to get the best out of everybody. Ray promised that when he arrived at his boat repairers he would start making enquiries about supplementing their workforce with another three couples, concentrating on a farmer, an engineer who would be responsible for all the machinery, and also a computer expert, although as Ray put it, if he didn't know the right guy no one would. Jim was careful to point out that he didn't want to find three men arrive and three extra women with no qualifications, given that Australian men seemed to think that women had only one position in life and that wasn't upright.

"You've got no worries on that score." interrupted Leah. "I've seen him hiring people before and I'll be standing right over his shoulder when the selections are made. If it were left to him we'd end up with three birds out of the Playboy magazine to go with us. But they wouldn't last long that far from civilisation."

Ray leered. "Yeah, but it'd be a good few weeks" This earned him a slap on the back of the head from Leah, who took the whole thing as a joke.

Later Jim spoke to Ray about the cover story he had told the smuggler and what he would do when they met him. "All I've told him is you want to meet someone in the Northern Territories and you don't want anyone knowing you're there. Then I said you're going to buy some property and maybe it's a bit dodgy about who gets ownership and you think it's better to keep a low profile while the negotiations are going on."

"Will he go for a story like that?" Jim asked.

"Don't see why not." Ray replied. "Guys like him always believe something if they think it's dodgy, it's in their nature."

"Where does he operate from then, on the coast?"

"Now you've beaten me." Ray confessed. "I haven't the first idea, all I know is if you ring his number someone takes a message and then a while later he'll ring you himself. It used to be from call boxes but now we live in the modern age he's got a mobile."

Jim would have gone on asking Ray questions but he forestalled Jim by saying. "Look, I'd better tell you everything I know and then you'll be able to judge for yourself. I met this guy some years ago, I was told about a load of computer parts that were coming on to the market at very reasonable rates, so I was given an address up the "Top End", to pommies like you that's up towards Darwin. In a place called Katherine. Now to someone who comes from a tiny little country like yours it might be hard to understand why I guy like me will travel for the best part of two thousand miles on the off chance of doing some business. But it happens. So I go up to meet this guy and sure enough he's there on the dot like he said he would be. We exchange money for goods, which I might add were excellent value for money, we had a few beers while I tried to pump him but got nowhere. I had a nights sleep and came home the next day, so the only thing I can tell you about this guy is that he lives up top somewhere, he's regular as far as I know, and now he answers the phone himself if he's not busy. I also know he's got his own boat and if it's needed he'll use it, considering what he does for a living his rates are reasonable and he takes on contracts himself so he knows who he can trust."

Ray leaned back. "That's about all I know about this guy."

Jim snorted. "I *need* to know a lot more than that but I don't think I'm going to find out much more am I?"

The next afternoon Ray who had been looking at the Global Positioning instrument said to Jim. "According to my reckoning were about two hundred miles off the coast in the Joseph Bonaparte Gulf, and I think it's time to give this guy a ring."

He promptly picked up his phone and a couple of beeps later he put the phone to his ear; he got through after several rings and nodded at Jim to tell him. He spoke to the phone for several minutes and then picked up his pen and jotted notes down while nodding to the unseen recipient of his call. He asked him to repeat one or two directions and then disconnected and put the phone down. After this he started to write out some of his notes more clearly until Jim in frustration snatched the pen out of his hand and said. "Are you going to tell me what's going on here or do I have to drag it out of you."

Ray laughed. "I was only having a bit of fun mate."

He pointed to the figures he had scribbled down. "The guy's going to meet us tomorrow night at this position here; it's about ten miles off the coast. He'll supposedly be fishing and I plan to get you aboard his boat with the minimum of fuss. You never know these days if anybody's watching what we do, like on the radar or something."

They spent the next day packing all the guns and ammunition down as tightly as they could and then turned their attention to their suitcases, finally everything was ready, Pat sank back on the bed with a sigh of relief. "Let me just go to sleep for a couple of hours." she put her hand over her eyes and breathed out slowly. Jim smiled down at her recumbent form and went out closing the door quietly. When he appeared on deck he found Andy waiting for him with a question. "Do you think we ought to carry some guns with us when we go ashore?"

"Once again." Jim groaned inwardly. "Why do we have to get into these situations when the answer must be perfectly obvious to you? If we go ashore carrying guns and get caught, what do you think the penalty is going to be?"

He answered himself. "We'll be serving a long time in prison and then we're going to get deported. If on the other hand, we get caught just entering the country we might be able to talk our way out of it."

Andy looked at Jim in astonishment. "Aren't you forgetting we're carrying a lot of guns there, do you think the police are going to turn a blind eye to that?

"No I don't expect they will turn a blind eye, but if we can get ashore we'll stand a better chance without getting caught carrying a gun, or worse still using it because everything goes wrong."

Finally Andy shrugged and said. "Have it your own way but don't blame me if things go wrong."

Breathing a sigh of relief Jim turned to sit down on the afterdeck next to Ray who had been listening with interest. "Young always think they can settle any problem with violence don't they?" he observed.

"Mm." Jim replied to a man who was barely five years older than his son. "If you remember he'd have had us swimming ashore in scuba gear, even if his mother can't swim."

"Don't knock him too much." Ray observed. "He did really

well in that fight we had with Diman."

"That he did." Jim answered with some feeling; if he hadn't been in position with the machine gun we'd have lost that fight and no doubt about that. But that doesn't make him a clever young man; it just makes him a brave young man."

They both observed each other and laughed; they had mostly recovered from their wounds and had the bandages off. Ray still had difficulty walking without limping and Jim's shoulder would be weak for some time. But they were fitter now and had more strength.

Jim asked Ray something he had meant to ask a long time previously. "What are you going to do about that mast breaking like that?"

"I'm going back to the place I got it and they're going to answer a lot of questions and then they're going to give me a new one free of charge."

"Yeah, you're right, I was thinking the other day you know, that mast caused the death of six men in its own way."

"It could have killed us all." Ray answered. "Not to mention what would have happened to the women."

They sat and pondered on this for a while and then Jim sat up quickly and looked around. "Can you hear something?"

They both looked around; the sun had set and dusk was just coming over the ocean, it was a lovely balmy evening and the water was almost flat calm. There was just enough wind to give them some way through the water but there was definitely some movement around them. Jim looked around to try and place the sound in a direction he could look but it was too indistinct. It was the time of day when everything they could see was a shade of grey, with no discernable colours to distinguish anything.

"I hope you two gentlemen aren't supposed to be the guard." A voice behind them spoke. "If you are, and I wasn't the nice guy I am you'd be copped and no mistake."

Ray gasped and Jim jumped round with a curse, Ray cried. "Jesus Blackie, you'd scare the devil himself, creeping up on a guy like that."

Jim said. "Who the hell is he?"

The rest of the crew came tumbling on deck when they heard the commotion; they were in various stages of disarray and none were fully dressed, as they had come on deck as fast as possible. Andy had his hands behind him and had hardly moved one pace when another voice came from behind him.

"The white-haired one's got a shotgun behind his back boss"

Jim looked over his shoulder in surprise to find an aboriginal man standing behind him holding a dilapidated gun on them. He hardly had time to think where he had come from, when almost as if by magic a gun appeared in the hands of the man who had been addressed as Blackie. The man changed as well, he went from friendly visitor to implacable foe in a split second. His eyes went hard and he crouched and levelled the rifle at them waving it slightly to cover them all and said. "Tell Blondie to drop the gun and tell him quick, he's making me nervous"

Andy nodded his acquiescence and slowly slid the shotgun on to the deck then stood and said to Blackie. "It's a strange visitor who comes on board carrying weapons."

Blackie studied him for a moment and then answered. "It's a strange man who greets visitors carrying a shotgun, but I'll be fair to you and give you the benefit of the doubt. In my line of work it's often better to be prepared for any tricks the customer might decide to play."

Ray stepped in to stop any more byplay between the two of them and said. "OK all of you, this is Blackie as you know by now and he's the guy I told you would be coming to take you ashore." He looked at Blackie and said. "I think you ought to put that gun away now we all know each other."

The tension went out of Blackie's stance and he visibly relaxed he allowed the gun to fall to his side but kept his hand near the trigger guard, a point noted by both Jim and Andy. He then looked around and said. "OK lads, it's all right for the time being.

Jim looked around in surprise as three other aborigine men stepped out from various places around them; they were all armed with rifles, which were levelled in their direction. They stood quite still and made no move towards them but had the alert look of people on their guard.

Pat and Leah who were standing close to each other reached out to touch the other one and give moral support and Dick and Andy glanced at each other to ready the other one if it was needed. As small as it was Blackie saw the movement and said to one of his men. "Give those men a going over and see what they're carrying."

He kept the rifle on them the whole time until the man had passed his hands over all the men, even feeling up their behinds, he stepped back when he found nothing and said. "They're clean boss."

He looked hopefully at the two women but his boss gave him a knowing grin and said. "Hard luck Jacko, those two aren't wearing enough clothes to be hiding anything so you don't get to frisk them today."

Jim looked at the two women and saw for himself what he meant; the pair of them only had on shorts and thin tops and were shivering slightly now the sun had gone down on them. They both involuntarily crossed their hands in front of their chest at this remark from Blackie, and Jacko grinned happily.

"Maybe I can check em out later boss, we can't never be too careful."

Blackie shook his head in disbelief. "You'll have to excuse the poor dumb abbo, he's always had a yen for white women, and it'll get him killed one of these days when he gets too close to the wrong one."

Jacko wasn't going to let him have the last word though. "Maybe if I get close enough I'll die happy, hey boss.'"

Jim watched this exchange between the two of them and knew it would be an ongoing joke between them until Jacko actually did get a white woman, then God knew what would happen. It came to him that Blackie was the only white man in the company, all the rest were Aboriginal. Even to call Blackie a white man was a bit of a misnomer as he had been burned to a deep mahogany colour by the sun. He had the lean look of a man who lived the best part of his life outdoors; Jim put his age as far as he could tell at about thirty-five. Jim smiled to himself; the man even looked like you would expect an Australian from the bush to look like, from the tip of his bushranger's hat to the boots on his feet.

For Jim, this was a first as he had never seen an Aboriginal up close and they came as a surprise because they weren't like the pictures he had seen, they were all dressed alike in scruffy trousers and shirts. He would have expected that they were dressed in loincloths and carrying spears, then he realised that the image he had was a stylised version of life in the outback, circa 1920. Two of them carried tribal scars on their faces but the others had no markings at all. The way they carried their guns spoke volumes about their way of life, they were all completely at ease with their weapons and looked ready to fire at any minute even though they had been told to relax.

Blackie now eased his position more and said to Ray. "You can break out the tinny's now mate so we can have a little chat, but don't go giving these dumb Abbo's here more than one, I don't want them drinking tonight."

Ray chuckled. "They can't hold it then Blackie."

"They can probably hold more than you mate, the only problem with them is they never know when to stop." He looked over his team and said. "Ain't that right you dumb asses."

They all burst out laughing loudly and agreeing in different ways with him. He waited for Pat and Leah to scurry down to the salon for more beers and when they returned with them they had managed to throw some clothes on to cover themselves. They handed the cans around and when everyone had taken a swig Blackie looked around and grunted. "Seems you've had a bit of trouble on the way don't it?"

Ray wasn't about to give too much away to him and only nodded and said. "Yeah, but it wasn't anything serious."

Blackie glanced around once more and observed. "I'd be careful where you take this for its next refit if I was you, or you'll have to answer a few too many questions."

Jim thought that with a man like Blackie it was probably be better to come clean, as he was evidently an observant man who wouldn't miss things like a broken mast and bullet holes all over the place. He was saved from stating the obvious by Ray grinning at Blackie and asking him where the best yard would be to get repairs done.

He scratched his head while he gave it a little thought, tipping his hat back so he could reach over his forehead, then taking his hat off with one hand he swept his hair back with the other and replaced the hat. When that was settled to his satisfaction he said. "I'm assuming you don't want any nosey coppers poking their nose in to see what's what. So I reckon the best guy for that job lives along the coast about twenty or so miles, he's got a nice secluded little boat yard on one of the creeks and a couple of sheds round the back where the interesting work gets done. I can get one of the boys to take you down there if you want. Some of their relations help out down there for a bit of drinking money."

"The boys." had been listening to this and one piped up and exclaimed. "I'll do that if you like boss I want to see one of my cousins about some family business."

Blackie cocked an eye at him. "Well I hope that "business" you're talking about isn't getting that young girl Natty into bed for a bit of fun."

"Oh nah boss, nothing like that, this is straight up I promise."

Blackie sniffed as if he knew better then turned to Ray and said. "He'll take you over there when we leave and introduce you, if you go in on your own you'll be out faster than an abbo looking for a drink when he's been in the bush for a week."

"I thought of maybe going down the coast a bit." Ray answered, more to test the way things were than in any attempt to put him off.

"You could do that." Blackie agreed. "But if you go round to Darwin or even further, you can find that it's so overcrowded and full of tourists that you won't get it done anyway or at least not without attracting a lot of attention. Speaking of which lets get our bit of business under way. Now as I understand it from you calling me you want three people to go ashore with their luggage."

He waited for Ray to agree and then pointed to Jim and Pat who were standing next to Andy. "Are these the three you want to go?"

Ray nodded and said. "Yeah."

Blackie looked them over while he nibbled a loose piece of skin on his lip. Then he said to Jim. "I'm doing this job blind but

I want to know you aren't going to bring down loads of trouble on my head."

Jim looked him straight in the eye and replied. "The only thing that can cause you trouble is bringing us in illegally and even that could be straightened out because we can say we're tourists and we cadged a lift ashore from you. Once we get our own transport we leave you and then there's no connection with you. The other thing is the "luggage", that can maybe cause you trouble and while it's with you it's your responsibility, but I assume that's what you normally do for a living so you can accept that as what you're paid for."

Blackie looked mildly perturbed then looked over to Ray and asked. "How much 'luggage' and what is it?"

Ray shuffled his feet and looked guilty, he had considered telling Blackie it was some tools or small machinery but when it came down to it he knew that Blackie would see through any lie he told. So he admitted that it was guns.

Blackie's reaction was surprising. "Yeah, I had you figured for guns, it's a good thing you told me cos I would've found out and I don't take kindly to people lying to me. I won't even ask what you want with a load of guns in Australia but I will tell you that if you use them and I don't like what you use them for I'll shop you as quick as look at you. Now here's the situation, I'm going to take you three ashore in my boat; I'll take you direct to a neat little hiding place where you won't be found. There's a lot of Abbos round here who tell the police a lot of things but they won't interfere with my guys and their business. The 'luggage' goes with my guys in the dinghy and I'll drop them off closer to shore. They'll store them out of sight until we can arrange delivery."

He stopped talking and started walking about ordering everybody to do his bidding until he had everything arranged to his satisfaction. Jim and Pat found themselves on board his boat with Andy, and when Jim examined it he found it was a large cabin cruiser with some very powerful engines. It was still a puzzle to Jim as to how he had managed to get all his men on board their yacht without anybody knowing they were there until it was far too late. He mentally made a note to enquire about that at the earliest opportunity. They had pulled in the dinghy and the rest of Blackie's crew jumped in with Ray, Dick Leah and the children. The 'luggage' was loaded as well. There was a meaningful glance between Andy and Leah as they parted but Ray was too occupied to see it because the children were making a nuisance of themselves. He resorted to threatening to send them to their aunt in Sydney before they quietened down and then it was time to leave. They cast off and went their separate ways.

Jim went to the cabin and watched Blackie for a while but when he spoke to him he only replied in monosyllables and he obviously didn't want to talk while he was taking them to the coast. After a while Jim went and sat at the rear next to Pat and Andy. Jacko was standing there holding on to a stanchion and Jim spoke to him.

"Your boss doesn't say much does he?"

The aboriginal turned to look at him and said nothing for a moment, and then he said. "He ain't my boss."

Jim was puzzled; "You called him that when you spoke to him on the other boat."

"Yeah, I know what I called him but that's his name not his job."

"You mean you call him boss but he isn't your boss so what is he?"

Jacko turned to Jim. "Right mate, I don't tell everybody this cos they don't understand. When we do a job like this someone has to be in charge and tell everybody what to do, that's him, and when he does that he's the boss. If he tells me to do something I don't want to do I tell him to piss off then he isn't the boss any more. Now do you understand?"

Jim scratched his head. "You've certainly given me something to think about for a while." he answered.

Jacko turned and stared at Jim for a long time and then he seemed to make his mind up about something and closed his eyes while he thought, then he rolled a cigarette from his pouch and sat down next to Jim. Jim was conscious of the smell of him so close up, it was a smell Jim had never experienced before, it was wood smoke and oil and cigarette smoke and something else he couldn't define but he put it down to the smell of Australia.

Jacko asked him. "How long you gonna stay here in Oz mate?"

"Probably a long time." Was the best Jim could come up with.

"Well, if you stay in the north up here you're gonna have to get used to the way we live up here. Now I've known him there." And he gestured in Blackie's direction. "For most of my life. We grew up as kids together, he don't know what colour I am and I don't know what colour he is. He's a bloody good bloke and he looks out for us, cos it's only in the last few years we get any sort of respect from the average Aussie. But he's lived in my house and I've lived in his, we drunk our first beer together and chased women together although he don't like men like me to get too close to white girls. But that isn't because he's prejudiced against Abbos but it's because he don't like mixed race children, he thinks they don't fit in anywhere and maybe he's right. I can't judge that. I know he don't mind it the other way round though as he's been with a few of the girls from my town that I know about."

Jim kept very quiet for the time, as he knew he was getting a rare insight into the way of life in this land he would be living in. Pat would have interrupted to ask questions about some aspect of what he was talking about but Jim put his hand on her arm and squeezed until she stopped, he didn't want the flow of words to dry up and he knew she had the ability to sidetrack the conversation until they would end up talking about nonsense such as where it was best to buy washing powder. If he noticed what had happened Jacko ignored it and carried on with his monologue.

"A few years ago in the "Wet," that's round about your Christmas. The roads around where we live get to be pretty impassable and my sister got sick. I don't know what she got but the doc on the radio said she had to go to hospital. Now you've got to understand that when its wet up here it's so wet nothing moves at all. Well he heard about it and turns up at my house with a four wheel drive and loads her on to it. I went with him and I swear he's the only man in the whole country who could have got us through to town, took us a day and a half to get there and then we had to wait two days before the doc's would let her out again. It took two days of hard driving to get her back and he looked after her like his own sister. When we got her back home he unloaded her and took her into the house then just walked out and went home without even stopping for a cuppa. I went to see him later and he didn't even let me offer to pay for some juice for the motor."

He stopped talking and Jim could see he was upset and near to tears with emotion, Pat reached over and laid her hand on his arm and he looked at her in surprise; he nodded and went on. "That's why I'll do anything for him, cos I know he'll do anything for me."

There was a movement from the wheelhouse and a shadow moved in the darkness and a voice said. "If you're telling that old story again Jacko I'll knock your bloody block off. I've told you time and again it's only because your sister is the best cook in the whole town that I did that. I didn't want to have to face your cooking any more."

He stopped talking as they all laughed to relieve the tension. And then Jim became aware that he could see in the distance a sprawling mass that was darker than the sea and he realised they were nearing land. The mingled scents of Australia came wafting over the waves to them and Jim felt that he really was a stranger arriving in a foreign country. He could identify none of them apart from the earthy smell of soil. All the rest were unidentifiable in the smell that was Australia. Slowly he became aware of the sound of waves landing on shore and myriad sounds that land has for the traveller. Blackie cut the engines down to a low mumble now and said to them. "I don't want any loud noises now for a bit as we've got to go past some obstacles."

He didn't enlighten them as to what the obstacles were but turned back to the wheel and guided them slowly into a bay between two headlands, Jim was aware that they had land on two sides of them as they went slowly forward. Blackie turned round and nodded to Jacko who leaned over the side and grasping the rope to the dinghy he pulled it in until he could untie it and let the dinghy free. The men inside waved and then they were swallowed up in the gloom, Jacko then turned to Jim and leaning forward whispered in his ear. "They'll find their own way home."

Jim nodded and then something made him turn round to see

Blackie frowning at him to keep quiet. They were still creeping forward and gradually the land came closer on both sides and the motion of the waves died down to be replaced with a calm as they went into what seemed like a river but could have been a tidal creek. Jim couldn't decide which it was. Suddenly Blackie cut the engine and they drifted forward silently until he signalled to Jacko and they got some paddles out of the side locker and leaning over the side they paddled gently forward. Jim could hardly believe his eyes, as it seemed too large a craft to move with paddles until he realised they were being helped by the tide and the paddles were more for guidance than momentum.

Once or twice Blackie and Jacko stopped paddling to look and listen to something Jim couldn't distinguish, but each time they carried on. It seemed like hours before they arrived at what to Jim's eyes looked like a river joining on the right side of the inlet. They turned into this and then Blackie started the engines again. They thrust forward up the river for several miles and Blackie spoke to Jim as they went. "We were lucky tonight, the tides up here can go thirty feet but we caught it just right before it floods and all that water pours in. It can swamp the surrounding area till you wonder about the geography of the place. We're going far enough upstream to lose the effect of that."

They motored on until the banks closed in to about twenty feet and just around a bend Blackie swung across into a small inlet that was invisible to Jim until they were in it, and up about five hundred yards to a small jetty protruding from the bank.

They could see nothing in the gloom and had to wait until Blackie and Jacko jumped out and secured the boat to the jetty, when this was accomplished, Blackie came back on board and addressed them all. "First things first. This place is only where I keep the boat. A lot of people know I've got it here and not many people come here to have a look, I've put the idea out that I take guys out to fish in the bay. That can explain why I go in and out with customers. Now I want you to get some kip and tomorrow we'll start out to my cabin. There are sleeping bags in those lockers over there."

With that he turned and jumped on to the jetty and strode off saying over his shoulder. "Don't wander around out there, we've got crocks roaming about and they'd like nothing better than a juicy Pom for supper."

Jim looked over at his crew and grunted. "You heard the man, get some sleep and tomorrow we start the big adventure."

It took only moments till they had a sleeping bag and settled down for the night and Jim looked over at Pat and whispered. "I wonder what we'll be doing in the near future?"

Pat smiled. "I know it's stupid, but what will be, will be."

Chapter Ten

Jim stirred in his sleep and suddenly realised they were not rocking in the boat, he sat up quickly, alarmed; until he remembered where they were. They were somewhere on the Northern coast of Australia on the banks of what appeared to be a river or tidal inlet; he wasn't quite sure on that matter. He had found it difficult to sleep as he was going over all their plans for the future and he twisted and turned for a long time until he had as much as possible worked out in his brain. He finally dropped off to sleep, his mind still in a turmoil where any one of a dozen things went wrong with their schemes. They were awakened the following morning by the sounds and smells of someone preparing breakfast in the galley. Jim made a dash for the toilet and washed quickly as best he could as all the toilet gear they had brought was still packed, then he went through to the galley to find Blackie standing at the stove with bacon and eggs sizzling in the pan, he nodded at Jim and said. "You'll find coffee in the pot, how do you like your eggs?"

Jim grinned in pleasure and answered. "Hot" then went and filled a glass with some orange juice he saw on the side of the cooker. He drained it in one gulp and helped himself to coffee, while he watched Blackie preparing the breakfast. He worked with the quick assurance of someone used to coping with his own cooking and soon he grunted and served up a plate with two eggs and bacon with several slices of toast to Jim. He glanced up as Andy and Pat came through and gave them the same.

He nodded at the cabin and said. "You can eat in there or outside, suit yourself."

He then popped some more eggs in the pan with bacon and in a few minutes he joined them on deck where they had opted to sit. Jim had had time to look around at their surroundings and was surprised to find it was lush from a point quite high and fairly barren in the vicinity of the water. Up on the bank was a small shack that was obviously used as a storage and sleeping area by Blackie. The sun had started its climb and Jim noticed that as they sat it was getting noticeably warmer, Blackie glanced up and said. "We'll make a start as soon as Jacko gets back, he's gone to check up on your, er." Luggage." The way he emphasised the word left no doubt in their minds as to what he was referring.

Jim was tempted to tell him why they had brought it with them but refrained from doing so because of the need for confidentiality. When they had finished breakfast Blackie took the dirty dishes and when Pat thanked him for breakfast merely said. "You're paying for it missus."

He went on. "I think Jacko'll be about another hour or so, if you want to have a walk you can, but watch out for the crocs, they aren't house trained and you could end up as dinner if you aren't careful."

Pat clutched at Jim's arm and quavered. "Have you got crocodiles around here?"

"Too true we have missus, and we've got some pretty big ones too, there's two kinds, the Salties and freshwater, the Salties are the dangerous ones, they'll hunt you. The others just take you if you can, they might even get out of your way. Just don't go too near to the waters edge and no swimming and you'll be OK. If you see one keep well clear as they can run pretty fast as well."

Jim stood up and said to Blackie." Thanks for the tip." He then turned to Pat and Andy and said. "Are you coming for that walk then?"

Andy nodded and stood but Pat refused to budge, Jim held out his hand and said. "Come on love this is our first day in this country lets go for a walk and see something of what it's like."

Pat's behind remained firmly glued to the seat and she shook her head and said. "No"

Jim looked at her in consternation. "Come on love you must want to step foot on dry land."

"I do, but not where there are crocodiles, they scare the living daylights out of me."

He clapped his hands to his forehead. "You've got to be kidding, and they're so big you can't miss them. We can easily avoid any we see."

He was distracted by a discreet cough from Blackie and when he looked in his direction he motioned with his eyes, he followed the direction and there in the water were two pairs of eyes looking at them. He looked at Blackie with a questioning frown and he answered in a low voice. "They're attracted by the smell of food, sometimes I tip the rubbish over the side. These two are almost tame." And he grinned. "Mind you I wouldn't like to go for a swim right now."

Now Jim was certain, this guy was going to tease them from day one and never stop. He looked back at Pat who had plucked up the courage to come over and peek over the side of the boat, unfortunately she chose the moment when one of the crocodiles yawned, exposing some of the largest teeth they had ever seen. Jim heard a sharp intake of breath and her hand flew over her mouth in terror. Right then he knew she would never go for a walk with him that day. They sat and waited for what to Jim seemed much longer than an hour and in all that time Pat stayed somewhere near the middle of the boat. She refused to even look over the side in case the crocodiles came near. Finally they heard the sound of an engine in low gear approaching through the trees and a four-wheel drive truck came along the track. It crept along until it came to a halt next to the boat and Jacko and another aborigine peered out of the cab. Jim could see it was a fairly new vehicle so thought to himself that business couldn't be so bad for them.

Blackie caught the look he gave him and grinned ruefully, spreading his arms, and said. "There isn't much else to spend the money on out here and we've got to have reliable transport as there aren't many people around here to keep them going."

He jumped out of the boat and strode over to the truck and spoke to Jacko, who nodded his head while he was talking to him and then gave some orders. When he came back to the boat he said. "We're going to go back to my cabin for a couple of days until I can get it sorted out to take you over to Katherine. If you don't know where that is it's about five hundred miles east of here."

This was the first time that Jim had any inkling of their position. Up till now all he had known was that they were on the northern coast of Australia, he had thought they were further along the coast but hadn't known the exact position, he asked him. "Can you show me the position on a map; I'd like to see it?"

Blackie shrugged and went to the cabin and returned with a battered road map of the Northern Territories. He laid it on the table and pointed to a spot on the coast and said. "We're approximately here, about fifty miles from anywhere and the only decent road to there." He pointed to another spot on the map with the town of Katherine on it. "Is fifty miles south of here along a bloody useless excuse of a road, so that's why I've bought that truck over there to get from here to there in some comfort; It's just as well it's not 'The Wet' right now or we wouldn't be doing much in the way of travelling."

He folded the map back in some semblance of order and returned it to its place in the cabin and said. "Not much call for maps out here; if you don't know where you are you're lost." He grinned at his own joke revealing a mouthful of even teeth. "And those useless buggers wouldn't know a map if they saw one." He grinned at Jacko and his friend who had entered the cabin while they had been talking.

Jacko wiped his nose with a grimy finger and said. "You showing those guys the white man's magic maps? I could take you from one end of this country to the other without trying and not one look at something like that, just using the knowledge my elders taught me."

"Yeah, and take a year doing it as well." Blackie responded. "How are your lads fixed?" He looked at the two of them.

"All done, just like you said boss." Jacko replied. The other two are shifting that other stuff. "He would have gone on but Blackie stopped him with a gesture and said. "You don't have to go into details right now we can talk about it later, now I want you to get the rest of the gear off this boat and put it in the truck, we're going to my cabin now and you two can come along and help."

Jim looked on this with interest; it was plain to see that the man was involved in several different arrangements at the same time. He recognised the need for discretion though and decided not interfere to as long as it didn't hinder his own plans. Blackie leaped over the side of the boat and inspected the truck all round and while he did that Jim made his own inspection with Andy. It was extremely well fitted out with extra water tanks on one side and fuel tanks on the other, it also had crash bars that although looking new were slightly dented. Their suitcases had been loaded into the back and some parcels that belonged to Blackie.

Blackie finished his inspection and called Jacko over to load some containers from the boat. He said to Jacko, "When we get to my cabin I want you to go on with these and give them to you know who. Don't take any money for them, I'll sort that out later, are we clear?"

"Sure thing Boss," Jacko grinned. "There'll be one big celebration tonight, I'll bet."

"Just don't go joining in, OK? You aren't supposed to touch that stuff anyway."

Jacko laughed again, "Cops ain't going to bother about that are they?"

"Just don't give them the chance is all." Blackie retorted.

It was the first time that Jim had seen close up that although Australians mostly had a respect for the law they also felt that it shouldn't intrude in their daily lives. He had seen this irreverence in the few Australians that he had met. And the two he had met now had both been willing to break the law and it seemed as if they did it as much for pleasure as profit. Blackie and his team had by now finished unloading the boat and transferring everything to the truck. Then they ran a cable from a reel on the front of the truck up to a shackle inside the cabin and back to the boat. They tied off on the boat and Blackie started the engine on the truck. Jacko cast off the ropes on the boat and they manoeuvred it till it was in line with the cabin.

While this was going on Pat sat in the truck and watched fearfully for crocodiles. When they had it lined up Blackie nodded at Jacko and he ran and brought a trolley with wheels down to the waters edge. They placed it ready, and Blackie winched the boat out of the water, and when it had inched it's way up the bank on to the trolley it wound its way in to the shack about fifty yards from the water. When this was accomplished they unhooked and closed the doors to the shack, Blackie wound the rest of the cable onto the drum and stepped back and looked at his watch. "Fifteen minutes, start to finish." He said. "Not bad, but maybe we can cut it down if we go for it next time."

Jacko looked at the sun and said. "I reckon you're right boss, I don't have one of those fancy things on my arm but maybe one day you'll tell an ignorant abbo like me why we've got to be so fast?"

"Don't worry about it Jacko, if you don't understand now you never will."

Blackie looked around. "Right, let's get this show on the road."

He stepped into the truck and crunched it into gear to Andy's dismay who had always prided himself on being a good driver. They drove off down the road with the four of them in front on the double seats and Jacko and his friend clinging to the back. The road, if it could have been called that was atrocious with deep ruts all over it and it was a constant struggle to keep it on line. They were still in second gear and looked like staying that way all the way down the road.

Blackie glanced around at them and said. "If we do get stopped anywhere here, let me do the talking and go along with anything I say, alright?"

The most they could do with all the bouncing around they were doing was nod in agreement. The jolting ride continued for what seemed like hours and in reality was probably about six. They stopped once for something to eat and drink and then carried on in the same slow way. Jim figured even at that they had probably only travelled about fifty miles, they then turned once again onto an almost invisible track and went a further three or four miles till they reached a farm gate. Jacko jumped down and opened it for them and they drove up the track to reach a cabin set back amongst some trees. It was a wood framed shack with a roof of shingles and clapboard panelling on the outside. It was sorely in need of a coat of something to protect the exterior but was evidently quite roomy, with a porch on the outside, roofed over, which ran along three sides so it could shade them from the sun.

The truck stopped in front of the cabin and they dismounted, feeling their bodies to check for bruises, and stretching to ease the kinks of sitting so long in one place, the silence at first was almost overpowering after the experience of the engine roaring in their ears. Then it was broken by the sound of music coming from the cabin and when he heard it Blackie's face hardened and he swung round to confront Jacko.

"I thought I told that sister of yours to stay away when I've got visitors coming."

Jacko's face if he had been white would have paled, but it went a shade of grey instead. He gulped and raised his voice and replied. "I swear I told her to stay away from here boss, but you know what she's like."

"I know what she's like OK; you wait till I get my hands on her." He turned and went to go to the door when it swung open and a aboriginal girl stood in the opening with a big smile on her face. Blackie stopped in his tracks for a moment and it gave them time to look at her. She was beautiful with a willowy figure and long black hair, which at the moment was tied into a ponytail behind her. Jim had never found the aboriginals in the pictures he had seen to be very attractive, but this one stood out and had something striking about her.

Blackie was obviously unimpressed by her beauty right now and advanced on her with a face like a thundercloud. "I told you to stay away until I sent for you didn't I?"

Her eyes flicked to Jacko with a look that said, help me. But as no help came from that quarter she faced him defiantly. "Not good enough for your white city friends am I? I'm good enough to cook and clean and lie in your bed when you ain't got anyone else here aren't I? Well I only came over to get some food ready and make up some beds for your visitors then I'll be on my way, you can get yourself sorted out cos I'm dammed if I'll make any bed for you."

She went back inside where she could be heard banging around and muttering to herself about selfish bastards who had no time for people who cared about them. Blackie looked about him in helpless confusion and it was left to Pat to mutter something about stupid men before marching in to talk to her. Blackie scratched his head and sat on the porch outside and motioned to them to sit with him while the noise gradually subsided as the two women sorted out the trouble with men in general.

Blackie spoke to Jacko. "I only wanted to keep her out of harms way until I knew the lie of the land with these guys here, and you know how she likes to gossip down at your village about what she's doing up here, some day someone's going to talk to the wrong man and my bacons going to be well and truly cooked."

"She don't mean no harm Blackie, you know what she's like, she thinks the sun shines out of your arse, and she only wants what's best for you."

Jim had caught the use of the first name when Jacko had spoken to Blackie and wondered about the relationship these two men had. It appeared it was as Jacko had told him previously that when they were working they were boss and worker, but when they were at home they were friends.

Blackie grunted. "You'd better get inside and tell her if she wants to she can make up my bed, I'll square it with her later, and while you're there get a few tinny's out here, my bloody throats so parched I couldn't raise a good spit if my life depended on it."

Although nothing more had been said, Jim had the impression that the girl was somehow being forgiven by Blackie, although that type of man found it difficult if not impossible to say sorry directly to the person concerned. Jacko grinned in relief and jumped up the steps to go into the door. He could be heard talking inside for a few minutes and then came back with some cans of beer dripping dew down the side. He handed them round to each of them and for a moment the only sound was the popping of cans and sighs of relief. Then Blackie looked up and said. "Well?"

Jacko shrugged. "You know what Chrissie's like boss, she ain't going to give up without an apology of some sort."

Blackie dropped his head and looked at the ground for a while; pondering his best way out and then looked up at Jacko. "You know how much I think of Chrissie don't you? Now why have I got to get down on my knees and apologise because she did something I told her not to do?"

Jacko spread both hands wide. "Don't look at me boss; I'm just an ignorant Abbo ain't I? But if you want an opinion, your best way out of this is to just apologise."

Blackie grunted in his bad tempered way and said nothing further until the two women came back out onto the porch to join them. They were carrying a large tray filled with sandwiches and drinks and placed them on a convenient table set up in the shade of the roof. They all moved over to make a start on the food and Chrissie said with her head down. "I guess I'd better be off then."

There was a sudden silence while they all waited for Blackie to say something and finally he spoke grudgingly. "Maybe it might be better if you stay over for a while to help out with the housekeeping while these people are here."

It wasn't an apology in any sense of the word but Chrissies face plainly indicated that she thought it was. It shone with joy and she looked up at him as she said. "Well, I'll stay if you think you need me around here for a bit."

"Christ, Chrissie serve the bloody grub up will you." he said gruffly. "You're more trouble than you're worth, going on all the time."

She smiled at Pat and they started to pass around the food. While they were eating Pat spoke to Blackie. "I couldn't help noticing two things about your house when I was inside."

Blackie stared back at her without comment until she spoke again. "First, I notice you've got a bathroom, and I haven't had a bath in fresh water for ages, do you mind?"

He nodded and waited again, she glanced over at Jim and said. "You've also got a computer there as well; can you access the Internet out here?"

He sighed and said. "Is that all?"

When she nodded back and said yes, He breathed a sigh of relief. "If only all my customers were as easily satisfied as that, my life would be ten times easier. OK first things first, water is a valuable commodity out here, by all means have a shower but make it quick. With all of you having baths it's going to go down pretty damn quick. The other thing is that that computer in there is connected to the Internet through the satellite link.

Jim stood. "Can I use it as soon as possible?" He asked. "I want to connect with all the other members of the party."

Blackie stood as well. "No reason why not." He answered. And led Jim into the house. It was quite large inside, built on piles and of wood in the Australian fashion; Jim was surprised as to how cool it was in the interior, but all the windows were open and the slight breeze blew through so it wasn't apparent after the heat outside how cool it really was under ordinary circumstances.

The computer stood on a desk against one wall and was a fairly basic model but appeared to have all the necessary components to make it work. Blackie bent down to switch it on and Jim became aware that he could hear the gentle rumble of a generator somewhere in the background. "Do you have that generator going all the time?" He asked.

"Nah, it'd cost too much to have that thing going day and night, there's a pressure switch on all the electric fittings so if you switch a light on it starts up, but it's only for the most powerful appliances. Small things like the clocks and things like that run on batteries, I can charge them up when the generator's going. There's a wind operated generator out there connected to the water pump but I have to supplement that with the diesel generator if the waters low and we've got no wind."

They could hear the shower start up and the sounds of Pat splashing in the water. Then her voice started in a most untuneful rendering of an Irish melody. Blackie winced. "Jeez mate, do you have to put up with that every day, if we had a pub near here I'd be down there as soon as she said she was going to wash. By the way I've got another shower out back with the tank above, that's always nice and warm because the sun shines on it all day, if you want to use that later it's just as good so feel free."

Jim thanked him and turned to the computer; he brought up the Internet Explorer programme and logged on. Then he said to Blackie. "Do you want to bring up your normal page and I can access the "Hotmail" connection? I might as well tell you now I'm only going to contact a few people and it's not private so I don't mind if you stay."

Blackie studied him for a moment and then said. "Why do

you think I thought you were going to do something illegal?"

"I thought that you might think that because of the way you brought us in here that we would be illegal immigrants here."

He shrugged his shoulders and shook his head. "I don't really know what you intend to do in Australia but I don't think you're the kind of bloke that does things wrong too much in your life. I figured you for some kind of guy who maybe wants to be here for a year or so without the permission of our paper oriented government. And you'd be surprised at the amount of people I bring in here with no papers on them. The only thing I draw the line at is in bringing in "coloured people". He made the phrase stand out when he said it. "And the only reason for that is they stand out too much in a crowd and they'll likely get me caught when they hit society."

Jim turned to the computer and spoke over his shoulder. "Each to his own, I won't interfere in your life and you sound as if you'll stay out of mine."

He quickly entered a message on the computer and then the addresses of Colette, Prof, and Victoria, pressed the send icon and watched as it connected and sent them on their way. Blackie had been watching this with interest.

"You know I can access that information any time I want, don't you?"

Jim smiled at him enigmatically. "I don't find that a problem, if you want to see what I've sent we can bring it back up now. If you find out what we're doing it won't be much of a problem anyway, the only problem is if the authorities found Pat and me here illegally. And I'm not sure we are *that* illegal. After all we've got valid passports and we're English, which helps. The only thing we've done wrong is enter without going through a port and registering with immigration. But we've got bank accounts here in Australia anyway so they know we aren't going to go on the dole. In time we might even make an application to become naturalised here then there wouldn't be any problem at all with being here."

"Blackie pondered on this for a while and then went over to one of his comfortable old armchairs and sat and relaxed. "So you're not worried if they find you here then?"

Jim responded with a shake of the head. "If they kick us out now it's going to be somewhat of a disaster, it'll totally mess up all our plans, still, you aren't going to turn us in are you Blackie? Because if you did I think you'd be in worse trouble than we are."

"Yeah, I'd already guessed that."

And Jim's implied threat had put the ball firmly in Blackie's court. At that moment Jim had serious doubts about the role of Blackie in this operation. He turned the conversation quite deliberately by asking him if he could have a look at the various energy sources that he had installed in the house. Blackie seemed to be happier discussing these than causing any more upsets in the relationship he was building with them. They went outside the better to see what he'd done and the first thing Blackie told him was that all the various sources of energy he had, were purchased piecemeal.

"One thing after the other, I just bought them as and when the money became available, if I had my way I'd prefer to have the generator going all the time, but it's far too expensive. I think the windmill is the best answer to energy as it keeps on going all day and night, the only problem is you can't be reliant on the wind."

"Why not get some solar panels and rechargeable batteries and wire everything into them and let them charge up all the time." This was a problem Jim had been going over for a long time in his head.

"Maybe you're right but it'd mean ripping out a lot of the existing wiring and doing it all over again, so you've got cost, and also some of the appliances use a lot of power like the freezer and the kettle, stuff like that."

"I can see your point." Jim answered. "But why not process your sewage and then you've got butane if you want it for running the generator."

"Do you know what systems like that cost?" Blackie exploded. "Look over there what do you see?" He pointed to a spot that had some brickwork surrounding it. "Do you know how much I had to lay out for that?" He didn't wait for an answer but carried straight on. "That's a state of the art cesspit, OK, it cost an arm and a leg, and you could, if you were that way inclined, drink the water that comes out of it. Now you say put in another treatment plant with all the maintenance and running costs and change over to a gas-powered generator to use it. Then I'd have to spend a good deal of the time playing about to keep it up to full working order. No, it's not a viable option for a working guy like me to do."

"OK, mate." Jim noticed he had started to slip into the vernacular of the region. "I didn't mean to get you all upset, the point I was trying to make was that if you start off with the right system it can actually work better for you than by doing it all piecemeal like you're doing now. And also it needn't cost all that much if you do a lot of the building work yourself."

Blackie grunted in disbelief. "Maybe for a builder like yourself it might work out that way but for someone like me it'd be plain stupid to try and build something like that. Anyway." He changed the subject completely to show he had no further comments in that direction. "I thought you wanted to get a shower to wash some of that dust and salt off you?"

"Yeah that'd be a good idea, salt water isn't the best thing for showers is it?"

They walked along until they reached a small enclosure with a tank suspended above it. It had a drainage channel cut into the ground leading off into the general direction of a garden with a variety of plants growing in it. Pointing at the garden Blackie said. "I don't take any praise for all that growing over there, that's all Chrissies work. I just supply the water from the shower and she does all the rest. The shower's easy, just turn the tap and she goes."

He turned and walked towards the house and Jim followed him to get his washing bag and go for his shower. He met Andy coming out of the door carrying his bag; Jim looked at him and said. "If you're using that shower out the back don't use all the water up before I have mine."

Andy did a double take and raised his eyebrows, and joked. "Humph, if your wife in there would only let someone else in to get washed I wouldn't be coming out here."

Jim grinned and went into the house, he knew his wife from way back, she would only emerge from the shower when she was good and ready and not a minute sooner, but eventually they all had a wash, including Jacko and Chrissie, Jacko's friend had disappeared by now. That evening they had a meal prepared by Chrissie. Then afterwards they sat out and watched the sunset on the porch. Blackie turned to Jim and asked. "You know, I'd really like to know what you're doing here in Oz."

Pat had been about to open her mouth but Jim shot her a look and said to him. "If it becomes necessary later I'll tell you all about it, but for the time being it's probably better for everyone if you don't know."

Blackie shot him a quizzical look that showed his feelings were hurt. But he said no more on the subject and turned to Jacko and started talking about the state of the track down to the nearest town.

They spent the next three days lazing around the farm and generally preparing themselves for the time ahead; if Blackie had any nervous feelings about them being there without permission from the authorities he never said or showed it in any way. The rest of the company had answered the mail on the Internet and sent the addresses where they could be reached. Fortunately they had all secured employment in Australia as they had hoped, the exception being Julia but she had hopes of a local school job when she and the Prof found accommodation. He had a job working in a college in Darwin and said he could probably travel to work if it wasn't too far. Victoria said she had a job working as a biology teacher in Cairns, Queensland. It would mean a long trip to visit but it was the only option right now so she said she would be willing to do it.

Her and Andy spent a lot of time talking on the Internet when they could but she appeared to be very busy and only communicated in the evening. Ray had been in touch and repairs were going along but "bloody expensive." As he put it. He and Dick had been out and purchased a four-wheel drive "Ute." and some extras for it to equip it for life in the outback.

Colette had been taken on as a doctor in Darwin and expected to be able to commute in company with the Prof and stay over when needed for night duty. Of course Jim knew all this depended on how accessible the farm was when they saw it and it was to this end he finally decided to go with Dick and see the property. He made arrangements to meet him in a hotel in Katherine, the nearest town of any size. When he broached the subject of a lift to Blackie he merely shrugged his shoulders and agreed. Jim didn't force the issue as to whether he could borrow the 4WD from him but it wasn't mentioned and when it happened he got Jacko as a driver. Before he left Blackie called him over and mentioned that if they ran into any sort of officialdom to let Jacko speak and to behave like a stupid tourist. Although as he put it." That won't be hard for you to do will it?"

They set of at first light with a full tank and water carriers on the side, Blackie saw them off and said to Jim. "Drink a lot of that water, there ain't no bars out there, and it'll keep you alive."

As they crawled off down the track Jim asked Jacko in a conversational way how far it was to Katherine, he received a shrug of the shoulder and the answer. "Don't really know mate, maybe a day, maybe two, depends on how well we get on down the track."

They drove all day but it was at a very slow rate as they only had a track through the bush to follow and as it was deeply rutted progress was really slow. The map had disappeared from the glove compartment so Jim had no way of telling how far they were travelling. The only idea he had was that their progress followed a generally eastern route, and the only indication of that was the slow passage of the sun. They kept all the windows shut to allow the air conditioning to work but it laboured in vain against the heat, which lay like an oppressive blanket over them. When night fell Jacko insisted on making camp by the roadside, as he didn't like driving at night. Jim felt a little dubious about this but had no knowledge to dispute what he said, after all they had had no trouble coming out to sea with Blackie and picking them up. Until now they hadn't seen another person in the whole day and Jim felt as if the scenario he had been awaiting with the others had finally come to pass and they hadn't heard about it.

Looking at Jacko over the embers of the fire he could understand how these people could feel about the white interlopers coming in and taking their country. He seemed to be as one with the land but when he broached the subject Jacko surprisingly disagreed with him. "We need the white man here now." He said. "Most of my people except for a few dedicated guys don't really know how to live in the bush any more, they don't want to go back to the old days, and they've got education and Doctors which they never had before. The only real bad problem is that our race has got a problem with the booze. Still, I hear that the Indians in America had the same and the guys in Iceland." He smiled. "Hey, I wonder what it's like to live in all that cold like that, I don't think I could put up with freezing all the time could you?"

Jim smiled himself at the irony and said. "I think they would have the same problem coming here, I don't think they could cope with all the heat like you." He looked around at the darkness and imagined an Eskimo in this country. "No, I don't think they could cope but I'd like to see someone try it for fun and see what the result would be."

"What do you think'd be the hardest? Living here or in Iceland." Jacko wanted to know.

Jim pursed his lips while he thought about it. "I think it'd be easier to live here if a man knew what he was doing. Wherever you go in this country you can find something to keep you alive, I know you have to know what you're doing but at least you can find something. But I've seen pictures of an Eskimo sitting for four hours over an ice hole waiting for a seal to come up to breath and he can't move because the seal can hear him. That's got to be hard hasn't it?"

"Phew." Was all that Jacko could think to say. "I wouldn't like to sit here for four hours without moving, not in the sort of sun we get round here. I reckon those guys must be pretty tough to live like that."

"They're much like your race now I think." Jim answered. "I don't think many of them live like the ancestors did any more."

They bedded down for the night after that and the following day they set off again at first light and a light breakfast. After about an hour of driving along a track that was only visible because of the ruts in the surface they suddenly came on a road running roughly east to west and they turned on to it in the easterly direction. "How far to civilisation now?" Jim asked.

"Bout five or six hours depending on what's happened to the road since last time." Jacko scratched the side of his nose.

"Never know what we'll find out here. In the 'wet' you can't use it sometimes."

'Seems a strange sort of life.' thought Jim. 'When you can't use roads because of rain,' he looked out at the countryside they were passing, it seemed ordinary enough. Jacko glanced at him and grinned in the way of a man about to impart some interesting news. "In January 98, they had nearly a metre of rain; a cyclone came over and dropped its load in less than a month. Caused a lot of trouble that time I can tell you. Katherine where we're going was under the water for a long time, the river there rose so much it came over the bridge and I think that stands twenty metres high."

They stopped for a while to brew some tea and had a bite to eat and then they went on, progress was slow with Jacko driving, as he liked to look out at the countryside as they passed through it. They met very few other travellers and the few they met merely waved as they went past. Jacko told him that if they had any trouble and sat by the road the next person to pass would stop and offer them any help they needed. "Especially." he added. "If we carry a load of beer with us."

"They don't care about drinking and driving then?" Jim joked.

Jacko looked puzzled. "Why would they care about that, the only person who gets hurt is the guy who causes it himself. If they drink too much along here they generally just pull off the road and get some kip till they sober up a bit."

About an hour later they saw a large cloud of dust coming towards them and Jacko said. "Oh, oh." and pulled off the road onto the side and waited. A few minutes later the cloud of dust resolved itself into a very large lorry pulling two trailers, Jim had heard about them and was interested to see one for the first time. He couldn't imagine driving one and would have worried all the time about making a wrong turn; it made him sweat just to think about trying to back one up. It went past at about sixty miles an hour in a shower of gravel and they got a blast of the klaxon as the driver waved his thanks out of the cab at them. Jacko waved back and pulled on to the road after he had gone. The dust seeped in to the cab as they drove along and when it had cleared a little Jacko said. "Got to give them bastards a wide birth, they've only got one speed and that's full pelt. They don't stop for nothing if they can help it, and they're half pissed most of the time as well."

The rest of the journey was uneventful and they pulled into the town of Katherine about 2-0-clock in the afternoon; their destination was a hotel come holiday village and they found it easily enough. Jim decanted himself with a sigh of relief and stepped out into the sweltering heat. He looked at Jacko as he got out and said. "I'm glad that's over, I'm going to take a room here for the night do you want me to book you in as well?"

Jacko looked appalled. "There's no way you're going to get me in there Boss, I'll kip down with some friends I've got around here and I'll come back for you in a couple of days." And with that and a parting wave he was gone. Jim hefted the small suitcase he had brought with him and went to book into the hotel. As he went in he saw a police car sitting in the car park with two men inside, the engine was running, and Jim assumed it was to keep the air-conditioning working. His assumption had he known it, was correct, but he would have been more intrigued to have known what was said. One turned to the other and said. "Now who the devil is that who just dropped that tourist off over there, I've not seen an abbo driving a rig like that in a long time."

The other man sighed and straightened his uniform before answering. "If you were in the force I might be inclined to expect you to know but as you're not I can tell you, that's Jacko, he runs around with Blackie from out west."

The first man nodded in understanding and looked as if he knew the names when told them. "I'll have to make a note about this and see if there's anything for me in it." He said. He tapped the side of his nose and went on. "Never know when the opportunity for a bit of extra money is going to crop up."

The police officer turned to him and stared straight at him with steady grey eyes. "You can do anything you want, but I'm telling you this much Gerard Schoonheid, this business we've got here is for a bit of fun and some extra cash. But if you bring any trouble to me I'll deal with it in a way you won't like."

Gerard Schoonheid looked straight back at him; he stood almost six feet tall when upright and was well built into the bargain.

Right now he was sweating slightly even though the air in the car was cool. He sneered at the officer and replied. "If you deal with me in anything I'll do the telling and don't forget it, you're in my pocket now." Having said that he climbed out of the car and letting a blast of the heat into it he leaned down and just before slamming the door said. "Why don't you go and check a few ID cards and earn your living the legal way for a bit."

The police officer sat and stared at his back retreating back as it headed away to go into the bar. He thought to himself how stupid he had been to let the man talk him into doing a deal with him for information, but it was done now and he knew the information had been used, so unless he kept his mouth shut from now on he could expect trouble, one way or the other.

Jim had entered the hotel and found the reception desk and booked a room for himself, and as he did so he asked the receptionist if anybody had left a message for him, she looked and said. "Not really a message but someone's waiting for you in the bar."

When he went through to the bar he found to his surprise that not only Dick had come, but Ray and Leah. They were standing behind foaming glasses of beer and gave a small cheer when he entered, then greeted him warmly. The next few minutes were taken up with the exchange of news about everybody else and Jim heard that Ray had almost punched his supplier when he tackled him about the broken mast. Leah was dressed almost conservatively in a mini skirt and blouse but still managed to show more flesh than most of the other women in the bar and was being glowered at by several of them for distracting their husbands. Dick asked after Andrew and Pat, and Jim regretted not bringing them. He was pleased to hear that Colette had left England and was on her way to join Dick with the baby. She had managed to secure a job as a doctor and would bring them up to date when she arrived. He told them about the Prof who had been in touch but mysteriously said not to contact him, he would reach them when necessary. He also brought them up to date on Victoria who was working as a teacher in a school in Cairns but she had applied for a job in a small university in Darwin or, as she put it. "I'll be spending more time on the road than one of those bloody road train drivers."

They moved over to a table where they could sit and talk for a while and had some beers brought over; the bar was fairly crowded with a mix of tourists and people who were obviously from the area. Jim learned that the 'Ute' was outside and Dick had made an appointment for them to go and see the farm the following day. As they were talking a large man had entered the bar and although not seeming to, he had paid some attention to them and as they made no secret of what they were talking about he must have heard what they were saying. When they moved to a table he gave them chance to settle themselves into chairs and order some beers then moved over to speak to them.

He wasted no time in talking to them. "Hi folks, I'd like to introduce myself to you, I'm Gerard Schoonheid and I'm a resident here, I couldn't help hearing your conversation just now, I want you to know that if you're thinking of moving into the district I'm the man to know around here. I've got several businesses' in the district and I know you'll need me sometime." he was standing directly behind Leah and was distracted for a moment looking down at her. Her blouse fell open slightly and he looked down at the rounded swell of her breasts. "Ahem." he went on. "If you want anything at all just let me know and I'll be only too glad to help out." He beamed at them as if he had just saved them all a lot of trouble.

Leah leaned back in her chair and gave him even more to be distracted with and said in her husky voice. "Why don't you come round here where I can get a good look at you sunshine, I want to see this saint in shining armour who can do anything."

He seemed a little taken aback at the way she spoke but moved round to stand where she could see him. She appraised him for a moment and Jim had been listening to this exchange with some interest got the feeling in his gut that this man would be trouble. He knew what the trouble was and didn't know any way he could change his feelings. The man spoke with a definite Belgian accent, Jim had worked a sufficiently long time in the country to be able to distinguish between a Belgian and Dutch accent. He felt the familiar anger rising in his throat and nothing could prevent him from wanting to take his revenge on this man simply because of his nationality. He leaned forward in his chair and said abruptly. "What country do you come from?"

The man looked a little nonplussed about this as if he was unsure what he should say, but nevertheless he answered. "Belgium."

"What part." Jim said brusquely.

The man answered. "Limburg, it's an area near to the Dutch border, do you know it?"

Jim knew it only too well as he had worked in the area for a while. It hadn't been a happy experience, it was too much for him, and he had no intention of doing any dealings with this man personally. But was curious as to the man's occupation. Schoonheid's face furrowed as he tried in vain to work out the significance of Jim's attitude, but Jim had no intention of letting him know his feelings. He nodded at him to let him know the information meant something and then leaned back and let Leah take over the conversation.

She said. "Well you seem a big enough man to say something like that but I wonder if you've got what it takes to carry it out."

His chest swelled as he tried to give the impression of sincerity, and Jim once again was struck by something in his manner that said he was a wheeler-dealer and they would be better off without him in their lives. Leah obviously felt the same way but took a slightly different tack. "Why don't you give us a business card sunshine and we'll let you know if you're needed."

He flushed and looked around the table at them. He got no help from any of them so reached in his pocket and produced a business card which he tried to give to Leah, but she merely glanced at it and left it to him to lay it on the table in front of her. When he had done so, she said. "Ok, sonny you've delivered your message, if we want you we'll call you, now you can leave us to get on with this conversation which I'm sure you'll understand is private."

She turned to Jim and started speaking to him about Pat and Schoonheid stood there discomfited and fidgeting while she steadily ignored him, until realising that the conversation was over and with some show of trying to assert himself he raised his hand in a half salute and said. "Well don't forget, if you need anything at all just give me a shout and I'll be there to help."

This time they all took their cue from her and ignored him until he walked away wondering where he went wrong. When he had gone out of earshot they all started laughing and Leah said. "He'll be putty in my hands if I start dealing with him."

Ray looked at Jim to see his reaction, and when there was none he asked. "Is it true then?"

"What's true?"

"That you've taken her on as chief gofer?"

Jim smiled at Ray. "You got any objection to that?"

Ray looked at Leah and Jim, then back again. "You fixed this up a long time ago didn't you, It's no surprise to you she said that, I can see. What makes you think she'll be good at the job?"

"From what I can gather about the house that you built, she did most of the organising on that while you went off and played with your boat."

Ray leaned forward intently. "She might think she did but all the decisions on that house were directed through me, not one of them was taken without the guys asking me if it was OK, did she tell you that?"

"I've had enough of this." Leah spoke up. "You." She pointed her finger at Ray. "Didn't have the first idea what to do on that house, I dealt with the architects the builders, the suppliers, and all the people who have a say in who does what and where. If you went back over the bloody plans and the organisation that went into the house you might have figured out that you didn't even know half the bloody people who built it for you. All you ever did was turn up once a fortnight and lord it over everybody like lord muck. But every man on that job came to me when you'd gone and asked me if it was OK to do what you said. If it had been left to you we'd still be waiting for it to be finished, so if he." She pointed at Jim. "Thinks I can do something useful, I'm going to do it without you interfering and trying to put me down in front of everybody else."

She nodded her head to show she had finished and sat back in her chair waiting for someone to say something, but Ray looked at Jim and said sardonically. "Puts me in my place doesn't it?" He shot a glance at Leah and said. "You have it your own way darling, but don't come to me when the going gets rough and these guys in this one horse town start playing you about."

Her eyes closed to little slits and she stared straight into his face and said. "You couldn't run a piss up in a brewery, who do you think ran your business all those years until you sold out, all you had was a good idea, it took someone like me to make it work, I know you think you ran it but it wouldn't have been a success if I hadn't sat in that office and told everyone what to do."

Jim slammed his drink on the table spilling some of the beer. "That's enough from you two, I made my decision a long time ago and I don't want you to start squabbling over things that you think happened a long time ago. We all have to do a job here and what I say goes, You." He gestured in Ray's direction. "Have the job of getting us some good reliable computer equipment and various other things in the electrical line, I think that'll keep you quite busy enough, and while you're at it I want you to remember that we've still got to have three other members and their wives to make it up to a full quota. I think we need two farmers and an engineer who knows what he's doing, so you can make a start on that as soon as possible. And for goodness sake make sure the farmers know about indoor farming, I don't want anyone turning up expecting to start working with a plough. Now that ought to keep you out of your wife's hair for a while."

Having said that he relaxed for a moment to let it sink in as he glanced around the table, he had given the appearance of anger when he had said this and had a job to stop smiling at them, as he wanted them to think of him as boss. To a man they all avoided looking into his eyes and stared at the table. Ray had been watching the door as he talked and observed that a police officer stood outside talking with the receptionist, he appeared to be quite casual but his eyes never stopped moving and rested on them several times. When he stopped yarning to her he touched the side of his head in a gesture that was almost a salute and then took it off to enter the bar. His eyes swept round the room and Ray stood and said to Jim. "Why don't you go and have a look at the Ute mate, I'll be along in a minute."

When they started to leave the policeman began to walk over in their direction but was stopped by Ray who started to ask him some inane question about the area. Jim walked past him and with Leah and Dick he went out of the door to go to the Ute. Ray followed a minute later and they all piled in and drove out of the car park with Dick driving.

Jim turned to Ray and said. "What was all that about? You got us out of there pretty damn quick if you don't mind me saying."

"Yeah I know, maybe I was being too cautious but you never can tell; when the guy was in the reception he seemed to be very interested in our little group and you haven't got a visa so I thought it best if we weren't about for him to ask about it."

Jim could see the sense of it but as he pointed out. "I have got a passport on me so I could maybe pass muster on the first attempt."

Ray nodded in agreement but went on. "I know that's true, but if you take chances you're going to get caught one day, there is a chance here now that you can apply for amnesty under a rule that says if you've been here some time you can get naturalisation. The trouble is I don't know how long you've got to be here for that to work. We'll have to find out because it's not going to do any of us any good if you do get kicked out too soon."

"I've still got to go back to that hotel though haven't I?" Jim answered. "And now if I do go back, he'll get to me there won't he?"

"Wait a minute." Ray thought for a moment. "You go in this hotel here for a drink and wait for me; I'll go back and check it out."

They pulled into a hotel along the main street that ran through Katherine and as they entered Ray drove off down the road back the way they had come. They settled themselves and Leah ordered some drinks from the barman who served them to a table in the shade outside. They only had to wait five minutes and had barely begun to drink when Ray returned. He stopped the Ute and came over with a big smile on his face. "Panic over." He announced. "The guy goes in every day to have a chat, he fancies the receptionist, and he was heading for the dunny when he came towards us. I hadn't noticed where it was. I've also found out that they have so many tourists around here in the season that there's no chance they can check on all of them."

Jim let his breath out, the incident had made him realise how precarious his position here in Australia really was. He resolved to try and do something about it as soon as it was possible, as he didn't like the possibility of deportation hanging over him.

"Maybe we ought to be getting on with the reason we're here." he said. "When are we going to get a look at this property?" He asked Dick.

"I've set up a meeting with the owner for tomorrow in the late afternoon as it's about two hundred and fifty miles out and the roads aren't all that good."

"Long way to go if you forget the matches then." Ray joked.

"Nothing for it but to get a meal, have an early night, and set off in the morning as early as possible." Jim said, he gave Dick a hard stare. "I want you to get that Ute ready for a long trip with plenty of water and petrol on board. Also I want enough supplies to last for several days. If it needs any servicing, do it. If it needs spares I want you to get them." He then looked at all of them. "I've heard it gets cold out there at night so we'll have to have camping gear and extra clothing so we'd better get on to it right now. I think we ought to have a radio as well."

Ray held his hand up. "Already thought about and installed, I took the liberty of putting in global positioning as well; never know when we'll need it eh?"

Jim dipped his head and pursed his lips in acknowledgement. "So you are good for something then Ray?"

"Oh yeah mate, I'm going with Dick here to see about stocking the Ute, why don't you and Leah go down to the shop and see if you can rustle up some camping equipment, have you got money on you?"

Jim had to confess he hadn't, so Ray tossed over a wad of notes and said. "You can get it back to me from the fund when we get it all sorted out."

He stood and went out of the door with Dick and Jim looked at Leah and said. "Shall we?"

Chapter Eleven

They set off the following day at six-o-clock after an early breakfast that felt as if the proprietor had been trying to feed an army and had food left over he wanted to get rid of. Jim had never felt so full for a long time. When he had mentioned it to him the hotelier merely commented. "You don't want to start off the day with an empty stomach mate; you'll get through most of the day on that."

They had stored the Ute in the garage inside as it had been full of supplies, and although crime was relatively low in Australia no one wished to take any chances with anything being stolen. Ray and Dick had done a good job on stocking up on spares and petrol, they had also bought some extra wheels and tyres as Ray had told them the roads in the country were mostly shale that could rip tyres to shreds. Jim and Leah had raided the local camping shop for clothing and they had outfitted everybody in tough boots and trousers. They all sported bush hats and Jim who had never worn a hat felt a little ridiculous in his, Leah stared at him when he put it on and said approvingly. "Suits you, now all you need are some corks to hang round the brim."

Jim smiled weakly and replied. "I think I'll rely on insect repellent."

Surveying all the stores they had loaded on, it became apparent that a camper van might have been better for their purpose but it was too late to change now so they left. The morning was cool before the sun had climbed too high and they made good progress at first. Then they turned on to the track leading towards the farm and their progress slowed considerably. The area they passed through appeared virtually deserted and only the track showed them that someone came along occasionally. Ray turned to Jim and said. "We'll have to sort something out at first, or when it's the "Wet" we won't be able to travel along here. It'll have to be a light plane I think or nothings going to move in or out of here."

Jim looked out at the countryside and nodded, it was hard to imagine now when everything was dry and parched.

"There is one form of transport that no one seems to consider for out here." He answered.

"Yeah, and what's that?"

"Hovercraft."

Ray looked disbelievingly at him. "You trying to tell me that they're any good?"

"Don't see why not." Jim answered. "The American army took them on for trials a few years ago."

"Maybe, but they aren't using them are they."

"That doesn't prove anything." Jim retorted. "They like to get back to the barracks every night if they can. That's why they use helicopters so much."

Unknowingly Ray had hit on one of Jim's weaknesses; he hated anything that wasted the earth's resources. His only consolation if it could be called that was that if the predicted volcanic eruption happened, it would solve the problem of global warming for centuries to come and allow the world a breathing space to settle down and equalise itself on to an even keel once again.

Leah had been listening to this exchange with interest. "I think we should at least give it some consideration, without blokes like you wanting to go around like macho man in his powerful Ute. Anything that lets us travel in the wet has got to be an improvement on sitting around waiting for the water to drain and the mud to dry out." She asked Jim. "How much can one of those things carry?"

He shrugged in answer. "It depends on how big you buy them, when I worked abroad we used to travel over the channel in them, and they could carry up to a hundred cars and vans with passengers."

She raised her eyebrows and stared at him and he went on apologetically. "I suppose the small ones could carry as much as a Ute, but I don't know whether you can drive one without licensing it on some way, they can't be steered like a car can they?"

"Do you think if you were taking someone vital supplies

over two hundred kilometres of mud, they'd care how it got there?"
She looked at Ray. "In his case if it was beer he'd offer to buy it
outright."

Ray grinned and said to Jim. "That hits the spot, why don't
you make some enquiries about them and see if they're suitable?"

They stopped twice to have a rest and refreshments and it
was nearly eight in the evening when they finally came on the farm,
a dilapidated gate swung crazily across the track and an equally
worn sign announced "Fred's Fruit Farm." the sign had all the signs
of being homemade and it only had one F, serving the three words.
The paint peeled from it and it no longer stood upright, rather it
leaned at an angle to the gate, creating an impression of being
uncared for.

They travelled up the track for about a mile before coming
to the farm proper, the house, such as it was stood surrounded by
fruit trees that had been neglected for a long time. It was a timber
built property that had seen better days and was in need of major
repairs. A man sat on the sagging porch with a beer bottle in his
hand and a belly to match; he had on scruffy clothes that needed
a good wash and was unshaven. He stood as they approached and
said. "Expected you earlier."

Jim looked around, although the property was in a general
state of disrepair it had all the signs of having been prosperous
at one time. This was born out by the man himself when he said.
"Used to be good around here when the wife was alive, but I can't
be bothered now she's gone, being stuck out here on your own ain't
no good for a man, better I sell up now and live somewhere near
civilisation."

Jim felt sympathy for him but still wanted them all to have
a good look round before they committed themselves. They asked
the man if it would be OK to walk round and have a look and when
he agreed they wandered off to see for themselves what it was like.
The house had been built in a hollow between two low foothills and
a path went up the rising hollow behind it. A windmill stood on the
brow of one hill and although the day was calm it was still turning
as the thermals from the surrounding area flowed over it. He could
hear water being pumped up to a large tank that stood next to the

windmill and surmised correctly that there was an underground stream flowing below. He knew the only thing to do with the house would be to demolish it as it had seen its best days and was useless for their purposes.

The fruit trees could be saved if they wished by hard pruning and if the water in the stream held out they could irrigate large areas and produce much better crops, with the plans that he had made he could visualise turning the place into a green and profitable holding. He knew that they would have to spend a great deal of their time building a place to pass the years when the earth was uninhabitable but even he who believed passionately that it would happen had no idea when.

On the opposite side of the compound which was about two hundred yards across from the house the ground rose as it went away from them and they went up with some difficulty, as it was very scrubby on the surface. It was a long climb and when they arrived at the top Jim gasped and looked out at a totally unexpected vista. The hill fell dramatically away from them in a steep escarpment down to a valley floor that lay at least 300 meters below them. He thought he could detect the glint of water at the bottom but it was thickly wooded and impossible to penetrate. He turned to the others who were as dumbstruck as himself. "I never thought I'd see something like this here." Dick said. Ray was silent but Leah said. "Would you look at that, I've never seen a vista like that for a long time and I didn't expect to see it here either."   Ray had been staring at the scene and spoke up musingly. "I reckon that ravine must be about five kilometres long from here and it goes back probably two or three, and if there's water down there it must have wildlife as well."

Looking back they could see the house and fruit trees surrounding it like a child's picture on the valley floor. At the best estimate Jim thought there would be about twenty acres of trees so it would be a full time occupation for them to begin. He could see that although it was hot and had been for some time there seemed sufficient water for their needs, but that had been promised in the brochure. Turning to the others he said, questioningly. "Well, what do you think?"

Glancing at each other and one by one they gave their

approval. He nodded his head and said. "All agreed then?"

Dick cleared his throat. "There is one drawback to all this, that hasn't been brought up. I like the set up here, and I think it's a great property with a lot of potential, especially if we demolish that shack of a house and build another. But how is anyone going to be able to reach it quickly and easily. If the Prof and Colette are working any where near Darwin it'll take hours by car and if Victoria's got to come from Cairns, that's going to take so long she'll never be able to come."

Jim had been expecting this and saw no way out for the time being other than to say they could only come at weekends, and would have said so but Ray stepped in. "A light plane might be useful, I've got my pilots licence and we could get a small plane to fly them in when we need to."

Jim frowned, he knew it would be a useful addition to the community but he felt that it could waste a lot of time and not to mention the money. Ray saw the indecision on his face and said. "I know what you're thinking mate, but you haven't got into the Aussie way of life out here. The distances are just too far and if you want something isolated you're gonna need some form of transport that's quicker than a Ute. Even with a plane it's gonna take about four hours to fly to Darwin and don't forget we can use it to get shopping as well. If it comes out of the general fund I reckon it could cost less than a good four-wheeler."

He knew he was probably right but Jim didn't want to see all the money going to buy a plane for convenience. "How much for a reasonable eight-seater then?"

Ray pursed his lips and thought about it. "Don't rightly know but we could get a second-hand plane without too many flying hours on it, the engines and maintenance can be done ourselves, any reasonable engineer can carry out servicing and we wouldn't be using it that much that we'd need to spend a lot of money after the initial outlay. And don't forget when it's flying it'll use less fuel than a Ute to go the same distance especially on that road back to Katherine." He looked down at the farm and went on. "If we put a landing strip over there we could get a good flight path for landing and take off."

Jim nodded. "OK, you've got me convinced, any objections from any of you?" He looked around at the others as he spoke. No one objected so he said to Ray. "Well, it seems like you've got a job then, you're the chief pilot." he stuck a finger in Ray's chest. "You'll find yourself pretty busy if you get this plane because you're going to have to teach a lot of people to fly it, it's no use having something only one person can use."

"Two people." The voice came from behind Jim. He swung round to confront Leah. "I can fly as well, got my licence at the same time as his lordship there."

"Well, well, well." Jim stuttered. "Is there no end to the talents that you two have?"

She shrugged. "You don't think I'd let him off to have flying lessons on his own do you? We had a week's holiday and learned at the same time."

Jim and Dick looked at each other and laughed. "If I didn't know any better I'd be saying these two are the original 'been there, seen it, done it,' pair wouldn't you? I expect you've got the T shirt as well" Jim said to them.

They sat there and started to work out their immediate needs in the next few weeks then went back down to speak to the owner. He accepted their offer with some reservation and said when they had agreed a price. "You've done the best out of this deal you know, when this place was going it was a regular gold mine."

Leah left him in no doubt though and replied. "It wasn't our fault you let it go downhill, if you stopped drinking that stuff." She pointed to his bottle of beer. "And got out there and did some work with a couple of helpers you might have been able to sell this place for a lot more. So don't moan at us old man, you caused it yourself."

He stared at her dumbstruck and then put his head back and roared with laughter. "Well, I'll give you that young lady you've got some balls, maybe if I'd have married you we might have made a go of it, but it's too late in my life to start all over so I reckon I'll leave you lot to it and let you have the work."

They shook hands all round and left him to his lonely life after agreeing a time and a place to meet and conclude arrangements.

None of them wanted to stay the night with him so they drove off down the road for a few miles and made a camp by the side of the road in a small grove of trees. Dick had got visibly agitated and if it had been left to him they would have probably driven on but common sense prevailed as driving over these roads at night was a prospect none of them wished to face. Jim knew that Colette was due in to Sydney airport the following day and was looking forward to seeing her himself so Dick must have been on tenterhooks after the long separation. He pointed out to Dick that they had arranged to go to Darwin to meet her when she flew up so he couldn't get closer to her, even if he travelled all night.

The following day when they broke camp it was still early and by pushing on with the driving and stopping only for a few minutes for refreshments they made it back to Katherine by midday. Dick had a quick shower and left for Darwin on the regular bus service, and Ray and Leah went to check on the boat. He had decided to leave it in Darwin, as that was the closest marina. Jim had made up his mind what to do and got in touch with everyone and called a meeting for three days from now to be held in the hotel in Katherine. He had made enquiries and hired a room for the day so they could thrash out the plans for the farm He determined to take the Ute back with him and bring Pat and Andrew back himself so he could save Jacko a trip. If he had been truthful to himself it would have been that he didn't want Blackie knowing any more of his business than was possible. The man sailed too close to the wind where the law was concerned, and he felt better knowing he had been kept at a distance.

He had been using the phone in his room to make the calls and rang Blackie to speak to Pat and Andrew. When he answered the phone, Blackie asked him when he wanted Jacko to come and pick him up. Pat came on the phone and he told her the news and said he'd be back the next day, and after putting down the phone he realised he'd have nothing to do for the rest of the day. Touring round beauty spots didn't appeal to him so he decided to have a shower and relax for a while with a beer. When he entered the bar he sat at a table where he could observe the room without turning his head, as he disliked sitting with his back to the door, so he was well placed to see the wheeler dealer Schoonheid come in.

Schoonheid looked around the room and nodding at a few acquaintances he made his way leisurely over to Jim. The last thing he wanted was this man for company but he decided to grin and bear it for a while to see what transpired. "G'day." The traditional Aussie greeting Jim thought. "Do you mind?" he said, indicating an empty chair and when Jim nodded he sat with a sigh. "Bloody weather never changes much does it?" he said conversationally.

Till now Jim had said nothing and now he waited again for the man to speak. "Beer?" Schoonheid asked. "Sure." Jim had a half of his beer still in front of him and Schoonheid called over to the waitress and had her bring them over. He waited till the beers had arrived and the girl had gone and then he brought up the reason for talking to Jim.

"I hear you're buying a place round here then?"

Jim leaned back in his chair feeling slightly unsettled, this town held about ten thousand people and yet this man Schoonheid had managed to find out what he was doing here, it became clearer when he went on. "I own one of the local 'Estate agents'? And I saw the sale of this property come in, so I decided to come down and talk to you personally. I guess you'll be looking to improve the property and I wondered if I can help you in any way?"

'The only help I'll get from you is to lighten my purse and make yours heavier' thought Jim but had to hold that in, as he knew that it would only cause difficulties to antagonize the man now. But he couldn't help disliking him. He wondered why the man got up his nose but he knew that he could never trust him in a business deal. The man's next words caused his heart to sink. "I own a local building supplies depot as well. I can get you anything you want in that line."

Although it went against the grain Jim knew he would have to deal with this man as it was going to be difficult to get supplies if he didn't. He would be quite capable of approaching the other suppliers and causing trouble if he was passed over in favour of someone else. There was a hint of menace about the man that discomfited him; he hoped it was only the pursuit of money that interested Schoonheid.

"Wishing to dissociate himself from contact with him he said. "You gave us a card the other day, when and if we need supplies I'll let my associate get in touch with you."

Schoonheid leaned forward with an oily smile and asked. "What are you going to do out there? There aren't enough fruit trees to make a living at, not after the price you're paying for it. And there seems to be an awful lot of people with you in this so what's going on?"

Jim felt the anger burning up inside him, what right did this moron have to question what they were doing. "Mr Schoonheid, let me make this absolutely clear to you, I am buying this place because I want to, for reasons of my own. If, and it is if, I decide to take you on as a supplier of building materials I will send my associate to you. She is perfectly capable of filling out an order form, and fixing prices. What we do with that property after we have bought it will remain our business and I'll thank you not to go poking your nose in where it isn't wanted. Now why don't you leave me alone to enjoy my life and you get on with yours."

Schoonheid's eyes narrowed, he didn't like to be put down. Most of his business dealings went the way he wanted them to go, and this man was going to have to be taught a lesson. He stood abruptly and said grimly. "I was only trying to ease the path you're walking along and do a bit of business at the same time, if you want it hard we can have it that way or we can come to some arrangement and do business like good honest citizens. You'll have to choose, but never forget that supplies come through me and when I say, so let's not fall out over this shall we? And by the way it's your shout."

Jim stared at the man in disbelief; he couldn't understand the mentality that could be so petty as to worry about whether a man bought a round of beer or not. He stood and walked over to the counter and bought a beer and then handed it to him. "There you are, that's your beer, and so I believe, we're even according to your counting method. And now." He looked him straight in the eye when he spoke. "If this project goes through I'm going to need a supplier I can trust, I will never put up with small time 'big shots' trying to dictate to me. If you want to do business with me you can get my orders when I give them or stand by and watch me deal with someone else, because a lot of money is going to be invested around here. So get your act together, I'm a potential customer and you'd better remember that."

Schoonheid stared at him with hatred in his eyes, he wanted to shout back to tell Jim to poke his business but he had a business mans nose and that came before any private feelings he might have. He held the glass up and took a swig saying "cheers", and placed the glass down on the counter, then took a deep breath and smiled smarmily at Jim. "What say we have a go at starting over again shall we? Never could stand arguing about business."

It was probably the most insincere statement Jim had heard for years but at the moment he needed the man and if it took some insincerity to achieve that aim then he would have to go along with it. "OK, let's give it a try." He replied. "But let's get one thing straight before we begin. I promise I won't interfere in your business, if you promise not to interfere in mine; that way everybody's happy."

Schoonheid smiled again and Jim was reminded of the wolf in Red Riding Hood, just before he pounced and tried to eat her. "Let's shake on that shall we?"

Jim regarded the hand that had been thrust in front of him and shook his head slowly. "Let's leave that until there's something to shake on shall we?"

He turned and walked out of the hotel leaving his beer on the counter, Schoonheid called out. "Here, you left you're…." His voice faded out as Jim disappeared from view and he looked at the beer himself, shrugged, and muttered. "Oh well, never look a gift horse." He picked up the beer and drained it in one go and walked out himself saying. "Nothing like a free one to perk you up."

Jim had jumped into the Ute and driven down the road until he found the garage and filled every available container he had on board with petrol and water, then went to a shop and bought more food to replace that which they had used on the trip to the farm. Then he drove along slowly until he found the sort of shop he was looking for. It held all sorts of stationary and he entered and chose some large pads, rulers, and writing articles. He also found a large-scale map of the area and a guidebook, which although it concentrated on the local beauty spot of Katherine Gorge had some interesting facts about the surrounding area. He took the lot back to the hotel with him and spent the rest of the day in his room poring over the maps and drawing up plans for the settlement he intended they should build.

The following morning he had eaten breakfast and was waiting outside when Jacko turned up to take him back to Blackies and he told him that he intended to drive the Ute back himself. Jacko looked dubious. "I don't like the idea of you lot driving around without anybody to look after you out there, it's bloody dangerous." He sidled closer to Jim and whispered in his ear. "Things happen out there, and there ain't any explanation why."

Jim grinned. "Come on Jacko, were living in the twenty first century now, and we're not a lot of superstitious Abbos are we?"

Jacko blanched, Jim was sure, if it had been possible to go white he would have done. He stared at Jim in horror, his whole demeanour changed and he glanced around superstitiously. "Don't go upsetting the spirits." He whispered. "There's a lot you don't understand."

"Oh come on Jacko, you know that there's no such thing."

"You don't know what you're messing with if you don't listen to the spirit world, I tell you the truth." Jacko was adamant, and Jim decided not to interfere too much with his beliefs. So he raised his hands in surrender. "OK Jacko, I give in, I'll pay more attention to what you say, and I'll behave myself when I think I see one."

Jacko looked at him. "You ain't ever going to see one, but you'll know they're there."

Jim smiled in disbelief, and looking round the deserted car park he suggested they get on the road before it got too late. Jacko said no more about the spirits but just nodded and told him to follow but not too close behind because he might have to stop quickly for an animal. They started off but didn't follow the same road as they had previously, and at first Jim was puzzled until he saw they were going in roughly the same direction, then he realised that when they had come previously Jacko had steered them on to the back roads to avoid being observed. They travelled about three hours before Jacko stopped for a drink and Jim had by this time swallowed about two litres of water. They drunk their tea and then started off again and drove for another two hours when they turned off and started to follow a track through the scrub. They went about an hour further on when he swerved on to the side and stopped. Jim stopped behind him and Jacko got out stretching to get the kinks out of his back and came over, he waited for the dust cloud to settle and said. "Time for a brew, mate."

Jim got out and following suit he stretched his legs as Jacko started to brew up, then he went to the cool box and produced some sandwiches, which they both consumed with relish. While they were eating Jim asked him. "How far to go, do you think?" Expecting Jacko to say about a day or so, but he replied. "Hundred miles give or take."

Jim gave him a hard stare. "How come it takes a day and a half to go, and one day to come back?"

Jacko smiled sheepishly. "Well Blackie wasn't too keen on you knowing exactly where he is, and he wanted you out of the eye of anyone nosing about. But he said you don't seem to be any trouble to him now, and he reckons if you're buying some property here you won't want any more bother so you'll keep quiet about him. He doesn't want any nosy buggers poking around in his backyard."

In the event they made it back by six in the evening and Jim climbed thankfully out of the driving seat. Everybody had come out to greet them and after Pat had given him a hug they all trooped inside to relax and catch up with the news. Jim brought them up to date about the farm and included Blackie in this as well. He knew that it was possible the rest of the armaments would be delivered through him anyway so they had no chance of concealing where it was or even what they were doing. Chrissie came out of the kitchen and called to them. "I've got some tucker ready if you want it."

Pat put her hand to her mouth and said to her. "I'm sorry love I meant to give you a hand."

Chrissie grinned back and answered. "No worries missus, it's easy to dish it up."

Jim looked questioningly at them and Blackie said. "Pat's been getting some food for us now and again, and if she ever decides she wants a job she can cook for us any time, she's been showing Chrissie there the way round the kitchen as well."

Chrissie laughed and answered. "I knew my way round this kitchen after five minutes here, and I reckon you haven't even found the door to it yet, I've never seen you in there since I arrived."

"Yeah, but I didn't want to disappoint you and show you up about the cooking love." Blackie joshed back.

It was easy to see they both had a lot of affection for each other and Pat smiled with them and said. "Leave you men to the cooking, and we'll all be having tinned food to eat."

They ate their meal and during the evening Jim brought Blackie up to date with all the developments and told him the location of the farm so he could deliver the rest of the armaments they had ordered. Blackie only had one question to all this and asked. "I know you're going to start a farm, as you like to call it and I know you'll have a lot of people there but what the hell do you need all these arms for? Most people in this area might have a gun for the occasional Roo, or fox, maybe even a croc, if you've got water, but what you've bought is for killing people not animals. Who do you think you're defending against?"

Jim surveyed the floor as he deliberated what to tell him. "Look." He said. "I hope we don't need them, it might never come to it, but if it does I want to know they'll be there for me to use. If what I think is going to happen does occur I want to be able to have these arms for defence only. So they'll only be used if someone comes looking for us, and for no other purpose." He looked at Blackie. "I haven't broached the subject with you because I didn't think you'd be interested, and anyway we only take in couples so that kind of lets you out doesn't it?"

Blackie scratched his head. "You'll have to run that past me again, why didn't you think I'd be interested, and why only couples?"

Jim sighed; he didn't really want to get into this as Blackie was possibly a future opponent in this scheme and if the scenario worked out it would take him about five minutes to figure out the plan. They were interrupted by a shout from Andrew, who had been watching the television. "I think you should take a look at this dad, it's going to be important."

Jim went over and stared at the television, a reporter had taken up position on the rocks in Yellowstone Park, and was saying the geyser 'Old Faithful' had started to behave erratically for the first time since it had been discovered. For years it had spouted at regular intervals of between 30 and ninety minutes, but now the intervals had started to come at fifteen and twenty minutes. This had coincided with a definite rising of the ground over a large area of the park and the bank at one end of the lake appeared to have risen by several feet. Scientists had been carrying out tests to determine whether the movement was natural or was heralding a new era in the life of the volcano. Surveyors were taking measurements to determine how much movement had taken place and they were being compared to measurements taken many years previously. One theory put forward had been that there were magma chambers beneath the surface that were filling gradually over thousands of years and creating the upward movement of the ground. The scientists were worried that the pressures could create a volcanic explosion of proportions never before seen by mankind. They referred to a programme seen before on television where the discovery had been made that this had occurred maybe twice before at six hundred thousand year intervals, and it was now long past the time for the next one.

Jim Andrew and Pat stared at each other in consternation, they had been imagining that they had lots of time to prepare and now they could feel the pressure of events crowding in on them. Blackie had been watching their faces with interest and now he asked. "Is this the reason for everything then?"

Jim nodded, and Blackie went on. "Why does something that's going to happen on the other side of the world concern you here in Oz? I don't get it."

Jim took the trouble to explain everything to him and after a long involved explanation Blackie simply said sarcastically. "You're bloody mad to do something like this on a long shot like that; you'd be as well off enjoying life until it happens. Because if you think you're going to survive underground for ten years you're making a big mistake. If any one in authority hears about this you'll have them down on you so quick you wouldn't have time to say 'piss off' before they took you over. This bloody government have already made preparations for a nuclear war with shelters out in the outback somewhere where nobody knows what they are."

Jim agreed. "I know that they've got them in England at various locations, because I had a mate who worked on the telecommunications and he had to install a lot of the telephone cables for them. But the point I'm making is that the type of person they want to put in them are all people who want to sit at the top of the pile and push everybody about. The trouble with that is they don't have any skills to contribute to the community so they end up dragging it down instead of supporting it. That's why I'm doing this my way and only people who are useful are going to get in. And also that's the reason for the arms, I want the means to defend myself and if necessary stop anybody else getting in, for whatever reason."

"Well you can count me out of that scheme mate." Blackie commented. "I'd rather take my chances out in the open than have to rely on a community like that to survive. You've got no guarantee it'll work out anyway, have you?"

"No." Jim admitted. "But it's the best chance if it does happen."

"Well." Blackie said. "I've seen the Abbos survive out in the desert, so if they can do it, I'd rather go with them and try, than be cooped up in there for ten years."

Somehow Jim had known that Blackie would opt for that course of action, he had never come across as a man who would take kindly to living inside, or even in a community, being an independent type of man. Still, he reflected, they would be better off without him, he had an air about him that suggested he wanted all his own way and that would never suit community life. He turned to Pat and Andrew who had been listening to this exchange and said bleakly. "We'll have to get a move on if we aren't going to get caught out by events, when we see the others we'll have to make plans to push on with building everything we need in the shortest possible time."

He asked Andy if he would go and get the Ute ready for the

return journey and settled Blackie up by agreeing the payment of all debts to an account that Blackie had set up to take care of his finances. They agreed that when they were ready for the delivery of the rest of the arms that Blackie could oversee the arrangements with Sulim as Jim felt dubious about letting him see where they had settled. To his surprise he found out that Blackie had heard of him and had done some dealings with his organisation peripherally, although he had never met him. How they were going to get the arms into the country Jim decided not to pry into, as from his point of view, the less he knew the better.

Andy came back and announced the Ute had been prepared for the journey with all the petrol and water loaded and sufficient supplies for several days, just in case something went wrong. They went to bed early and next morning set off at dawn on the long journey to Katherine. All the people on the property were out to see them off and Chrissie in particular started to wail when Pat said goodbye to her. Pat mollified her by saying she could come and visit later when they had got settled, and Blackie was coerced into promising to bring her. On the journey back the only trouble they had was when the air conditioning went on the blink, but decided to try and fix it when they arrived back as none of them wanted to play about with mechanical things on the road. The rest of the journey passed with them all sweating profusely, and trying to make the Ute go faster to stir up some wind. On arrival in Katherine they booked the Ute into the garage and went directly to the hotel.

When they entered the hotel, they booked in, and Jim found several messages waiting for them, he took them and they went directly to their rooms to shower and change after the long day. While Pat took her shower first, Jim read the messages. They were all much the same, they informed him that all the members of their group had arrived and were waiting for them. While he was reading them someone knocked on the door, and when he opened it, Colette stood outside holding her child in her arms and a big smile on her face. He grabbed the little one and gave her a big hug and told her to come in. Then she kissed him and they hugged each other while Dick stood behind waiting for them to stop making a fuss. Pat came back in, still wet from the shower and Emma wriggled from his grip to go to her grandmother and jumped into her arms where she clung and wouldn't let go. Pat tried to make a fuss of her at the same time as talking to Colette but all that ensued was a happy babble of voices all trying to drown each other out, and tell all the others the news. Another knock came and it was the Prof with Julia and then Ray and Leah came and had to be introduced to them, as they had never met before, Victoria arrived as she had been attracted to the noise and after introductions she huddled with Andrew on the only sofa in the room. For a while it was bedlam and Jim escaped thankfully to get a shower himself.

When he emerged he found the room still full and from somewhere some wine and beer had appeared and they were drinking from a variety of cups and glasses purloined from various bathrooms and cupboards along the corridor. Emma, who was four now and growing tall, still clung to Pat's arms and looked as if she had no intention of letting go, but when Jim reappeared she slid down and toddled over to him to be picked up and cuddled. She put her thumb in her mouth and watched them all trying to talk at once. George and Jeannie came along then and Jeannie stared at Colette in awe as she stood next to Dick, not wanting to admit that her idol had found someone else, quite forgetting that he had already been married before she had met him.

Colette dropped a bombshell a few minutes later when she refused a drink and said. "I can't, thank you very much, I don't want to damage the baby."

The room went quiet when Pat screamed. "Are you expecting again." and when Colette smiled she threw her arms around her and shouted. "It's going to be a boy I know it."

Colette only smiled at her mother's enthusiasm and said. "It's going to make life a bit difficult at first."

"Oh pshaw." Pat said. "What's so difficult about having a baby with all the women we've got around here?" What she left unsaid was that she would be taking over this baby if it killed her, her instincts had been aroused, and picking Emma out of Jim's arms she said. "We'll look after the baby together won't we darling?"

The hubbub started again as they all tried to congratulate Colette at once and it became obvious that the noise was going to be too much. Jim became aware that he was being plied with drinks on an empty stomach so he called them all to order and when the room quietened down he said. "I don't know what you lot feel like but I'm starving and I'm drinking when I ought to be eating, so I suggest we all go down to the restaurant and get something to plug the gap."

The Prof looked at Julia and said. "We'd better give our two a call and get them down for something to eat as well."

Jim called down to the restaurant and told them they wanted a table for all of them and they went down a few minutes later to find everything arranged at the back of the dining room. He looked around as Julia's children Kevin and Pauline came in shyly to meet them and she introduced them to the people they didn't know. After they had been introduced Jim told them to sit with George and Jeannie to get to know them. It was something of a strange mix as Pauline was one year older than Jeannie and Kevin one year younger than George, so they mixed with each other, but warily.

They all had to accept what the waitress called meal of the day as the time had gone on and the cook had no intention of preparing a lot of different meals. Jim watched and noticed although Victoria accepted the meal she made sure to give her portion of meat to Andy. By the time the meal was over and they finished coffee it was time to go to bed so Jim suggested that the children could go sightseeing the next day while they got started with preparations and had their meeting in the morning. Ray volunteered to find a child minder to take the children to Katherine gorge, a local beauty spot, for the day.

The following morning they climbed out of bed with the expected hangovers but Jim decided to have the general meeting regardless; he saw the manager and hired the conference room in the hotel for the day, then told everyone to be there at ten without the children who had to go sightseeing with the minder Ray had hired.

There was a knock on the door and when Jim opened it he found the Prof and Julia waiting outside. He welcomed them in and when they were all seated he looked at them expectantly. "I've got something to tell you I feel you should know."

Jim looked at him puzzled. So the Prof began. "You might have wondered why I left England so abruptly, the truth is that the Customs and Excise were on my case and I had to get out."

Jim's brow furrowed. "I don't understand; you're a teacher. How did you get involved with them?"

The Prof grinned. "There's something you don't know about me. I'm a metalwork teacher, right? And a deal came my way with a lot of money behind it and I took the chance." He sighed. "I went in feet first without asking questions and almost got left holding the baby. From the start, a guy approached me, he knew I lived in a big property that's fairly secluded. He told me he had some gold bars that he wanted to get rid of but they were still warm. I took it to mean they were the results of a robbery. He told me he had been sitting on these for about ten years. But the trouble was they were hallmarked and even a sniff of the numbers stamped on them would bring the police down on him like a ton of bricks. He wanted me to melt them down and make trinkets out of them and ship them out to India where they could be processed again. The trouble was that 'some' turned out to be 40 and on the open market would be worth anything up to 1.5 million Pounds."

He spread his hands. "What would you do? I was promised £250.000 to convert them all into trinkets, so I hired another guy I had met at trade school and over the next few weeks we worked evenings and weekends melting them all down and casting them into a variety of objects. When we had done that, the guy turned up and took delivery of them and promised to pay me in India. Then he left. I heard later that the Indian authorities had found them but let him go as he was innocent in India. But as a matter of course they told the English Customs about the affair. They in their turn started making enquiries in England. It was only going to be a matter of time before they got round to me because of the smelting equipment I had. When you proposed coming here it was like a godsend and I hotfooted it out as quickly as possible. I went to India collected my money and got new ID cards made up for us two and came into OZ through the normal channels. End of story."

Jim reflected on this for a time, it was something of a shock but then he compared this to his own law breaking. He grinned and leaned forward. "If this disaster does happen, who's going to be any the wiser? You won't be punished, but on the other hand the money's going to be useless to you."

With that he stood and went on. "Best not tell the others yet and just carry on as usual, now we've got a meeting to go to." He resolved to think this over some more and see what conclusions could be drawn.

When they had all gathered in the conference room, Jim looked around the table; he sat at the end, and the others were scattered round it in various seats with no order to them at all. They were all in various conversations and paid him no attention until he stood and called out. "Can I have a bit of quiet here please?"

When they had quietened down he shuffled his papers and said. "I want to bring this meeting to order now, as we've got a lot of business to get through. Now I've given this some thought and I've come to the conclusion that although I'm against authority in a lot of ways." He was interrupted by Ray who murmured. "Hear, hear."

He carried on. "The fact remains that someone has to take responsibility for all the decisions that are going to be made in the next period in our lives. I've decided to take that on myself if that's OK with you?"

He paused and looked around the table at them, Dick held his hand up slowly, and Jim acknowledged him with a nod. "I thought we'd all have some input into the decisions."

"That's true." Jim replied. "It will happen that way, everybody's views are important but one person has to take the final decision about what to do but it will only happen if the majority want it. What I'm suggesting is that, for example." He pointed at the Prof and Julia. "They won't be here a lot of the time and neither will Colette or even Victoria at first so somebody has to have authority when they aren't here. Now we all know that we've got a Limited Company, and what I propose is that we have a Secretary for taking notes of meetings. Also we should have a Treasurer for countersigning checks, and maybe a couple more to form a committee to see that all our decisions are fair. Now, has anybody got any objection to that?"

When he looked around the table it was Pat, who put her hand up, he mentally cursed and thought to himself, 'What the hell does she want to say?'

She cleared her throat and started to say. "It's all very well you wanting to take all the decisions around here but some of us might want to have some say in what goes on or you men would probably start building a brewery before you got round to growing crops. And anyway, what makes you so suitable to make all the decisions"

Jim could feel the anger start to grow and thought. 'Why is it she can get under my skin so easily?' He controlled himself from answering too quickly by taking a sip from the water glass on the table. He looked around the table before he answered. "Does anybody else feel like this?"

Leah held her hand up. "I don't necessarily feel like Pat, but I would like to have a chance to say what I want to happen."

"OK." Jim said. He looked at Pat. "I've never done anything in my life without consulting you and you know it." He put the palm of his hand up to stop her speaking. "Listen first. What I want to do is bring in as many people as possible to help with the big decisions but the small ones can be dealt with by anyone with any common sense. Now right at the moment I reckon there are only six people here who can be counted on to be here constantly. That's Pat, Dick, Andrew, Ray, Leah, and me. All the rest are working somewhere else at this time except Julia, who can if she wants, stay here and help out with the building."

Julia looked at the Prof who nodded and she said. "We've already discussed this and we've come to the conclusion that I won't earn much working as a supply teacher so it's probably better if I work on the farm and see Prof at the weekend."

Jim looked around the table. "Any one else got anything to say on this subject? OK, so what I propose is this, we form a committee, with me as chairman, or person if you want me to be politically correct." This had been directed at Leah who had been making her feminist views known. "The committee can be composed of Pat, Leah, Andrew, Dick, Ray and Julia. That avoids the possibility of decisions being stalemated. Although I don't expect we'll argue much anyway." Jim said with a grin. "To go on, I want to have one of the committee to be able to sign cheques, with a counter signature, probably me. And I want one other to act as secretary and write up the minutes of all the meetings so that everyone can be seen to vote and all the committee have to sign so if any person isn't satisfied we'll have everything in order for them to see. Is there any query about that?"

When he looked around the table he found to his surprise that no one had any problems with what he had said. "I want to have a vote on this so that it can go in the minutes."

They got on with the tiresome business of proposing and seconding the motions and at the end of it all, they had Julia as Secretary, Ray as Treasurer, and Jim as Managing Director. The other members of the committee were Pat, Dick, Andrew, and Leah.

Jim stood when all this part of the business had been concluded, he stared around at them solemnly for a moment, and then his face split into a wide grin. "Congratulations to you all, we're now an officially designated company and all the legal rules and palaver are concluded. Now my first action as Chairman is to call a recess and propose we have a drink to celebrate."

He reached under the table where he had earlier secreted a basket with some sparkling wine and some glasses. To cheers from the rest of them he opened the first bottle with a bang and poured some foaming drink into the glasses, soon there was enough for everyone and he toasted them all with the words. "Success."

Ray shouted to him above the hubbub of the excited conversation that broke out. "Would you have broken out the champers if the vote had gone against you?"

Jim thought about that for a moment before replying, and then he said. "But it didn't did it?"

They were about to continue when there came a knock on the door, Jim strode over and opened it a crack and looked through to find Schoonheid standing outside. "Just wondered if there's anything I can do to help out." He said. He would have gone on speaking but Jim stopped him his face dark with anger.

"I thought I told you I would get in touch with you if I needed you, I don't know what you think you're going to gain from keeping on pushing but if it carries on I'll make sure you get no business at all. Do you understand?"

Schoonheid flushed and started to say. "I only wanted to...." He might have gone on but he found the door closed in his face. Jim locked it from his side and went back into the room with all the humour of the previous minutes dissipated, and he was in a sombre mood when he faced them again. "OK, let's get back to business."

Leah touched him on the arm. "Don't let him get to you, I'll deal with him in my own way when we start working, he won't be so pushy then. Especially when I ring him at two in the morning demanding materials."

Jim laughed at that prospect and looked at them with a lighter expression on his face. "OK, let's settle down and I'll start off by giving you some figures to work on. I've been in touch with the bank and we've got an account here in Katherine, it's only a small branch but most of the business is done by cheque anyway so we can just pay as we go with no real problem. I'm pleased to say that we've arrived here with more money than we started with as the interest has been building up and we've paid for all fares and travel expenses up to now. Our original investment was about Two and a half million and that's still there plus some interest. The best part of the whole enterprise must be allowing Ray and Leah to join, they've put in about a million in £'s so now we stand at 3 ½ million quid."

There was a gasp from some of the audience who hadn't until then, realised how much they had contributed. He went on. "From now on though we are going to start spending with a vengeance, I've got to go and pay for the fruit farm soon and then we've got to start to equip the place. Now this is what I propose and hear me out before you criticize. We need to live out there for some time while we're building the accommodation blocks so I think we could buy or rent some residential caravans, for each family. We're definitely going to need a digger of some sort and various ground moving tools. We should build some sort of landing strip out there for a plane, as we have to buy one for fast delivery of personnel, especially at weekends." He looked at Prof and Victoria when he said this and smiled at them. "Also I want it to be able to carry larger than average loads as I think we'll have to use it for shopping, which I want Pat and Julia to handle." He looked at the two of them. "You'll have think about frozen food as well and don't forget we'll need a fair-sized freezer to take it all. You can't just go to the local supermarket and buy something. It's about a days travel and not easy. "When it comes to materials for the actual building, the list is endless and I've done some figures but Leah will have to start working on that Schoonheid bloke to get his firm to make deliveries as quickly as possible, if he won't, I might hire our own lorry and do it ourselves. This brings me to a point I've been thinking about for a long time. The sort of building we want to build has got to be strong and well built, and our labour isn't going to be enough. It's going to be physically impossible to do it all in a reasonable time frame so I think we should consider bringing in some shovel hands and not from Katherine, I don't want too much speculation about what we're doing here. But we are going to need at least four more men for about six months. Now I know I said we should tell people we are building an indoor farm, but I think now a better explanation is research establishment. It'll explain all the indoor cultivating we're doing."

Victoria looked up and nodded her head in agreement with this. "I've got something to add to this when it's my turn to speak."

"OK", Jim started to speak again. "I've arranged for a windmill to be delivered and we'll erect it as soon as possible but in the meantime we'll have to rely on a good old fashioned diesel generator. We can build it in to the structure when we want, as we may need one in the future." He looked over at Dick and said. "You're the engineer and you'll have to work out how we're going to build this place, I can get work done but I need a plan to work to and that's where you come in."

Dick smiled, and tapped his forehead. "It's all in here, been thinking about it for weeks. I can rough out some drawings and have them ready within a week." His brow furrowed. "One thing I'd like to know, is it necessary to get any sort of permission to start work on the place or not?"

Everybody glanced around at each other, and looked mystified. It became obvious that no one knew the answer to that question. Even Ray had nothing to say, it was left to Leah to come up with a partial answer. "If we build it without permission who the hell is going to come all the way out there and say we can't. I don't see some of these official geezers wanting to leave the air-conditioned luxury of their offices to sweat it out over that distance to check on what we're doing. And even if they do go as far as that, it could be just another storage area like a barn."

They had to make do with that answer and Jim thought to himself that once again they had gone into a situation without the proper thought and something like this could land them in serious trouble. He resolved to take a little more care with forward planning and make sure they knew all the facts before making a decision. He then said to them. "I want you all to think about what we need in this building and talk to Dick about it, when you've all had time to consider; we can incorporate all the features we need into it. We can't afford to leave anything out at this stage as it will mean altering everything at a later date and we don't want that to happen." He ticked the points off on his fingers. "Accommodation, kitchens, washrooms, toilets, heating, lighting, waste disposal, food growing areas, education area, entertainment area. The list goes on and we've all got to think very hard about our requirements."

He stopped talking and sat down saying. "I want to hand over the meeting to Colette now."

She stood and opened a briefcase, looking round at them she said. "This part is going to be easy in one way and hard the next." She handed round several sheets of paper to everyone there. "I want you all to fill this questionnaire and I'm telling you now, I want you to be perfectly honest with me, I'm the only person in the community who's going to see the answers you give but don't forget what I'm going to tell you now. If you come into this community with some incurable disease it's going to kill you because we can't expend precious medical supplies to try and make things easier for you. Every person here has one object in life from now on and that is to produce children, once that obligation is over you are expendable."

She looked over at Jim. "That goes for you and Mum just as much as everybody else, you are valuable now but when the place is built you're going to be just so much excess baggage. I know that you're my parents but at the end of the day if you are ill you'll have to go the same road as everybody else." She looked round the room. "I want you all to remember that the only compassion I will have is for the survival of the children. These questionnaires ask you for your medical history, and also for the history of your parents. If they died of a heart attack at least tell me, it won't bar you from coming but it will help me later in my job. I want you all to see me in the next day or so as I want to take some samples, I'm going to send them away for analysis so don't try and conceal something that could come out in the tests as it won't look too good on your record will it?"

Several of them had been studying the questionnaire as she spoke and Leah spoke up. "You seem to want to know a lot about our general health and if we've had any diseases, I can understand that but what about viruses? My understanding is that all of us carry viruses of one sort or another, and what about the aids virus?"

Colette's face hardened. "If I find the aid's virus in anybody's samples that's going to be an automatic exclusion, we won't have the facilities to care for them and we can't take the chance they'll spread it to the others. As for the ordinary viruses like herpes, I think we'll have to accept that they've been around for a long time and most people have them with very few problems. I will be buying a lot of patent medicines and I'm going to institute a programme for inoculation against most illnesses but there comes a time especially later, when we will come into contact with other people who can be carrying things which we won't have any immunity against. Remember the American Indian was almost wiped out by measles. Hawaii lost almost 90% of their population to measles and syphilis, brought by, I might add, the Europeans starting with Captain Cook. The tests will be as comprehensive as I can make them, and I warn you I will be thorough."

She looked around to see if any of them had any further questions and when nobody had, she said. "Don't worry too much, everybody has something wrong with their health and my only concern is if we can get our children to grow up strong and healthy. Now if you can fill in these questionnaires today and let me have them tomorrow I can get on with the analysis during the next week."

She sat down and Jim asked. "Has anybody got anything to add to this subject before we go on?" He glanced around the table and when he got no response he said. "Victoria, I think it's your turn to speak now." She stood slowly putting a fat briefcase on the table, and clearing her throat she glanced shyly around. "First of all, I'd like to say that I'm pleased to be in this position and to meet you all. Now I've done a great deal of research into this subject while you lot have been swanning around all over the southern oceans." She grinned, and several smiled back at her in acknowledgement. "The subject is too big to go into here but I'll give you a small run down of the requirements we will have to have, then I'll hand a folder over to Jim and Dick so they can incorporate all the designs into the overall plan."

"First of all I'd like to try and introduce another person here who I believe can help us a great deal. He is possibly one of five people in Australia who is an authority on botany and he runs his own nursery growing plants, both for sale and for study. He is married and has two children, I've talked to him about this subject, but I've given him no details. I would like to ask him if he wants to come into the community as I think he will be invaluable, but maybe you might be able to approach him."

She had said this to Jim and looked appealingly at him to get his approval, he looked at the others raising his eyebrows and when they nodded he said. "I'll put him down for a meeting if you give me his name and telephone number after this meeting Victoria, well done anyway, we need someone to run the growing of the food as well as yourself, and experts are always welcome. Do you think he would fit in with us?"

Victoria simply answered. "Oh yes, I'm sure he'd fit in OK."

She turned her attention to the papers before her on the table. "First of all I've done some research into the mechanics of actually growing all our own food and although we can grow a lot I think at the end of the day we'll have to give up some things as impossible to supply in any quantity. We've all come to expect a varied diet as part of modern living, but we will have to concentrate on items that grow quickly and easily. I also think we can grow on two levels if we put in a good artificial lighting system on the lower floor and control it for maximum output. That'll leave the top floor for growing crops in the sunlight." She looked at Jim. "I know you think we won't have sunlight but it will be lighter during the day and crops can survive if we keep them warm. I've also given some thought to animals as well, I can foresee that we'll need three types for food and products; these are cows, pigs, and sheep. If we build this place right we can incorporate them into the scheme of things." She smiled wryly. "I know I've admitted before that I'm a vegetarian, but now I can't see us doing without them, we need cows for the milk, butter and cheese. We need sheep for the wool, and porkers can eat a lot of the waste and turn it into protein. I have been thinking we can isolate them in a separate section so we don't get any cross infection from them. The only thing that I want you to discuss is a horse; we could accommodate a breeding pair, as we will need something when we come out to start us off on farming the land. We can't be sure of having power in any form when we come out, and not only that, on compassionate grounds we ought to do something to stop the species dying out."

There was a general nodding of heads in agreement with these sentiments and Jim could see that everybody agreed with this, she handed a folder with several sheets of paper in it to Jim and said, "I've also got some measurements I want to go over with you later Jim but these will have to do for the time being, I think the growing area has got to be quite large as we have to process a lot of the waste to make a growing medium so that the whole process becomes self sustaining. From eating to processing to growing, it's got to be much like a spaceship with nothing wasted. There is one thing I'd like to mention, and that is we will be producing a lot of natural gas when we process the waste products and we should find some way of harnessing that and making the generator and vehicles run on it. That way we don't have to rely too heavily on the windmill, but it must be pointed out that the power requirements are going to be quite large so we need to be certain we can get it in one form or another."

Jim said. "From what I've seen we're going to need a small

nuclear reactor to get this little town self sustaining." He looked around at their horrified faces. "It's a joke, I didn't mean it."

Ray piped up. "I'm looking into the possibility of solar panels to see if they can be used in low light situations, but the problem is if there's a lot of dust they would need cleaning regularly and that means going outside for some time to do it."

"We're going to have to go outside some of the time anyway." answered Jim. "Some products we have won't recycle at all and we'll have to go out and dispose of them. And if you think about it we won't be able to let our waste pipes stand there for years on end without maintenance."

Andrew held his hand up, "I can use BA equipment because I've been trained in its use when I was in the army, the air can be just pumped into the cylinder, and it only needs a compressor and the right connections. Scuba diving uses the same technology."

"OK, that's settled then, we'll have to see what we can do about getting it in place." Jim looked around and said. "Anybody got any more subjects to bring up?"

Ray stood up and said. "I've got something to say." He waited until the room quietened a little and then went on. "I've been in touch with a supplier I knew when I was in the business and he can supply all the computer equipment we need and it'll be the latest models and all the programmes we need to run the whole place. He's going to let me have loads of programmes like encyclopaedias and general knowledge so we can run the school. I'm also looking into the possibility of having re-writable pads so the kids don't need too much paper in the school. He's going to give me a total price for the whole shebang and I'm sure I can squeeze a good discount out of him."

Andrew leaned forward. "You'd better get loads of games and films as after a while we're going to run out of things to do in our spare time."

Victoria gave him a small smile. "I can think of some better ways of passing the time than playing games on a computer."

There was a chorus of jeering and gentle comments about the expression on Andrews face when she said that, and he shook his head in despair when he regarded her with an embarrassed look on his face.

Julia leaned forward in her chair. "I know you lot keep on talking about computers and games and so on but I think you're all missing a point here, I concede computers have their place but have you given any thought to what happens when you come out. What happens in twenty or thirty years when they're clapped out? How are you going to teach the children or how are you going to access knowledge? You have got to make provision for books, and you have to make sure the children can use them in the proper way. I say you've got to place as many books as you can in storage so they can be used after we come out. You'll never be able to build computers again, not for years, as they are, after all, a product of a highly advanced society."

The Prof; sitting on the other side of the table said. "I agree with what you say darling, but we have to use what we can while we've got it and you know that you can store all the books in the library on a few discs, we'll just have to find a way to keep the computers going."

Julia's eyes flashed as she stood abruptly and putting her hands on the table leaned over to face him. "If you agree with what I'm saying why do you insist on thinking like a stupid moron? What happens if the CD player or whatever you call it goes on the blink? Who the hell is going to repair that? Most people don't even know what it looks like on the inside."

She sat down again helplessly and the Prof regarded her for a moment before standing heavily to his feet. He was just about to speak and Jim sensing that what he would say could cause a lot of offence to his wife; stepped in and said. "Before you two get your knickers in a twist over this, and let me say I agree with you both. Although we've got to keep the computers running as long as possible, and we've got to store books; the one thing that sticks in my mind is that when we come out we will in reality be a farming community and at first the level of technology is going to be quite low, we need knowledge about farming but we do have experts coming with us anyway, so at the end of the day, education, although it's useful doesn't serve anyone very well to begin with. We can try and access books later, I don't believe that all the library's will be a pile of rubble after ten or so years and I think that most librarians would close them before going off."

It was left to Ray to try and have the last word. "I can see your point Julia about The CD player packing up, but you ought to know that we intend to put a lot of extra spares in so we can keep them running for a long time."

Julia looked at him in despair. "You don't understand this situation at all do you? There are certain things that we are going to want to have but we won't be able to. There's no way that a farming community is going to be able to produce some of the items we take for granted now." She looked at him patiently. "If I can explain in words of one syllable what I'm getting at. Take the situation maybe several thousand years ago; the Egyptians didn't have the wheel. They just got along without it, but when they saw it first they probably thought to themselves that's great, we'll have a go at making that. That's because the concept is easy to understand, and replicate. But a computer is something else, that's the product of hundreds of different inventions so it's as impossible for us to make one, as the Abbos down the road. We'll never have the technology, and I think if this does happen, in fifty years we'll be back to the era of the Middle Ages."

She sat back in her chair and looked around at the rest of them. There was silence around the table for a while then Jim spoke up. "Well that puts us in our place Julia, I hope we can cope a bit better than that, but we can only hope a lot more people survive than just us. Then there'll be a chance that some of today's technology can be used."

He looked around at them and asked. "Has anyone got anything else to say about these things that have been raised today?" He waited for an answer and when none was forthcoming he said. "OK, I propose we close this meeting and reconvene tomorrow afternoon as I've got to go and complete the deal on the fruit farm tomorrow morning. I'd like Victoria, Dick, Leah, and Ray to stay for a bit but the rest of you can have a break if you want. All except you Julia, can you get the minutes of this meeting written up?" She nodded and he smiled his thanks.

They all started to troop out except Pat who said with a little ice in her voice. "I know you didn't want me to stay but would you like me to get some coffee for you?"

Jim knew instantly he had made a mistake so attempted to rectify it by making excuses. "I didn't know you wanted to stay, it was only to discuss the building and what goes in it; I didn't think you'd be interested."

"Well ask first." She retorted. "I might just want to stay and put in my penny worth." she turned and walked out without waiting for an answer to her question.

Jim raised his eyebrows and waggled them in chagrin. Leah snorted. "You men, you've got no idea how to treat a woman have you?"

"How could we when all you women seem to think of is personalities and whether us men are putting you down. Why don't you just accept sometimes that all we want to do is get on with something and not worry about whether the wife is going to agree with it or not. Now all I wanted to do right now was make some decisions about the size of the establishment not worry about whether my wife was going to get offended if I left her out of something I didn't think she'd be interested in, in the first place. Now can we get on with some work and forget about personalities."

The others had been listening to this exchange between them with some amusement but now Victoria laid her folder on the desk and opened it. She waited for Jim to look at the figures she had previously given him and then waited for his reaction. It was one of astonishment. "I didn't think it would be this large." He said.

The building designated for the farm needed about 10,000 sq meters on each of two floors, and on the upper floor she had asked for glass. The area for animals had been placed of to the rear of the main building. Living accommodation was all at the front of the property, and the processing plant for waste at the back. Dick had been looking over Jim's shoulder with Ray and Leah alongside; he leaned forward for a closer look and said. "Building this is a major operation and we're going to have to work really hard to complete it quickly. It's about the size I was expecting though and we can build it fairly easily if we get the proper equipment."

They were still discussing it when the door opened and Pat

came in and placed the coffee on the table and went out without a word. Jim looked up and said. "Thank you" which was ignored by her and she departed with back straight and stiff.

Ray smiled and commented. "Join the club mate, I know how you feel."

Leah drawled. "You'll be in the same boat if you don't watch your tongue." Ray groaned to himself but wisely refrained from speaking and they got on with the business in hand.

At the end of the session, it had been decided to buy as much of the heavy equipment as possible and also some caravans for living accommodation. Ray would be chief buyer for that and also he had to find a plane for them as well and Jim asked if he could try and buy a hovercraft. An idea that brought a wry smile to Ray's face. Leah had to arrange for supplies of building materials and other small equipment like shovels and tools. Jim had to make up the list of things needed and also he had to look for a generator capable of giving them enough power at first, then he had to arrange for the delivery of the windmill and enough spare parts to enable it to work for a long period. Dick was given the job of drawing up plans and also he had to oversee the actual building and surveying of the ground. Victoria had possibly the most important job as she was to be in charge of the indoor farming and had to arrange the growing beds, seeds, and plants they needed.

Julia and Pat had to forage for supplies and work out how much bedding and household materials they needed. Jim promised to send Andrew off to see his supplier for stocks of his beloved 'meals ready to eat' although they all groaned at the thought of actually eating it. Colette had the task of getting in sufficient medical supplies, with the accent on dry supplies in powder form and tablets that had some chance of surviving for some time. Ray had to accompany Jim to buy the property in his role of treasurer.

The next day Jim was out of bed and had breakfast long before anyone appeared, as he could never sleep well before an important period in his life. He had finished before Ray and Pat came into the dining room with Julia and he was engrossed in a paper on the terrace. They joined him there and ordered breakfast to be served outside, as it was still a little cool there before the sun rose and started its burning path across the sky. When they had eaten they decided to walk to the estate agents, as it was still an hour to the appointed time. They reached the office far too early and decided to have a coffee across the road in a small coffee shop. They were sitting there when they spied Schoonheid entering the office accompanied by a well-dressed man who looked as if he used his brain to earn a living rather than his hands. About ten minutes later they saw the owner of the fruit farm arrive and enter, so they stood and went over themselves.

They found the three of them in the office and the well-dressed man turned out to be a lawyer brought in to legalise the transaction. When it came to putting the name of the new owners on the document and Jim told the lawyer the name of the Company it caused some raised eyebrows with Schoonheid, as he had until then no idea that they were working as a Company. And it came as a further surprise to him when he found out it was an English company. He refrained from commenting on it until after all the business had been dealt with and they were the owners of the property. Fred the ex-owner turned to them when he had the cheque in his hands and said. "Well I wish you the best of luck out there, it's got a lot of potential, and I just didn't work it properly. Maybe you'll do better than me, anyway good luck."

He shook hands all round and headed out of the office in the direction of the nearest drink. The lawyer made his excuses, wished them luck, and said he would be in touch to finalise the legalities as soon as possible and then followed him. Schoonheid grinned and said. "Typical of a lawyer, he's trying to get his hands on that money before it all goes down the drain. That old guys not going to stop buying drink until it's all gone."

"Maybe he'll do some good if he can stop him wasting it all on drink." Pat had got back on her hobbyhorse about drink again, and before she could start again Jim decided to get them out of the office. As they left Schoonheid said. "Don't forget to come and see me about supplies, I can do you a good deal you know."

Jim went out of the office without answering and Ray followed him out into the street with Pat and Julia. Schoonheid followed them as they went off down the street and watched as they went back to the hotel. Then he turned and went over to the pub the lawyer had disappeared into.

Ray turned to Jim and said. "Persistent bastard that Schoonheid isn't he?"

"He gets right up my nose, if you want to know." Jim answered. "The problem with it though is we need him, and I can only stay away from him and let Leah deal with it. If I do it myself I'll probably end up decking him."

Ray roared with laughter. "Give the guy a break; he's only trying to make a bob or two."

"That's not what worries me, I get the strong feeling that he'll try and get his profit any way he can, and he's not too fussy about the legality of what he does, or for that matter the methods he uses. I just get this feeling that says stay away from him."

"You can't worry too much about the Aussie way of doing business mate." Ray said. "We've all got a touch of larceny in us, it's not done in a malicious way, and it's mostly to see what we can get away with. There ain't any harm in it."

Jim nodded; he had seen plenty of examples of this peculiarly Australian way of thinking. Pat and Julia suddenly veered off and started walking away from them and Jim looked back questioningly. Pat smiled and pointed to a small supermarket over the road and mouthed. "See you later."

Ray looked over in mock alarm. "I hope they haven't got any money on them." He joked. "If they're anything like Leah they'll never know when to stop."

"Research mate." Jim answered. "Just research."

By this time they had arrived back at the hotel and settling down for a beer they saw the rest of the company come in to see how they were doing. Colette and Dick came in with Andrew, and Victoria came in with Leah. Knowing what he knew about Andrew's life Jim wondered what they would find to talk about but kept his council. The Prof walked in just as they were starting and sat down heavily to one side. When they had settled themselves around a table in the corner Jim looked questioningly at Dick who smiled and produced a working sketch of the plan. He gave it to Jim and said. "I've based it on the ideas that Victoria gave to me and used those as a basis for estimating how big we need to build it.

Jim took the drawings and asked. "When can we have definite plans?"

"About two weeks, I think."

"OK, I'll work something out about materials based on these; we can still make a start on getting some of them ordered." Jim looked at Leah. "This is your chance to start using the skills that you've told us about. You'll have to go and see that Schoonheid bloke and get him to give you some idea when he can start delivery of materials to the site. Set up an account with him and stress we want priority deliveries, and we don't want to be robbed either." He looked around. "This is to let all of you know; from now on we're researching farming methods to enable the world to produce more food. We're privately funded through the company, that's all they need to know. Is that OK with everyone?"

He laid the papers down on the table "I think it'll be a good idea if anyone who hasn't seen the place to have a trip out there tomorrow, we'll take some stakes and measures and place them so we can see where we'll put the main buildings, we can also assess whether we can convert the fruit trees back to full production again."

Pat and Julia came in as they were finishing and told them that the market they had visited had promised to deliver as much food as they needed as long as they ordered two days in advance, although they couldn't guarantee to deliver in 'the wet'. Ray looked at all the preparations and advised Jim to think seriously about hiring a coach to make the trip out to the farm, as the Ute would be seriously overcrowded. Jim thought that was a good idea and promised to go and consult the local travel agent. Ray also said that as he had seen the farm he was going to shoot off on a shopping trip to try and sort out some of the equipment they needed. The Prof and Victoria had been having a private conversation and offered to go out with them in the Ute to take as much supplies as they could, and as they had a few days of their holiday left, they would stay there and start the task of preparing to take delivery of any items that could be sent quickly.

Leah stood up and asked Jim. "When are you setting off

for the farm? I want to go and see that Schoonheid guy and get something sorted out."

Jim looked at the list of items he had roughed out and tore it off the pad and gave it to her. "I think I'll arrange to hire a coach for first thing tomorrow if we can get enough supplies to last us for a few days, I don't think water's going to be too much of a problem but we're going to need a lot of other things like a generator at first. We might be able to take some camping equipment with us till we get some static caravans lined up."

Ray jumped to his feet. "That comes under my job description mate." He said. "I'm going now to get a start." He looked at Leah. "I'm going to take our FWD for now, and I'll meet you out there as soon as I can, OK?"

"Hold on there just a minute." Leah jumped to her feet. "What the hell do you think I'm going to be driving while you're swanning around the countryside in *our* FWD? I helped to pay for that and I want to have something to run around in myself."

Ray grinned at her, "I've already thought about that Luvvie, I've had some transport delivered for you, and the keys are in reception. Don't try and take it out to the farm though, it's not suitable for running around in the outback. Find somewhere to park around here so you can use it when you come in for buying supplies." He looked round at them all and said. "Well I'm off, see you all later when I get back. I'll go directly to the farm unless I hear anything to the contrary while I'm away."

Having said that he leaned over Leah and kissed her on the cheek. "See you soon darling."

As he disappeared through the door; Leah looked after him with a worried frown on her face. "Something's not quite right around here, he's acting just a bit too shifty for my liking, I'm going to have a look at that car he's left me."

She walked out of the door with Pat and Julia in tow, who were trying to get her to take them to the supermarket to get some supplies in for the trip out to the farm. Jim said to Dick. "I didn't consider it too much before but we'll have to sort out some form of extra transport for all of us to use for a while, I don't mean a car for everyone but we'll need some extra ones anyway."

Dick nodded. "It needn't be that many, you've got one and Rays OK, I don't know what Leah's got but as Ray said she shouldn't take it far it can't be much, I think about one car to every two people ought to be right. So you'd need to have three more at the moment. Also, I don't think anybody should travel that road to the farm unless they have someone with them. It goes through some pretty rough country."

"Yeah I think you're about right there." Jim answered. He looked around the rest of the team trying to assess who to give the job to, and his eyes came to rest on Andrew, he called him over and said. "I've got a job for you." Andrew groaned and said. "Why do I think I'm not going to like this?"

"I think you're going to eat those words in a minute sonny boy." Jim joked. "Now I want you to go outside and take a look at the "Ute" that Ray and Dick bought for us and I want you then to go and buy three more just like it, and when you buy them I want you to get enough spares for them to last some time, and that includes tyres because the roads out there can be pretty nasty on them. I also want you to fit them up with jerry cans for water and fuel. If you can, buy good second hand ones, but if you can't, get new, but screw them down on price. We want them delivered out to the farm and make it clear that if our mechanic isn't satisfied they all go back at their expense."

Andrew looked at Jim in puzzlement. "Who's the mechanic?"

Jim stared back at him straight faced. "That's not important, what is important is they think we've got one. Anyway, if those vehicles reach the farm that'll be a good test of their roadworthiness won't it? When you've got those vehicles on order I want you to get off and see your friend and start negotiations for delivery of all those 'Meals ready to eat' you've been on about. And don't forget we're only paying on delivery not on some promise of they'll be alright mate, do I make myself clear?"

Andrew clicked his heels. "Crystal, dad crystal. Don't worry; I won't let you down. Where do you think I should buy the Ute's?"

"I'd have thought that was obvious. "Jim answered. "There must be a dealer here in Katherine and if you can't get any satisfaction go to Darwin that's the nearest big town. Or go and ask out at the reception where you can find a dealer. There's a lot of Ute's out there, being driven around and they're buying them from somewhere, so go and find something for us to drive."

Andrews's eyes had started to glaze over after the first few words and he showed every sign of impatience with his father, finally he couldn't stop himself. "I only thought you might have had an idea of where you want to buy them. I didn't need chapter and verse about choosing a car salesman from you."

This had every sign of starting to upset Jim but Colette suddenly stood up and pushed in between them. "Why don't you take me with you?" she asked her brother. "The idea of screwing a salesman down appeals to me." She turned and called little Emma over to her and looked at Andrew. He seemed distinctly displeased at having her along, but he knew better than to try and go against her so he shrugged his shoulders and went off with her.

Jim looked round and found the room was quite empty now with only the Prof and Dick left with some children who showed every sign of being bored but Jim felt he had no time to entertain them, so he asked Dick if he would take them out for a while. Dick accepted with bad grace as he said. "I was hoping to get on with drawing some plans up for the farm this afternoon?"

"Yeah, but they can be drawn up later can't they?" Jim answered. "I want to get on the phone and order some things for delivery to the farm. And I need the Prof here to help me get them organised because we're going out there tomorrow morning and until we get ourselves organised we've got no communications out there, and mobile phones although they're useful only work when you can charge the batteries, and you know we haven't even got a generator yet. So please look after the kids for a while and you can start your drawing tomorrow or the next day"

Dick groaned but went out after getting the children together, the only one who looked anything like happy about this arrangement was Jeannie who still carried a torch for him. Jim looked at Prof and said. "We've got to do quite a lot this afternoon and I want to go up to the room and get on the phone to some suppliers, can you sort out a phone book for us so we can make some calls. We'll have to look into making E-mail letters from here as well because if we call England it's the middle of the night there."

There was a small cough from behind them and Jim looked around to see Victoria standing there. "Have I gone invisible? Or don't you have anything for me to do?"

Jim looked at his feet in embarrassment; he had forgotten her in the general scheme of things but wouldn't admit it to her. "I'm sorry Victoria, but I just haven't got a job for you right now, but I can tell you that in the long run your work is crucial to our survival. So why don't you get your writing paper out and compile a list of all the plants you think we're going to need. And while you're doing that it might be an idea to get in touch with your botanist and ask him to come down here for an interview?"

She looked at Jim puzzled. "I already told you I've done a lot of work on the design of the place and that included me estimating what sort of plants go in there. I can ring the botanist guy and ask him about the possibility of coming here for an interview but do you want to see him here or at the farm."

"I'd rather see him at the farm so he can have a look over the plans but will he be able to find the place? No." He held his hand up. "I've got a better idea, why don't one of us pick him up here and take him out to the farm then we can at least be sure he'll get there, or we could even arrange a lift on one of the delivery lorries that that guy Schoonheid is supposed to send. And to answer you about plants Victoria I'd like to ask you about the possibility of incorporating some of the medicinal herbs into a special section because we might need something like that later."

Victoria looked at Jim with a frown. "I thought Colette was going to bring as much medicine as she could?"

"That's true." Jim replied. But what's going to happen in a few years time when those run out, we'll have to make our own then won't we? And it would be nice to have the plants we need ready to hand, so we can try."

She scratched her head while she thought this over and then said. "I don't know the first thing about herbal remedies, I'll have to go down the library and see if I can find some books about the subject."

Jim smiled. "I've heard they've got quite a nice library here in Katherine, and the woman who runs it is quite a fund of information, so I'm sure she'll help you."

"You sound as if you've been there before Jim, but I know you haven't had the time to go, so how do you know that?"

Jim's smile got even broader. "Wonders of the internet dear, I was in contact with her long before I came to Australia."

It was Victoria's turn to smile. "So you've been swotting up on the quiet then, and all the time we thought you were just a common old builder with no interest in the modern way of life."

"Go on get off up the library and have a look for those books." Jim pushed her on the shoulder in the direction of the door.

She went off and called over her shoulder. "It won't matter too much because if that botanist comes he'll have all that sort of knowledge anyway. But it'll be a good idea to have some books with us so we can look things up and maybe have someone specialise in it."

Jim looked at Prof; "You know that isn't such a bad idea, to have someone specialise in making remedies out of herbs because it's going to be really important at a later date. Right shall we get on with contacting some suppliers?"

They went off to start composing E-mails to different people and Leah marched into the room with Pat and Julia just after they left. Her face was set in a display of temper and she flung herself into a chair and called over to the barman and shouted. "Get me a nice big gin and tonic over here sharpish young man and give these two ladies what they want."

She fumed to them. "That bloody husband of mine's going to feel the edge of my tongue when I see him next, fancy leaving me a pile of rubbish like that car out there. I haven't driven anything that awful since I was a student."

Pat smiled at Julia, and then said to Leah. "It wasn't that bad really Leah, at least it didn't break down and it went where you pointed."

"Yeah, I suppose you're right, it just galls me to think he swans off with that lovely big 4WD and leaves me here with a pile of rubbish that hasn't even got air conditioning. And was it hot this afternoon or not, or was I just dreaming about sweating it out in the nearest thing to a tin can I've been in for a long time?"

The barman appeared at her elbow with a tray of drinks and placed them on the table, and then silently left, Leah watched him go with one eye on his rear then picked up her glass and took a large swig and smacked her lips. "I needed that." she said with relish.

Later that afternoon they all met on the terrace in the cool, although the term was relative as if it had been in England it would have been considered a heat wave. All of them had something to report and it seemed everybody had managed to arrange to get his or her share done. Jim had arranged to get the windmill delivered later and had also got a supplier of construction equipment to hire some caravans to them, they weren't the most luxurious but as the man had pointed out to them, he would at least take them back when they were finished with them. Ray had rung to say some heavy equipment would be delivered in a few days and he had feelers out for a plane and he had bought a hovercraft. Leah had got a promise out of Schoonheid to deliver some of the essentials of a building site to them such as water pipe and electricity cables, he was also going to supply them with all the small tools such as shovels and trowels and levels, because Jim had had to leave all those essentials in England when he left. In the next few days he was going to deliver cement and ballast in quite large quantities. Andrew and Colette had screwed a supplier of Ute's down to a contract and they were due for delivery the following week. Pat and Julia had some supplies coming and also had managed to get hold of some large freezers.

Andrew was due to disappear the following day to see his supplier of MRE, so it was with a mood of optimism that they all gathered together for the drinks. Jim knew that however well they planned, something had to go wrong; but with the best will in the world he couldn't foresee everything so had decided to take life as it came. Although they had had a lot of money to start, it went out fast enough when they started to sign cheques and Ray had taken to joking that he would suffer from writer's cramp before they had everything they needed.

Victoria had arranged that her friend the botanist was going to visit them in a few days and she was coming in with Andrew to bring him to the farm. Ray and Jim had interviewed a man to help with all the electrical cables they were using, with a view to asking him if he wanted to join later. The guy had told them he was a single man and he lived with a partner and of all the people Jim had met so far; this man had been the only one he didn't trust. He couldn't put his finger on it but something just didn't gel right with Jim.

They had put out feelers for men to help with the building of the structure and several men had expressed an interest in working for a few months. Jim had had to abandon his idea of bringing in labour from any distance away as most men were reluctant to travel to work when they had sufficient closer to home. He had also been very surprised when the demands for the working conditions had been laid out for him and it came as a cultural shock to him to find out what the labour unions had insisted was minimum conditions for living and working on a site. He had had to comply, but thought privately that if England had these rules there, the men would soon find a way to exploit them. As these men were local they all knew where the farm was located and had opted to travel out under their own steam so they had transport to go home when they needed to.

Pat and Julia had decided between them that they would do all the cooking and cleaning between them to save the men from having to stop work to do it themselves. The Prof reluctantly had to go back to his job the following day so wouldn't be able to accompany them down to the farm as he had hoped. At present it was necessary for him to do this and Colette and Victoria also had to work, as they had to establish a presence in Australia that was legal.

Jim still felt unsure about his position in the country but had hopes that sometimes the authorities declared a general amnesty for all illegal entrants into the land and naturalised all who came forward to be considered. Still, that was all in the future and now called for silence for a moment, they had several other families to watch them but he ignored that and said. "I've just got a couple of things to say and then we can get on with our business, first of all, we'll be going out to the farm tomorrow and so you'll have your first sight of it then, but now I want you to raise your glasses and join me in a toast to the start of a wonderful enterprise and here's to good luck and if that doesn't help us, work harder."

He drained his glass to the cheers and jeers of them all and then sat down to enjoy the rest of the last day before the work commenced

Chapter Twelve

Jim looked around in satisfaction; they were three months into the project and he considered they had done wonders in that time. They had hired four men to help them and with everyone mucking in where they were able, the work had gone much easier than they would have imagined. The static caravans had been delivered within two days of their arrival on the farm and although they were of a basic design Pat and Julia had transformed them into habitable units. They had had to put up with the constant drone of a generator for several weeks until the windmill had arrived but they took the time available to lay a foundation for it and when it arrived, it had been accompanied by a construction crew who had assembled it in a matter of days. It stood now on top of the hill turning constantly in the breeze and worked as well as the salesman had promised Jim all that time ago. The electrician Ray had hired had run cables down to all the caravans and wired up a pump to the well so a constant stream of water was pumped up to the enormous tank they had constructed on the top of the slope behind the buildings.

The heavy earthmoving machinery had arrived at the same time as the caravans and had proved invaluable apart from the fact that Andrew had had to learn to drive it and took a day to do it, but he had in the end mastered the controls and now many jobs requiring a hydraulic shovel could be carried out easily. They had also managed to have the hovercraft delivered which Jim wanted to store as he felt that it would be a good form of transport in the 'Wet'.

Dick's plans had proved simplicity itself and the workers they had hired were going on apace with the construction of the side walls; they had hired shuttering and would start to pour concrete to form the floor above within a day or so. Jim would have laughed out loud when the construction workers arrived except it would have annoyed Pat too much. They had evidently pooled their resources together to save money and came in what was to Jim's eyes the biggest Ute he had ever seen. Although they had brought sufficient tools for their work they only took a small amount of the available space, the rest of the Ute had been filled with case after case of what a certain Australian would have referred to as the, 'Amber Nectar'. They were stubbies of beer but of a size he had never seen before, he wasn't sure how much each one held but they disappeared so rapidly Jim was hard put to keep an eye on them. To a man they had beer bellies and seemed to drink the stuff non-stop.

If he had noticed any mans work suffer because of drunkenness he would have sacked him on the spot, but they all worked as hard as they were expected to without complaint and Jim supposed the liquid intake was coming out in the sweat each of them was constantly bathed in. Their fridge in the caravan had the shelves groaning with bottles and they took them out in rotation to ensure the beer was as cold as possible.

Pat looked on all this activity with tight lips but said not one word about their habits. She merely said to them on the first day. "You men can drink as much as you want for all I care, but I will not have your empties spread all over the place, you pick them up and take them away with you when you go. And you will under no circumstances give beer to any of the children around here."

This they had willingly agreed to and the matter of the children had been solved as the children for the most part were staying in Darwin with Prof. Colette had moved in with him as well during the week and Ray who had by now bought the plane which was a six seater, and had the runway of shale laid out, went up every weekend to bring them all home.

Leah had taken over the small office Jim had created and her organisational abilities had come to the fore. She had seemingly tamed Schoonheid and he had kept them supplied with all the materials they needed, he still asked a lot of questions about the project but until now she had managed to field them. He had turned up one day with a delivery lorry, but Jim had totally ignored his presence and left it to Leah to deal with him. He had certainly had a good look round and made several remarks about how it didn't add up to build something this big to grow crops when the weather around here was so good for growing outside. She had explained they were for research but it was plain he didn't believe her, and he went off shaking his head and muttering to himself about the stupidity of some people.

The botanist that Victoria had recommended had turned up and had a good look round just after they had started and had wavered about to start with, as Jim had been unsure whether to tell him the whole story at first, but they had had a long chat and although he didn't really agree that the volcanic explosion would happen he had decided to come out and work alongside Victoria for several years to gain experience in the ideas they were carrying out. He said. "I'll give you five years so I can carry out my research into indoor farming but I want your assurance that if I come in now, I want my money back if I decide to go." Jim had been forced to accept his terms and the man was coming out in three weeks when the first storey was built. He would bring his family but as far as Jim could ascertain he hadn't put all his money in or sold his nursery where he had quite a good income. Jim had wondered whether he should crack a whip and force him to choose but in this instance he had decided the man would be too valuable with all his knowledge so let the matter lie for now. He had at least made a considerable contribution and as Ray had done he had kept some back so Jim had put himself into a cleft stick. They had issued shares to him on the basis of his contribution and that as far as Jim was concerned, was where the matter had to end for the moment.

Jim smiled to himself and said to Ray and Dick who were standing with Andrew to one side looking over the construction site plans. "You're going to have to tell me what day it is, out here I loose track of time." They looked up in surprise. "It's Wednesday," replied Ray. "dead simple when you think of it, follows Tuesday, every week on the dot."

"Very funny, I need your humour round here to keep me from thinking I've gone off my head. So you go to town tomorrow to collect everybody?" It was a regular flight for Ray and one he looked forward to making, as it got him away from the drudgery of construction work which he admitted he didn't enjoy at all. Andrew perked up at this, as it was his turn to go with Ray and learn some flying. Jim suspected they took it in turns to have a bit of a binge but thought what the hell he could do with one himself. He had had a plan lurking around in the back of his head for some time now and decided it was time to put it into operation. He said to Ray. "I'm going to be coming with you tomorrow, I've got some things I want to buy in Darwin that I can't order over the phone."

Ray and Andrew looked in consternation at each other. "Don't worry." Jim went on. "I'm not going to get in your way, all you do is drop me off and I'll see you when you come back with Prof and Colette."

It was obvious Andrew was a little put out about this and he said. "Why don't you let us buy what you want and save yourself a trip?"

"Because I want a few hours off to myself and maybe have a few beers like you." Jim told them. "Lets get back to work, I want to see some progress today, and if we stand around those guys over there stand around as well." he nodded in the direction of the construction workers who were standing by a cement mixer. He walked over to them and shouted. "Come on you lazy bastards, don't let that spinning drum on the mixer hypnotise you, we've got some work to do today. I want to be ready to pour concrete next week."

The self appointed spokesman for the group grinned at Jim. "No worries boss man; we know what we've got to do. It'll be all right."

Jim looked down at his spreading waistline and leaning forward patted it. "That beer belly is growing by the day mate, if you stay out here much longer working for us you're going to have a hard job explaining it to your wife."

"She'll be all right mate, when that cash gets back home and she's got something to go down the shop with, she doesn't much care whether I'm out here or not."

This had been a running theme of conversation with him, as he seemed to be more interested in work and beer than getting home. They all worked for ten days straight through so as to have four days off and have a long weekend. They behaved like men who were glad of the chance to get out of the house for a few days and drink a bit while they worked. Pat came to the door of one of the caravans and shouted across. "Are you men going to get some work done today, so I can get on with cleaning up around here?"

She had taken on the task of making sure the caravans were clean and went in with Julia while everyone was at work. She had said to Jim. "We might be out in the wilderness but that's no reason to suppose we have to live like animals, it prevents infection as well. If you left it to that lazy lot over there the place would look like a tip."

Slowly the men drifted off to begin the days work, the sun had started it's climb to the heavens and the temperature was rising by the minute, Jim would have preferred the continental way of working where they would start at first light and have a siesta at midday then work later in the night, but he had been voted down on that one. As the men drifted off to work a cloud of dust from the road attracted his eye, and it seemed the eyes of everyone in the camp. A lorry came grinding up the road towards them and Jim could see three men sitting in the front.

He could recognise instantly the lean tall shape of Blackie and his adversary Schoonheid who was grinning evilly. The man sitting alongside him proved difficult to place until the lorry rolled to a stop and the door opened to reveal Diman. The last time Jim had spotted him had been on the wrong end of a rocket launcher and the memory had never left him. He involuntarily reached for a gun he knew wasn't there and the other man saw the movement and smiled at Jim in triumph. "So, we meet again at last." He said. He glanced down at the gun in his hand and cocked it. "The circumstances are a little more in my favour now though aren't they?"

For a moment Jim was too disturbed to answer, he had thought that he would never set eyes on this man again and now he had appeared like a spectre from hell. "Well you're certainly one for surprises, I must say that." He replied. "I thought you died on that boat."

"It will take a better man than you to do that." Diman answered. "But I might be able to help you on the way."

He raised the gun until the barrel formed a round black hole facing Jim's face, his finger tightened slightly on the trigger and

Jim stared at him paralysed. Suddenly Diman stiffened and a voice said from behind him. "If you want to start looking through that hole in the back of your head just carry on pulling that trigger, it'll be your last act in this life."

Diman slowly started to lower the gun and when it was safely pointed at the floor a hand came out and touched it. "Drop it." a voice commanded. He clicked the safety and dropped the gun to the floor and the owner of the voice came round the side of the truck. It belonged to Jacko and his face beamed as he looked at them.

"He don't seem to like you very much does he boss." He joked.

Jim felt the anger burning through him and stepping forward until he could reach Diman he slammed his fist into the man's face, the pain shot through his hand and at first he thought he had broken it. Diman stumbled back with his hand over his nose, which had started to steam blood and spat one of his teeth on to the dust of the floor. He lay sprawled for a while with the blood dripping from his face and Jim heard a voice say. "Calm down Jim, you two have got to do some business here today." He looked round and saw Blackie standing next to him. Schoonheid came round, a smarmy grin on his face, and said. "When you start on someone you really mean it don't you?"

Turning to Blackie Jim asked. "How does this bloke get in on the act around here?"

Schoonheid answered for Blackie. "There isn't much that goes through this part of the country without my knowledge mate, and if it wasn't for me this 'merchandise' wouldn't arrive here now."

Jim felt helpless at the indignity of Schoonheid even knowing what the 'merchandise' was but realised that the die had been cast and now the only way forward would be through him. He looked around and found just about everybody in the camp was staring at them and hanging on to every word and action as it unfolded. He waved his arms and shouted. "You lot get back to work." then he turned to Ray and Dick standing next to Andrew, you three hold fast here, I want your help."

Bending down Blackie hauled Diman to his feet and gave

him a piece of rag that had seen better days to wipe his face, Diman glared at Jim and muttered. "Our business isn't over yet, I'll make you pay for that."

Jim ignored him and went over to Jacko, he put his hand on the man's shoulder and said. "I want to thank you for what you did there, I thought that was going to be the last of me."

"T'ain't nothing." The little aborigine replied. If you want the truth of it, I don't think he was going to pull the trigger at all. He had to know we'd kill him if he did. I reckon he was just trying to scare you so you'd lose face."

Jim laughed mirthlessly. "If that's true he succeeded, I'll have to start wearing brown corduroy trousers if this goes on."

The pair of them started laughing together and after a moment of staring at each other everybody else joined in. Diman just stood still while this was going on. Blackie waited until the laughter died down and then said. "We ought to get on with business before long, and we've got a long way to go when we've finished up here."

Jim nodded and looking around he counted how many people were involved in the transaction and finally said. "I want Blackie, Schoonheid, Ray and me to have a talk then we'll decide what we're going to do."

Schoonheid leaned forward and said. "You can't leave him out." He indicated Diman. "He brought the 'merchandise' here and he's got to be dealt with and paid."

Jim reluctantly conceded he had a point and agreed that Diman should join them in the caravan. Pat had only just finished cleaning it and glared at them when they entered but wisely decided to say no more and went outside after telling Jim she could be found in one of the other caravans. As they sat at the table Schoonheid made sure he sat next to Jim at the head of the table. Jim felt uncomfortable with this arrangement but helpless to change it without causing any more trouble. Diman went over to the sink in the corner and wet the rag to wipe his face and then sat at the other end where he continued to glare at Jim.

Ray went over to the fridge in the corner and broke out some bottles of beer and handed them round, they all swigged them and Jim felt a little guilty at drinking so early in the morning but the others paid no heed and drunk heartily. That over and no more formalities to be completed Ray looked around and asked. "Well what have you brought us then?" Diman had finished cleaning himself and looked at him. "I've brought you everything you asked for and ordered, all the arms are here but before we go on I want payment of the supplementary charges.. And we've brought no ammunition with us so if you want the delivery in full you can pay me now and the rest of the ammunition will be delivered in two days. Here's the bill for the whole shipment."

Ray leaned forward and picked up the bill from the table, and then he looked at Diman with the anger showing clearly in his eyes. "You cheating bastard." He shouted. "This is fifty per cent more than we agreed."

Diman shrugged his shoulders, and spread his hands. "Our costs have gone up since we agreed the price, we have to pay a lot of people to guarantee shipment." He looked meaningly at Schoonheid, who raised his eyebrows and said. "Everybody's got costs, I have to pay people off as well."

Ray glowered at them and Jim reached over and gently took the offending bill out of his hands. Looking at it he could see the price had been altered slightly from the original and another entered over the top. He cleared his throat and said to Diman. "I think we'll have to phone your boss and verify what the true cost is for these items."

Diman shrugged; his demeanour one of a man who couldn't care less. Jim asked Ray. "Have you still got that number Sulim gave you when we bought the merchandise on that freighter?" Ray grinned and said. "Sure, he said it was his private number and to ring him any time if we had any queries."

He took a cell phone from the shelf and started to search in the memory for the number, Diman blanched a little and held his hand up to stop him. "Can you let me have a moment please? I might have made a mistake with copying out the bill." He practically snatched the bill from Jim and hurried from the caravan with Schoonheid in pursuit. They could be seen arguing furiously outside the window and Jim turned to Ray and said. "Who were you ringing then?"

Ray almost laughed out loud and said. "My stockbroker, I didn't know any one else to ring."

"He'd have got a shock if you started to talk about delivering guns to us wouldn't he? Jim said. "Do you think he'll catch on?" he gestured in the direction of Diman.

"Nah, the only way he can is if he rings his boss himself, and if he does it gives the game away doesn't it? How did you catch on so quick to what he was doing?"

"Simple really." Jim answered. "First it was what I would have expected from him and second if you remember, Sulim told us his word was his bond, so if he'd gone back on it, we wouldn't have trusted him any more would we?"

The two men re-entered the caravan and Diman spoke for both of them. "There was a slight mistake on the bill, but we have had extra expenses on the delivery so we want a little more to cover those, would a figure of ten per cent more be acceptable?"

Ray and Jim agreed so Jim said. "We agree to the terms but you get the money when we have the ammunition and not before."

He could see that Diman had it in mind to argue so he went on, "if you want a compromise, I want to go into Darwin to see somebody so I'll meet you there and pay you when I know we've got all our shipment." He looked at Blackie, who had been watching the negotiations with some amusement. "Will you go to wherever the shipment comes ashore and bring it back here?"

Blackie looked at him and answered. "You pay me my going rate and I'll ship whatever you like wherever you want."

Business concluded, they all trooped out into the sunshine and Schoonheid made sure he could speak to Jim. "This business gets more and more curious, if you don't mind me saying. First of all I couldn't figure what you're doing building this bloody great warehouse out here, and now you're buying arms. What the hell are you up to?"

"It's none of your business is it?" Jim answered. "And I do mind you saying. Why don't you keep your nose out of my affairs? What we're doing isn't going to hurt any one here in Australia, so keep out of it and take your profit. Do I make myself clear?"

Schoonheid walked away saying. "OK, keep your hair on, I was only asking out of friendly curiosity."

Jim knew it was more than that as Schoonheid was one of life's chancers and wouldn't rest until he could figure out a way to turn a profit out of the situation. He worried a little whether Blackie would enlighten him about their plans but from the viewpoint of a third party he thought that on the balance of probabilities, Blackie had no more love for Schoonheid than himself. 'Nothing more to say' he thought to himself. 'Just have to let the situation go on and see what happens.'

They all went to the lorry and with everybody helping it was soon unloaded. They placed it at the back of Jim's caravan under some tarpaulin for the time being as they had no other shelter possible for it. He made arrangements to meet Diman in Darwin the following day and then the lorry trundled off down the dusty road back to civilisation. Breathing a sigh of relief they all went back to the caravan to enjoy a drink to celebrate.

Ray looked at Jim as they sat for a while, and said. "You're going to have to be a bit more cautious in your dealings with that Schoonheid guy you know, he's got something on us now and I think he'll use the information without a second thought. The only thing we've got going for us is he doesn't know what were doing, so he doesn't know how to turn it to a profit."

Jim agreed with him but commented. "I thought maybe if we had a word in his ear about what happens to guys who try to go against us and put the thought in his head that it might be damaging to his health if word gets out. He knows what we've got here now doesn't he? Maybe he might believe we won't be afraid to use them."

Ray shook his head. "I think he'll use the police or someone to get at us, he isn't the sort of guy to try it on his own."

Andrew had been listening to this and sat up in his seat. "Maybe he needs to think that whichever one of us is free he'll get it in the neck if he's responsible for anything."

"What do you propose?" asked Jim.

"Maybe something on the lines of what Dick did to that boat." Andrew answered. Dick looked up from his position further along the seat. "I'd enjoy that, maybe I could explode his car just before he gets in it, that'd put the shits up him."

"Yeah, and send him running for the nearest copper." Jim answered. "We've got to be a lot more subtle than that, let me have a think on it and see what I can come up with. Now don't you think we've wasted enough time for now? We'll have to get those arms under better cover than that as soon as possible. If any coppers happen out this way because someone's tipped them off our feet won't touch on the way to a cell."

They went out and walked over to start work on the building and the contractors' spokesman grinned at Jim and asked. "What was all that about Jim? That feller pointed a gun at your head."

"Don't take any notice; it was more a bit of fun than anything."

"Didn't look like fun from here mate, and you didn't look like you enjoyed it one little bit. Especially when you flattened him with that crack in the mouth."

Jim glared at him and said. "He got that for asking too many questions, now do you want to go on asking bloody inane questions as well?"

The man backed off immediately. "Hey, what you do around here is your business, I don't want to interfere in that, I was just curious that's all."

He walked off in the direction of the others and picked up his tools to start work again. Jim glanced round but no one wanted to meet his eye and they started working again. Jim picked up his own tools and looking at Ray and the others he said. "We'll get that merchandise under cover when we've got the weekend to do it; no one can tip the police off before then anyway." He looked at Ray. "I want to set up some CCTV cameras around the perimeter, maybe four miles out and someone to watch them all the time, I don't want any nasty surprises from now on."

The next day before the contractors left for the weekend Pat made sure they went round and loaded every bottle on to the Ute, with the admonition. "You aren't leaving any of those around here." then after they left at midday they saw them off down the road and waited until they had the whole place to themselves. When he was sure they had gone Jim turned to the others. "I know it's going to make us late going to pick up the Prof and Colette but I want to get all those guns hidden from any prying eyes that happen to come here."

They all groaned but Jim insisted and they loaded the arms on to one of the 4WD Ute's. It was hard work but finally it was full. Jim loaded some ropes and timber on the top of it and then they drove it to the top of the escarpment opposite the front of the site. When they arrived there they unloaded everything and Jim tied a rope to the Ute and threw the end over the edge, the others, Ray, Andrew and Dick, looked at him in disbelief. It was a sheer drop for three hundred metres and the rope wasn't long enough to reach the bottom. "What do you think you're up to for Christ's sake?" Ray gasped.

Jim grinned at him. "Follow me down, and you'll see." He tied a safety line round his waist and swung himself over the edge and slithered slowly down the rope, with his legs wrapped round it tightly. He could do a lot of things but heights bothered him, so he clung to the rope much tighter than necessary. He slid down until he found what he was looking for, a small cave about forty metres down from the top, there were scrubby bushes growing round the mouth and it was almost impossible to find. Jim had spotted it a few weeks before when he had been down to explore the valley. He had had his binoculars with him and had found it by painstakingly examining the cliff face minutely. This was the first time he had approached it though, and now when he entered he found it was going to be perfect for his purposes, it was little more that a crack in the surface but it ran back about ten metres to a solid wall at the back. There were a few bones and nests scattered about as though animals and birds of prey had used it in the past but nothing else.

He heard a scrabbling sound at the entrance and Ray came into the cave on hands and knees. He raised himself as much as possible as the inside of the cave gave no headroom to either of them and stooping together they examined the interior. "Well what do you think?" Jim asked.

Ray nodded and succeeded in banging his head on the ceiling. "I wondered where you planned on hiding this lot until we've completed building. It's going to be a sod to get them all down here though isn't it?"

"I don't think so." Jim gestured upwards. "With what we've got up there to work with, a small scaffold held back with a couple of braces and a pulley wheel we can have it down in here in a couple of hours. They went back to the surface and set to with the others to construct the scaffolding. When it was completed Jim went down with Ray and they unloaded the cases as the others sent them down. When they were all stacked in the cave they threw a plastic cover over them and tied it down to keep animals out, then they went outside and hanging on the ropes they brushed the entrance until it was practically indistinguishable from the surrounding cliff. They went to the top again and dismantled the scaffold, and then when the Ute had been driven off down to the bottom of the hill they followed behind brushing the ground with long branches to obliterate all the tracks. As Jim had forecast it had been hard work but only took two hours.

They reached the bottom and looking back Jim nodded in satisfaction, from here it seemed as if nothing had ever been on the side of the hill. When Jim saw Pat she told him that she had prepared some food and had rung Colette to tell her they were going to be late picking her up. Jim told her he was going in with Ray and Andrew but that he intended to stop over and come back on Sunday when Ray came back. He made the excuse that he had to meet Diman and pay him off but he meant to do some private shopping for himself.

They ate their meal and then Jim, Ray, and Andrew went out to the plane to set off and pick up Colette and the Prof. Pat stood and watched Jim ready himself and said. "None of that getting drunk and making a fool of yourself, you know what we've heard they're like in Darwin."

"No chance of that." Jim said grimly. "Not with the business I've got to do there. If that Diman thinks I'm weak in any way, he'll climb all over me."

"Well Blackie should be there, he'll probably make sure you're OK, I think he likes you"

Jim wondered how much a man had to like you before it

interfered with the making of money, but let it pass, as he didn't want to alarm her. He knew that Diman had no love for him but he had a boss as well and it wouldn't do for him to lose a valuable customer because he wanted revenge. He kissed her on the cheek and climbed in, Ray had a shopping list thrust in his hand by Leah and Andrew settled himself into the pilot's seat. Jim looked at him in surprise. "Are you flying this thing when we take off?"

Andrew looked over his shoulder at Jim, a smile on his face. "It's not hard to take off dad, it's the getting down that's hard."

Jim groaned. "I wish we'd bought some parachutes when we bought this plane."

"Wouldn't do any good, you'd probably kill yourself if you jumped out with one of those things on." Andrew joked.

"OK, you two." Ray interjected. "We aren't going to crash whatever you say. So let's get on with it shall we?"

Andrew turned back to the controls and the plane ran forward quickly gathering speed over the slightly bumpy ground and finally to Jim's relief the bumping stopped to be replaced with a much smoother passage through the air. Andrew circled round to make some height for himself and Jim was treated to an aerial view of the runway and the tiny figures standing on it watching them. He waved from the small window but got no response and decided they couldn't distinguish him from there. As the plane dipped its wings and flew over the hill he saw Pat raise her hand slightly and wave gently as they disappeared. The rest of the flight passed quickly for Jim and he spent the time watching the countryside disappear under their wing.

They arrived all too quickly at the small runway just outside the town and Ray took over for the final landing, much to Jim's relief. Like many fathers it took him a long time to accept that his son was competent at anything and he worried when he had to rely on him to do something. Colette, Victoria and the Prof were waiting for them when they arrived and they had the children with them, Colette hugged Jim and asked why he was there and Jim had to answer that he was off to do some shopping, so he wouldn't return with them. She groaned and said. "I told all the kids you'd be there and maybe take them out for a bit to see some of the country."

"Sorry to disappoint you darling." He replied. But I've got to go and get this shopping sooner than later, and I don't want to put it off too long in case they have to order the things in."

There was a collective groan from the children as he had established himself as someone who came up with exciting things to do and although they loved Pat she tended to concentrate on being a better person and not so much on fun. Colette's Emma had no such compunction, she loved hanging on to Pat's coattails and helping her in her own way to do all the chores around the camp.

He ignored Colette's questioning look when he didn't say what he wanted to buy and simply asked Prof to give him the keys to the Ute.

He started it up and drove off in the direction of Darwin waving to them as he went. As he passed them grouped around the plane, he shouted. "I'll be waiting here for you on Sunday when you come back." It was getting late when he finally drove into the town of Darwin and he looked for a place to sleep immediately. He found one but would have been hard put to say where it was as he was tired and only wanted a place to stay for the night. He asked for some food and ate it when it was delivered, then took a shower and collapsed into bed and within a few minutes he was asleep.

He woke the next morning feeling completely refreshed and as he ate a hearty breakfast he thought over the previous day and realised that it had been a long one from start to finish. Then he shrugged his shoulders and thought to himself that life has to go on. He asked one of the waiters where he could buy the sort of thing he was searching for and then, when he had this information he asked the man to get him a taxi. When it arrived he gave the taxi driver the address and they set off. He knew that Darwin had been completely rebuilt after a cyclone had struck but was hazy on the dates, but the town impressed him for it bore no sign of any damage, and he idly wondered who pays when a cyclone strikes. In America he thought, the people have to pay for their own rebuilding, but maybe they got some help here. He hoped they had, as it must be a catastrophe to anyone's finances to have to build a new house if the old one got demolished. They travelled through the town until they reached a side street with several bars and shops along it and the driver pointed up it and told him it was just a hundred meters along the road.

He found the shop and when he entered he saw straight away they had exactly what he wanted. He spoke to the assistant and examined the articles and when he discussed the relative merits of them he opted for the top of the range and looking at the assistant he told him he wanted four. The man raised his eyebrows and looked surprised as they cost a lot of money. He took his credit card from his pocket and paid the man who proceeded to pack them all into a case for him. He gave him the case as a gesture of 'goodwill', as he said, and Jim asked him to call a taxi. When it arrived he left the shop with the thing weighing his arm down, and dumped it on the seat. Back at the hotel he had a porter deliver the case to his room and went to eat something in the restaurant.

While it was coming he rang Blackie on his mobile and asked if he had the 'merchandise' as Diman had promised. "Sure have mate." Blackie answered. "Just tell me where to bring it and I'll see you there." As Jim had no real idea of where anything was in this town they decided to meet at the Hospital in three hours. When he had eaten Jim took a stroll back to his 4WD and as he went along the road he was surprised to note how cosmopolitan the town was. It seemed to him that many of the nations surrounding this corner of Australia had somehow managed to be represented here. He retrieved the Ute and when he was seated in the driving seat he looked in his wallet for a piece of paper that Ray had given him before he left.

This is going to be the trickiest part of the operation he thought to himself. He rang a number and when a man answered he said into the mouthpiece the words. "I'm a survivor." The reply when it came was a precise set of directions to reach a house in the suburbs. He found a map in the glove compartment and saw he didn't have far to go, so he drove off to search for it. When he arrived it was to find it was a secluded house set back a way from the road with shrubs growing in profusion around it. Picking up a small case he walked up the path and knocked on the door. A large unsmiling man answered, Jim noticed he had his hand behind his back and he stared at Jim as he waited for him to speak.

Jim said. "Ray told me to come here when I wanted something." The man said nothing and continued staring at him. Jim smiled apologetically and then said. "I need some spare parts for the Ute." The man broke into a large smile and said. "Come in mate, I might be able to help you there."

He took his hand from behind his back revealing that he had been armed and said. "Can't be too careful can we?" They stepped inside to a cool reception hall and Jim felt the cold draught of an air conditioner, the man walked away from Jim and said over his shoulder. "Wanna beer mate?" Jim knew enough about the hospitality in this country now to know that the man would be offended if he refused, so he nodded his thanks and the man reached into the fridge and pulled a can out and pushed it into his hand. He took one for himself and swigged a large part of it down; wiping his mouth with the back of his hand he gestured to a stool by a breakfast bar and said to Jim. "Take a load off mate and I'll go and get you those 'spare parts' you want." He exited the room saying. "Ray told me to expect you sometime today so I got it out ready for you."

He came back a moment later with an attaché case and plonked it down in front of Jim. "There you are old son, now give me a minute to get out and you can open it in private." He left the room and Jim looked at the case for a moment and then turned the combination lock on the front. It sprang open revealing that it was crammed full of notes, he took out enough to pay for the arms and ammunition plus the extra commission agreed with Diman and then locked it again. Stuffing the notes into the small case he locked that and put it on the floor beside him and called out to the man. "OK mate, thanks, I'm finished now."

The man returned to the room and sat down opposite Jim. "Better introduce myself hadn't I? I'm known as big Mal, for obvious reasons I suppose. I used to be a copper until I retired; now I do anything I want to in the security line. Ray asked me to look after the case for him because he knows there ain't a man out there I'm afraid of. And none of em would dare try anything on with me."

Looking at him Jim could believe this as the man radiated confidence in himself. When Jim didn't answer he carried on. "I knew Ray back when he had his own company and I used to run some of the security angles for him."

He got up and without asking plonked another beer in front of Jim. He cracked another for himself and they drank quickly before Jim looked at his watch and said. "I've got to be going, I've got someone to meet."

"Yeah, I know." big Mal answered. "You're off to meet up with Blackie and that guy, Diman." He raised a huge ham like hand. "Look out for that Diman, I reckon he can be dangerous, Blackie's OK for a crook. He'll keep his word for the right kind of incentive and in his own way he's got a good sense of fair play. But that Diman will double cross you for sure if you take your eye of him for a minute. So be warned."

Jim had listened to this tirade with surprise and when the man had finished he asked. "Where did you find out who I was meeting? As far as I know only a few people have been told it was going to happen today."

The man smiled at Jim and tapped the side of his nose. "Never mind how I know, there isn't much goes on up the 'top end' I don't know about." He glanced up at the clock on the wall and said. "You'd better be getting along or you'll be late."

Jim stood and they shook hands before he went out of the house, he walked down the path to the Ute shaking his head in wonder at the ability of people to surprise him with their knowledge of his movements. He drove down the road until he found a sign directing him to the Hospital and found the car park easily enough. When he drove in he looked for Blackie's Ute and saw it parked as far from the Hospital as possible in the corner of the parking lot.

Blackie and Diman were standing by the Ute and when he got out of his vehicle they waited for him to walk to them. Blackie grinned, but Diman just glowered at him. Jim couldn't resist one little dig and said. "Not much chance for an ambush out here is there Diman?"

Diman regarded him from brows lowered like thunder and his eyes smouldered with hatred. "You might feel like you've won mister." he grated. "But the chance will come again, for us to meet. It always does in this life."

"Maybe you're right." Jim retorted. "But don't forget, it might not go the way you want it to."

Diman flushed, and even though his skin was naturally dark, Jim could se the colour darken and his eyes glinted like coal dust on a sunny day. He would have made some move on Jim but Blackie had tired of this little by-play and stepped between them. "Right, that's enough from you two, we're here to conduct business so let's get on with it shall we?"

Jim stepped back and waited for Diman to do the same, which he did after some hesitation and Jim thought to himself, 'why does he hate me so much? What did I do to him that made him so revengeful?' No answer was forthcoming so he contented himself with asking Blackie if everything was there.

Blackie shrugged. "None of my business mate." He answered. "Round here, I'm just the delivery boy. I went with him to pick this lot up, but it's for you, and not me."

Diman walked round to the back of the Ute and would have opened it when another car approached through the car park. For a moment Jim thought it was going to be the police but when it slowed to a stop he could see it belonged to Schoonheid. 'Christ,' He thought to himself, 'this lot follow me round everywhere I go. I'll never get away from them'.

Schoonheid climbed out of the car and Jim could see the perspiration form on his brow as soon as he got the full warmth of the sun on his face. He took out an oversized handkerchief and mopped his face. "I just thought I should keep an eye on my investment." He said it to no one and everyone.

Diman evidently thought he should have been the one to run this transaction and yanked the back doors viciously, they stayed resolutely shut and everyone except Diman grinned to themselves.

Blackie jangled his keys and chuckled. "They work better with this mate; you didn't think I was going to run around with the back doors open did you?"

Diman scowled but said nothing as Blackie opened the doors to allow Jim to enter the back. Schoonheid would have got in as well but was stopped by Jim's finger in his chest. "You might be getting a cut of this shipment Schoonheid but it's me that's paying and I'll thank you to keep out of this and let me examine it myself."

It seemed for a moment as if Schoonheid would argue but he must have contented himself with the thought of the profit coming and stepped back reluctantly to let Jim enter. When he got in, it took Jim a moment to let his eyes adjust to the gloom in the back, but they finally did he could see the floor had been completely covered with boxes, he gasped as he saw for the first time how much they had bought. Most of them were unopened and looked like they had never been opened from the factory to here, Jim felt grateful for that, as the first time anybody knew whether ammunition was good or not was when it was first fired. He had no chance of testing any here so had to accept them as they were delivered.

He got out and said to Diman. "I accept them as they are, because I can't test them, you come with me and I'll get you're money."

They started to walk over to Jim's Ute and Schoonheid turned to walk with them, but felt a hand on his shoulder and Blackie said. "That business is between them, you'll get your chance in a minute."

Schoonheid stopped short and swung round to face Blackie, his face suffused with anger. "You'd better watch your step mate, I don't like blokes like you interfering in my business." None the less he waited with Blackie while Jim paid Diman his money.

Jim had let Diman into the Ute and put the case on the seat between them, he opened it and let Diman put his hands inside to try and pull the money out with a greedy look on his face. Jim pushed the top of the case down trapping his hands and said to him. "Before you get into a mess counting that, it'll be easier to accept that it's all there, the last thing I'd do is try and short change you. So why don't you close it and keep the case as a present. I've got one thing to say to you though, if I get back and any of that ammo's duff, you're going to have me to deal with and I'll make sure I find you down some dark alley one day, and the ammo I'll be using will be good. Do I make myself absolutely clear?"

It appeared Diman wasn't having a good day but he nodded without speaking and Jim eased off the pressure and released his hands. Then they got out of the Ute together with Diman carrying the case. He walked over to Schoonheid and they both got in to his car and drove off without even a wave goodbye. At first it shocked Jim and then he realised that once the business had been concluded Diman had no way of leaving without Schoonheid to give him a lift. Anyway he reasoned that Schoonheid wouldn't want to let the cash too far out of his sight until he could get his hands on his share.

Blackie said without looking round. "OK Jacko, you can come out now." Jim looked round in surprise and a figure rose silently out of the ground behind some bushes only about five metres from where they were standing, it was Jacko holding a small rifle in his hands. "All right boss, you win. Now tell me how long I've been there?"

They were playing some game that only the two of them knew about. "I've known you were there ever since you moved that little branch over there." he pointed at the bushes some twenty metres from them.

"You couldn't have seen that." Jacko exclaimed. "You were looking the other way." Then realising what he had just said he stopped talking.

Blackie grinned and said. "That's going to cost you another stubby when we get back Jacko."

He asked Jim. "What do you want to do with all this stuff I've got in the back here?"

"I want you to take it out to the farm for me if you will; I can't take it with me because when I go back I'll be in the plane."

"Glorified delivery boy, that's all I am." rejoined Blackie.

"Money's good though isn't it?" Snapped Jim. The incident with Schoonheid and Diman had unsettled him.

"Keep your hair on mate, it was only a joke, I don't ever complain when I'm earning my daily bread, you know that." Blackie replied meanly.

Jim felt sorry he had snapped at him because as he had rightly pointed out to him he didn't complain when asked to do anything. "Yeah you're right Blackie, I shouldn't lose it, it's just that Schoonheid guy gets right up my nose, and that Diman's no better. He acts like I'm going to be dead next time I run across him, all I get from him is aggravation."

"You might get more than that one day." Blackie answered. "I think if he gets the chance he'll do you some real harm, so keep an eye open when you're around him. It's a pity you can't take some action first but he'll only try and take you down if he goes, so you can only hope you never see him again."

Jim nodded, his mind going elsewhere as he thought about his next move; suddenly a thought crossed his mind, and swinging round he said to Jacko. "What were you doing there, anyway Jacko? Hiding in those bushes, and armed as well."

"Aw nothing really, I was just keeping an eye open for boss man there, he thinks he can handle anything, but he'll get caught out one day if no one looks out for him, and anyway I couldn't take the aggravation if I went home and told Chrissie something had happened to him."

Blackie scuffled his feet and kicked a clod of earth lying close by, plainly embarrassed with the fact that anybody thought so much of him. "Hmm." He said. "Better be getting on if we're going to get stocked up for travelling out to the farm tomorrow." his voice was gruffer than usual and Jim thought he could hear something in the back of his throat, that sounded suspiciously like emotion.

They bade each other goodbye and then they got in the Ute and drove out of the car park. Jim followed slowly and went back to his hotel. He was at a loose end now for the next twenty four hours so he went out and did some sight seeing and in the evening he got himself some beers, only one thing led to another and by the time he got in bed that night he had definitely had more than was good for him, he woke the next morning feeling the usual shame and felt glad his wife couldn't see him and give him the ear bashing he normally got when he over indulged. His head was pounding and the first thing he did was eat some breakfast and take some of his favourite painkillers.

By ten in the morning after a shower he felt ready to face the world and got the Ute out of the car park and drove off down to the town of Katherine to meet Ray when he came back with the Prof and Colette. When he arrived there he filled the Ute with stores and petrol for the journey they would have to make and then waited patiently in a bar drinking water until they came in to the airfield.

They had no time to talk, as Ray, who was accompanied this time by Dick, wanted to get back as soon as possible.

He gave Colette a hug and gave the children a kiss and handed the keys to the Ute over to Prof and they left. "Well that was short and sweet, I must say." He commented. "I thought I'd get more than a few minutes with my daughter when I saw her."

"Don't forget she's my wife as well." Dick interjected. "I wish she could be out there all the time."

"Yeah, but from what I know about marriage." Ray said. "You'll wish she wasn't when she is there."

He leaned forward and started the engine up and watched the propellers spinning in front of them, and then slowly brought the plane round on to the runway and they sped down it until they soared into the air. He turned and beamed at Jim. "Whatever you say, I know this is only supposed to be a milk run, but I get a real thrill from just getting into the air and going somewhere. I reckon those guys who fly those airliners aren't working, there're enjoying their hobby."

"I wonder how much you'll enjoy it when you start giving me lessons after these two get their pilots licences." Jim watched his face as the words sunk into his head and then Ray deliberately turned his head to look back at Jim.

"Are you serious?"

"Never been more serious in my life, why? Don't you think I'm capable of doing it? I've watched you and these two trying and I don't see anything hard in it at all."

"Well it's not as easy as all that, there's a bit more to it than just getting up and down."

"From what I've been told, they say if you can drive a car you can fly, all it needs is a bit of confidence, and one thing is definitely sure, I can try if I want can't I?"

The consternation was plain to see on Ray's face now and Jim took some delight in taunting him. "Don't say you're scared to try and teach me, you taught these two with no bother and I reckon I can do anything those two can do." He looked at them and said. "And another thing, none of you has done any navigation yet, all you do is follow the road until you see the farm. If you had to go across country you'd be lost in five minutes."

Ray looked round at him and laughed. "I reckon we'll have to have navigation classes in the evening from now on."

Dick groaned out loud. "More maths, I suppose."

"You never know when you're going to need to use something like that, think of what's going to happen if this volcano blows and we do have to fly, if it's impossible to see the ground, how do you find your way?"

Dick had to concede the point and they agreed to start lessons in navigation as soon as possible. Pat and Julia had prepared a meal for them when they arrived back and they sat down to eat it. It was finished soon enough and Jim glanced out and saw they had about two hours of daylight left. He looked at Andrew and said. "I want you to come with me for a walk Andy, I've got some business to sort out."

He walked out with a puzzled Andrew following him and all the rest looked at each other with quizzical expressions on their faces. No one knew anything so Pat called out after Jim's retreating back. "Where are you going Jim?"

He waved and said. "Don't bother about it, it's not so important I need an audience." He didn't stop and carried on until he reached the plane, opening the door he pulled his mysterious packages out and said to Andrew. "Let's get these things loaded on to one of the Ute's."

They put them in the flat bed of the Ute and Jim jumped in and started the engine and drove out of the camp. He drove for about a mile and then stopped, getting out he looked around but so far from camp he knew he was free from prying eyes. "Now I'm going to tell you what all the mystery has been about." He said. "I've been thinking of doing this from the very first day." As he spoke he had been unwrapping one of the packages, and now it was revealed. Andy's eyes shone as he bent down and picked it up, it was about two feet long and looked deadly, as indeed it was. It was a crossbow in some sort of fibre material. It had a fast load system and telescopic sights, there were a hundred arrows packed in a cylinder as well. Andy stroked it in admiration. "That's some piece of workmanship dad." He exclaimed.

He put it to his eye and sighted through the lens and tweaked the trigger with his finger. "What's the range?" he asked, clearly reluctant to put it down.

"Well the guy in the shop assured me they can be fired accurately to a hundred yards, and if you practice and get used to it you can manage two hundred yards, but it does have a range greater than that but not accurately."

"OK dad, all well and good but the question remains, why? What the hell have you bought them for?"

Jim scratched his nose while he thought about the answer, then he said. "I can envisage a time in the future that we will be attacked if people find out what we're doing here and that volcano blows. It's going to take the dust maybe a few months to spread right over the whole globe. At least that's the best information I can come up with. In that time there'll be lots of opportunity for someone to remember us and what's happening here. Take Schoonheid for example, he knows we're here and he knows we could be in a position to survive, don't you think someone like that is going to have a good try at getting in and kicking us out. That's why I agreed to buy the guns. Another thing that occurred to me is that maybe someone like him would recruit some help to get us out as well, and it makes me wonder who that could be. Now I know we could threaten to destroy the place and make it unusable but that defeats the object of building the place at all, and leaves us with nowhere to go. So I've been looking at all possible means of defence and one of the principles of good defence as you know is attack. But what happens if we get stuck outside for some reason with no arms? Well that's where these come in, for emergencies. Now I want to hide these things out here, but they could be lying here for ten years, maybe more, would you like to come out here and collect a gun that's been buried for ten years?"

Andy stared at his father. "You crafty old devil." He said admiringly. "I didn't think you had it in you. Do you reckon this Schoonheid will come if it happens?"

Jim shrugged his shoulders. "If not him, there could be others, people talk and who knows will know about this place, I wouldn't put it past some of these politicians or local council officials to try and muscle in if they thought they'd have a better chance of survival out here. I'm going to tell you something I've known about for years from one of my friends who worked on the Telephone Company. He told me there's a secret place near our town that's set up for a nuclear attack; he fitted all the telephones there. Now tell me, in your honest opinion, who's going to get the chance to go into there? Do you think they'll let Mr Joe public in? Not a chance in hell. It'll be packed to the roof with worthy civil servants and their families who'll swear on a stack of bibles that there're necessary to the running of the place after a catastrophe. So when it comes down to it, I'm the same. And we're going to defend this place till the bitter end if needed."

Jim stopped talking as he realised he had got back on one of his favourite hobbyhorses again. He flushed under his sun tan. "Sorry, but when I start I can't stop, I've always hated people who use privilege as a right, just the same as I hate cheats and liars."

Andy laughed at Jim's ideas, but answered. "I know you've got a bee in your bonnet about this Dad, but in fact I agree with you, at least we're putting our money down to prepare for something and if we choose to live out in the wilds of Australia for that reason we ought to reap the benefits of what we do. Now I've got something to ask. Where the hell are we going to put these crossbows?"

Jim looked around and said. "I think they should be scattered round the farm at about a mile away on four sides, since we've got four of them, we can pick out a landmark like a tree or a rock and mark it so we don't forget. It might be a long time before they're needed and we'll need to know with some accuracy where they are." He pointed at the bundle Andy was holding and went on. "The guy in the shop said these are the best thing to wrap them in, they'll keep for years in these if we get them deep enough."

He stopped what he was doing and stared hard at Andy. "I've just remembered something in all this preparation, what are we going to do about Ray? I've got an idea we should let him know what we're doing."

"For what it's worth, I think you're right, we can let him know tomorrow, OK?"

As the time had gone by so quickly while they discussed all

this, they only had time enough to bury the first one and agreed to come out the following day to finish the job. Jim threw the shovel in the back of the Ute and Andy marked the tree where they had buried it. He took out his knife and cut a blaze that looked suspiciously like an umbrella, and under this he carved the figure Fourteen to signify that the bow was buried fourteen metres from the base of the trunk, in the direction of the mark. Although the blaze looked very white Jim knew that in time it would fade as the tree repaired itself, but the mark would remain. Marking down on the map where exactly the tree was proved difficult, and Andy joked. "We ought to have that Global positioning device Ray's got on the boat. It'd be a piece of cake with that."

"Mmm." Jim was distracted and barely paid attention, and then he looked up, and said angrily. "You know we can't use that, what if it gets damaged, the best thing to do is use the old fashioned method as used in the pirate stories. We'll have to pace it out."

They solemnly paced out the position, only mildly arguing over the length of their strides and when they had finished Jim took a good look round and told Andy to do the same and try and impress the spot on his memory. "After all." he said. "It could be a long time till we come out here to find them."

The sun had begun to set over the hills by the time they finally made their way home and when they arrived, work had finished and most of the community were sitting outside in the dying rays of the sun with a drink and chewing the fat. The construction workers had come and set themselves up again which in their case meant unloading the stubbies, which were of a size that meant they had to move all the shelves in the fridges to accommodate them. Still it had been accomplished and they had dragged their chairs out to sit with everyone else.

Ray looked up when they climbed out of the Ute and said loudly. "What have you two been up to then?"

Naturally every eye turned on them to listen to the answer. "Aw, not much" Jim said casually. He turned to enter his caravan and tipped Ray with a wink. "I'll tell you about it in the morning, right now I want a shower."

The following morning when work had started, the men had

got to the point where they could pour concrete but first they had to erect shuttering to hold the upper floor together and lay reinforcing bars across so Jim beckoned to Ray to come with him. He grinned in real pleasure when Jim showed him the crossbows and told him what he intended to do, and replied. "That makes two of us don't it mate, I reckon these'll be pretty good to have around if things do happen. They look like they're indestructible."

"They're not far off that, they'll certainly last a long time in the wild and even if the rain gets to them they should survive, I only hope they can last as long as the guy in the shop said they would."

Andy came round the side of the Ute. "Thought I'd find you two here, the electrician's arrived and he's brought those CCTV camera's you wanted, he wants to know where to site them."

"How many has he brought?" Jim asked.

"Three, I think." Andy answered.

"Well tell him I want one out on the road about four miles out, and the rest to give us a view of the whole site from the top of that hill over there, and a view from the top of that one over there. The roads the only important one right now and the others are just luxury for the time being. They may come in more useful as time goes on. Oh, and tell him I want them put up so nobody can see them with a casual look. If they know they're there, we'll have every visitor trying to come in round another way to see if they can beat the system."

"I'll have to give him a hand with that you know, he won't be happy about running a cable out four miles." Andy looked peeved to think he would have to dig a trench four miles long and lay cable into it.

"Don't try and get it too deep then and make sure it doesn't show when you've finished either, the best place to lay it is by the side of the road, so the vehicles will run over it and disguise it."

"Can't we hang it on the trees till it gets out there?"

Jim felt helpless for a minute; he disliked having to explain everything to someone who should know better. "If you do that it'll be like an arrow pointing straight at the camera and that'll make it useless for our purposes."

Andy groaned. "I believe you're right, I'd better get on with it I suppose."

"OK." Jim answered. "By the way, I've decided to go out with Ray and put them in place, we'll let you know where they are later, OK?"

Andy nodded in the affirmative and Jim and Ray climbed into the Ute and drove out of the camp towards the second of the sites they had chosen as suitable. It was the work of several hours to bury the crossbows and mark all the places on a map they made of the area. Jim gazed at it when they had finished and said. "Looks like that should be OK, I just hope we never have to use them."

"Nothing like being prepared though is there." Ray opined. "How many times in your life have you said, 'if only'?"

"More than I like to admit." Jim said with feeling, "right." He looked around and fixed the layout of the ground in his mind. "Lets be getting back, I could do with something to eat and drink."

It was midday when they arrived back and the day had a different hue to it, instead of the sun beating down endlessly it had a halo round it that presaged a change in the weather, Ray glanced up and around at the camp and offered his view on this change. "It's going to piss down soon, if we want to keep going in the wet, we'd better start getting organised round here. We need to think about getting as many supplies in as possible and some boards laid on the ground so we can walk around would be a good idea."

As they talked, Leah came over and heard what he was saying. "Most of what you've just said has already been done, I've been in touch with that supplier Schoonheid and we've got two or three loads of materials coming in and more if needed. He said he won't let us down and if it gets too wet he'll do his best."

To Jim this sounded like someone who was trying too hard and he wondered what the man could be up to, but no one else felt his suspicions so he let it pass. Leah went on. "By the way, Victoria rang, and she's coming out at the weekend with her friend the biologist so she wants to be picked up Friday evening. She'll confirm that when she rings later."

Jim felt satisfied that something was moving in that direction and was about to answer when Pat poked her head out of the door. "While you lot have been running around having fun some of us have to work, I've made something to eat so you'd better get in here a bit quick and I'll serve it before it gets so many flies over it they'll be doubling in number."

It had been a perennial problem for them from day one, as the Australians had no dung beetles in the country to feed on the dung, consequently the grubs of the flies had no predators to eat them and multiplied rapidly. This meant that flies attacked anything that moved outside with a ferocity that left newcomers to Australia breathless. Jim sympathised with the Australians as several species of animals had been introduced by well meaning people in the past with sometimes disastrous results. The rabbit had been one and a species of frog another, both were now serious threats to the balance of nature and now they didn't want to introduce something else for fear of causing more damage to the fragile state of nature. They went in to the caravan they used as a mess hall and the construction workers followed in as well, Andy came in with the electrician and Pat asked Leah to help with the serving and soon they were eating their fill.

They had just finished the meal when the phone rang; Pat answered and listened in silence, a puzzled look on her face. When the person on the other end had finished speaking she said. "Thanks very much, I'll get in touch with you later." She replaced the phone and turned to Jim who was waiting for her to enlighten him about the mysterious call.

"That was Blackie; he's given us some information and wants us to act on it straight away." She turned to the workmen, who as expected in a small community where nothing much happened were hanging on to every word, and said. "You lot had better go and get on with some work hadn't you?" She said sharply.

They reluctantly got up and started to file out slowly, as he went past the foreman said to Jim. "If you need a hand with anything let us know mate."

Jim nodded his thanks and smiled hesitantly to show he appreciated it. Pat stopped Ray and Andy as they went past and whispered. "You two had better stay and hear this, it concerns you as well."

Finally, Leah who had sensed it was something she needed

to know joined them, they sat down and listened as Pat explained the situation. "As I said, that was Blackie and he told me that there's a copper on his way to have a look round. Blackie only found out about it by accident because one of Jacko's relatives is with him, he's brought him so he can see if he can find anything out about those guns we've got."

Jim frowned, 'How the hell did they find out about those,' he thought. Then it crossed his mind it could have been Diman as he had no liking for him and he had been paid and had nothing to lose. It could have been Schoonheid as well but he didn't really consider that, as the guy still wanted the business.

The news had fallen like a bombshell on them and while they tried to absorb the information Pat said. "Blackie said he thinks he'll be here in about three hours."

"Hang on a minute." Ray said nastily. "If he gets here that late, have we got to put him up for the night? That's carrying hospitality a bit too far, isn't it? If he comes here to investigate what were doing and we have to give them lodging." He slammed his hand on the table. "He gets nothing from me."

Leah was bobbing her head in agreement when Pat said calmly. "I think you're missing the point here; first, what about Jim and myself? We're not here legally yet so they can't be allowed to find us here, and second all those workers over there saw that little charade with the delivery of the arms. They'll know something was delivered and they won't have to look too far to find them either, not with an Abbo looking for them."

"Is there any way of getting to that Abbo at all?" Jim was beginning to hate the way that Pat kept on asking questions but knew she was right to bring these subjects up.

"Maybe there's another way." Andy interjected.

Jim looked at him sharply. "What have you got up your sleeve?"

"Well it occurred to me that if you and Mum weren't here they couldn't question you about anything, although if you faced them out and said you're a Managing Director of a big English Company and you've brought a load of money into Australia, they'd have a lot of trouble kicking you out. But suppose I flew out with you and we went to another place for a day or two until this blows over, that'd solve that problem. But what I really want to know is if we offered the Abbo enough incentive do you think he'd turn a blind eye?"

"The hard part there is getting to him without the copper getting wise to the situation." Jim said. "Have we got anything here we can give him in the way of incentive?"

"We've got some money left over from buying the ammunition." Ray said. "If you remember I put it away in the cash box."

"Is there enough for say, six months salary for the Abbo?" Jim asked.

Ray nodded in the affirmative.

"Right then." Jim went on. "The way I see it is this, he'll find that store of guns if he looks hard enough, but maybe we could make his choices a little easier. If we point him gently in that direction and leave something for him he's got two chances."

"If he makes the wrong one he'll regret it I can tell you." Ray broke in.

"Yeah." Jim drawled. "I bet he will." He knew they had no other choice in the short term as time was going on. He looked over at the construction workers who to a man were working but only with half an eye on the job, the other was firmly trained on them to try and ascertain what was happening. "We'll have to do something about them as well." He said. "They saw that shipment come in the other day and it had disappeared when they came back after the weekend, they aren't stupid are they?"

Ray joined him in looking at them. "How about if I have a word about a bonus for working extra hard and not seeing anything that goes on?"

Jim agreed, he knew better than most that construction work had a great many people who only just made a living out of all the hard work and a little extra in the pay packet never went amiss. "That's probably the only way we can play this as far as I can see, Christ knows what's going to happen if the Abbo doesn't like the idea. We'll be up shit creek and no mistake."

"No worries, we'll sort it out." Ray sounded confident and

Jim shrugged to himself, 'nothing else to do,' he thought.

Aloud he said. "My biggest problem hasn't been mentioned yet." He looked over at Andy who started grinning when he clicked on to what Jim was about to say. He pointed at him. "He hasn't qualified to fly that plane yet has he?"

"Dick broke in. "Maybe he hasn't, but I'm more qualified than he is."

Leah asked. "Why don't you let Ray fly you then there's no problem?"

Jim looked at Andy. "I'd rather we had someone like Ray here to sort out any problems if they arise, can you fly that plane or not?"

"I can fly it Dad, don't worry." Andy spoke confidently. Ray, when he saw the worried look on Jim's face said. "He'll be alright if you go in the daylight and don't do any night flying." Dick looked disappointed but Ray went on. "I'd rather have you stay here Dick than these because you at least have got some reason to be here in Oz, and if the cops see those." He nodded in Jim's direction. "We might have some explaining to do."

Pat said. "If we're going we'd better get a start, I want to be out of here before any police car comes up that road."

Jim looked at Ray and said. "Good luck, I hope everything goes OK. I wish I could stay here and help you out; I don't like leaving a mess for someone else."

"It'll be alright." Ray replied. "I'll sort it out one way or another, now, you'd better be going, I don't want any sign of you here when they come and I've got some things to prepare anyway."

Pat ran into the caravan and drawers could be heard being opened and shut, then she reappeared a few moments later with an overnight bag in her hand, she stared hard at Jim and Andy. "You'd two had better pick up a few things and get out here ready to go."

They both went off to do as they were told and Pat asked Ray "Is that plane ready to go?"

"Sure, no problem, I always keep it fuelled up. Where do you think you'll go?"

She smiled. "Do you really want to know the answer to that? Especially if we go into a regular airport and him with no licence."

"Ray sucked between his teeth and ran his tongue round his lips, he hadn't given it a thought and now it occurred to him they could still be in trouble if they ran into anyone in authority. "Better not go to a regular airport, if I was you I'd head for a cattle ranch or something and say you're just visiting."

She smiled to put him at his ease and waved in a gesture that encompassed all the surrounding countryside. "There are plenty of places to go out there, we'll be alright."

The two men came back and wished Leah and the others goodbye and then they jumped into the Ute for Ray to take them to the plane. The construction workers were craning their necks by this time to see what was happening and Jim smiled to himself as they went down the road. Ray would have to do some really fast explaining when he got back. They got to the plane with Ray giving Andy some last minute instructions, which Jim thought was probably a bit too late. Andy was nodding his head. But he made a brave show of nonchalance as he climbed in and started the pre flight checks. Jim watched him closely from the other side as Pat sat herself in the back. When Jim glanced at her she smiled and crossed herself and held her hands up with her fingers crossed also. He could see she was tense but could do no more than wink at her to show he wasn't worried, the sound of the engine starting up made him turn and look at Andy who sat in the pilot's seat. He leant over and patted him lightly on the shoulder. "It's going to be OK son." He said reassuringly. "You're not doing anything you haven't done before."

Andy visibly relaxed at the soothing words and bending slightly he ran the throttles up and took hold of the wheel as the plane started to roll forward. The rest of the takeoff was textbook and as they soared into the air Jim saw the look of triumph on his face at his achievement. They banked and flew round to gain height and Andy looked out of the side window at Ray on the ground who was jumping up and down waving his arms. As they passed over him he held both thumbs up in the air to signify he was pleased.

"So far so good." commented Jim. "Now all we have to do is find somewhere to go for a few days."

Pat leaned forward and spoke between their shoulders. "You

men think you're so bloody clever don't you, not one of you has thought of the obvious choice of place to go, have you?"

Jim turned to look at her expectantly and she went on. "We can't go into Katherine can we? Too many people know us there don't they? We can't really go to a cattle ranch and just land and walk in, but there is another choice isn't there?" She answered her own question. "We could go to Blackie's ranch couldn't we?" The plane dipped slightly as Andy turned to look at there as well. She put her hand out and pushed his head round with her finger. "I'd just as soon you keep your eyes in font of you for the moment young man."

They could hear the worry in his voice as he said. "It might not have occurred to you but first I'm not sure I could find it, and any way he hasn't got a landing strip has he?"

In answer to both his questions she said. "We could find it by going to a place on the track we know and following it back to his ranch and when we were there he showed me a place that he said would make a good landing strip if he ever got enough money together to put one down and buy the plane."

Jim was astonished. "I know the place you mean, and it's still got shrubs growing on it."

"You've got your phone on you haven't you? It'll take about two hours to fly there won't it, give him a ring, and ask him to go out and cut the worst down. Little ones shouldn't bother you should they?" This last was to Andy who was flying automatically now as he considered her plan.

"You know, it might work mum, and it'd be a good place to hole up for a day or two, no one's going to come out there and bother us are they?"

They looked at each other for several moments and then burst into hysterical laughter as they contemplated the position they had found themselves in. It finished as quickly as it started as Andy jerked the wheel as he flew along. Jim reached down and took his mobile phone out and dialled Blackie's number, tapping his fingers on the seat while he waited for him to answer. It took only a few seconds and then he was through. When he explained the situation it was plain that Blackie thought they were crazy and Jim had to do some rapid talking to convince him they were serious. When he finished talking he disconnected and looked at them. "He said he'll do his best but it's not only shrubs that's a problem but rocks as well. He'll have to get all the boys out there to help him and he's not sure he'll be ready."

There was nothing more to do, but fly on, and hope that Blackie could ready the strip for them. They had flown a course that took them away from the road the police were coming on so this wasn't a worry, but the fact that they were flying over uncharted areas was. Pat in particular, worried they wouldn't find the road and have to come down in the bush. It proved an unfounded concern though, as they spotted the road after about an hour, Andy turned and began to follow the track towards Blackie's but it wound so much he climbed higher and followed the outline in a straight line.

They saw the buildings from a long way out and a cloud of dust was rising as the men worked frantically to clear the ground, they stopped working for a moment to look at the plane, and it became obvious it wasn't ready for them. As they got closer they could se the tall form of Blackie waving his arms at them and when they re-started work he pulled the phone from his pocket. A moment later Jim's phone rang and when he answered they could see Blackie speaking into his. "How much flying time have you got?" he asked.

Jim indicated to Andy he wanted to know the state of the fuel. "I think we've got enough for a couple of hours yet, but I want some extra time to practice landing, so I can't let it go too long."

Jim thought it was a good time to worry about his landing technique but let it pass, as he didn't want to upset him. Pat had no such inhibitions though and snapped. "I thought you knew how to fly this thing, I don't want you practising landing I want to get my feet on that ground down there."

Jim waved his hand to her to shut her up and stop worrying Andy, and then he said to Blackie that they could let him have an hour or so to finish up. Blackie waved his thanks and switched off the phone then carried on working with his men on the clearance. Andy flew over once more and waggled his wings as he went, although no one took any notice, as they were far too busy. He flew out several miles and then turned to Jim and said. "I'm going to practice landing at three thousand feet, as if the landing strip was there so I'll go up to four thousand and descend to three. I want you to call out the height on the altimeter in hundreds of feet and then in tens until I hit three thousand. OK?"

Jim agreed and Andy flew round steadily gaining height until he reached four thousand feet. When he did, he levelled out and flew in a straight line and then he nodded to Jim and flew round in a half circle and throttled back slightly to lose the necessary height. Jim's eyes widened a little as he saw how quickly they lost height and he called it out for Andy as they came down. They were about two hundred feet above three thousand when the stall warning started to beep loudly, Pat grasped Jim's arm tightly but Andy merely pushed the throttle and side slipped a little to gain speed. Pat gasped as the ground seemed to rush up at her but then they soared back up until Andy felt able to relax again. He turned to her and said. "Don't worry it happens to everyone the first time."

"If you only knew how much that frightened me you wouldn't be so casual about it." She replied.

Jim knew that at this point Andy was probably enjoying the experience and saw no way of impressing on him that he had passengers who badly wanted to live while he was playing with his new toy. He leaned over and said grimly. "I want you to get it right this time son; I'm fed up with being flown by amateurs."

The shot hit home right where he wanted it to, Andy glanced over at him, and he saw the lines of determination deepen as Andy clenched his mouth, he ran his tongue over his mouth and said to Pat. "Did you put anything in to drink, before we left?"

She said nothing but rummaged in her bag and pulled out a bottle of water, Jim idly wondered where women manage to find the room for all the items they crammed into their bags, then let it go as Andy gave the bottle back and nodded at him that he was ready to start again. They went through the same procedure again but this time he kept the airspeed up and they successfully completed the practice landing. He went round and did it twice more before the phone rang and Blackie announced they had done their best and to come in and give it a try.

Andy turned to his mother. "Better get those 'Hail Mary's' going Mum." He joked. "This time it's for real."

She looked pained, as he had never been as religious as she had wanted him to; preferring instead to take it lightly. "You get us down in one piece and I'll say some for you." she joked, Jim knew from her attitude she was frightened stiff but had kept a brave face on it for this long. She looked at him and smiled uncertainly, he could see the worry etched in her face and leaned over to put his hand on hers, she clasped his with a force that surprised him and together they waited for Andy to start his manoeuvres. He glanced round at them and joked. "If you want to get out and walk from here, I'll understand."

They flew over the strip to survey it before landing and looking down Andy swore softly to himself under his breath, Jim looked down to see what he had observed and it immediately became obvious what was wrong. In his haste to get it ready, Blackie had not bothered to eye it up from the end and it had a definite dog leg in the middle, the worst of it was that right in the middle of the bend was a substantial shrub which looked strong enough to rip the wing off if it came in contact with it. The strip was also fairly narrow so there seemed no leeway for error.

Andy scowled at them; "He doesn't make it easy does he?" He remarked, before turning and flying out about a mile to give himself plenty of room. There seemed to be no wind for the moment so it didn't seem to matter which way they landed. He turned in to the strip in a classic move designed to lose airspeed and height in one easy go and Jim felt Pat's hand tighten on his as they appeared to sway all over the place. Jim could see he was trying to land on one side of the strip so he could still go straight across the inside edge of the bend. They swooped down and just when Jim thought they would have to hit some bushes on the side they skimmed past them and touched down as lightly as at any time Jim had ever felt before.

Andy immediately applied the brakes and practically stamped on them in an effort to stop quickly. The bend loomed up on the side of the plane and he released the brakes for a moment and as it freewheeled past it he turned the wheel just a touch and the plane sped past it just grazing the shrub as it went. The moment they had passed it he turned the wheel back and as soon as they had straightened he stamped once more on the brakes. The plane rocked from side to side threatening to touch one of the wings on the floor but then righted itself. Jim was staring fixedly out of the windscreen watching the rough shrubbery at the end coming ever closer to them and Andy seemed to be almost standing on the brakes as he started to mutter "Come on, stop; stop you bastard."

Pat's hands were like a vice clamped on Jim and unknowingly he had gripped hers so tightly the blood had stopped flowing to her hands. The plane started to stop its headlong rush into the bushes at the end and Jim could see there were rocks and deep gouges in the soil there to trap the unwary. As they neared them the plane skidded slightly as Andy applied so much pressure to the brakes but it had some effect and they finally came to a halt with the propeller buried in a shrub. It was still turning and bits of the branches were flying around as it chopped pieces off them. Andy reached forward with shaking hands and turned the key to switch off, and the noise from the engine stopped, leaving a silence behind that was only broken by some ticking from the engine as it started to cool and the metal contracted.

They sat there unbelieving at the luck they had had until suddenly the door was wrenched open and Blackie thrust his head through it with a large grin plastered on his face. "You like to cut it a bit fine don't you?" Were his first words. He got to say no more as he was pulled aside by someone' hands and Chrissie pushed her black face into the opening, she jumped up and somehow got into the plane and then grabbed Pat in a bear hug that threatened to choke her. She had tears running down her cheeks cutting tracks in the dust on her face. "I sure thought you weren't going to make it down when you came in." She cried.

Pat was surprised at the intensity of her welcome from Chrissie, but on reflection it was probably because apart from Blackie no one had ever treated her well. Jim turned and started to try and get out and they all finally made it to terra firma. They stood in a circle with big grins on their faces as the reality of their situation sunk in. They had made it but only just, and looking at

Andy, Jim realised he had been far more worried than he had at first shown. His hands were shaking and he rubbed his face in his hands to loosen muscles that had grown stiff from holding them tight while he flew the plane. Pat went to Blackie and hugged him. "Thanks for doing that Blackie that was a real emergency in the end wasn't it?"

Andy stepped forward and gesturing up the runway he said to Blackie. "Next time maybe you can build one in a circle so we can land sideways."

Blackie looked at him in puzzlement. "What are you talking about?"

"Can't you see it." Andy asked. "It dog legs about half way down."

Blackie swung round and stared up the strip. "Where?" Was his first reaction. Then he caught the sight of the side of the strip and staring hard he lined it up with his eyes. "Jesus, you're right, I never saw it before." He swung round to Jacko who was standing with his friend Charlie. "You stupid dumb abbo, that's what comes from using a race of people who invented the boomerang."

Jacko looked so downcast and kicking his feet in the dust he started to mumble something about how hard it had been to get the shrub out and he thought it would be better to leave it and do it later. The explanation sounded so ridiculous that they all started to laugh until Jacko stomped off back to the house with Charlie in tow. They followed along when Blackie said. "Let's get something to eat, after all that I'm starving."

The next day, early in the morning sunshine of what promised to be another hot day, Jim strolled outside with Pat and two cups of coffee in their hands to find Jacko and Blackie sitting in the early morning sun when it happened.

"Everybody stand still," A voice boomed out on a bullhorn. Everybody froze and stared as a large man in uniform stepped out into the clearing in front of the house. Blackie would have had his gun out but it had been placed into a leather holster inside the cabin. Jacko had a gun but another man appeared and pushed his rifle into Jacko's back, then relieved him of his gun.

"OK Lads, you can come out now," The man with the bullhorn

bellowed.

About ten other men stepped out of their cover, they were all armed and grinning at Blackie.

"Got you bang to rights," The big man boasted, "I've always wanted to say that Blackie, especially to you. Now I can put you away where you belong, you've had it your own way for too long in my book, but now I've got you. And what are all these other folks doing here? Not illegal immigrants I hope, that'll be some more time you'll do."

"Christ, what sort of an idiot are you Tom?" Blackie laughed. "What the hell do you think you're going to charge me with? A bit of pot, I'll only be getting a suspended sentence for that."

Tom blinked, and then said, "You brought in some containers a couple of days ago, and I want them, now where have you got them stashed?"

"I told you that was only a bit of pot, what did you think was in them?"

The sergeant said nastily, "I bet you haven't had a look in those containers have you? Your mate who you've been doing favours for, is going down for ten years and he fingered you for the import of his drugs, mostly heroin I believe. Now where are the containers? And don't mess me about, I know there're still here."

Blackie looked astounded, the surprise written all over his face. Tom ignored him and went over to Jim, "Who are you and what are you doing here?" He asked.

. "I'm Sergeant Tom Wilkins, by the way." He snapped officiously. "I'm responsible for Law Enforcement in this Territory." He glanced over at Blackie and went on, "I've been after that bastard over there for a long time now and I reckon I've got him. Why haven't you answered my question? I asked you what you're doing here?" Jim reached into his pocket, pulled out his passport and handed it to him

Then he answered slowly, "I'm a tourist and English, so what's the problem?"

"The 'problem' mate, is that as far as I know you haven't gone through immigration to get into our fair country, so I reckon you've broken the law somewhere along the road, and I'm taking the lot of you in until I get time to sort it all out."

He was about to issue further orders when there was a bang from inside the house and the sergeants cap flew off his head and landed in the dust behind him. Immediately all the policemen opened fire and bullets flew all across the front of the building. Pat screamed, "Andy's in there stop firing."

"Hold your fire," the sergeant bellowed. Then shouted the same thing a few seconds later when several of his men carried on firing. When they finally stopped the sergeant called out, "Come on out you two, you ain't going to do any good using that rifle, you'll only end up getting yourself killed. You're in enough trouble as it is for firing at me, and you are definitely going to buy me a new cap. I might even try and get you on attempted murder if I don't see you in five seconds."

Blackie growled, "Thanks very much for shooting the whole place up Tom, I suppose it's too much to ask if you intend to repay me for the damage isn't it?" He turned to the house, "Get yourself out here Charlie and you Andy," He yelled. "We aren't going to make a breakout, and I'm certainly not going on the run, it's all over for a while. So give it up."

Pat was wringing her hands in terror by now, she grabbed Jim by the shoulder and shouted, "Do you realise my son's in there?"

There was no answer from the house for several long minutes, then Jacko offered, "Shall I go in and bring them out?"

The sergeant nodded and Jacko went forward to climb the stairs, at the bottom he called out, "It's all right, its only Jacko, I'm coming in to see you,"

There was no answer so he went up the remaining steps and entered the building. He was inside only a few moments and then reappeared on the top of the steps, "Congratulations sergeant," He said bitterly. "You've only gone and done for him haven't you, he's lying in there with a bullet through his head."

Pat's hand flew to her mouth in horror, and she attempted to run up the steps into the building. The sergeant grabbed her by the arm and held her tight, "You, hold on to her, I don't want her in the house yet." He said to one of his constables.

He went quickly up the steps then came out and shouted to

one of his men, "Send for an Ambulance, but tell them there's no hurry, nothing anybody can do."

Pats face went white, she strode over to the sergeant and ground out slowly, "If my son doesn't walk out of there you had better watch out because I'll be looking for you one dark night, and you won't like it if I find you."

The sergeant regarded her morosely, "If your son's copped it missus, that'll be your own fault, so don't start trying to blame me, it's you that's breaking the law."

He looked at Blackie, "Don't even think about trying to lay this at my door mate, someone's dead because you were smuggling and he was attempting to protect you. And what about that plane that landed here yesterday? Is that part of the plan to smuggle them further along the route?" He pointed at Jim and Pat, "What's their part in all this?"

"What's happened to my son?" Pat screamed

The sergeant looked over his shoulder and said to the constable holding her, "Get that woman out of here will you? she's getting on my nerves. And take that man there as well," indicating Jim.

The constable dragged Pat who was wailing sorrowfully down the road to the waiting Police Vans with Jim in tow. Then the sergeant accosted Blackie.

"What's those two's part in all this?"

Blackie regarded him bleakly, then answered. "Their part is to visit us here and that's all, if you've been watching us all this time you'd have seen us building that strip out there so that puts your grand plan about an organised route in a cocked hat don't it?"

Tom sneered, "Something's up here and I'm going to get to the bottom of it,"

He then bellowed out to his men to search the house and outbuildings. They scattered round and searched every building but came back empty handed. When the last one had reported to Tom they had found nothing he glared round at his prisoners, and said venomously. "I'll find them drugs if I have to search the whole of the Northern Territories."

He went over to Blackie and shook his finger in his face, "I know you brought some containers in two days ago, I've only been waiting for you to make a move. Now tell me where they are and it'll go easier for you in Court."

Blackie's face turned white with anger, "If you had used your bloody common sense, you'd have known I don't deal in hard drugs, I'll admit to a bit of pot now and again but you can sod off now because you've got nothing on me."

The sergeant leaned forward, his face inches from Blackie's, "I'll have you yet you conniving bastard, I reckon you've got that stuff hidden in one of the Abbo's houses, I saw some of them sneak off yesterday," He turned to some his men and shouted, "Get off down the road you four and search all these Abbo's houses, and find me those drugs, I know they're around here somewhere."

The he shouted to the rest of his men. "Load everyone here on to our transport and take the lot down to the station," When they had all been loaded, he sergeant then looked at Jim and said, "You'd better be able to prove you had nothing to do with those drugs or you're in for a long stretch as well."

Once again Pat screamed, "Where's my son you bastard? What's happened to him?"

The sergeant, who seemed to take an evil delight in taunting her, laughed. "You'll find out in good time dearie."

Two men were ordered to wait for the ambulance and then come in with the body.

Inside the police van Blackie exchanged looks with Jacko, "Are they safe?" He whispered. Jacko nodded and said no more, Blackie subsided back into his seat satisfied that his shipment was in safe hands.

Pat looked at Jim angrily, "You've done nothing to help me either," She moaned. "If he's dead because of your mad cap schemes, I'll see to it that this whole project is finished and that's a promise."

"You stupid woman," he ground out between thin lips. "There were two men in that house and Andy isn't reckless enough to take a pot shot at a policeman, it'll be that Charlie who fired."

"Well where's Andy then?" She challenged.

Behind them Chrissie strolled out of the bush just as the police van rolled off down the track. The two policemen regarded her sadly, "You can't go in the house yet Chrissie, someone got shot and we're waiting for an ambulance to take him into town." One of them offered.

Chrissie looked at him with eyes that had seen a lot of her countrymen suffer at the hands of the white man. "I've got eyes enough to see what happened here, but I expect by the time it gets into a report it'll all be Charlie's fault," She said morosely. "I'll wait here for you to take the guy out and then I'll clean the house and stay here until Blackie comes back."

The policeman shook his head, "By the time that Tom Wilkins has finished with him Blackie won't be coming back for a long time and those friends of his are gonna get deported I reckon."

Chrissie's head shot up and she shouted, "You ain't got nuthin on him, he'll get out of this you wait and see."

Jim sat on the seat in despair, his son maybe dead, his wife threatening to stop the project, his brain was working overtime trying all the options. But he could see no way out of their predicament yet, so resolved the only course open to him was to let events take their course. And see what happened when they arrived at the police station.

The End

Everything will be explained in
The Survivalists Book 2
(available soon).

Find out what happens when the world ends.

You can find out more at www.franciswait.com

Lightning Source UK Ltd.
Milton Keynes UK
UKOW03f0330220813

215771UK00001B/3/P